Archer of the Heathland

—∞—

Book One

—∞—

Deliverance

J.W. Elliot

Bent Bow
Publishing, LLC

Bent Bow Publishing
P.O. Box 1426
Middleboro, MA 02346

ISBN-13: 9781718149526

Cover Design by Brandi Doane McCann

If you enjoy this book, please consider leaving an honest review on Amazon and sharing on your social media sites.

Please sign up for my newletters where you can get a free short story and more great, free content at: www.jwelliot.com

TO SAM AND BERNICE,
MY LOVING PARENTS

Book One

Deliverance

MAP OF
FREI-OCK ISLES

Chapter 1
Blood in the Snow

Stay here." Weyland placed his good hand on Brion's arm. His hand was pink with cold and still slick with the fat of the mink he had been skinning. The overpowering stench from the mink's scent glands filled Brion's nostrils, and he pulled away from Weyland's hand.

"Not so close to my face," Brion said with a smirk of disgust. But Weyland wasn't paying attention to him.

Brion followed his father's gaze to the south road where a troop of soldiers marched around the bend and swung east toward the city of Mailag. Their weapons and armor glinted in the slanting light of the evening sun. Rank after rank churned the snow to a muddy slush. The royal banner snapped in the breeze over their heads—two crossed swords with a boar underneath. This was a sight rarely seen in the wild country of the Great Oban Plain. Why were they here?

A rider paused and gazed toward the shed where Brion and Weyland had been skinning and stretching the hides from the day's catch. The rider wore the sky-blue colors of one of the noble families from the south. Even from the shed, Brion could see the bold, white streak of hair that cut across one side of the stranger's head.

The rider's horse stomped its feet and danced sideways, blowing white mist out its nostrils. Weyland's crippled arm dangled at his side as he strode past the cabin. He wiped his good hand on his leather apron as he approached the rider. Brion shook the thick, brown hair from his eyes as the stranger bent low over his horse's neck to whisper to Weyland.

Weyland glanced sharply back at Brion, and the expression on his face sent a shiver through Brion's entire body. His father was afraid—really afraid. In all of his seventeen years, Brion had never seen his father afraid of anything. Brion stepped around the table to approach the rider, but Weyland waved him back with an angry gesture. Brion wiped his hands

1

on his leather apron and took another step toward Weyland when a clatter at the fence behind him made him turn.

His younger sister, Brigid, clambered between the rails of the fence into the stall to stroke the neck of her old cow. A calf nosed at the cow's udder, but the cow kicked it away. The chill breeze curled Brigid's fiery-red hair about her throat and wrapped her skirt around her legs as she peered over the cow's neck.

"Who's that?" she asked. She stepped around the cow to lean on the fence next to Brion.

"Don't know." Brion didn't try to conceal his irritation as he studied the rider and Weyland. He couldn't decide if he should ignore his father and find out what the man wanted. If Weyland was afraid, then Brion had a right to know why. Didn't he?

"Did I hear someone else on the road?" Brigid asked.

Brion glanced around at Brigid. The old cow was nudging her shoulder. The calf had followed the cow over, and Brion dropped a hand to rub its head.

"It's time we butchered this useless cow of yours," Brion said.

Brigid reached over the fence and slapped Brion on the back of the head.

"You don't eat pets," she said.

"She won't even care for her own calf."

"We didn't eat that ugly, old dog you liked so much."

"A dog's not a cow. You eat cows."

Brigid cuffed Brion again, less playfully this time, climbed through the fence, and disappeared around the corner of the cabin.

Brion looked back to the road. The rider kicked his horse into a gallop and disappeared over the rise after the soldiers. Weyland stood motionless. His whole body seemed to droop. Then he pivoted and slogged away from the cabin towards the woods by the south pasture. He never raised his gaze from the muddy road. His crippled arm dangled useless at his side.

Brion glanced back up the road to where the soldiers had disappeared. He considered going after Weyland, but he knew from long experience that it would do no good to ask him what the man had wanted when Weyland was in a sour mood. So Brion returned to the table by the shed, grabbed up a mink and began to peel the hide back while releasing it from the underlying fat with deft strokes of his knife.

Deliverance

As he worked, he kept thinking of the line of soldiers and how their weapons glinted in the afternoon light. He had never followed the south road to its end. He had never even been to Mailag. His world was so small. There had been at least three hundred men in that troop. How many people did he know? Ninety maybe, if you threw in the old midwife that lived in the cave outside of Wexford. And where had he been? Nowhere.

By the time Brion finished skinning, stretching, and scraping that day's catch, the sun had long since gone to bed. Weyland hadn't returned to the shed after he disappeared into the woods. So Brion was surprised, and rather irritated, to find him seated beside the fire in the cabin, running a fine stone over his sword. The blade rested on his lap, and he passed the stone over it with his good hand. The steel sang as the stone honed the edge. It was an excellent short sword with a plain, brass pommel. His father seldom took it out of the trunk.

Brion yanked the door closed with a bang and stalked over to the table. The aroma of roasted pork and rye bread from the evening meal lingered in the cabin. Brion threw off his cloak with a quiet snort of annoyance. He stopped at the table long enough to tear a piece of bread from the loaf and skewer a piece of roasted pork with his knife before collapsing onto the rug before the fire. The flickering light of the fire and several candles cast a wavering light around the cabin.

"Finola asked about you," Brigid called from the corner where she helped their mother, Rosland, stretch the warp on the loom.

Brion refused to take the bait. Brigid was trying to goad him because he had mentioned butchering the ornery, old cow again.

"It's gonna freeze tonight," Brion said as he kicked off his boots and wiggled his cold toes toward the fire.

"I want that roof patched tomorrow," Rosland said.

Brion nudged the old, orange tomcat with his toe. The cat blinked at him lazily.

"I have to check the traps first."

"Did you feed Lila?" Brigid asked.

"I fed your stupid cow." Brion scowled at Brigid. She was always going on about her useless cow.

3

Weyland wiped the sword with an oily cloth and sheathed it. He picked up the poker and sat beside Brion on the rug. He rested his crippled arm in his lap and turned to study Brion. In the dim light of the cabin, Weyland's pale, silver eyes seemed to glow.

"I need to speak with you," his father said. But his voice was low as if he didn't want the women to hear.

Brion watched his father in growing confusion. Weyland was still afraid. The fear seemed to emanate from him. It filled his eyes and wrinkled his brow. It bore down upon him, making him hunch his shoulders. But this was the man who, despite his crippled arm, had faced down a charging bull and fought off a spitting wildcat.

Brion's gaze fell to the withered hand. He tried to imagine away the long, jagged scar and the awkward angle at which the arm lay across his father's thigh. He tried to imagine his father drawing back the heavy string of a longbow with that hand and sending an arrow into a Salassani heart. But Brion couldn't do it. The shriveled hand was all he had ever known. It had always been there, taunting him with its promise of what his father should have been.

Brion raised his gaze back to his father's weathered face. A shock of muddy-brown hair fell into Weyland's eyes. But it couldn't hide the fear. Weyland lifted his withered hand and stared at it as if he had read Brion's thoughts.

"What did that rider want?" Brion asked.

Weyland shot Brion a surprised glance, but ignored the question.

"It's coming around again," he said.

"What?"

Weyland shook the hair from his eyes. "War," he said. "And we're in a bad place."

While Brion tried to sort out what that was supposed to mean, Weyland's gaze swept the room as if he expected someone to overhear him. Rosland and Brigid were deep in conversation about the recent rumors of weddings and affairs in Wexford.

"But she's only sixteen like I am," Brigid was saying.

Weyland shuffled closer to Brion.

"I haven't talked much about my time as a warrior," Weyland began. He paused as if considering. "Look, you can't tell anyone what I'm about to tell you."

"Sure," Brion said.

"Not Brigid, not Neahl, no one. Do you understand?"

"I guess so."

Weyland's frown deepened. "If they ever found out, they'd. . ." He pinched his lips tight, paused, and spoke in a whisper. "Promise me, no matter what happens."

Brion nodded again, trying to still the growing alarm that warmed his chest and rolled his stomach into a knot.

"What I'm about to tell you is very dangerous. It's treason." Weyland breathed the last word as if it left a bad taste in his mouth. "I wasn't just a warrior," he said. "I worked for someone very powerful, and he gave me some things to keep safe."

Weyland swallowed. "He'll be coming for them now—soon."

Weyland glanced around at Rosland and Brigid.

"Things are in motion, Brion. Dangerous things. And we're mixed up in them." Weyland glanced down at his arm again. "It's going to be hard for you to understand, but don't judge us too harshly. We did what was best."

Weyland raised his head to peer at Brion. He wasn't just afraid. He was in pain. His eyes brimmed with tears. "Forgive me," he said. "I—"

"What are you two whispering about?" Brigid said as she scooped up the old tomcat and dropped to the floor beside Brion. She cradled the cat in her skirt and scratched its ears.

Weyland scowled and turned his back on her to stir the fire with the poker.

"What?" Brigid asked.

"Tomorrow," Weyland said.

Brion tossed his last crumb of bread at Brigid in frustration. His father had never talked about his days as a warrior even though Brion had asked. Now Brigid had broken the moment.

Brion poised between two worlds with the axe loose in his grasp. The clear, blue sky spread out above him, the icy roof of a frozen world. The open grassland that rolled up and over the hills beyond his home invited him. It tempted him with its promise of something new and exciting just beyond the horizon. The other world of beech trees and oaks crowded into the little valleys. It was dark and mysterious—a world of woods and shadows brooding on the ageless eons of decay. It enticed him with the promise of danger lurking in every hollow, dancing in every vale, and peering from behind every tree.

"War is coming again," his father had said. But Brigid's interruption had sealed his lips. That morning Weyland had refused to talk about it. After they had checked the traps and brought in the catch, Weyland had sent Brion to the far end of the south field to chop down the old beech tree. Usually they skinned and cleaned the morning catch together, but not today. As they parted, Brion had seen the haunted expression on Weyland's face. What secret could be too dangerous to reveal even to his family? Treason? War? What would a crippled fur trapper living far from any place of importance on the edge of the great Oban Plain know of anything that mattered?

Brion returned to the task of felling the old tree that had guarded the edge of the south field since his childhood. His breath rose in clouds of steam to disappear against the icy blue of the winter sky. His father's cryptic conversation by the fire had filled him with a desire to strike out, to try something new. If a war was coming, maybe he could become a warrior like his father had been.

It wasn't that he didn't like trapping and living off the land. He loved it, especially the trapping. He was free—really free—unlike the village dwellers who had to live elbow-to-elbow and cheek-to-jowl. It was worse in cities like Mailag, or so people told him. It's just that he wanted a vacation now and then. He wanted to test himself to see what he could do. But with his father's crippled arm, he would probably never get the chance.

Brion swung the axe with such violence that it bit deep into the old, rotten trunk. Huge chunks of wood jumped away to fall heavy on the snow. The tree shivered above him. But the rush of satisfaction was smothered amid the echoing shriek that ripped through the still, morning air and lingered amid the snow-heavy trees.

Brion jerked his head around to listen. Wood chips clung to his sweater. Steam rose from his sweat-darkened hair. The axe paused in mid-stroke. Brion's gaze scanned the trees, searching for the source of the cry. The clash of steel, the cries of battle, and another scream of terror drove all other thoughts from his mind.

"Brigid," he breathed in desperation.

Brion sprang over the split-rail fence and sprinted through the snow, still clutching the axe in his hands. The sounds of battle rang through the woods. Fear gripped at his stomach. Fear like he had never known.

The trail bent. The smokehouse came into view. The smell of wood smoke filled the air. Horses' hooves pounded the frozen ground.

"Brigid!" he yelled.

The blood throbbed in his ears as he rounded the last bend in the trail and slipped in the wet snow, sprawling headfirst. He scrambled to his feet, scraping the slush from his eyes.

The pounding of hooves faded into the distance. Brion raced around the front of the cottage. His father lay prostrate in the trampled snow by the open door, a red pool staining the snow by his head. The jagged shaft of a broken arrow protruded from his shoulder. His sword lay clutched in his good hand. A crimson stain covered the tip. Weyland's fingers spasmed against the grip as if they struggled to raise it again.

Brion stared for a moment in mute horror. Burning pain began to spread in his chest. He stooped.

"Papa?" He shook Weyland's shoulder. "Papa."

Weyland groaned.

Brion rolled him to his back. The sword slipped from Weyland's hand. Weyland blinked slowly as if his eyelids were sticky with glue. Weyland opened his mouth and struggled to speak.

"I told you," Weyland whispered. "I told you they would come." He blinked and tried to swallow. "They didn't get it."

Brion struggled to regain his internal balance. He had no idea what his father was talking about. He had heard Brigid scream. Where was she?

"Keep it safe," Weyland said.

"What?" Brion asked, unable to stifle the rising desperation.

Weyland blinked and tried to wet his lips. "You're all they have left, Brion. Don't desert them."

"I won't."

"Take it." Weyland raised his withered hand. A large, golden ring encircled is father's index finger. Brion stared at it. He had never seen it before.

"Take it."

Brion slipped the ring off his father's hand.

"Promise me," Weyland said. "Promise me you won't let them . . ."

A long sigh escaped Weyland's lips, and he lay still.

"No!" Brion whispered.

He laid a trembling hand on his father's chest, willing it to rise and fall, but his father never stirred. Brion saw the brutal wound in his father's head. It leaked blood and something gray into the thick, brown hair. Tears slipped from Brion's eyes. He wiped savagely at them, terrified for his mother and Brigid. Where were they? Why hadn't they come?

He lunged to his feet, shoving the ring into this pocket and stepped back from his father's body.

"Momma?" he called. "Brigid?"

Silence greeted his words.

A cow's hoof twitched from where it poked out from underneath the fence where the muddy snow was stained red.

"Momma?" he yelled again as he rushed into the cabin.

No one answered. Panic tightened his throat. He darted into the back room and choked on the sob. His mother lay prostrate on the floor staring up at the ceiling—a great purple bruise by her eye, a dribble of blood on her ear, a knife in her hand.

"Momma?"

He dropped the axe, frantic with unconstrained horror. He couldn't breathe. Brion knelt and lifted his mother's head into his lap. It rolled to one side.

She didn't blink or smile or breathe. Her face remained peaceful and impassive. The auburn hair spread out like a fan over his trousers. She might have been asleep. Brion's mind reeled. What had happened? Who could have done this? Why?

The pile of orange fur crumpled against the trunk drew his attention. The body of the old tomcat lay twisted in death. They had even killed the cat.

A boot scraped on the floorboards. Brion swept up the axe as he lunged to his feet with a savage growl.

Neahl, his nearest neighbor and his father's best friend, stood in the doorway studying him. He had no cloak, his linen shirt was torn, and his boots were caked with mud. Brion searched his wizened face. Neahl's gaze flicked to where Brion's mother lay on the floor.

Brion let the axe fall to the floorboards with a thud, trying to blink the tears from his eyes.

"I . . ." he began. "They're . . ." How could he tell Neahl that he had failed to protect his entire family? "I wasn't here," Brion said.

Neahl panted as if he had just sprinted a mile. But he knelt beside Brion's mother for a moment before he stood and faced Brion again. Brion saw the pained expression slip across Neahl's face before he could mask it. Neahl placed a hand on Brion's shoulder. It was his right hand—the one that was missing the tips of the fingers.

"They took Brigid," Neahl said.

It took Brion a moment to understand what he meant.

"Who?" he demanded, as he wiped at his eyes.

Only then did he notice the blood shining on Neahl's face and caked in his grizzled hair. He glanced down to see the bloody knife still clutched in Neahl's left hand.

He searched Neahl's face for an explanation.

"The Salassani," Neahl said, as if this truth was too obvious to require mentioning.

Brion's eyes opened wide. He snatched up the axe, pushed past Neahl and rushed from the cabin, jumping over his father's body as he cleared the doorway. Now he saw the tracks in the snow. Several horses had milled about. He noted their direction, hefted the axe, and sprang after them.

Chapter 2
The Cold Grave

Brion stood gazing out over the frozen river, one hand clutching at the pain in his side, when Neahl found him. The river wasn't wide or deep, and, sometimes in the summer, it dried to a trickle. But now it was a slushy, impassible death trap for a man without a horse.

The river had cut through the plain, creating shallow bluffs on either side. Clumps of sage and bayberry and the occasional cottonwood sent up thin, bone-like limbs to reach toward the steel-gray sky.

"Which way did they go?" Brion asked, rounding on Neahl as he approached.

Neahl placed his hand on Brion's shoulder again. "These aren't the ones you want."

Now Brion gaped at him. "What? I followed them here."

Neahl shook his head and lowered his arm. "The ones you want left this trail a mile back." He nodded toward the river. "These are the ones that raided the village."

Brion scowled. "How do you know?"

"Because I took the time to read the trail instead of chasing any horse track I found in the snow."

Tears brimmed in Brion's eyes as he shrank under the weight of his despair.

"They're dead, Neahl. The Salassani took Brigid. I have to go after them."

Neahl nodded and patted Brion's shoulder. "We will, lad. But not today."

Brion straightened. "What? They'll get away. We have to go now!"

"They already got away," Neahl said. "We need to get ready to go after them. Come spring we'll follow."

"Spring? Why not now?"

Neahl sighed. "Look at yourself. You've got no food, no water, no weapon save a crude axe, and no proper winter clothes for a long journey. You'd be dead in a week, if not sooner. And you'd be dead for sure if you caught up with them alone and armed with nothing more than an axe."

Brion glanced at the axe. He had almost forgotten it. "But what about Brigid, Neahl? They'll . . ." He couldn't say it. The tears still swam in his eyes.

Neahl nodded. "I know. Believe me, I know." Neahl paused. "Let's go see to your parents. There are things you need to know."

"I can't," Brion said.

Neahl frowned. "You have to."

"Neahl, please."

Brion had known Neahl all of his life. Neahl had been there when his father had been crippled by the sword stroke that severed the tendons in his arm. Neahl had helped his father scratch a poor living selling the pelts they tanned to merchants in Mailag. Neahl had been there when Brion's parents had wed. Neahl had been there when Brion made his first kill with a bow. Neahl had always been there.

Brion turned back to the river. He didn't want to admit the truth of Neahl's words. To do so meant abandoning Brigid. Brion shook his head. "I can't leave her."

"Well, suit yourself," Neahl waved an angry hand at Brion. "If you're not back in a week, I'll come looking for your body."

Neahl turned and stomped off down the road. "I'll pick up whatever the Salassani and the wolves leave behind," he called over his shoulder.

Brion perched on the edge of indecision until Neahl disappeared over the hill. At last, he admitted to himself that he didn't stand a chance alone in the wild heathland.

Brion wiped at the tears before he stole one last, longing look at the slushy river and turned his back on it and on Brigid. He had failed her. She would be searching the horizon, expecting him to come to her rescue. But he wouldn't be there. Maybe he would never be there.

Back at the cabin, Neahl and Brion scraped a single, large grave from the frozen earth. Brion worked without feeling. His mind ground to a halt on three simple questions: How could his world have evaporated so quickly? How could he live a life without his parents, knowing that his little sister toiled as a captive among the savage Salassani? And what did this have to do with his father's secret?

They laid his parents together in the grave, side by side, the way they had lived their lives. If it hadn't been for the blood that matted Weyland's hair, they might have been sleeping together in bed the way Brion had seen them countless times. Brion brushed a lock of hair from Rosland's face and remembered a time when she had lain sweating and shivering with a fever. He had wiped her brow with a damp cloth, and she had grabbed his hands and squeezed. "I bless the day you came to us," she had said. "You gave me a reason to live."

Brion had never understood what she had meant by that last line, but it made his failure today all the more agonizing. He hadn't saved them—any of them. Brion swallowed the knot in his throat and stood to place Rosland's prized tablecloth over them. The close weave of pure white displayed delicate blue flowers woven carefully into the cloth. He laid the old tomcat beside her and picked up his father's sword to lay it on the cloth.

"Not the sword," Neahl said. "You'll be needing it."

Brion glanced at him and back at the sword. Brion had rarely used a real sword. He usually played with the wooden cudgels his father had used to teach him how to fight.

This thought gave him pause. His father had had time to go to the trunk, unwrap the sword from its oiled cloth, and make it to the front door in time to intercept the Salassani. And he had warned Brion the night before.

Brion turned to Neahl. "He knew they were coming," he said.

Neahl considered and nodded. "Weyland was no fool."

"But who were they? Why would they care about us?"

Neahl shrugged. "Let's just finish here," he said.

Brion faced the shallow pit where his parents lay. Bitterness and shame tightened his throat and stung his eyes. Weyland had tried to warn Brion, to prepare him. And Brion had failed. He hadn't been there to help his father. He hadn't been there to protect to them.

Brion lifted the shovel to cast the dirt over his parent's bodies. He couldn't watch the muddy soil fall into his mother's hair and onto his father's chest. It was too final. He averted his gaze, but he couldn't avoid the sound of the hollow thump as the mud hit their bodies. Bile rose in his throat. He coughed and swallowed, struggling to keep his stomach

Deliverance

from turning itself inside out.

Brion knelt beside the mound of muddy earth searching for the strength to let his parents go—struggling to comprehend how he could ever be worthy of their memory. After long minutes, he stood and faced Neahl. He wiped at the last of the tears and tried to stand taller. His father had taught him that a man learns to accept what he cannot change and goes on living. A boy kicks against the pricks until his feet are bloody.

"What were you going to tell me?" Brion asked.

Neahl glanced at the dead cow still lying in the corral.

"Are you going to butcher her?"

Brion followed his gaze. "You don't eat pets," he said.

Neahl stood and motioned for Brion to follow him as he set off down the road towards his own house. Brion took several steps and then stopped. There, in the shadow of the trees, stood the old midwife. Brion had seen her occasionally around the farm and in the town. She had never spoken to him—just watched him. Her clothes sagged about her like rags. She held a tree branch in her hands. Brion took a step toward her, but she raised the branch, turned, and disappeared into the trees.

Brion ran to catch up with Neahl, but Neahl didn't go more than a hundred paces before he veered off the road and into the trees. Brion followed.

Neahl stopped beside a large, black mare that nibbled on the low-hanging twigs of a beech tree. Her reins trailed in the snow. Not far from the horse sprawled a man dressed in loose-fitting, dun-colored clothing with a sword clutched in his hand. His black cloak draped over his legs. Bright-red splashes stained the trampled snow.

Chapter 3
Ghosts of the Past

Brion gave Neahl a questioning glance. Neahl gestured to the man.

"He's a Salassani from the northern fens," he said. "On horseback, it would've taken him two to three weeks to come this far south."

Blue and red paint lined the man's forehead in the shape of two, large, blue-black eyes with red pupils. The effect was startling. It made the man appear as if he had four eyes.

"What happened?" Brion asked, tearing his gaze from the man's still form.

"I was in the west field when they came over the hill," Neahl said. "There were about five or six of them. This one came after me." He said the last phrase with a small shrug.

"Why are they down here? I mean, they haven't been this far south since, well, since I was a kid."

"Probably just raiding," Neahl said. "A bigger party hit the village. They'll be back in the heathland by tomorrow morning and back to the fens by the new moon. We would never catch them."

"But—"

"It's cold," Neahl said with a shake of his head. "Let's talk where we can get warm."

Neahl bent and pulled the man's sword-belt free, sheathed the sword, and checked the man for any other items he would no longer need. He retrieved a small bag of coins that clinked when he shook it and a large, wide-bladed knife stuffed in the man's boot. Neahl grabbed up the horse's reins. The horse reached over to sniff at the dead Salassani and followed.

"Aren't we going to bury him?" Brion asked.

Neahl stopped and glanced back at the corpse as if considering. He shook his head.

"What for? He's just Salassani scum."

14

Neahl led the horse away.

Brion paused. The man had seemed so innocent as he lay in the snow. But Neahl's words reminded Brion that this man and his friends had come to kill his family. They had carried Brigid away, and Brion had been helpless to stop any of it. Frustration, anger, and despair roared up inside him. He wanted to strike back, to do something. Brion ground his teeth and kicked the Salassani. Then he spat on him and wheeled around to follow Neahl out of the woods.

Neahl handed Brion the axe and gestured toward the pile of logs. He sat on a stool beside the cabin, pulled out his bloodstained knife, and began cleaning it.

"I thought we were going inside to get warm," Brion said.

"This will keep you warm."

"Weren't you going to tell me something?" Brion asked.

Neahl gestured toward the wood.

"No sense wasting time while we talk," he said.

Brion grabbed a chunk of wood and propped it up on the splitting log. He split it in one, smooth stroke and reached for another.

"Did Weyland ever tell you about the wars?" Neahl said as he spat on his blade and wiped the last of the dried blood away with a cloth.

Brion shook his head and split another log. "Not much," he said.

Nothing really, he thought. His father had mentioned it only twice in his entire life, and the last time he had spoken of it, he had forbidden Brion to tell anyone.

Neahl stood and stepped into the house. Brion expected Neahl to bring him some relic of the war, but Neahl came out with his big whetstone and set it on a log beside the stool. He bent over it and began running the blade over the stone in long, even strokes.

"Well," Neahl continued. "It's time you understood. If you're going to go into the heathland, you need to know."

Brion paused and Neahl pointed to another log. He waited for Brion to pick it up.

"Weyland wasn't much older than you," Neahl said, "when we set out to join the army of the Duke of Saylen."

"He fought with the Duke of Saylen?" Brion blurted in surprise.

Every boy in the Kingdom of Coll had heard of the Duke of Saylen.

He had saved Coll from ruin by his valiant stand against overwhelming odds in the Laro Forest. His courage and heroism were legend. And Brion had had no idea that his own father had fought with him.

Neahl nodded. "Many times. In fact, Weyland saved his life."

"What?" Brion paused, resting the axe on his shoulder. How could his father have kept this a secret all of his life? Why?

"Keep splitting," Neahl said, pointing to the pile of logs.

Brion grabbed a log as Neahl bent back to sharpening his blade.

"Your father shot from the other side of the battlefield," Neahl explained, "and felled the Dunkeldi swine as he raised his sword to kill the Duke. It was an amazing shot, even for Weyland, who was the best archer in the army."

Brion could only stare. The axe dangled loosely in his hand. He had lived all his life under the same roof with his father and had never known. He struggled to imagine his father as a great archer, but he couldn't imagine away the withered and twisted arm Brion had known all his life. Nor could he forget the secret shame it had always caused him.

Neahl pointed to the logs and waited until Brion picked one up.

"The Duke took a special liking to Weyland after that," Neahl said. "He often visited Weyland, and I think Weyland did some favors for him." Neahl's gaze strayed to the fields. "The Duke gave Weyland this land in payment for his services."

Brion split the log with a rising fury. Bitterness filled his throat. He had lived seventeen years with his father only to find that he was a stranger to him. Maybe this is what his father had wanted to tell him. But it didn't seem so dangerous. What other secrets had his father kept?

Neahl inspected the edge of the knife. He tested it on the hairs of his arm and set it back on the whetstone.

"It was a chaotic time," Neahl said. "The royal family had been murdered, the Salassani were sweeping the southern heathland, pushing us south, and some terrible disease from the continent swept over the islands. People were dying everywhere. No one knew what to do with the bodies."

Brion had heard of the Great Death. He had seen the bones poking up from the shallow mass graves where the bodies had been dumped outside of Wexford.

Neahl surveyed Brion with raised eyebrows until Brion picked up another log. Brion could barely restrain the anger. Why couldn't Neahl just tell him without making him split the stupid logs?

"You were born the year of the coup. Brigid was born before the wars were over."

Neahl tried the edge again. It shaved the hair clean away.

"Weyland and I grew up together in the village of Comrie on Com Lake just at the foothills of the Aveen Mountains."

Neahl stood and entered the house. Brion fumed. Why couldn't Neahl just say what he had to say without interruptions? Neahl came back with a little bottle and a cloth. He sat back on the stool and tipped the bottle onto the cloth. He stared at Brion, waiting for him to continue splitting.

"Just say it," Brion said.

Neahl pointed to the logs.

Brion cursed, but he picked up another log and slammed it onto the splitting log.

Neahl continued.

"One early spring day, the Salassani swept into our village. We put up a fight, but they drove us back into the heather. They killed everyone they didn't carry off into slavery—men, women, and children."

Neahl wiped the oil along the blade.

"They killed my mother and burned my grandmother to death in the house. My little brother survived because he hid under a rock along the lake shore. And they kidnapped my wife."

Brion stopped chopping. Neahl married?

Neahl said this without any emotion in his voice. But he paused and lifted his gaze to survey the field.

"We gathered our men and went after them," Neahl said. "We caught them high up on the southern reaches of the Daven Fens where the heather is small and the land is dry and cold. We drove them off and recovered our womenfolk and the children."

Neahl turned his gaze to Brion. Pain slipped across Neahl's face for just a moment, the way it had a few hours ago.

"But my wife didn't survive."

Neahl stood, went back into the cabin and came back with his short sword. He stared at Brion until Brion picked up another log. Brion swallowed the knot in his throat and continued splitting.

"Weyland survived," Neahl continued, "and took those we had recovered back to the village. But I pursued the Salassani, hunting them like rabbits. I harassed them for days, deep into the fens before they caught me. I don't know why they didn't kill me, but they took out their fury on me."

He raised his right hand. The three fingers had not been cleanly cut. They had been severed in a downward slant toward the small finger. This left most of the index finger from the third knuckle down and the ring finger from the second knuckle down. The pinky was almost gone. Neahl also pointed to several long, white scars on his face and arms.

"They almost let me bleed to death. But they kept me alive in the end to send me back as a warning, I guess, to anyone who might be left."

Neahl took a deep breath and pointed to the logs. Brion cursed again and kept splitting.

"So I met up with Weyland and my brother at a neighboring village. We came south to offer our services to the Duke. Your father and my brother served as archers. I tracked and scouted, because, well . . ." Neahl glanced down at his crippled hand. "We spent three long years in the Duke's army. We fought in every battle."

"What happened to your brother?" Brion asked as the axe bit deep into the splitting log.

Neahl sneered. "When the Salassani trapped us in a narrow valley on the edge of the Laro Forest, he turned coward and ran."

"Why?"

Neahl shrugged and wiped the oilcloth over the sword. "He didn't think we should be killing the Salassani anymore. He even let one go after a Salassani archer pinned him down for an entire day, trying to kill him. I thought he had betrayed me." Neahl shrugged. "By the end of the war, he had changed. He said he didn't want to die fighting for an impostor king. He had said that it was foolhardy and dangerous and that we would live to regret it." Neahl shrugged again. "Well, he may have been right. But he abandoned us when we needed his bow." Neahl examined the sword and slid it back into the sheath. "And now it's time to prepare for another foolhardy journey into the heathland."

He stood and motioned for Brion to follow him into the cabin. He retrieved a pot of steaming water from the fire, poured two mugs, and dumped a few bits of dried leaves and flowers into them. He gestured to the table and pushed one toward Brion.

"Stir it in for a bit. Then drink it. It'll make you feel better."

Brion obeyed. The warm liquid spilled into his stomach, sending a reassuring warmth throughout his entire body.

Deliverance

"What is it?" Brion asked.

"An herbal remedy I picked up from a Salassani prisoner. Just keep sipping it while I tell you what we're going to do."

Neahl sipped his tea.

"First," he said, "while I'm gone to the village, I want you to go back to your house and collect your things. Bring them back here and wait for me. Chop firewood if you're restless. I'll be back in about an hour or so."

"Why can't I come with you?"

"Because you need some time alone, and I have a few favors to call in that would best be called without any witnesses. I won't be gone long."

"But what if they hit the village hard? Shouldn't I come to help out?"

Neahl considered for a moment and shook his head.

"If they need help, we'll go back later. Let me check it out first."

Brion scowled. Neahl wasn't telling him something. Brion wanted to visit the village because he needed to know that Finola was all right. She might be feisty enough to give any kidnapper grief, but he still needed to be sure that she was okay.

Neahl stood without another word and stepped out the door. He broke the ice in the water barrel, dunked his head, scrubbed off the blood, shook his head like a wet dog and strode off up the road. Neahl cut through the wood toward the village, while Brion followed the road to his own home.

The familiar open fields spread out around him with the blackened stubble of last year's growth poking up through the slushy snow. The thick woodland, now stripped of leaves, filled the hollows in between and wiggled its way toward the river to the north while fanning out towards the Great Oban Plain to the south. This land had been his home for almost eighteen years. Now it seemed foreign and forlorn. A wasteland of buried hopes and dreams.

At first, he just stood beside the fresh grave, wondering what he could have done to prevent this—wondering how, in the time it had taken him to race from the south field, his entire family could be kidnapped or killed. Why had his father been at the house at all? He had gone into town, or so Brion thought.

Brion swallowed the lump in his throat and wiped at his eyes as he stepped into the house, being careful not to tread in the red snow. The phantom memories of his mother bent over the fire, Brigid singing to the ugly, old tomcat, and his father teaching him to read pursued him

19

about the house, nipping at him like a selfish puppy, hunting him.

He tried to ignore the memories as he collected his clothes and his bedding along with his leather flask and hunting knife, his bow, his arm guard, and shooting gloves. He didn't have much else. So he went to his parent's room, retrieved the keys to the trunk from the loose floorboard in the corner and opened the trunk. It surprised him that it was locked. Had his father even put the sword away after sharpening it last night?

One by one, Brion withdrew the treasured objects. Some of them had no meaning to him, like the small doll he found wrapped in the corner. But he found his mother's silver necklace in the little maple box his father had made before he lost the use of his hand. Brion slipped the necklace over his head and promised himself that he wouldn't remove it until he could drape it around Brigid's neck.

A rush of affection for his parents engulfed him. He had lived his entire life without ever once imagining that he would find himself alone, facing empty years they would no longer share. His parents were still young and strong. They were so capable and wise. He had depended on them for everything. Now he was alone with the terrible burden of knowing that his sister had no one else left in the world.

Brion closed the trunk and dropped the key into its hiding place. Something made a sound like dried leaves. Brion peered into the little hollow where the floorboard had been and found a bundle of papers. He withdrew them. The bundle smelled of age and mildew. Why hadn't the rats found them?

His father had known how to read and had insisted on teaching his children. He used to say that "a man who can't read is easily tricked by one who can. When other men know you can read, it encourages them to be honest."

Brion thumbed through the papers. Some were notes to his mother. One was a deed of ownership for the land his father had owned. But the last document was several pages long and was written in a language Brion couldn't read. But he understood the seal well enough. It was the coat of arms of the Duke of Saylen—a stag in a teardrop shield.

Why would his father, a crippled trapper, have papers sealed with a nobleman's seal? Could it have something to do with the fact that his father had saved the Duke's life? Had his father done some secret work for the Duke? Brion puzzled over the strange writing before stuffing the wad of papers inside his tunic.

Deliverance

Brion pulled from his pocket the ring he had taken from his father's bloody hand. The plain gold had an oval surface into which a coat of arms had been engraved. The key feature of the coat of arms was an eagle with outstretched wings—the same symbol had been scratched onto the margin of one of the papers in the bundle Brion had just found. Though Brion had seen only one other ring like it on the headman's finger, this ring was clearly a seal of some kind. Suspicion played at the back of his mind. If this was his father's secret, why would anyone kill him for it?

As Brion left the cabin, he paused at the door with his hand on the latch. He cast one last yearning glance at his boyhood home. Brigid's bonnet dangled on a peg by the door as if she had just come in. His mother had the loom set up as if she had just stepped away to tend to the cooking. The ghosts of the past chased him from the cabin. He pulled the door closed and let the latch fall with a click of finality.

Chapter 4
Love Lost

pen it."

Neahl laid a long, oiled, canvas bag on the table and swung the large quiver filled with two dozen arrows beside it.

Brion knew what it was. He always kept his own bow unstrung and in its oiled sack. Moisture was a bow's enemy and it was even worse for the flax strings that became heavy and sluggish when they got wet. Brion pulled the longbow from the sack and hefted it. He glanced up at Neahl to make sure that he understood what this meant.

"I brought my old bow," Brion said.

Neahl nodded.

"It's time you shot a man's bow. This bow will send a bodkin through chain mail at a hundred paces and, at fifteen, through plate armor."

Brion examined the beautiful, yew longbow with its black, horn tips sharpened to a fine point. The cream-colored sap wood formed the back and the red heartwood the belly. Brion knew that the sapwood was springy but resisted stretching, while the heartwood resisted compressing. Together the two woods worked to create a very fast and powerful bow. It was thick—much thicker than his own.

"What if I can't draw it?" he asked.

"Then you'll draw it until you can."

Brion rubbed his hand over the glossy surface. The yew wood had been smoothed and oiled to a high polish. He caught the faint scent of honey and knew that the last layer to be rubbed in had been of warmed beeswax mixed with oil.

"It's beautiful. Thank you."

"Well, it isn't the beauty that counts, but it makes a man feel proud to carry a weapon like that." Neahl paused. "So string it. It's time you got started."

Brion stood and hefted the bow in his left hand. It felt good. He bent all his strength to string the bow.

"Wow, that's heavy. What does it draw?"

Neahl smiled. "It's only seventy pounds."

"Seventy pounds. My bow's fifty-five, and I've never drawn over sixty."

"Then it's time to get to work," Neahl said. "Put on that arm guard and that glove and follow me."

"What about the village?"

Neahl frowned and waved at Brion to follow him outside as he started walking toward the fields.

"About twenty-five raiders hit the village," Neahl said. "They carried off two more young ladies and three lads—probably to sell them up north as slaves. They killed old Jonah when he tried to stop them from taking his little boy."

"Who else did they take?" Brion asked.

Neahl glanced at him.

Brion stopped. "Who else did they take, Neahl?"

Suspicion at Neahl's hesitation tightened Brion's throat. His fist closed more tightly around the bow.

"They took little Maggie, Rob, Jonas, Billy, and . . ." Neahl paused. "Finola."

"What?"

Brion wanted to shout. He and Finola had been friends ever since she slapped his hands when he had tried to sneak a sweet roll from the bakery when he was seven. The blonde, young woman with the pale, blue eyes had become more than a friend in the last couple of years. And now Finola had been kidnapped by the savages that had murdered his parents and stolen his sister. It was too much to be borne.

"We don't have time for this, Neahl." Brion shook the bow in Neahl's face. "Let's go after them. Now."

Neahl sighed and shook his head. He had apparently anticipated Brion's response.

"Thirty men already went after them. If they can be caught, the men will bring them back. But the ones who kidnapped Brigid didn't go the same way as the others. I checked the trail."

Neahl squatted down and scratched a map in the snow on the edge of the field where Brion had stopped.

"The ones who hit the village followed the river for a few miles before they crossed and headed straight north." He dragged the stick through the snow. "If they continued in that direction, it would take them between Mailag and Brechin. But the ones who took Brigid didn't cross. They stayed on this side and were careful to conceal their trail." Neahl jabbed the stick into the ground.

Brion's face burned. His pulse throbbed in his neck. He struggled to contain his fury and desperation. "It's too much. I can't stand it," he said. "How will you follow their trail once it's cold?"

"I don't have to. I know where they came from." Neahl rose to his feet and started toward the field again.

"What?" Brion hurried after him.

"Did you notice the pattern of the dead Salassani's paint?"

"What, the eyes?"

"Yes," Neahl said. "The Salassani may be just Salassani to us, but they make distinctions among themselves. The Bracari, Aldina, and Taurini are from the far north, and the Carpentini live along the west coastal moor and in the Aveen Mountains. The Dunkeldi come from the east coast and the oldest and smallest tribe, the Salassani, from the Daven Fens. We just simplify things and call them all Salassani."

"So?"

"Most Salassani paint their faces while raiding. By the different designs you can tell that we had at least three bands in the raid. My guess is that the ones who came here had quarreled with the others and sought their own prize. They were from a different band, I think.

"But you know where their village is?" This seemed like the most important piece of information, and Neahl was avoiding it.

Neahl nodded. "More or less."

"Then why not go after them now? We could cut them off and get ahead of them."

Neahl shook his head. "Two reasons. One, the snow has already covered their trail. Two, you are not ready."

"I am ready. I'm ready now. My father trained me to hunt and shoot a bow."

Neahl spun on Brion making him come to an abrupt halt. Neahl stepped uncomfortably close and stood taller and broader. Brion held his ground. He was serious. He wanted to leave now.

"But did he train you to be a warrior?" Neahl asked. "To kill and to be prepared to die? Did he train you to survive on your own when others hunt you? That's what you have to be ready for, Brion. Don't think you can just chase down the Salassani and shoot them without them having something to say about it."

Neahl held up his crippled hand as if in evidence.

Brion kicked a clod of mud. "It's hard. I want to do something."

Neahl placed his crippled hand on Brion's shoulder. "You *are* doing something," he said. "You're preparing yourself to survive when we go get Brigid and Finola."

Brion stared at Neahl, trying to conceal the wretched pain that filled his chest.

"Will they—" he swallowed.

Neahl frowned. "I don't know. I'm betting nothing will happen to them until the great trade fair they hold once a year on the shores of Aldina Lake. They call it the Great Keldi."

Neahl set off into the field again.

"You're betting?"

Neahl stopped and regarded him. "Virgins bring a higher price, Brion. So it's a safe bet."

Brion bowed his head as Neahl continued walking.

"The tribes come from all around under the King's Peace—" Neahl explained, "a general agreement that no one will seek to resolve any old grievances. Sometimes the King of the Dunkeldi himself attends. I don't think they'll do anything to lessen the value of their prize."

"You think? But you don't know?" Brion shouted as he struggled to constrain the rage and frustration. How could Neahl be so casual? It seemed as if he didn't care what happened to the girls.

Neahl stopped again and scowled at Brion. "I've told you. You're not ready. But you obviously think you know more than I do. So I'll make you a deal. We fight right here and right now, and if you can hold your own, we'll leave before the sun sets."

Brion took a step back. He was large for a seventeen-year-old, but Neahl was a big, burly man with many years' experience. Still, at that moment, all of Brion's rage was directed at Neahl, who seemed to be intent on letting the Salassani have their way with Finola and Brigid.

Brion dropped the bow and quiver and lunged, swinging his fists. Neahl stepped in to block the fists and brought a knee up into Brion's gut. Pain lanced through Brion's body as the air rushed from his lungs. Before he knew what was happening, he was face down in the muddy slush with an arm wrenched painfully behind his back.

"I think this means we wait until spring," Neahl said.

Neahl let Brion drag himself to his feet and then pointed to an old stump a good fifty paces out in the muddy field. "You've got two dozen arrows," he said. "Shoot until you can get all two dozen in the stump."

Brion held a hand to his stomach. He wanted to keep arguing, to convince Neahl they had to go but knew better than to push his luck any further. Brion hefted the bow. He knew he wouldn't be able to draw it. But he pulled the quiver over his head, withdrew an arrow and slipped the nock onto the string.

He raised the bow, made sure his grip was loose, the way his father had taught him, and that the grip of the bow nestled on the pad of his palm. He pushed the nock down against the small knot of string tied there to ensure he had a consistent nock point and placed one finger above and two beneath the nock.

He drew the bow, canting it sideways so he could aim. To his surprise, he could get the string most of the way back, but he couldn't reach his anchor point on his cheek. He let the arrow fly anyway, and it flew wide and fell short.

Neahl grunted. "I'll call ya for dinner."

Neahl didn't come back until the sun drooped over the horizon. Brion's entire upper body ached. His hands trembled from fatigue. He couldn't even get the bow to half-draw anymore. But he stubbornly kept shooting, determined to show Neahl that he didn't quit—that he could be a warrior. Neahl watched him shoot his last arrow and accompanied him to retrieve them. Half a dozen arrows had hit the stump. The rest scattered around its base.

"It's a start," Neahl said.

"You know I could hit that stump nine times out of ten with my bow."

"I know," Neahl said. "But you need a war bow now, and you need to be able draw it all day without getting tired. We're building muscles now. In a month, you'll be coming to full draw. Then we'll start perfecting your form."

They swung around to stroll back toward the house and found a man standing beside the door with a braced bow in his hands. Neahl stopped and surveyed the intruder as if sizing him up before striding forward.

"Evening stranger," Neahl said.

Neahl was never what you would call an inviting person, but he put on a welcoming smile and tried to sound friendly. Brion glanced at Neahl. After what had happened today, he would not be so trusting. Brion slipped an arrow from his back quiver and placed it on the string. The stranger took no notice—which meant he was overconfident or dangerous.

The man nodded his grizzled head and resumed his leisurely stance. He wore forest greens and browns and carried a quiver full of arrows on his back and a large satchel over the other shoulder. A short sword dangled in his belt and a large knife protruded from under his cloak opposite the sword. He didn't make any movement, but Brion knew by the way he stood, relaxed and ready, that this man knew how to take care of himself.

When they reached him, Neahl stretched out his hand and stopped. The smile faded. He paused, stepped backward and shook his head. "Not you," he whispered.

"Why not?" the stranger replied. "Don't you think it's about time we came to terms?"

Neahl sneered, stepping toward the man while bringing up his fists. "I'll come to terms," he growled.

The stranger raised one hand in surrender, though he still clutched the bow in the other. "I won't fight you, Neahl. I ask only that you hear me out."

"Why should I listen to a coward and a traitor?"

"Because I'm your brother," the stranger said. "Hear me, and if you're not satisfied, I'll leave and never trouble you again." The stranger glanced at Brion. "But I have a feeling you may need my help," he said.

Neahl snorted and strode into the house.

Chapter 5
Captured

Brigid sat on the damp ground with her back to the rock as the daylight faded from the sky. She wrapped her skirt around her knees and cradled the little bowl of broth in her hands. The chill breeze played with her bright red hair and penetrated her thin, woolen blouse. She scanned the horizon from the direction they had come while occasionally sipping the broth. The dreary, barren landscape stretched as far as she could see, all brown and gray, except for the occasional green juniper. Small mountains rose up amid the gray sky to the northwest. They had ridden hard all day, staying close to the river and the cover of trees that clung to its banks before disappearing into the rolling valleys of the heathland.

By now, the whole village had to know that she had been kidnapped. Her mother would have raised the alarm. Brion would have heard her scream as she had seen her father lying in a pool of blood. But where were the men who should have come after her?

She blinked back the tears. She would not despair. Her father and mother would not want her to despair. They were tough trappers and frontier folk, bred to a life of toil. They had raised her to work hard without complaint and to accept whatever struggles life sent her way. They would be patching their wounds and deciding how to rescue her. Brigid would not believe that they would just go on without her. She could not.

Raised voices came from the circle of men gathered around the fire in the gathering dusk. Brigid glanced at the young warrior who had carried her on his horse all day. He had blue and red paint over his face in what appeared to be a wolf's open mouth with fangs. But he couldn't be much older than Brion. His loose-fitting, dun-colored clothing couldn't hide his slender build and the fluid movements that made him appear overconfident. His hair was a light sandy color, where the other men all had black hair.

The big man with white face paint and a bloody bandage on his arm

28

was yelling at him, gesturing in her direction. The young man glanced at her. Her gaze met his. She noted something intense, even threatening in his expression—something that made her shiver.

He faced the angry man again and said something in Salassani, without raising his voice. The big man leapt to his feet and drew his sword. His cloak billowed out behind him. The young man glanced at the blade and shook his head. He rose slowly to his feet. He pointed at Brigid and placed a hand on his chest as he spoke.

Brigid watched the gesture and understood that he had claimed her. He had been the one to lift her up into the saddle when the other men wanted to kill her. He had been the one to give her food and water, while the others hung back and glared at her.

The terror clawed its way into her belly and wrapped a coil around her chest, squeezing all the air from her lungs. She grasped the wooden bowl more tightly, trying to stop her hands from trembling.

The angry man bellowed and raised his sword for a swing, but the young man moved so fast that Brigid wasn't sure what he had done. Somehow he had closed the distance while drawing a long knife and slashed three or four times. The big man's roar of rage turned to a cry of pain and surprise.

The big man stumbled backwards. The sword fell with a clang to the stony ground. Blood gushed from the terrible wounds as the man gaped at them. Then he raised his head to stare at the young man who stood impassive before him.

The young man gave his knife a shake, wiped it on his pant leg, and jammed it back in its sheath at his side. The big man's eyes grew wider and wider. He fell to his knees, grasping at his ragged flesh in a desperate attempt to stem the flow of blood. The young man gazed at each of the other men in turn as if questioning their intentions. No one stirred. They all watched the big man bleed to death beside the little glowing fire.

Brigid sipped the broth and tried to swallow it as she turned away from the horror of the scene, but her stomach wouldn't let her. She knew little about the Salassani, but she did know that they raided for slaves and for wives. She extended her foot so that her boot pulled tight against the little dagger concealed there. If she had to, she would use it. Her father had been a warrior, and he had trained both his son and daughter to defend themselves. Brigid remembered what he had told her.

"I've seen too many women and girls perish under a blade because they didn't know how to use one. What you lack in strength you can make up for in cunning and skill."

She managed a wry smile as she remembered his scarred face and crippled arm and the many hours she spent learning to use the dagger, the bow, the lance, and the short sword.

"A well-placed arrow, even from a light hunting bow, can kill the largest man," he had said. "But you'll never be able to withstand the strength of a man with a great sword. It's best to stay out of reach or come in close for the kill."

Brigid understood the skill her captor had just displayed with the knife. But she had never seen anyone killed so brutally before. She couldn't drink the broth. She spat it out, set the bowl on the ground, and watched one of the men drag the dead man away from the camp and roll him down the hill. They all returned to the fire and began conversing in low tones as if nothing had happened—as if slaughter was an everyday experience.

Brigid brushed at the hair the evening wind blew into her face. She turned away from the men, their smokeless fire, and the horror of what she had seen. She gazed back the way she had come—back towards her home—a home she may never see again.

She had never been so far from Wexford. And she had no idea how to get back. All of this meant that her wild daydreams of escape were just that—dreams. Even if she could get away, where would she go? How would she survive on her own? How would she find her way back to her own people? It was no use. Her only hope lay in rescue.

Chapter 6
Cold Steel

rion stared, dumbfounded at Neahl and this strange man with the longbow. For some reason, even though Neahl had told him he had a brother, Brion was having a hard time seeing Neahl as anything but a loner—a one-man show. Neahl seemed old, weathered, and solid, like the hard, prairie earth. Brion hurried to follow the two men into the cabin. In his haste, he forgot about the arrow on the string until it caught on the door as he rushed in. It popped off and fell with a clatter. When Brion rose after picking it up, both men watched him. The stranger smiled with the side of his mouth. Neahl scowled.

Brion replaced the arrow in the quiver and unstrung the bow while the other two stepped toward the fire. Neahl hung a pot over the flames and sat down, gesturing for Redmond to sit opposite him.

Neahl waited until Brion had pulled off the quiver and sat on the ground beside his chair and then gestured to the stranger. "Meet my younger brother, Redmond."

Brion stared as Redmond pulled off his green cap and nodded to Brion. The two men had the same strong jaw and steady eyes, but they didn't look alike. Redmond was more wiry and taller than Neahl. His eyes were hazel. His hair was grizzled. Brion noted the thin, white scars on his hands and face.

"Well?" Neahl said.

Redmond sighed. "I didn't betray you."

Neahl scoffed.

"No, listen," Redmond said. "I knew that as long as I stayed by you, you would pursue the Salassani until we were all dead. I did everything I could to dissuade you. Weyland had a family to consider. I had Lara and her family to worry about. The Salassani were hunting us. How long until they went after the people we loved?"

Brion wanted to ask who Lara was, but the scowl on Neahl's face silenced him.

31

"So you just turned coward and abandoned us in the middle of a battle?" Neahl's face twisted in rage.

Redmond bristled. "I wasn't a coward," he said. "I would have stood beside you and died with you even though I never approved of the coup or your vendetta, as you well know."

Neahl lifted his lip in a sneer. "You're not convincing me to change my mind."

Redmond clasped his hands in front of him as if he were resisting the urge to draw his blade or to reach out and strangle Neahl. The muscles in his jaw twitched.

"My horse took an arrow in the flank during the battle and bolted," he said with exaggerated calm. "My boot slipped through the stirrup so I couldn't dismount. I had little choice but to cling to him until he calmed. I hurried back, but when I returned, you were gone. I fought my way south in search of you only to hear rumors that you had sworn to kill me for my cowardice."

He paused as if he expected Neahl to deny the assertion. Neahl stood up and stirred the fire with a poker.

Redmond's gaze followed his movements, and he continued speaking. "Well, I felt betrayed in my turn," he said, "and I realized that the only way to stop you was to kill you or to leave you. So I left. I left so that Weyland's son could have a father. So that Lara and her family could live unmolested by the assassins that were coming after us."

Neahl leaned on the fireplace and stared into the flames as if he had not heard. So Redmond continued.

"Besides, you would have killed me on sight, and Weyland would have shot me before I came within hailing distance. I was young and angry and desperate—maybe even foolish. So I left the island, and I've been wandering in the southlands ever since."

"Weyland wouldn't have shot you." Neahl spoke without taking his gaze from the dancing flames.

Redmond glanced at Brion and raised an eyebrow in obvious disbelief.

"They crippled his right arm in the fight," Neahl said. "We almost didn't save it. He couldn't use it much."

Redmond frowned. "Too bad. He was a gifted archer. Where is he now?"

Redmond glanced at Brion. Neahl turned to face Redmond.

"Weyland died this very morning at the hands of the Salassani," Neahl said. "This is his son, Brion."

Brion nodded and tried to swallow the knot that rose in his throat at the mention of his parents. He had almost forgotten them in the hours that Neahl had kept him busy digging graves, chopping wood, and shooting his new bow. Maybe that's what Neahl had intended all along.

Redmond stared at Brion in open shock. Brion thought he saw tears spring to Redmond's eyes.

Redmond cleared his throat. "Sorry to hear it," he said. "Very sorry."

Neahl returned to his seat, clasped his hands together in his lap, and watched his thumbs twirling around each other.

"Why have you waited so long to come back if your story is true?" he asked.

Redmond shrugged. "I heard rumors of war," he said, "and I wanted to see if you were all safe. Besides, lately, I've grown weary of the southern heat, and I wanted to return to my own folk. I wanted to come home." He paused. "I hoped the long years would have done something to soothe your anger."

Neahl bent forward, his shoulders hunched as if a great weariness had settled over him. He glanced at Redmond, then at the fire, and finally at his own hands. He turned his right hand over to stare at the stubs of his missing fingers. He grunted and raised his gaze to Redmond's face. He shook his head.

"Now that I face you," he said, "it doesn't seem to matter anymore."

Neahl leaned forward and reached over to grasp Redmond's hand.

The Salassani bent over Brion with a wide grin that twisted the ghastly, blue face paint. Blood dripped from the knife as he raised it for the kill. Terror and rage blossomed in Brion's chest as he lashed out with fist and feet. The Salassani laughed and stepped back to let Brion see his parent's bodies lying sprawled in the snow, stained red with their blood. His father's voice echoed in his ears. "Take it. Take it. Do not desert them."

Brion awoke to a sharp slap on his head. He opened his eyes, blinking into the darkness. He had curled up on the floor beside the fire, wrapped in his cloak against the chill as Neahl and Redmond continued to talk late into the night. The fire had died down to a pile of red coals. Brion could make out Neahl's hulking shape bending over him. Neahl nudged him with his foot.

"Get up," he said. "There's work to do."

Brion had grown up running trap lines, which meant he rose long before the sun, but he could swear he had been asleep only a few hours. He couldn't even see the hint of morning.

"What?" he groaned.

Brion rubbed his eyes and struggled to sit up while keeping the cloak tight. He grimaced at the stiffness and pain in his shoulders and arms. He would pay for drawing that heavy bow all day.

"Get up, string your bow, and come outside."

"Now?"

Neahl strode out the door, leaving it open. A cold draft blew in to stir the coals in the fireplace.

Brion pulled the cloak about his shoulders and fell over with a grunt. Neahl could not be serious. It wasn't even the crack of dawn yet. He was exhausted and so stiff that he couldn't move without pain.

Brion was jerked off the floor and held suspended in air for an instant, his legs and arms churning. All he could see in the darkness of the cabin were Neahl's boots firmly planted on the floor.

"Let's go," Neahl yelled.

The cloak flapped about Brion like bat's wings as he flew through the door. He landed hard and sprawled on the frozen earth. When he untangled himself from the cloak, he found Neahl standing in the doorway.

"What's the matter with you?" Brion shouted as he scrambled to his feet.

"I told you to get up, and I meant it. Get that bow strung, now."

"What for?"

"Because I said so, and, if you don't, I'll thrash you until you do."

Brion knew from long experience that Neahl did not make idle threats. And the thumping Neahl had given him the day before was still fresh in his mind. Brion kicked at a patch of snow only to find that it was frozen solid.

He cursed at the pain, hopped on one foot a few times, and then stomped into the cabin. Stringing the bow proved far more painful than he wanted to admit, but he would not let Neahl know how sore he was. He grabbed up his cloak and came back out of the cabin with the bow and the quiver in his hands.

"Okay," Brion said. "Here I am in the middle of the night when I should be asleep, with my bow strung standing in front of your house.

Do you want me to shoot the stump in the dark, just for fun?"

He didn't try to keep any of the sarcasm out of his voice.

Neahl ignored him and marched toward the road. Brion growled and followed.

Neahl stopped by the small path that led into the wood. He pointed at the trail.

"See those tracks?"

Brion glanced at the trail and back at Neahl.

"It's black as pitch out here and freezing cold. How in the name of the King's beard am I supposed to see anything?"

Neahl pointed again.

"Look until you do see them and find him. Don't come back until you do."

"Find who?"

Neahl ignored him and strode to the cabin.

"Neahl, who am I tracking, and why am I doing it?"

Neahl kept walking.

"It's cold. Can't we do this in the morning? Neahl?"

Brion stood in impotent rage for a moment while he considered picking up a rock and chucking it at the back of Neahl's head. But he knew it would be a bad idea. He fumed, screamed Neahl's name again, and then gave up. It wasn't any use, and he knew it.

He bent to the path. The dim light cast from the thin sliver of moon overhead did little to illuminate the trail. He could just make out the imprint of a boot in the frozen mud. He tried to think, but his brain was clouded with sleep and his muscles screamed for mercy every time he moved. He cursed Neahl again and began following the darker shadow of the trail as it wound through the impenetrable blackness of the forest like a snake on the prowl.

The thin crust of slush and mud cracked under his boots. His breath rose in clouds of white against the darkness, and he pulled his cloak tighter. What was Neahl playing at?

Brion stopped periodically to search for the footprints. When he found one, he straightened and continued down the trail. He went on like this for a good hour until he lost the bootprint.

After a string of curses, he crawled back searching for the last track. But in his carelessness he had left his own scuff marks all over the trail, making it nearly impossible to find them again.

The crust of frozen mud cracked and cut his hands. His fingers began to turn numb and the sharp taste of earth and oak coated his tongue.

Brion finally found another series of footprints that left the trail. He had missed them in his careless stomping in the darkness. Brion veered off to follow them until he became entangled in the brush. His bow and quiver snagged at every branch and twig.

In the end, he gave up just as the faint gray of dawn began to filter through the trees. He leaned his back against a large oak and closed his eyes to try and soothe their burning. He pulled the cloak about him, trying to gather a little warmth against the cold. After a bit of a rest, he would go back and tell Neahl he could go find whoever he had lost by himself.

The next thing Brion knew, cold steel pressed against his throat. He came awake—wide awake.

Chapter 7
Decision

Don't move," the voice whispered hot in Brion's ear. Wild images of Salassani lurking about in the woods flashed through his mind. Maybe the Salassani yesterday had just been a scouting party. Neahl must have been mistaken. The Salassani were still here, or maybe they had come back searching for their fallen comrade. Brion tried to swallow and considered going for his own knife. But the blade convinced him that it wouldn't be wise to attempt it.

"Don't do anything stupid," the voice said as if the owner of the voice had read his mind. "Get up slowly."

Brion rose and his bow slipped to the ground. He tried to turn his head to see who was behind him, but the knife pricked his neck. Brion stiffened.

"I said don't do anything stupid." The voice spoke harsh in his ear. "Look straight ahead and don't move."

Rough hands grabbed Brion's wrists and tied them behind him. Then a blindfold dropped over his eyes. Brion struggled to keep the quaking out of his voice as he spoke.

"What are you going to do with me?" he asked.

"You'll find out soon enough, now move."

Sharp pain stabbed into his back, and he stumbled forward. He had been so disoriented by the appearance of the stranger that he now had no idea which way they were headed. He knew the trail wound through the wood for some miles before it crossed a small stream. He also knew that many paths forked off of it. For all he knew, his captor might be taking him to some secret lair in the heart of the woods.

All along the trail, he stumbled over roots and stones. When he fell, he rolled to one side so that his shoulders would take the blow instead of his head or his face. Each fall sent the agony screaming through his already sore muscles. His captor dragged him to his feet, gave him a few good switches with a rod, and pushed him along, never saying a word.

Brion thought of Brigid and Finola and how terrified they must have been to see their own people slain and to be carried off like sacks of potatoes by the Salassani. Maybe he would follow them into slavery. Maybe now he could understand how they felt.

As he staggered up the path, Brion could see the light of day growing slowly brighter even through the blindfold. He wondered how long Neahl would wait for him to come back. As stubborn as Neahl was, he probably wouldn't even notice Brion was missing until dinner. It would be just like him to let Brion suffer all day with no food or water.

But the air changed from the close dampness of the forest. A breeze blew across his cheeks. The rich odors of the forest fell away. The trail became less broken, and he could step forward with more sureness. He tried to imagine what part of the trail would be open and smooth, but he couldn't be sure. He had no idea how far or in what direction they had walked.

Maybe Neahl wouldn't be coming after him at all. If the brigands had done their work well, Neahl would be stretched on the ground the same way he had found his father.

"Where are we?" Brion asked.

"Don't you know?"

Brion shook his head. Then he stopped. He smelled the smoke of a fire and the muddy earth. Footsteps slapped against the ground. Brion tensed, not knowing what to expect.

"This isn't what I meant when I said don't come back until you've found him."

"Neahl?"

Rough fingers jerked the blindfold down. Brion blinked into Neahl's glowering face. Brion craned his head around to find Redmond smiling at him with a long, pointed stick in his hand.

"What the . . ." Brion's head swiveled back and forth as the blood rose hot in his cheeks.

Neahl shook his head, pursed his lips, and clicked his tongue. "This is not a good start."

"What's the matter with you?" Brion shouted. "Are you crazy?"

"Funny, I was going to ask you the same questions."

"Don't be too hard on him, Neahl," Redmond said. "He won't forget that march through the woods anytime soon." Redmond grinned and rolled the switch in his hand.

Deliverance

Neahl stepped close to Brion. "You listen and you listen good," he said in a whisper. His hot breath washed over Brion's face. Brion flinched despite himself at the cold, hard anger in Neahl's eyes. "You are a dead man if this is how you plan on going after your sister. And you'll get your companions killed, as well."

He paused to give Brion time to absorb what he had said. Brion opened his mouth to speak, but Neahl spoke over him.

"This isn't some harmless archery competition," Neahl said. "We'll be playing for keeps, and one mistake, one moment of hesitation, one fit of laziness or cowardice, and you'll be dead. Do you understand me?"

Brion nodded.

"And make no mistake, what we'll teach you will keep you alive when most other men will die—that's if you're not too bullheaded to learn it." Neahl poked him in the chest. "The Salassani will show no mercy. And I'll not travel into the heathland with a lazy, snot-nosed boy. Either you train to be a warrior like your father or you go back to trapping and forget about rescuing your sister. You commit to your course here and now. Which will it be?"

As Neahl spoke, Brion found his anger rapidly replaced by shame. His cheeks now burned for a different reason. He bowed his head. He *had* been lazy and immature. He *had* been selfish and weak. What Neahl said was true. He raised his gaze to meet Neahl's.

"I'll be a warrior. I'll do whatever it takes."

"I would expect no less of Weyland's son."

Chapter 8
The Art of Tracking

Well, that was pleasant," Redmond said. "Sorry, I had to do that to you, lad."

He cut the rope binding Brion's hands. Brion grimaced as the blood flowed into them. Now everything was stiff and bruised.

Brion shrugged. "I deserved it."

Redmond pulled Brion around to face him. "Look," he said. "If Neahl didn't think you had what it took to be a warrior like your father, he wouldn't waste his time on you. Take some courage in that, and don't let your guard down again. I could have slit your throat as easily as not." Redmond tossed the stick away. "Neahl may appear harsh, but he has to prepare you for far worse."

Redmond handed Brion his bow and quiver of arrows before following Neahl into the cabin. Brion watched him go. Did he have what it took? Could he live up to his father's reputation? He didn't think so. He had already failed him once.

Brion sighed, shouldered the quiver of arrows, and trudged back to the stump. He might as well start now.

That morning's practice proved to be nothing more than an experiment in agony. The beating he had received on the trail that morning combined with the already painfully sore muscles to make every shot torture. But Brion kept shooting. He never did get the bow to full draw, but the arrows started to cluster the way they used to when he shot his lighter bow.

A couple of hours later, Neahl came out from the cabin and watched him shoot a round of twenty-four arrows. He waited while Brion retrieved them. Then he gestured for Brion to follow him back to the cabin. Hot stew and warm bread waited for him on the table. Brion fell to it with such an appetite that he had finished three bowls and an entire loaf before he sat back and let out a long sigh of contentment. He closed his eyes, thinking that now would be a good time to catch up on the sleep he had been so rudely denied.

Neahl cleared the table as Redmond placed a large map of Coll and the surrounding islands on it. Neahl kicked Brion's foot. "No time for napping, boy."

Brion's eyes popped open, but he suppressed the complaint that rose in his throat. He had made his decision, and he would stick with it.

"If you're going to be a warrior and a tracker, you have to understand the lands through which you move," Neahl said. "The best way to learn it is to travel over it. But since we can't afford the time to travel all of the Frei-Ock Isles, we're going to have to settle for the second-best method."

Neahl paused and stared down at the map with raised eyebrows.

Brion understood what he meant, though he had never seen a map so complicated before. He had seen the rough sketch of the village that the headman had on his wall, and he knew that he lived on a large island called Frei-Ock Isle, but he had never seen it represented. Nor had he seen the other islands. He sat forward eagerly.

"Where are we?" he asked.

Neahl placed his finger near a river just southeast of Mailag. "Wexford is about here."

"Wow, how far are we from the sea?"

The distance appeared short on the map, less than the length of his forefinger. Brion had always wanted to go to the sea. He couldn't understand how a body of water could extend as far as a person could see into the horizon.

"It's a good five days' travel to the west and an entire fortnight to the east."

"Five days? How long will it take us to get to the lands of the Salassani? Where are they?"

Neahl poked his finger just south of a mountain chain near the northern end of the island.

"If we don't stir up any trouble, we'll be in their lands in a week and at Aldina Lake in another two to three weeks, depending on the condition of the pass."

Brion sat back. "It could take us a month just to get there?"

Redmond and Neahl both nodded.

"I didn't realize it would take that long."

Neahl sniffed. "What? You thought they just lived next door?

"No, I—"

41

Redmond laughed.

"Well, it will take that long," Neahl said. "So you're going to spend some time memorizing the location of every mountain range, river, forest, plain, heath, and group of people. You need to have this in your head before we start out. You'll fill in the details from your own experience."

"Are we just going to go straight across Hackel Heath?"

Redmond shook his head and traced a path on the map that followed a long, narrow mountain range labeled Aveen to its northern end and across Bracken Moor to the mountains that surrounded Aldina Lake.

"It's better to stay off the open heathland," he said. "The Salassani don't tend to venture into those hills, because they're the enemies of the Carpentini who have recently occupied them. So, we'll skirt them."

Brion started to ask another question, but Neahl interrupted him.

"That's all you need to know for now. Start memorizing. I want this map stuck in your head so well that you can draw it out." Neahl stood. "We'll be back in a few hours."

"Where are you going?"

"That's none of your concern. Just memorize."

Redmond followed Neahl out.

Exhaustion lurked behind Brion's eyes. His eyelids drooped, his head bobbed, and his brain ached. After nearly falling from the chair a few times, Brion began jumping up and down, jogging around the cabin, and flapping his arms—anything to get the blood flowing. Then, he would go back to the map.

By the time Neahl and Redmond came back, all of the excitement of seeing the map had worn off. Names and coastlines swam before his eyes and swirled around in his head like a visual stew.

"Well?" Neahl queried.

Brion blinked and rubbed his eyes.

"Well?" Neahl repeated. "What's the northern most island?"

"Perth."

"Who lives there?"

"The Parsini."

"Where is the capitol of the Kingdom of Coll?"

Brion glanced down at the map, but Neahl snatched it from the table, giving him a sneer as if this display of weakness should be beneath him.

Brion grunted and screwed up his face. "Uh, Chullish is south near the mouth of the Tilt River on the edge of the Laro Forest."

Neahl nodded. "The Kingdom of the Dunkeldi?"

"Between the Fife Fens and Heron Moor. Capitol city is Ballach."

Neahl grunted. "That'll do for starters. I want you to study this map every day until it becomes a part of you."

Brion nodded and suppressed a laugh. Neahl had expected him to get them wrong.

"And," Neahl continued, "it's time you started learning to read, write, and speak Salassani."

Brion gaped at him. "You can read Salassani?" He had never even heard Salassani spoken, let alone seen it written. Everyone in Coll spoke the common tongue with the exception of a few clans deep in the Taber Wood.

Redmond grabbed the map and rolled it up. "Speaking and writing Salassani may not help much in killing them, but it can come in useful when you want to avoid dying," he said.

The next morning, Neahl hefted a long spear while Brion and Redmond shouldered their bows and quivers. Neahl led them far down the road away from the village into a part of the wood that Brion hadn't trapped in several years. After a few hours listening to those two woodsmen talk about what they saw and heard in the woods, Brion realized that he had always seen the woods as a blurred whole. He had missed many of the subtle details that communicated vast amounts of information to those who knew how to read it. Scuff marks, overturned leaves, bent limbs, broken spider webs, sounds, and smells all communicated information. Brion realized that, even though Weyland had trained him well, he still had much to learn.

They stopped to study a muddy spot in the trail filled with a variety of animal sign. Redmond began listing off all the different types of sign from tracks to bits of hair and even smells. Brion glanced at the muddy imprints.

"That's a lot to remember in one go," he said.

"Precisely," Neahl said. "And that's why you're going to practice interpreting sign every day in every possible weather and light condition. It's the only way to learn."

Brion sighed. "Somehow, I get the feeling that you are going to enjoy making this difficult," he said.

They examined deer, fox, coyote, opossum, and even some bird tracks before they continued down the trail—all the while, Redmond and Neahl instructing him in the secrets of successful tracking.

When they came across a fresh deer trail, Neahl stopped them.

"Now's your chance to show us what you've learned," he said. He stepped back to give Brion the lead.

Brion nodded and bent to the trail. He had followed many a game trail in his life, but he knew that Redmond and Neahl wanted something more than a basic assessment. He examined the ridge in between the print of the hooves and found that it was sharp. The walls were smooth and no debris had collected along the floor cut. Some of the tracks had splayed out in the mud as the deer slid to one side. He peered up and down the trail. The tracks proceeded in a straight line.

"Well," he said. "I figure the deer passed here not long ago, maybe within the last couple of hours. It's a young, medium-size doe, and it's not in much of a hurry."

He glanced up and found both men nodding.

"Not bad," Neahl said. "Let's go." He gestured toward the trail with the spear.

Brion followed the tracks onto a narrow game trail. The soggy ground and the patches of snow made the track easy to follow. Within a hundred paces, they came across a large pile of deer scat. Brion stopped and picked up a few of the oval droppings. He smashed one between his fingers.

He glanced up at Neahl and Redmond.

"It's still warm, really warm," Brion whispered.

Neahl grunted and gestured to the pile of scat with his injured hand. "Now take that warm scat and rub it all over your clothes," he said.

Chapter 9
The Hunt

rion glanced at him sharply. "My clothes?"

"That's what I said." Neahl grinned.

"Um, that's just a bit nasty, don't you think?"

"Maybe," Redmond said. "But if you want to get close enough for a good shot, the best thing you can do is smell like a deer."

"Ah, I see. I thought Neahl just wanted to get me filthier than I already am so that he could make me wash all of our clothes tonight."

Neahl smiled. "Not a bad idea."

Brion smirked.

Redmond and Neahl both bent and picked up handfuls of the droppings and smeared them all over their clothes. So Brion followed their example before continuing down the trail. The warm droppings smelled horsey and musky. Soon the aroma overwhelmed every other odor of the forest.

Ten minutes later, Redmond stopped him and pointed through the trees ahead. A white tail flicked about thirty paces away. Then the deer materialized from out of the undergrowth. It pawed at the ground under a large oak tree.

Neahl nudged him and bent over to breathe into Brion's ear. "Go touch it."

Brion gaped at Neahl. Had he had lost his mind? But Neahl nudged him forward anyway. Brion glanced at Redmond, who raised his eyebrows. Brion had never tried to get this close to a living, breathing deer before. He didn't have any idea what the deer might do. But the challenge of seeing how close he could get intrigued him. So he carefully and slowly placed one foot in front of the other.

The wind rustled through the dried leaves that still clung to the beeches and oaks, which helped cover up the slight noises he made. He tried not to breathe. He came around a large, serviceberry bush so that nothing lay between him and the deer but three, short paces.

45

Just then, the top of his bow caught on the branches of the service-berry bush and shook them. The deer exploded into action in a burst of sound. Brion tumbled backwards onto his backside with a grunt. The deer stopped after three more bounds and peered back at them with a flick of her tail.

Brion froze when the deer looked right at him. She waggled her head and surveyed him as if to say, "That was rude." Brion held his breath. The deer studied him for a moment and stepped down the trail with a disdainful flick of her tail.

Roars of laughter sent it crashing into the trees. Neahl and Redmond stumbled out of the brush toward where Brion sat.

"I think she startled you as much as you startled her," Redmond said.

"Laugh it up," Brion said. He rose and dusted himself off. "You knew she would do that."

Neahl nodded and wiped at the tears on his cheeks.

Brion wandered over and leaned against the big oak, trying to retain some of his dignity.

Redmond stopped laughing first and came over to him.

"See, I told you. Don't smell like a predator, and you'll have more success hunting."

Brion nodded. "And don't hunt with you two if I want to have any self-respect left."

Redmond restrained a laugh. "Don't take it so hard. You got close for a beginner. I didn't even get within five paces before mine bolted."

"You mean Neahl did this to you, too?"

Redmond smiled and nodded. "It's a lesson you won't ever forget."

"Or do you mean it's a lesson he won't ever *let* me forget?"

"That too," Redmond laughed and clapped Brion on the shoulder.

Neahl finally staggered over to them. "Oh, that was choice," he said between chuckles. "I haven't pulled that trick on anybody in years. It never gets old."

"Are you finished having sport with me, yet?" Brion asked.

Neahl nodded. "For now," he said. "That one will last for a while."

"Well," Redmond said. "I don't know about you two, but I'm ready for a nice, hot supper and a warm bed. I didn't get much sleep up that tree."

"Don't expect me to feel sorry for you," Brion said.

Neahl kicked Brion's foot as Brion's head bobbed over his bowl. The warm stew had made Brion so sleepy he almost fell into it.

"Not yet," Neahl said.

Brion blinked and rubbed his eyes.

"If you intend to keep me awake all night after what you did to me yesterday, I'm going to start calling you an executioner instead of a trainer."

"When it comes to Neahl's style of training," Redmond said, "there's a fine line between the two."

Neahl grunted. But Brion could tell that he wasn't annoyed.

"I expect you to be up before first light. I want venison for breakfast."

Brion rolled his eyes.

"Of course you do. Any particular size or sex?"

A smile twitched at the edge of Neahl's mouth. "Make it young and tender," he said.

Brion gave a mock bow. "As you wish, my lord. Now can I get some sleep?"

Neahl nodded, but Redmond cut in.

"Not just yet."

They both watched him.

"I've been considering taking on a pupil of my own." Redmond grinned at their puzzled faces. "I know an old crank who wants to relearn how to shoot a bow."

Neahl frowned. Brion just stared at the two of them, uncertain what to do. An uncomfortable silence filled the cabin.

Redmond stopped smiling and placed a black circle on the table that caught the firelight on its polished surface. It looked like a funny ring with a long tongue on it.

"While I traveled on the continent, I ran into a group of archers who didn't shoot with their fingers like we do. They shoot with this thing. They call it a thumb ring."

He picked it up and slid it onto his thumb so that the tongue nestled on the inside. "They wrap the thumb around the string and hold it this way." He folded his forefinger over his thumb. "And they get very smooth, very fast releases with it."

He held it out to Neahl. "Wanna give it a try?"

Neahl's face darkened. "This your idea of joke?"

Redmond didn't smile. "I'm dead serious. The best horseback archers in the world use the thumb ring. They draw heavy weights with it, and they are dead accurate at a full gallop. I've seen them do it."

Redmond glanced at Neahl's crippled right hand, which he had unconsciously covered with his left hand.

"You still have enough of your index finger left to make it work. Men with less finger than you have done it."

Neahl continued to frown, but Brion noted a change in his expression. Brion's father had told him that Neahl had been a gifted archer—especially expert in long-distance shots. As a young man, he had been able to place half a dozen arrows in succession into a man-size target at one hundred paces. Brion could only guess what it had cost Neahl to lose his fingers and the ability to shoot.

Neahl picked up the thumb ring that Redmond had placed on the table, examined it briefly, and pulled it onto his right thumb. He placed what remained of his index finger over the thumb and glanced up at Redmond for confirmation.

Redmond smiled. "I think you can do it."

Neahl nodded.

"But there's one more adjustment you'll have to make," Redmond said. "You have to shoot off the right side with the arrow resting on your thumb. Otherwise, it won't work."

Neahl nodded again. But he didn't say anything. Brion could only guess what thoughts might be parading through his mind.

When Brion entered the woods the next morning under a canopy of stars, he stopped in the shadow of the oaks to see if anyone had followed him. He might as well start practicing the caution and care Neahl expected of him. No one appeared, so he set off down the trail, trying to keep every sense alert while still moving in silence.

The darkness of the woods settled over him like a great woolen cloak. Sounds lingered in the still air. The hooting of an owl, the whisper of the wind, the creak of branches all came sharp and clear to his ears. The trail appeared as a ghostly line, snaking its way through the shadows.

Brion smeared himself with deer droppings from several piles of scat he found along the trail and settled in at the edge of a clearing where a stream trickled through the forest. He pulled the cloak tight against the chill.

For the first time since his parent's death, he found his mind unoccupied. He let it wander to Brigid and Finola. The fierce desperation he had felt as he stood staring at the icy waters of the river expanded inside him. The horror of seeing his parents lying still, their eyes vacant and staring, choked him. The hatred that had been growing since he kicked the dead Salassani gripped his throat. He would have his revenge—someday.

The full light of morning filtered through the oaks and beeches when five deer stepped into the clearing in front of Brion. They scattered about to nibble at the leaves and the grass. Two went to the stream and bent to drink. A medium-size doe stood broadside to him not fifteen paces away. She flicked her ears, swished her tail, and bent to nibble the grass.

Brion lifted the bow. The deer raised its head and swiveled it around to stare right at him. Brion froze until she bent to the water again. He drew the feathered shaft as far back as he could. His stiff muscles complained, but he held it, peering down the shaft to rest the point directly behind the doe's shoulder. His fingers relaxed.

At the same instant his bow sang, he heard the thrum of another string and felt the swish of a feathered shaft as it zipped just over his head, lifting his hair as it passed.

Chapter 10
The Unexpected Archer

rion ducked instinctively and spun, whipping an arrow from his quiver and trying to nock it. He fumbled with the arrow and dropped it. He grabbed for another as Neahl stepped from behind the tree.

"What's the matter with you?" Brion yelled. "I could have shot you!"

"Not the way you were fumbling with those arrows," Neahl said. A smile twitched at the edge of his lips.

"Or you could have shot me," Brion said. "That arrow barely missed my head."

Only then did Brion realize that Neahl clutched a huge longbow in his left hand. He gaped at it in shock for a moment and pointed.

"You shot that?"

Neahl's grin widened. Brion had never seen him so openly pleased.

Neahl held up the right hand and showed Brion the black ring. "I've been practicing all night. So when I saw you leave, I thought I'd test myself."

"You were asleep when I got up."

Neahl shook his head and stepped up to peer over the bush. "No, I was in the field. You should've looked more closely."

Brion let out a long sigh. He would never be able to predict what this man would do.

"I think we bagged two of them," Neahl said.

After cleaning the deer, they threw them over their backs and trooped back toward the cabin. Even dressed, the deer still weighed over one hundred pounds. Brion's muscles complained.

"How did you do it?" Brion asked.

Neahl cast him a sideways glance. "Do what?"

"Relearn how to shoot after so many years and with that ring thing and off the wrong side of the bow in one night."

"Practice, Brion. I practiced."

Brion shook his head in annoyance. "But you only had one night. You must have lost all your arrows in the dark."

"Nope. I started shooting close and didn't step back until I had the feel of it."

Neahl fell silent for a moment and then said, "It makes me feel like a man again."

Brion glanced at him, but didn't say anything. He had some idea how Neahl must feel.

They trudged along in silence under their heavy loads for about a mile before they dropped the deer on the ground and sat down for a break. Brion unwrapped his bread and offered a piece to Neahl.

"You did the right thing this morning," Neahl said between mouthfuls.

"What?"

"Stopping under the shadow of the trees to see if you were being followed."

Brion frowned and paused with a piece of bread to his mouth. "So how come I didn't see you?"

"Because I expected you to do it."

Brion stared at him in exasperation. "So how did you follow me without me knowing?"

Neahl took a bite of bread. "Because you didn't look back. And you weren't listening when I came up behind you."

Brion tore a piece of bread. "But I would have heard you. Nobody can go through the woods without making a sound."

"I did make sounds. But you weren't listening."

It was true. Brion stuffed the bread in his mouth and chewed while he pondered. He swallowed. "But how can I tell the normal sounds of the forest from the ones that don't belong?"

Neahl took a long swig from Brion's waterskin and wiped his mouth with the back of his hand. "If you listen long enough and hard enough to the sounds of the forest, you can come to recognize the ones that don't belong. It takes time to learn."

A squirrel gave two short and one long chirp somewhere in the trees. Neahl froze. His hand edged slowly to his bow. His nostrils flared, and his eyes opened wide.

"You don't have to try and scare me, I get the point," Brion said.

Neahl raised his hand and shook his head. His face was tense.

Neahl waved Brion back into the trees, slipped an arrow from his quiver, and fitted it to the string.

Brion obeyed, but placed an arrow on his own string, as well.

The squirrel chirped again and another one picked up the call. The birds had gone quiet. The entire forest held its breath in anticipation.

Brion saw the movement before he heard the slap of the string.

Chapter 11
Alone

The young warrior rose from his place beside the fire and stepped over to Brigid. He extended a piece of meat he had skewered on his long knife. She pulled the meat from the point. The greasy heat felt good on her cold fingers. He watched her tear off a bite.

Then he gestured back the way they had come. "Your people will not come for you." He spoke in the common tongue, which surprised her. She had heard him speak nothing but Salassani.

The miles had rolled beneath Brigid and her captors as they rode northeast at a steady trot. The bone-jarring pace drew the huge mountains nearer as the landscape rose up to meet them. As the mountains loomed, Brigid's hopes had shriveled. Where were Brion and Neahl? Where were the townsmen who always bragged about hunting Salassani? The further north they traveled, the less likely her escape from this quiet, young warrior who watched her with his penetrating, honey-colored eyes. By now, Brigid understood that he was the leader. She had seen how the others deferred to him.

The young warrior waited to see that she understood him. "They're dead," he said.

His declaration drove to her heart like a knife. He had said the words she had refused to say to herself, though she had been unable to suppress the doubts and fears. She struggled not to show any emotion while his gaze rested upon her.

He turned to go back to the fire, but stopped and faced her again. His hand dropped to catch at his cloak as the wind whipped it around his legs. "I'm sorry," he said.

Brigid swallowed hard and struggled to keep her face expressionless. He watched her as if trying to read her thoughts.

Brigid turned away, pulling her cloak tight against the chill wind. But a cold worse than the biting wind filled her. She trembled. Tears spilled down her cheeks. How could she know if he were telling the truth?

She had been slung over her captor's shoulder and had fought so fiercely to get free that she hadn't seen what finally happened to her father or her mother. As they rode away, she had seen her father lying on the ground with his blood staining the snow, but that was all. The doubts rose up hot and furious. Had the Salassani lied to her to rob her of what little hope she had left?

He had said your people. Could he mean that they had killed her mother and Brion as well? But why would they bother? They would both have been valuable slaves. He must have lied. She had to believe that he lied, because she could not bear the alternative.

That night, the young Salassani tied her hands and feet as before, but this time he left her by the fire with an extra cloak draped around her shoulders. And he didn't tie her to his ankle as he had been accustomed to doing.

Sleep came slowly as Brigid wrestled with the fears and doubts. When sleep did come, the flash and crash of steel, her father's silent, solemn face, and the terrifying painted men danced before her. She could smell their stink, taste the dirt, and hear their low, guttural voices. Then, a tall, handsome youth rode into her dreams on a great horse, carrying a bow.

The pain from the leather straps cutting into her wrists roused her to wakefulness before the sun climbed over the horizon to the east. She couldn't feel her hands or her feet. She wriggled, searching for a more comfortable position. One of the men rose from a clump of heather where he must have been watching her. He grabbed her by the hair and pulled her to a sitting position. She swallowed the scream of pain.

He untied her and motioned her towards the fire. But as the blood rushed into her numb hands and feet, she could only sit and grit her teeth. The fiery needles of pain brought tears to her eyes, but she held them back. He grunted and left her.

The feeling returned to her fingers as the sun began to peek over the cold horizon. Even in her despair, she couldn't contemplate the orange glow with anything but amazement. The heathland spread out in all directions to break like waves upon the mountains to the west and the north. Clumps of small heather, bunches of stiff, brown grass, broken ground, stunted trees, and rolling hills surrounded her. It was a beautiful land for all of its savagery, but it depressed her spirits with its vast, brooding solitude.

The young warrior approached her and sat cross-legged in front of her. "My name is Emyr," he said.

Brigid said nothing.

"Your people can't come for you." He watched her, but she struggled to betray no emotion. "You must learn the Salassani ways and language if you wish to survive. Do you understand me?"

Brigid hesitated and nodded.

He turned to leave.

"Why did you kill that man?" Brigid asked.

Emyr surveyed her in open surprise at the question. Then, he nodded as if coming to a decision. "He challenged my leadership and threatened to kill you, because I wasn't supposed to leave anyone alive."

Brigid swallowed. Emyr watched her for a moment and leaned toward her. His face tightened.

"There may be others," he said. "I'll protect you if I can. But you must do as I say."

Brigid nodded again, finding that she had nothing to say. If he had meant to make her feel better, it hadn't worked. Wasn't it bad enough that he had stolen her from her family? Now he was telling her that people were going try to kill her and he offered her protection. Why would he apologize for destroying her family when that was the reason he had gone on the raid in the first place? What had appeared to be nothing more than another savage Salassani raid now seemed different, and much more ominous. Brigid sensed that she was swimming in deep waters, and she had no idea what lurked at the bottom of this lake.

After days of steady progression northward, Emyr signaled for Brigid to dismount in a little vale where several warriors had constructed temporary shelters amid the dwarfish junipers. Brigid glanced around, uncomfortable at all the staring eyes. One young man with no paint watched her closely. When she boldly returned his gaze, he looked away. Emyr gestured her towards a shelter built of twisted limbs woven into a dome shape with a leather flap over the doorway.

Brigid ducked to peer into the warm shelter. The odor of dead animals and human filth assailed her nostrils from the darkness within. Something shuffled. A voice whispered—a female voice—and it didn't speak Salassani. Brigid knelt and crawled part way into the shelter. Someone gasped.

Chapter 12
Reunion

s Brigid's vision adjusted to the light, she found herself staring into the wide, pale blue eyes of Finola, the baker's daughter. Her blonde hair was pulled back and secured with a piece of leather. Beside her sat a small boy of maybe seven or eight years old.

Brigid simply gawked for a long moment as shock and relief swept over her. Finola's skirt and blouse were torn and dirty, but the dirt couldn't hide the determined gaze of a young woman who knew her own mind. The dirt also couldn't hide the split lip and the large, purple bruise surrounding her eye. Finola grinned and reached for Brigid.

"I can't believe you're here!" Brigid said as she crawled into the shelter and hugged Finola fiercely. "Are you all right?"

Finola returned her embrace and nodded. "We're fine." She gestured to the little boy who sat watching them with big, dark eyes.

"What happened? How did they get you?" Brigid asked.

Finola shook her head. She picked at a clump of burrs that clung to her skirt. "I don't even know. I had just opened the shop when the horseman stormed into the village and began snatching people and clubbing the ones they didn't grab. The whole village started screaming and running for cover. One of them tried to grab little Sarah, so I hit him with the only thing I had in my hands. It was a rolling pin."

Finola gave Brigid that mischievous grin that drove the boys in the village crazy.

"He didn't like it much. He hit me over the head with a cudgel, and the next thing I knew I was tied over the front of his horse being jerked half to death as he galloped off into the heather."

Her lips dropped into a frown, and she crawled toward the doorway. She pulled the flap aside. "He's the fat one by the fire—the beast. His name is Ithel."

Brigid peeked through the slit. A big man with a wide face and a messy patch of black hair lifted a leather tankard to his mouth.

Finola let the flap fall back into place as she continued. "He kept me tied to him for days. Guess he thought I might try to get away. I tried for his knife once, but he didn't like that either. So he beat me a bit." She said this as if it was of no importance. "What about you? Did they get Brion too?" Finola asked.

Finola peered past Brigid to the tent's entrance as if she expected Brion's head to appear in the doorway.

Brigid stared down at her skirt. "No, Brion was off in the fields. I couldn't see what happened, but Emyr said . . ." Brigid stopped and swallowed. "He told me that my people were all dead."

Finola raised a hand to her mouth. "Do you think they killed them all, even Brion?" Finola whispered his name.

Brigid shrugged miserably. She had thought she had better control of her emotions after so many days, but saying the words out loud for the first time and to someone she knew made them all come back in a rush.

Finola embraced her, and they clung to each other for a time. Brigid couldn't keep the sobs from tearing from her throat. Her family was gone. How could they be gone?

Finally, Brigid pulled away and glanced at the little boy who sat beside Finola with his legs crossed. "Who's this?" she asked. She smiled at the child as she wiped the tears from her cheeks.

He kept his gaze upon her, but made no expression or movement.

Finola touched him gently. "I don't know his name," said Finola. "I call him Johnny. He understands me, but he won't talk. I think Ithel did something to his family, because he doesn't like him much. But I don't know. He certainly isn't Salassani."

Brigid studied him with pity. What if he had seen his family slaughtered? What must be going through his little mind? His eyes were dark, but his hair was sandy brown. He might have been Brion, if he were nine or ten years older.

She reached out to touch his hand, but he pulled away.

"It's okay," she said. "We'll look after you."

That evening, another band rode into camp. Wrapped in their cloaks, Finola and Brigid tried to melt into the shadows cast by the dancing firelight, but one of the men saw them and strode over to examine them. Ithel and Emyr exchanged glances. Ithel stood up and fingered the hilt of his sword.

The stranger stood over the girls for a moment before he bent to touch Brigid's hair. She pulled away. He laughed. Up close, Brigid could see that his face was horribly disfigured. Even under the paint, the twisted and distorted flesh drew one's attention. The reek of a sweating man and horse assailed her nostrils.

He sauntered over to the fire and sat across from Emyr. Brigid understood only the word for girl, but it was obvious what he wanted. Emyr shook his head while he gestured toward her and then in the direction they were traveling. The small man held up a bag that clinked. But still, Emyr shook his head.

"Guess he likes redheads," Finola whispered.

Brigid shot her an annoyed glance. "You think it's funny being haggled over like a piece of meat?" she said.

Finola frowned, but her attention shifted back to the argument as it grew louder.

Emyr sat unruffled and apparently disinterested in the entire affair as the stranger began to rage. The man's hand strayed to his knife. Brigid tensed, expecting Emyr to deal with him as he had the last man who had challenged him.

Other men began casting furtive glances at each other until Emyr tossed a stick into the fire and stood. Silence filled the valley. Emyr said something quiet, and then turned his back on the man as if he were going to tend to his horse. Whatever Emyr said had infuriated the man. He jerked his sword from his sheath, but he hadn't even raised it by the time Emyr had dropped into a crouch and spun, sweeping the man's feet from underneath him with an outstretched leg. The man fell heavy and hard onto the rocky ground. The sword bounced from his hand.

Chapter 13
Slaves

s the stranger started to sit up, he found Emyr's blade at his throat. They faced each other like this for some time until Emyr gestured for the man to rise. After another brief exchange, the man and his followers saddled their horses and rode out of the valley.

"Well, that was entertaining," Finola said. "Looks like your captor likes you."

"Stop kidding around," Brigid retorted.

"What's the other option?" Finola asked. "Cry and pull out my hair? I, for one, am not going to be sold to anyone. I won't be here long enough."

Brigid opened her mouth to respond when she realized that Emyr stood over her. She looked up. Emyr gave her a knowing glance before sheathing his sword and going back to the fire. She knew he meant to tell her that he had been right—that she needed to learn to be a Salassani if she wanted to survive.

After this exchange, Emyr became even more insistent that Brigid learn to speak Salassani. He rode beside Brigid and Finola as they traveled, drilling them on pronunciation and grammar.

"I'm not wasting my time learning to speak with murderers and thieves," Finola told Emyr.

Emyr gave her an appraising glance.

"Suit yourself," he said. "But if you refuse to speak Salassani, you'll be sold across the sea as a slave to the Hallstat. They aren't so kind to their slaves."

"You call *this* kind?" Finola asked.

Emyr smiled. "I call this kind compared to life in the galleys or in a house of pleasure." He let that idea sink in for a moment before he continued. "The Salassani allow slaves to join their society. The Hallstat don't. Once a slave, you remain a slave until you die."

Finola pinched her lips together and focused on the horizon. But she didn't argue anymore.

One of the Salassani named Deryn fashioned a boy-sized bow and some arrows for Johnny and gave them to him one evening while they sat around the fire. Little Johnny didn't show any obvious emotion, but Brigid could see the excited tension in his face. To everyone's amazement, Johnny charged up to Ithel and shot him in the back.

Ithel cursed and spun around, his wide face twisted in anger. But he froze when he found the little boy with another arrow nocked and drawn, pointing right at his face. Ithel flinched while the entire camp roared with laughter. Someone called out something Brigid didn't understand, and the men all laughed again.

Johnny loosed the arrow. It caught Ithel full in the chest. Ithel cursed again and stepped toward Johnny with murder in his expression. Johnny stood his ground while trying to nock another arrow. Deryn stepped in and swept Johnny off his feet, laughing as he did. He said something to Ithel, ruffled Johnny's hair, and carried him back to his seat by the fire. From that moment on, Johnny rode with his new mentor.

"They're trying to turn him into a Salassani," Finola complained to Brigid.

"That's the idea," Brigid said. "They're going to turn us all into Salassani."

"Not me," Finola said. "I'll die first."

Brigid considered telling her that if she kept this up she was probably right, but didn't feel like having an argument over it.

Chapter 14
Assassin

n arrow slapped into the carcass of the deer that sat next to Brion. Neahl leapt to his feet and loosed an arrow. Brion raised his bow, but couldn't find a target. A face flashed in the leaves and another arrow slammed into the tree right beside Brion's head. The shaft shattered. Splinters flew into Brion's face. He dodged behind the tree, sank to the ground, and crawled behind a pile of stones. He listened to the crashing that echoed through the woods.

"Stay there," Neahl called and sprinted into the undergrowth. Brion heard the slap of Neahl's string and a strangled cry. But the crashing persisted. Hooves beat the ground. Branches snapped.

Brion stood, backed into a big oak, and watched. While he waited, he scanned the forest around him, anxious not to be surprised by another attacker. His gaze focused on the shape of the pile of stones. It was about two feet long and a foot wide. A larger stone stood at one end. Brion knelt to examine the shallow letters scratched into the stone. "B.W." it read.

"A grave? Out here?" Brion said to himself. He didn't have time to consider its meaning because Neahl jogged up to him.

"That was no Salassani," Neahl said.

Brion sliced a long strip of flesh from a deer's flank. The blood dripped from the wooden board to muddy the dirt beneath.

"If it wasn't a Salassani, who was it?" Brion asked.

Neahl's knife slammed into the cutting block. "He didn't wear any family colors or crests that I could see," Neahl said. "But he knew how to use a bow and how to conceal himself. He was trained."

"The arrow you brought back could belong to any hunter," Redmond said as he finished smearing the brains over the flesh side of the hide.

"I didn't get a good look at him," Neahl said. "But he used a longbow, and he didn't hold his arrows in his hands the way the Salassani do when they're hunting."

"What do you think it means?" Redmond asked. He rolled up the hide and stepped into the cabin to place it over the fireplace beside the other one to cure.

Neahl sighed. "It means," he said, "that we're dealing with something more than a simple Salassani raid. That raid on your cabin was planned, and whoever planned it knows that you are still alive and sent an assassin to kill you."

Brion's knife slipped and sliced his finger. "Ouch! Me?" He gaped at them.

"Keep an eye on your blade or your hand will look like mine," Neahl said. He threw Brion a rag and carved off another strip of meat.

Neahl continued. "They didn't come to my house and that assassin probably could have hit me if he hadn't wasted his second shot on you."

"I don't understand," Brion said. He sucked on his finger. He couldn't tell them, but he thought he had some idea. It had to do with the ring and his father's secret.

"Neither do I," Neahl said. "But this means we're going to have to accelerate your training and keep our wits about us. There may be others."

The next day, Neahl leaned back in his chair after breakfast. "Well," he said. "It's time to accelerate."

Brion paused with a piece of roasted venison halfway to his mouth. He glanced at Neahl and Redmond. They ignored him. Brion decided that he should prepare for more pain.

"Today," Neahl said, after taking a long swig from his mug, "we'll begin your training in hand-to-hand fighting, and Redmond here has agreed to be your trainer."

Redmond grinned from the other side of the table.

Brion raised his eyebrows. He had been in more than one fight growing up so near the village, and he hadn't lost many of those. He sized up Redmond and thought that with luck he might get in a few good whacks before he was down.

Neahl saw the expression and harrumphed.

"Your first lesson is never, and I mean never, underestimate your opponent. Size can be important, but a trained fighter will know how to compensate for any apparent deficiencies."

"Tell him," Redmond said. He nodded his head toward Brion.

Neahl grunted, but stood without saying anything.

"Come on, Neahl. You had your sport with him the other day. Turn about among friends is fair play."

Neahl glared and stomped out of the door.

"What?" Brion asked.

Redmond chuckled.

"What?" Brion asked again.

"When we were still boys, Neahl must have been fifteen or sixteen; he was the size of a full-grown man even then. Once he pushed a man aside who had crowded in front of him at the tavern, thinking the man was just another boy. The man couldn't have been more than five feet tall." Redmond raised his hand to indicate the height. "He turned around to size up Neahl. Neahl realized his mistake, but he was too bullheaded to apologize since he thought he was in the right. The man moved so fast, I'm still not sure where he hit Neahl first."

Redmond pantomimed the fight. "That little man broke Neahl's nose and his pride. I don't think he's ever gotten over it." Redmond paused while he laughed out loud. "And he's never forgotten the lesson. Well," Redmond sighed, "we'd better get to it before Neahl comes back and finds us loafing."

Neahl returned hours later with a pack on his back and a new companion. Brion and Redmond were covered in mud, sweat, and blood as they reviewed the fluid kicking style of fighting that Redmond had been teaching Brion. Neahl watched them for a while before setting down the load he had been carrying and nodding to the man beside him. He stepped forward after a quick exchange in which Redmond landed a solid strike to Brion's ribs. They stopped. Their chests heaved. They wiped the sweat from their eyes. Brion held his ribs and glared at Redmond. Redmond grinned.

"Took you long enough," Redmond said. "You've missed all the fun."

Neahl nodded and said, "Looks like it. I guess I'll have a go."

Redmond really grinned this time and passed the back of his hand across his mouth. "He's meaner than he looks," Redmond said.

Brion raised his hands. "Look, I've had enough. Redmond has been wailing on me for hours."

"Good," Neahl said. "Let's see if he's managed to pound anything into that thick skull."

Brion let out a sigh. "We're pulling our punches," Brion said.

Not only was Neahl fresh, but he was the size of a bull and twice as mean. Brion had already tangled with Neahl and come out the sorry loser. He didn't want to be on the receiving end of one of those big fists.

Neahl nodded again and began to circle.

Brion shadowed his movement, waiting. In his mind, he ran through all of the principles Redmond had been pounding into him. Neahl lunged with a right hook. Brion stepped in to block it and brought in a right jab of his own. But Neahl wasn't there. Brion realized that he had fallen for a feint just as his feet were swept from underneath him, and he fell hard on his back. He lay there for a while gasping for breath and trying to figure out how Neahl had fooled him. When he finally had the answer, he sat up.

"Felt real nice," Brion said as he came to his feet. "Somehow Redmond didn't teach me that little trick yet."

"No, but I did teach you to quarter your attacker," Redmond said.

"I know."

"What else did you do wrong?" Neahl asked.

Brion tried to smile, but somehow it just wouldn't come to his lips. If all of Neahl's lessons were going to be so painful and so embarrassing, he was starting to think he didn't want to learn them anymore. Had his father been this slow at learning how to fight? Probably not.

"Three things," Brion said. "First, I underestimated your ability to move quickly. Second, I looked into your eyes. And third, I led with a right jab like I did when you were watching."

Now Neahl smiled and slapped him on the back.

"Exactly. Fix all three, and you might survive."

"Great," Brion said with plain sarcasm. "Just those three little things in addition to the ten thousand other things I have to learn between now and spring."

"Yep," Neahl said. He stepped towards the man who had accompanied him. "Well, Mullen, what do you think of our student?"

Brion knew Mullen by sight but hadn't ever interacted with him. He worked as the town cooper and was widely known for the quality of his barrels. He was a stocky man with thin, brown hair and a square face, but the way he held his eyes made him appear hesitant and uncertain. Today, he had a bandage on his right hand and one on his head.

"I think he'll do fine," Mullen said.

Neahl retrieved his large pack, and they all followed him into the house. Brion and Redmond washed up in the basin, while Neahl prepared the stew. They engaged in small talk until they had finished eating and pushed back their chairs.

"Now we come to the point," Neahl said, as if they had been discussing something specific for hours. Neahl stood, handed Brion his bow, and tossed him a block of beeswax and a bottle of oil.

"Neahl—" Brion began, but Neahl waved an impatient hand at him. So Brion strung the bow and began running the beeswax up and down the string.

"You probably know that Mullen is Maggie's father," Neahl said.

Brion nodded and kept rubbing the wax into the string.

"But I didn't tell you that he was in the rescue party that just returned."

Brion dropped the wax.

"Did you find them?" Brion asked as he bent to pick it up. He sat up red-faced and staring. He tried not to betray his anxiety to know about Finola. Brigid hadn't been in the party the village men had been tracking, but Finola had.

Mullen nodded his balding head.

"We caught up with them past Com Lake after four days of hard riding," he said. "We encircled them and attacked at daylight. We caught them completely by surprise, but they were fast." He reached up a hand to touch the bandage on his head. "A large group broke through with some captives and rode away. They left a rear guard that slowed us down for the rest of the day. Then they disappeared into the night. We lost five men with most of the rest wounded."

"And the prisoners?" Brion struggled against the rising anticipation.

"The bowstring," Neahl interrupted.

Brion ran his fingers over the string to warm the wax and force it into the fibers, but he never removed his gaze from Mullen's face.

Mullen shook his head in answer to Brion's question. "We recovered two of the boys, but they carried Maggie, Finola, and one other boy away at the beginning of the battle."

He blinked at Brion. "I'm sorry, lad. We tried to follow after the rearguard disappeared, but we were worn out and wounded. The Salassani didn't stop after that."

Brion noted the thickness in Mullen's voice.

"I'm sorry," Brion said.

The emptiness he had been fighting to keep at bay opened up inside him like a great, black pit. Finola was gone. His last hope fell into the emptiness. Finola and Brigid were gone, and here he was sitting comfortable and safe, waxing a bowstring. He should be out there with them. He should be suffering like they were.

"I've come to offer myself to ride with you come spring when you go after them," Mullen said.

Brion glanced at Neahl. Did the whole town know they planned to ride into the heathland?

Neahl shook his head and pointed to the bow.

Brion gritted his teeth in frustration, but he picked up the rag, poured some oil on it and began rubbing it into the yew bow.

"You've got a family, Mullen," Neahl said. "You can't risk your life again."

Mullen's face flushed. "She's my only daughter, Neahl. And she is barely four years old. I'll not sit here while those villains . . ." He didn't finish the thought.

"We can't let you ride with us, Mullen, but you can help us in other ways."

Mullen's face fell. He didn't try to conceal his disappointment. But he sat up straighter as if he had expected this conclusion. Apparently, he had already had this discussion with Neahl.

"Name it," he said.

"Somebody needs to carry news of this raid to the High Sheriff at Mailag so that he can inform King Geric. I also need someone to bring back some supplies for us that I can only get at Mailag. And I need two good horses built to cover distance at speed."

Mullen nodded. "I'm your man," he said. "Give me a couple of weeks to set my house in order, and I'll go."

Mullen pinched his lips into a thin line, and Brion read the frustrated resignation in his posture. He knew what it felt like to be prevented from going to the rescue of those you loved.

Mullen excused himself and mounted his horse. Brion stared after him in growing despair as Mullen disappeared up the road. If an entire rescue party had been unable to save the girls, how were three men—no, two men and one boy—going to accomplish it?

Deliverance

After the assassination attempt and the beating he had taken that day, his confidence in his fighting ability had drained out of him like water from a leaky barrel. The more he learned about being a warrior, the more he knew that he would never be able to live up to his father's reputation. Besides, he had never fought with a sword or a knife, and he had never killed another human being.

Neahl called them in once Mullen had disappeared over the hill.

"There's something I didn't tell you," he said. "The assassin we met in the woods visited the headman before he left the village."

Chapter 15
Separation

Brigid surveyed the village of Durk as they paused at the crest of the last rise. The village clustered on a wide, grassy plain where two, broad rivers joined and veered to the east. Fields and grazing herds of horses and sheep spread out to where the heathland rose up, gray and brown in the evening light. A thick stand of evergreens fanned out up the far hillside to the north, casting a splash of color to the winter landscape. It was a beautiful site, and it made Brigid feel sick.

It had taken them another week of hard riding to reach the village. And now that she gazed down upon it, her captivity seemed more real than ever before. She struggled against the despair. How could she ever hope to see her own land and people again? She glanced at Finola and saw the scowl on her face. This made her smile. With Finola there to constantly talk of escape, she might be able to keep her hopes up. If nothing else, Finola was a piece of home.

The odors of cooking food and burning wood rose on the columns of smoke that drifted leisurely into the steel-gray sky as the company descended to the village. It almost smelled like Wexford. This thought surprised Brigid. Somehow she had imagined that the Salassani lived in skin tents and roamed about the heathland like wild animals. The Salassani themselves were a mixed lot with many dark heads intermingled with a few blondes. Most were of medium height and build, wearing a mixture of skins and woven cloth to fend off the cold. Most wore capes and many women wore trousers like the men.

Emyr and Ithel led the party to the center of town where the villagers crowded around. Emyr dismounted and signaled for them to do the same. The crowd surged forward to gawk at them. Rough hands reached out to feel Brigid's hair. One little rogue yanked a few strands from her head and scampered away. He held them up as a trophy. A few people tried to rub the freckles from her hands and face.

The crowd soon parted for an old woman bearing a long, flat board.

Deliverance

Without a word, she started beating them on the backside with it. Brigid yelped in surprise and danced sideways. After a couple of strikes, she managed to jump out of the way. But the woman struck Finola only once before Finola spun to face the old woman, red with rage.

When the woman swung the board again, Finola jumped in and wrestled it from her hands. The crowd roared with pleasure and began stamping their feet. Finola glared at the woman who raised her hands to the sky, said something that made everyone laugh, and then shuffled back to the crowd.

Emyr approached them with a broad grin. "You two go with the old woman now. She'll take care of you," he said.

Finola glared at him. "If she tries to hit me again, I'll use this board on her."

Emyr threw back his head and laughed. "You're as fierce as a she-cat, but don't worry. The hitting is done."

Finola grabbed Johnny's hand, but Emyr shook his head.

"The boy stays with me."

Finola glared at him. "What are you going to do with him?"

Emyr shook his head. "Don't worry. He's okay."

Johnny gazed up at Finola with his big, round eyes. His lips were pulled into a thin line. He withdrew his hand from Finola's grasp. The boy had made his choice. He would become a Salassani. Tears glistened in Finola's eyes as Johnny went to stand beside Emyr. Finola stepped after him, but Brigid grabbed Finola's arm and pulled her toward the old woman that stood waiting for them.

They followed her through the village to a small hut where the woman motioned for them to enter. A fire burned in the center where a pot of steaming water hung from a tripod. The woman rummaged around in a chest and tossed each of them a change of clothing.

"Wash and change," she said. "I'll return for you."

Brigid glanced at her sharply. The woman spoke with no accent at all.

"What's to become of us?" Brigid asked.

The woman shrugged. "You'll be taught how to be a good Salassani woman and then sold at the great gathering. It is the way."

"When is the gathering?" Finola asked.

The woman waved a hand at them impatiently. "Wash and change. There will be time for talk later."

"What do we do now?" Brigid asked as she and Finola sat brushing their hair before the fire, enjoying the warmth after so many days riding against a cold wind. They had already slipped into the long shirts, trousers, and boots the woman had tossed at them.

Finola shrugged.

"Do you think anyone will come for us?" Brigid asked.

Finola stopped brushing her hair. "They already did," she said.

Brigid's heart sank. Finola had told her about the rescue attempt and how Ithel had galloped off with her and let the others do the fighting and dying. Finola didn't know about the other captives, but she had seen Maggie carried away about the same time Ithel had dragged her to his horse.

"Then you don't think anyone else is going to come after us?"

Finola shook her head. "How would they find us?" she said. "Even if they did, they would need an army to get us out of a place like this. We're on our own."

They brushed and braided their hair in silence until Brigid spoke. "I'm not going to give up."

Finola tied her hair off. "Who said I'd given up? I'm just facing reality."

"What about Brion?" Brigid asked.

Finola paused. "Do you think he's still alive?" Her voice thickened with emotion.

Brigid considered for a moment before answering. Obviously, she couldn't know. But he hadn't been at the house. The men were in too much of a hurry to have time to find him—unless he rushed in after she had screamed. Or maybe they had killed him before even coming to the house. The thought sickened her. She blinked at her own tears.

"I think he is," Brigid said. "They hit us so fast, they didn't have time to go find him. I just don't think he's dead."

Finola coughed and blinked rapidly. "Well, I'm not going to wait around for him or anyone else to come find us," Finola said. "First chance I get, I'm escaping."

Brigid smiled. This was the spunk that Brion had so liked in Finola.

"How are you going to find your way back and do it without getting caught?"

Finola shrugged. "I'll work that out when I come to it. But I'm not going to become the wife of some Salassani pig. I'd rather die."

The door opened. The girls spun to face it. The old woman came in followed by Emyr and Ithel. Emyr motioned for Brigid to follow him. She hesitated.

"Why can't we stay together?"

The old woman slapped her. Finola sprang forward, but Ithel caught her and held her tight.

"I told you, you have been too soft on them," Ithel said.

Ithel dragged Finola from the house. Emyr motioned to Brigid again. This time she followed. Finola craned her head to stare at Brigid as Ithel dragged Finola away.

"We're on our own now," Finola called. "We're on our own."

Chapter 16
The Sheriff

ullen traveled to Mailag several times over the ensuing weeks bringing them supplies and news. But when he returned after his last trip, he didn't come alone. Brion had almost forgotten about Mullen in the long days of training that rapidly bled into two months. The tall man that accompanied him sported a mail hauberk that caught the light of the afternoon sun. The man's black cloak spread out over the horse's flank. The pommel of his great sword glittered. Neahl went out to meet them.

"Lord Sheriff. We didn't expect you."

The man wore a close-cut, grizzled beard that matched his hair. His face was long and lean. He dismounted and flipped the reins at Brion. Brion caught them and scowled.

"Sorry to come unannounced, Neahl," he said.

He stepped forward and shook hands with Neahl.

"It's been a long time," the Sheriff said.

Neahl smiled. "Long before you became the Lord Sheriff."

Neahl led him towards the house. Mullen handed Brion the reins to his horse.

"Thanks, Brion." Mullen said.

The Sheriff turned back to Brion. "Give them a good brushing lad," he said.

Redmond came around the corner of the house in time to see them enter. He gave Brion a questioning glance.

"It's the Sheriff," Brion whispered. "What's he come all the way down here for?"

Redmond shrugged and jabbed a thumb toward the stables.

"Best see to their horses," he said before hurrying into the house.

Brion snorted and jerked the reins.

"No, thank you for offering, Redmond," he said in mock conversation as he led the horses toward the barn. "But I can take care of the horses myself. Why don't you just go inside, have a nice glass of mead, and relax your tired feet? I've been wanting to care for two, big horses and a pack mule all day. Don't let me keep you."

The better part of an hour passed before he had unsaddled the two horses, unpacked the mule, given them a quick brushing, and fed and watered the lot. He hefted the two big packs, slung them over his shoulder and trudged toward the house.

He found them all seated around the table with the map spread out before them. Neahl pointed to the Daven Fens.

As Brion entered, the Sheriff scrutinized him. He nodded to Brion, and Brion nodded in reply.

"Sorry to hear about your father and mother, lad. I'm truly sorry."

"Thank you, sir," he said.

But something in the way the Sheriff said this made Brion watch him more carefully. The Sheriff had refused to meet his gaze. Brion glanced at Neahl and Redmond to see if they had noticed, but they showed no sign if they had.

The Sheriff pursed his lips. "So, you all plan to go after them then?"

"Yes," Neahl said.

"You know that I can't offer you any support. King Geric can't afford to be linked to any raids into Salassani territory, even in retaliation for a raid. So you're on your own. I can't come to your aid if you get into trouble."

He paused to see that they had all understood. As his gaze passed over Brion, Brion noted again the Sheriff's hesitation to look him in the eye.

"I never expected any royal support," Neahl said. "But can we count on you not to interfere?"

The Sheriff smiled and spread his hands. "I have no intention of interfering. In fact, I've come with a request from the King himself."

"Really?" Neahl raised his eyebrows in surprise. He exchanged glances with Redmond.

"There's been a lot of activity around Dunkeldi Castle the last few months," the Sheriff said. "We know something is afoot, but we don't have many informants in Dunkeldi. So the King would be obliged if you could keep your ears open for any news or unusual movements among the Salassani."

"Of course," Neahl replied. "But I want it understood that our first priority is to recover the girls. I won't go into the heathland with my hands tied by royal agreements and protocol."

He watched the Sheriff as if waiting to see that he understood his meaning.

The Sheriff nodded and said, "I never expected anything else from you. Just be careful that you don't start a war. Make sure the Salassani understand that you're acting on your own."

Neahl grinned. "Oh, they'll know. I'll make sure they know."

"Good. When do you leave?"

"Not until the snow melts. We still have more work to do before we're ready."

The Sheriff looked at Brion. He smiled. But the smile did not reach his eyes. "You don't look much like your father, boy. Did you inherit his gift with the bow?"

Brion shook his head. "No, sir."

"He's being modest," Redmond said. "He may not be there yet, but he will be."

"You'll need it where you're going." The Sheriff cleared his throat and turned to Neahl. "I'm going to speak plainly, Neahl," he said. "I understand why you have to do this, but I don't think it's wise. By the time you get there, the Salassani will be gathered in Aldina Valley. You can't possibly hope to stroll in there, grab those children that the Salassani expect to sell for a profit, and walk out again." The Sheriff shook his head. "I think it's a suicide mission, Neahl. I can't say it more plainly. I don't expect you to come out alive."

In the ensuing silence, Brion watched Neahl, afraid that he might change his mind, afraid that he would have to go into the heathland alone, and knowing he couldn't do it. Neahl kept his gaze on the table with his hands clasped before him. He spoke without raising his head.

"I'm aware of the danger, Cluny. But I will not abandon Weyland's child to the Salassani."

He raised his head to stare the Sheriff directly in the eyes. He said nothing else, but his meaning was plain to see. Even if it cost him his life, he was going to try.

The Sheriff nodded. He appeared satisfied. "Well then, I wish you luck. If anyone can do it, you can. We'll look for you by midsummer."

"Well," Redmond said as the Sheriff and Mullen disappeared over the hill into the golden glow of the setting sun, "Cluny still knows how to inspire and instill courage for a difficult task, doesn't he?"

Deliverance

Neahl glanced around at him with half a smile. "He never was what you would call optimistic."

Redmond shook his head. "No, but he is a good man to have in a fight, though he still likes that ridiculous longsword."

"How do you two know the High Sheriff?" Brion asked.

Neahl grunted. "He wasn't always the High Sheriff. Old Cluny was a simple man-at-arms when the war began, but since he came from the lower nobility and he was a fine swordsman, he quickly rose in rank as the Salassani killed off the officers. We've seen many a battle together, and he's as stout a man as you'll ever find."

"He became the officer in charge of the scouts," Redmond added, seeing that Brion wasn't satisfied with Neahl's answer. "That's how we know him. But I didn't know he was the High Sheriff. When did that happen?"

"About five years ago," Neahl said. "He was Sheriff of Dunfermine before that."

"Do you think he's right?" Brion asked. "I mean about our chances."

Neahl and Redmond exchanged glances. Neahl shrugged. "It doesn't matter what he thinks. What matters is what's up here and what's in here," he said, touching Brion's head and then his heart. "You get those two things prepared and the impossible can happen."

"I don't like him," Brion said.

Neahl blinked and looked at Redmond who kept his gaze on Brion.

When neither of them spoke, Brion continued. "He wouldn't look me in the eye."

Neahl stepped forward, his brow furrowed.

"Cluny's a good man, Brion. Your father admired him," he said.

"The Cluny we knew was," Redmond said. "But a Cluny who can't look a boy in the eye when his parents have been murdered is a different animal."

Chapter 17
Foiled

Finola curled up in the little hollow created where the roots of the tree had been ripped from the ground as it fell. She pulled her knees up to her chest and wrapped the cloak tightly around her. The rich smell of damp earth surrounded her. She had planned her escape the best she could and had taken the time to gather food, a knife, some waterskins, and the woolen cloak that Ithel had given her to wear. When Ithel and Addie, Ithel's wife, had both gone to the market, she had quietly slipped out the other end of the village and had stolen into the heather. She had been running all day. She needed rest.

She would find Brigid, and together they would work their way south. Tonight, she would shelter under the bundle of roots, get a bite to eat, and get some sleep. Tomorrow or the next day, she would be at Brigid's village.

Two long months had dragged by since she had been captured. The snow no longer fell, and the nights were not so cold. She had heard Ithel's plans to sell her at the gathering they called the Great Keldi. And she was not going to wait around for that to happen. By escaping now, she had a long spring and summer to work her way back home, if it took that long.

Despite her words to Brigid, she had waited for Brion or other men from the village to attempt another rescue. But that hope had slowly died in the long, lingering weeks—smothered by a growing despair. So she had taken matters into her own hands.

If she returned to Wexford and found that Brion had been living comfortably in his little cabin, she would beat him to within an inch of his life and then send him packing. A man who wouldn't risk his life to save his woman was not worth having.

She swallowed the lump that rose in her throat and hugged her knees tighter. Maybe he hadn't followed because he couldn't. Maybe he was— she wouldn't think it. She remembered how they had played as little children on the festival days and how he had always paid a visit to the bakery whenever his family came into town.

She remembered how he had looked at her after winning the town archery competition. It had reminded her of a child seeking approval. She remembered the first time they had held hands while they strolled through the forest. And she remembered the time she had watched him from the bakery window as he had lifted the little girl from the mud puddle where she had fallen, wiped her clean with his own shirt, and held her until she stopped crying. Only then had she decided that he was worth marrying.

But those days were long gone. Now she huddled alone in a dark wood, trying to run back home—back to him. She leaned against a long, thick root and closed her eyes. She wouldn't succumb to the despair that sought to drag her down. Things would be better in the morning. They always were.

Finola awoke with a start. Something had crashed near her. She grasped the knife she had stolen from Ithel's house and gripped it hard against her palm. The cold, gray light of dawn struggled to infiltrate the forest.

Voices murmured. Something snapped. Someone cursed. Her heart leapt into her mouth. Could it be Ithel, already? He couldn't have found her so quickly. Or could he? The crashing and voices grew louder. Finola tried to become smaller as she pushed back further under the overhanging roots. She nearly screamed when a painted face poked around the roots to peer right at her. A wicked smirk formed on the lips. Then another head appeared. It was Ithel.

"Get out of there," he said in Salassani.

Finola raised the knife.

Ithel reached for her, but she stabbed the knife toward his arm. The other man shot in his hand to grab her wrist. She resisted, but he bent it back and down until she cried out in pain and dropped the knife. He dragged her from under the tree and tied her hands roughly behind her back. Ithel stepped up to her and slapped her hard across the face. She tasted blood in her mouth and felt the fire of his blow on her cheek.

"If you run away again, I'll kill you," he said.

Brigid experienced a sudden, wild tinge of fear. She paused on the trail with the large basket of clothes on her hip. Little patches of snow still clung to the shadows, but the day had turned unseasonably warm as a balmy wind blew in from the east. The water might be cold, but it was faster and much less work to carry the clothes to the river rather than to haul the water to the house. Nothing unusual occurred, so Brigid continued on down the trail to the river.

Early March had arrived with a blast of warm wind that swept the snow from the ground. The snowpack in the Aldina Mountains filled the river with icy water that rolled towards the rapids with a gentle roar. The smell of fish and wet earth filled the air. Brigid avoided the large group of gossiping women at the big rock and stepped off up river to find a spot where she could be alone.

She settled into the rhythm of scrubbing and pounding and wringing until her fingers were numb. She sat back to rest when the uneasy feeling settled over her again. She scanned the area. The women trailed off toward the village. The sun burned behind the drifting clouds. Birds chirped and sang in the trees. The dull roar of the rapids further below reached her. Everything was as it had been, so she bent back to her work.

She finished the last shirt, wrung it out, and tossed it into the basket before she stood and tried to stretch the stiffness from her joints. A strong arm encircled her, pinning her arms to her side. A calloused hand clamped over her mouth to cut off her scream. She struggled to reach the knife in her boot, but couldn't.

The sudden, paralyzing terror of being kidnapped again burned in her chest. It gave way to a desperate panic as she kicked and clawed while her captor dragged her back into the shadows of the trees. He threw her face down and yanked her hands painfully behind her back. She opened her mouth to call for help, but a knee forced her face down into the dirt. Her hands were tied behind her, a piece of cloth was stuffed into her mouth and a cloth tied over it to keep it in place. A blindfold followed.

She was thrown over a horse's back. Her captor leapt up behind her and kicked the horse into a canter. All the terror she had experienced that day at her family's cabin came rushing back, hot and furious, together with the certainty that her life was about to get a lot worse, if she survived.

Emyr looked down at the overturned basket and the wet clothes scattered in the mud. He had come in search of Brigid when she hadn't appeared to help Dealla with the lunch. He followed the signs of a struggle into the trees. When he saw the horse hooves leading up the river, he spun and sprinted back to the village.

He saddled his horse, grabbed his weapons and several days' worth of food, spoke briefly to Dealla, and rode out of the village. He returned to the site of the struggle, bent low over his horse's side and followed the trail. It wasn't hard to see. Whoever had stolen his slave girl had made no attempt to conceal his trail, which struck Emyr as either foolhardy or intentional. Perhaps they had come back to finish the job he could not.

While he rode, Emyr struggled to understand his emotions. He had been so angry at first that he hadn't noticed the anxiety. But as he bent to the task of tracking down the thief, he was surprised how much he worried for the welfare of his slave girl.

She had been a good slave, it was true. He had never had to discipline her, though his mother sometimes did just to keep her in her place. But the redheaded, green-eyed, young woman had become more than a mere slave to him. He had never considered this before, and it astonished him. He had saved her life out of a sense of moral indignation and because he couldn't stand to see such a beautiful creature destroyed for no good reason. Then he had decided to sell her at the great gathering. But if he lost her now, he would lose both his profit, and . . . . He left the thought unfinished because he didn't know how he felt.

As he followed the trail that wound on up the river towards the mountains, Emyr tried to imagine who might have kidnapped the girl. The two men who had offered to buy her might have decided to steal what they could not buy. It might simply be another young Taurini or even Aldina on his own little raid. Anyone could see why a young man might want such a slave girl, but anyone who knew that Emyr was the girl's master should have had second thoughts about stealing his slave girl. Still, doubt filled his mind.

Brigid collapsed onto the grass and leaves. They had only stopped once to rest when her captor set her upright in the saddle and wrapped his arms around her. His body had pressed close to her, filling her nostrils with the stink of his sweat.

As he now lifted the blindfold from her eyes, she blinked. The soft, golden rays of the setting sun fell upon the face of the young man she had first seen in the encampment where she had found Finola. He was young and well-muscled, but the placement of his eyes and the set of his jaw gave him an odd appearance, as if someone had just posed a difficult question and he was trying to work it out.

He studied her for a while, the way a hungry boy might survey a steaming loaf of sweet bread, before he removed the gag and cut the cords that bound her wrists. Fiery pain rushed into her hands. She gasped. Tears sprang to her eyes. Gingerly, she touched her hands together. Needles prickled up and down her fingers. So she let them rest limply in her lap, trying not to move them.

The young man watched her for a moment longer before he began setting up camp. Brigid worked her tongue around to moisten her mouth and spat out the grit and dirt. She considered running into the woods, but she knew that she was in no condition at the moment to go far. So she sat and watched, terrified that she knew what this young man wanted-ed. She also wondered what Emyr might do and if he had already discovered what had happened. Would he come after her? She didn't know.

The young man cooked a quick supper over the fire. He offered her a small bowl of stew. She ate it and drank her fill of water. The pain in her hands and wrists subsided to a dull ache. The headache she had developed also subsided. The young man didn't speak to her. He just watched her with that greedy, hungry expression that made her skin crawl.

A damp chill began to settle into the little vale as the light faded. The young man unrolled two sleeping rolls and handed her a cloak. She wrapped up in it, never taking her eyes off of him.

He sat down beside the fire and began poking the glowing red coals with a stick. Brigid concluded that he was either deciding what to do or building up the courage to do it. She shifted, feeling the knife in her boot push against her leg. She moved again to make sure that she could get it quickly while using the cloak to conceal both her hand and her boot. She started trembling again and tried to swallow the terror that kept rising in her throat.

The gray of evening slowly faded into the dark of night. The boy finally stirred. He came to sit beside her. Brigid stiffened. He reached out a hand to touch her hair. She flinched away from him. Anger flashed in his eyes. He grabbed her shoulder and spun her to face him. He spoke in Salassani.

"You're mine now."

Deliverance

He had a different accent than the people from Emyr's village, but Brigid understood him.

She shook her head.

"No. I belong to Emyr. He captured me," she said in Salassani.

"And I have taken you from him. You're mine."

He paused and reached for her hair again. This time she let him touch it, her mind racing. It seemed clear what he intended, and she would rather die. She drew her knees up under the cloak. Her right hand slipped down to the side of her boot.

"By Salassani law, you are mine, and I will make you my woman."

Brigid stared with wide eyes. Fear tightened her stomach. He touched her shoulder. She jumped up with the knife in her hand, but still concealed by the long cloak.

"I won't be your woman. Take me back."

The young man stood up slowly with a broad smile on his face.

"It's too late for that."

Brigid shook her head. He stepped forward. She backed away.

"Stay away from me," she said. She struggled to control the trembling in her voice.

"Let's talk about it," he said.

But as soon as the words left his mouth, he rushed in to grab her. A cry of surprise escaped Brigid's lips as she brought the knife up in a backhand swipe across his chest the way her father had taught her. His eyes opened wide in shock and dismay. His momentum carried him into her, but she sidestepped and shoved him away. Her knife opened another long wound along the inside of his arm. He stumbled on for a few steps and stopped to gaze at the gash in his chest. Blood soaked his tunic and dripped from his arm.

Brigid struggled to keep the tears in. The blood pounded in her ears. The breath caught in her throat. The knife felt slippery in her hand.

He pivoted slowly toward her and blinked. His expression surprised her. He seemed more confused than angry. Brigid held the knife at the ready.

"I said stay away from me."

His eyes narrowed. The shock changed to rage. He yanked his own knife from its sheath and rushed her. Brigid jumped to the side as his blade sliced a thin cut on her shoulder. She spun swinging her knife into his back. It scraped on bone as it sank up to the hilt. Brigid jerked it free and whirled to face him again, revulsion and terror surging through her in equal measure. He sank to his knees with a groan of pain.

Tears streamed down Brigid's face. The nausea rose in her throat, and she trembled. It was all she could do to stay on her feet.

"I'll kill you," he said. He staggered to his feet and stumbled toward his horse.

Brigid watched wide-eyed as he fumbled with the short bow he had strapped to the saddle. When he withdrew an arrow from the quiver, she spun and fled for the cover of the wood. The cloak fell from her shoulders. Stumbling footsteps followed her. She sped downhill several dozen paces until she came to a shallow cutaway that sliced through the forest. She paused and jumped into the darkness at the same moment that the bowstring sang.

Chapter 18
Blood Trail

A shout and a cry shattered the stillness. Emyr reined his horse to a stop. He had tracked the single horse all day until the sun had gone down and the trail had disappeared into the shadows. He had been pondering his next move when the cry reverberated through the trees. Emyr kicked his horse toward the sound. Voices drifted to him. The rich aroma of burning wood reached him before he saw the orange twinkle through the trees.

He dismounted, loosened his sword in the scabbard and nocked an arrow on his short bow. He ghosted from shadow to shadow, always staying downwind so that the stranger's horse wouldn't get his scent and give the alarm as most Salassani horses were trained to do.

The sounds of a struggle reached him. Leaves rustled. A bowstring thrummed. Something crashed. A bowstring thrummed again and the crashing and thrashing slowly died away. A growing dread began to creep into his chest, but he refused to believe that someone would go to all the trouble of capturing Brigid, only to kill her outright. So he crept through the deepening gloom, moving as silently as he could.

Emyr reached the circle of firelight and stood watching, waiting. No one was in the circle. The horse stood grazing on the grass to one side. Two blanket rolls lay crumpled on the ground. The fire had not been fed. The flames burned low, the wood almost spent. Cooking utensils lay scattered about.

Faltering steps came from the far side of the clearing. Emyr melted into the shadows again. He pulled the bowstring taut, ready to shoot. A man stumbled into the firelight. One hand clutched at his chest, while the other dragged a bow. At first, Emyr didn't recognize him. But as the man staggered to the fire and fell to his knees, the ruddy flames illuminated his face. He had no paint, so Emyr knew that he had not been successful in a war party yet. But he was surely old enough to have participated in more than one. Emyr recognized him as the boy in the camp where they had met the remnants of the group that had raided the village of Wexford.

In the light of the fire, Emyr noted the dark stain on his chest. He searched the clearing for Brigid. Emyr knew that she had to be there somewhere. She had not left the trail along the way. He was certain of it. So he hesitated. He didn't know who had injured this young man. They might still be lurking about. Someone had attacked him and probably taken Brigid with them.

He watched the young man's horse, whose nostrils flared at the smell of blood, but otherwise it showed no sign of disturbance. Emyr called out to the boy while still remaining in the shadows, his bow ready.

"Who are you?" he called.

The young man's head shot up. He reached over his shoulder for an arrow, but the quiver wasn't on his back. It was still tied to his saddle. He struggled to his feet.

"Don't try it," Emyr called. "I can see that you're injured. Throw your weapons away."

The young man paused. He dropped the bow, pulled his knife from its sheath, and tossed it away.

"Get rid of any weapons I can't see," Emyr called.

The young man shrugged and raised his hands. They shook violently from the effort. As Emyr stepped into the clearing, the young man's face showed recognition. He dropped to his knees again.

"She's a demon," he whispered.

"Where is she?" Emyr asked. He stepped closer.

The young man waved a hand back the way he had entered the clearing. "Gone."

Rage filled Emyr. He stepped toward the boy ready to kick some fear into him when he saw the great gash opened across the young man's chest. Ribs showed through, pale and white. It was a horrible wound. Blood bubbled a red froth as he breathed. It soaked his shirt and pants. The young man crumpled sideways.

Emyr glanced around again and stepped up to him. He set his bow on the grass just within his reach, but beyond the reach of the young man. Now he also saw the hemorrhaging wound in the young man's back where more bloody bubbles blossomed. The injury might have cut the spleen and maybe the liver, but it surely punctured the lung. Emyr rolled him over. The boy's breathing was shallow.

Deliverance

"What happened?" Emyr asked. "Why did you take her?"

An ironic smile slipped across the young man's lips. "I thought to make her my woman," he said. "But she fights like a she-bear." He coughed, closed his eyes, and died.

Emyr sat back on his haunches and shook his head. What should he do? If he tried to track her at night, he would certainly lose her trail. But if she was injured, she could die before morning without help. He glanced down at the young man.

Fool. He should have known that even had he succeeded, Emyr would have killed him. He could not let an insult like this go unpunished. Not if he ever wanted to live in peace in the village. A shamed man had no peace. It was better to die.

He picked up his bow and strode to the edge of the clearing. The young man had shot at least two arrows, and he was apparently aiming at Brigid. What if one of them had found its mark?

Emyr decided that he could not wait until morning. But he couldn't go blundering about in the dark either. He returned to the fire, built it up, retrieved his own horse, hobbled it, and set about making torches. The pine trees on this slope of the Aldinas were called fire pine by the locals because the slightest injury to the bark caused them to weep copious amounts of thick, amber resin. So Emyr collected all the pine pitch, birch bark, and dried grass he could find—enough for half a dozen torches. He packed a bag with medical supplies and food, lit a torch, and faced the forest. The preparations had taken him the better part of an hour.

Still, he felt sure that he had made the right decision. Bending low to the ground, he began searching for sign. It was difficult to find in the shadows of the trees, but he could make out a trail of disturbed leaves and droplets of blood heading downhill. He soon came to a gully that dropped four or five feet down. Emyr left the blood trail and climbed up the gully about ten paces before dropping over the side. He didn't want to jump down and land on any sign the fleeing girl might have left behind.

He found where she had landed and rolled. He picked up the broken point of an arrow. It was still sticky with blood. His heart sank. He searched for the other half of the arrow, but it wasn't there. Brigid had been shot and part of the shaft was still lodged in her body. With a wound like that, she couldn't have made it far.

With a new sense of urgency and dread, Emyr hurried along beside the trail, careful not to disturb the sign. His torch sputtered and spit clouds of smoke that stung his nostrils, burned his eyes, and blurred his vision.

Emyr soon came to a large tree where he found a pool of blood. She must have rested here. Bloody feathers poked up from a huckleberry bush. Emyr lifted it by the shaft. The blood was still tacky. She must have torn it out. He hurried on, bent low over the trail in search of any sign his feeble light would illuminate.

Now her trail meandered as if she struggled to keep her sense of direction, but it always tended downhill. Upturned leaves, broken branches, the tell-tale sign of a boot in some soft patch of earth or snow, scuff marks in the green moss on the rocks, and the occasional splattering of blood led him on.

As the trail lengthened, he became more and more convinced that she had not been seriously injured. If some vital organ had been punctured, she could not have lasted this long. And he could not be far behind her, but the necessity of pausing frequently to puzzle out the trail with his sputtering torches slowed him down.

The occasional cry of a wildcat made him shiver at the thought of the wounded girl, smelling of blood, wandering through the forest. He hurried as quickly as possible, but in his haste he lost the trail and had to double back.

After an exhausting night, the gray dawn found Emyr standing on the bank of a gurgling creek, peering over the water. He had tracked her to the cobblestone bed and had lost her trail. He was bone-tired, and he marveled at this girl's toughness. Most women he knew would have given up in despair long ago. But this young woman had killed her attacker and fled into the night, going on hour after hour. By all rights, he should have caught up with her by now. She couldn't have kept going all night.

But maybe he misjudged her. Maybe she had decided to conceal her trail when she came to the water. His torches had burned out long ago, and he had crawled on hands and knees so as not to lose the trail. Without the torches, he didn't dare continue past the creek in the darkness. He had to wait for the light of day so that he could examine the moss-covered rocks and the little sandy pools for any sign of her passing. If he crashed on into the woods without a clear idea of where she had gone, he would lose her for sure.

Emyr went back to where the trail dropped over the small embankment into the streambed. In the early light of day, he could now see the

Deliverance

blood stains on the stones. But these were not droplets. Bloody fabric had been pressed against the rock. Several more marks like it could be seen in an irregular pattern as if the maker had no clear idea of direction. Then they disappeared amid a wandering trail of overturned stones. Emyr picked his way up the creek bed, following the trail. It went to the water's edge before veering upstream. He knelt to examine the stones just beyond the water's edge for any sign of her passing when a terrible cry split the still, morning air.

Chapter 19
Unlikely Friends

myr jerked his head up at the chilling cry. At first, he wasn't sure if the cry had been human or animal until the distinctive scream of the wildcat lifted on the air again. It came from upstream around the bend.

An unreasoning, sickening dread swooped into Emyr's stomach. He nocked an arrow and bounded up the cobble-strewn bed, heedless of his own safety. The dread was born of the certainty that the wildcat had found the wounded girl. Maybe she was still alive and fighting.

He sprinted around the bend to find the wildcat swatting at an overhang of brambles. A rock flew out but missed to clatter harmlessly amid the stones. The cat hissed and swatted again. Emyr slid to a stop amid a clatter of stones, raised the bow and loosed. The arrow bit deep into the cat's side just behind the shoulder blade. The great cat twisted back on itself hissing and spitting. It rolled and rolled, breaking the shaft, before careening off up the riverbed in a wild panic to escape the biting pain of death.

Emyr approached the cutaway. "Brigid," he called softly. "Brigid, it's me, Emyr."

He bent down to peer through the brambles. His gaze focused on the bloody point of a knife. Then he saw her eyes. They were ablaze, almost crazed. Emyr sat back on his haunches and raised his hands.

"It's okay," he said. "He's dead. You can come out. I'll take you home." Brigid hesitated. The wild light faded from her eyes.

"Come out," he said. "You're safe now."

Brigid blinked and lowered the knife before crawling out of the cutaway. Emyr resisted the urge to snatch her up into his arms and offered her his hand instead. She grabbed it with surprising strength and struggled to her feet.

She regarded him now with steady, green eyes. "He's dead?" she asked.

Emyr nodded. "He was dying when I found him. You didn't need to keep running."

She considered for a moment and shrugged. "How was I supposed to know?"

Emyr restrained a smile of relief and amazement as he saw the gash on her arm, the bloody rag wrapped around her right hand, the fiery hair matted with dried sweat and tangled with leaves and twigs. He marveled at the strength and courage of this apparently frail, young woman.

"Let's clean your wounds," he said.

Brigid cradled the cup of tea Emyr had given her in her good hand. She sipped it and gagged.

"That's nasty," she said.

"It'll dull the pain a bit."

Emyr unwrapped her wounded hand while Brigid grimaced. The arrow had pierced her hand in the fleshy part between the thumb and forefinger.

"Will I be able to use it again?" Brigid asked, trying not to wince. Even with the tea Emyr had given her, the pain was almost unbearable.

"I think so," he said. "It's a good thing he grabbed a small game point and not a broadhead. A broadhead probably would have crippled you."

"It still hurts," she said. She figured she should remind him of that in case he forgot.

"No doubt," Emyr said.

But she hadn't needed to worry. Emyr was very gentle. Brigid watched in interest as he tenderly cleansed the wound, confused by the sense of relief she had felt when she saw him peering into her little shelter and confused at the sense of safety and strength his presence brought her.

"Will you tell me what happened?" Emyr asked. His fingers moved nimbly over the wound, removing bits of grass and dirt and pouring more water over it.

Brigid bit her lip against the pain, nodded, and recounted how the young man had grabbed her from behind. Her face burned when she explained why he had kidnapped her, but Emyr didn't seem to notice. He kept his gaze on her wound and nodded as if he understood.

"It is the way," he said. "If he had succeeded, you would have been forced to stay with him."

"Why?"

"Because it is the Salassani way," Emyr explained. "A woman who has been with a man can't be with any other until that man dies or he gives her to another—or in my village, until she divorces him. But a slave can't divorce, and he could have kept you forever."

Brigid bristled. "That's barbaric," she said. "In the south, a boy who kidnapped and raped a girl would be executed. She wouldn't be forced to marry him. It's disgusting."

Emyr glanced at her. He extracted a little pouch from his bag and untied it.

"Yes, it is," he replied. "But it is the way." He paused as he sprinkled a red ocher powder over her wound. "If it were any other woman, he might have succeeded. But he didn't count on you fighting him."

He glanced up at her and gave her an approving smile. "Where did you learn to fight with knives? That looked like a professional job."

"My father taught me." Brigid examined the pines over his head, trying not to think of her father or of the throbbing pain in her hand.

Emyr began wrapping her hand in a clean cloth.

"Wise man, your father." Then he frowned. "I'm sorry for what happened to your family."

Brigid scowled. What was that supposed to mean? She stared at him. "But you're not sorry for stealing me from them," she demanded.

He finished wrapping her hand and sat back on his heels. He shook his head. "No, I'm not sorry for taking you, because, if I hadn't, you would have been killed."

"Why?" she asked the question that had been bothering her for months. "Why would you kill perfectly good slaves?"

Emyr looked tired. "We were hired to kill your entire family. We weren't supposed to leave anyone alive."

Chapter 20
Questions

rigid opened her mouth, but no words could form in her mind. Hired? Who would want her family killed? Why? They were nothing but simple trappers.

Emyr shook his head and reached a hand up to examine her arm. "May I?" he asked. When Brigid nodded, he cut the sleeve away and began cleaning the wound.

"Your father had powerful enemies."

"What?" Brigid looked down at her throbbing bandaged hand.

"Someone with a lot of money and good connections arranged for a raid on your village. We were supposed to make it look like just another border raid."

"But why?"

"I don't know." Emyr dipped a cloth in the hot water and gently scrubbed her wound.

Brigid sucked in her breath, and bit her lip. She kept talking to keep from screaming. "So you just took the money and killed my family?"

Emyr paused, looked at her, and nodded. "I led the raid, so I'm responsible. It is the way."

"I don't care about your stupid way!" Brigid screamed. "I want my family back. I want to go home!" Tears slipped down her cheeks.

Emyr sprinkled the red powder on her arm without looking at her.

"I know," he said. "I'm sorry."

Brigid nearly exploded in fury. She jerked her arm away from his grasp.

"How can you know?" she shouted. The rage and despair ripped through her. She wanted to break a rock over his head.

"Because I wasn't born a Salassani," he said.

Brigid stared at him, open-mouthed. She tried to decide if he was lying. But in the last three months, she had never known him to tell a lie or even to stretch the truth. He wore the Salassani paint, and he was well-respected in the village. She had seen people seek him out for advice even

91

though he was so young. He couldn't be more than twenty years old. She had even heard one of the women in the village whisper that he would be the next village headman.

"I was born in Coll," Emyr said, "and taken when I was three or four years old."

"What about your mother, Dealla?"

Emyr shook his head as he wrapped her arm in a clean cloth.

"She's not my mother. I was adopted by a great warrior after he saw me in a fight. Dealla was his mother. He died in battle a year ago, and I've been taking care of her ever since." He bent to put his things back into his bag.

Brigid struggled to come to terms with what he had just told her. She wanted to hate him. She wanted to snatch up a stone and pound him to a pulp. She wanted to do something to let out the fury that tightened her throat and made the blood pound in her ears.

"How can you enslave people after what happened to you?" she said.

Emyr shrugged and leaned over the fire to check the stew that had been simmering while he had treated Brigid's wounds. He tasted it and lifted it off the fire.

"It is the way," he said.

"It's not my people's way," Brigid replied.

Emyr handed her a bowl of stew with a wooden spoon. She cradled it in her lap. She didn't want to eat—not after what Emyr had just told her. But she had eaten so little yesterday and pushed herself so hard that she knew she had to eat. So she lifted the spoon with her left hand.

"No," he said. "Your people don't keep slaves; they just sell them to the Salassani. They just hire us to do their dirty work. They just push other people off their land, and, when they fight back, they kill them."

Brigid was incredulous and smirked at him.

"Why do you think the Carpentini have fled their plains for the mountains?" Emyr asked. "Because your farmers wanted their land to grow wheat and barley. Why do you think the southern heathland is empty of people? Because your King Geric killed everyone who lived on the southern Hackel Heath and Heron Moor. He said it was to protect his borders by keeping the savages at a distance. Where do you think the Carpentini children went who were captured in the raids on their villages?" He didn't give her time to answer. "They were sold to the Hallstat or the Perthians as slaves. Why? Because it is the way."

Deliverance

Brigid had not known any of this, and she didn't want to believe him. Her world had been turned upside down already, and she hadn't had time to make sense of it. She sipped at her stew to avoid having to say anything. Emyr also said no more, though he glanced at her occasionally while they ate.

When they had finished, Emyr addressed her. "How do you feel?" he asked as she handed him her empty bowl.

"Better," she said.

"Do you think you can walk back to the clearing?"

Brigid nodded. Her hand and shoulder still throbbed, but the pain was much less.

"It would be good for us to camp there tonight. We can ride back to the village tomorrow."

Emyr packed up his gear and led her back the way she had come. But the climb proved more difficult than Brigid had imagined. She hadn't counted on the fact that she had had little sleep, and, though the injuries were not life threatening, they still sapped her strength. Her legs trembled at the effort, and she rested often. Emyr didn't try to rush her. He waited patiently until she was ready to continue. By the time they reached the top of the hill, the twilight of evening had settled in the clearing.

Emyr made her stop and rest in the shadow of a large maple just beyond sight of the clearing. The cool breeze swirled about, and Brigid caught a terrible odor on the breath of wind. As Emyr entered the clearing, a chorus of birds complained. They flew off with much flapping of wings and cries of fright. Brigid closed her eyes. She didn't want to think about what had been happening—but the images of hungry birds pecking at oozing wounds and staring eyes nearly made her sick. Twenty minutes later, Emyr returned for her and helped her back to the clearing. A dark stain smeared the flattened grass beside the fire, but the body was gone.

She glanced at Emyr. He just shook his head as if telling her not to ask and set about making her comfortable. She lay back on the sleeping roll gratefully. Her hand and shoulder were stiff and sore. The jostling they had received during the climb had brought the pounding ache back with a vengeance. Every beat of her heart caused the injuries to throb with pain.

Emyr brought her a cup full of the same bitter tea he had given her that morning, and the pain began to subside.

They hadn't spoken much during their climb back to the clearing. But Brigid was not satisfied. Even if there was cruelty in the world that didn't mean one had to participate in it. Couldn't a person simply refuse? And how could he sit there so casually and tell her that he had been hired to kill her and her family?

When Emyr brought her dinner, all these questions came pouring out of her.

He nodded. "You're right," he said. "But I ask you to consider what would have happened to me had I refused to participate when I was first kidnapped? Or if I refused to participate in raids and in battle?"

Brigid shrugged.

Emyr smiled a cold, mirthless smile and kicked at the dirt.

"I would have been worked to death as a slave or simply killed outright. A man who can't or won't follow the way will be shunned. He will become the prey of any who wishes to have sport with him. The only way to gain and hold this honor is to follow a warrior's path—and that is a path of blood and suffering."

"How old are you?" she asked.

Emyr gave her a puzzled expression before responding. "I've seen about fourteen winters among the Salassani, and I think four or five before that, but I'm not sure."

"Why do all the Salassani men paint their faces?"

Emyr grinned. "You've been holding in all these questions all this time?"

Brigid nodded. "Slaves aren't supposed to have questions."

Emyr gave a short laugh. "No, they're not," he said. "But I'll tell you. When a young Salassani man makes his first successful raid, he's allowed to choose a design from among the spirits that he believes may protect him and give him courage. After each successful raid or act of bravery, he may elaborate the design. Colors and designs, however, are specific to each band. The Carpentini don't use them."

"Why did you choose a wolf?"

"Because I wanted to *be* a wolf. He's the most cunning animal in the heathland."

The blue, crystal-clear sky threw out its great arms to embrace the wide, rolling land as Emyr and Brigid rode out of the pines onto the

Deliverance

high, open heathland. A crisp breeze whispered in Brigid's hair. Antelope bounded over the horizon in front of them. Brigid wondered how she had never perceived the brooding majesty of this lonely land. In all the weeks of her captivity, she had seen only despair.

A few hours' riding brought them back to the river, where it murmured in its channel. Brigid followed Emyr down a well-worn trail riding the same horse that had carried her away two days before. After all, the young man wouldn't need it anymore.

"Tell me about your family," Emyr said as they rode down the river path.

Brigid cast him a sideways glance, still trying to decide if she hated him or not and knowing that she should. She hadn't forgotten the terror of being ripped from her family, of having her whole life and her hopes for the future dashed to pieces in a few moments.

She couldn't forget the ringing clash of steel as her father fought desperately to protect his family with only one good arm. She couldn't forget her mother's desperate attempts to hide her before the Salassani rushed into the room. The agony was still exquisite even after all these weeks. And here was the man who had taken money to tear her away and make her a slave. But he was also the man who had just saved her life—apparently for the second or third time. What was she supposed to think? How was she supposed to feel?

With considerable hesitation, she told him that her father had been a great warrior who had lost the use of his arm. She told how her mother had taught her to keep a house and weave cloth. She told of her father's friend, Neahl, and how he had the fingers on his right hand cut off. Once she started, the words tumbled out of her as if they had been waiting for the chance to spill from her tongue. And with them came the slow, dripping tears.

Even with all her talking, Brigid didn't tell Emyr that she had a brother whom she hoped to be alive and well and whom she dreamed would come to rescue her. She didn't know if Brion was still alive, but she couldn't give up that hope. She clung to it with a desperation that bordered on madness. Because it was all that she had. And she didn't want Emyr watching over his shoulder, just in case Brion did come.

She talked more than she had intended, but it had been many weeks since she had been able to talk to anyone. Finola was far away in a different village, and she had heard nothing of her or from her. Emyr didn't interrupt. He rode quietly beside her with his gaze fixed on the road ahead.

When she had finished, he finally spoke. "I am sorry," he said. "I would change things if I could."

Emyr turned his head to gaze at her with a pleading expression as if he wanted her to forgive him. The expression sent her mind reeling again. What did he want from her? What was she supposed to do? What could she possibly say? They rode on in silence.

Brigid knew they were nearing the village when the dull roar of the rapids drifted to meet them on the still air. The sun had already set behind the mountains, leaving a lingering, copper glow. The shadows had grown long and the air chill.

After Brigid's long explanation of her family, Emyr had been quiet for several hours. As the village came into view, he stirred and glanced over at her.

"I want you to keep that knife close, in case you need it again," he said.

"Why might I need it again?"

Emyr shrugged. "I wouldn't have thought you would have needed it at all, but you did. My mind is not easy. Just keep it close."

Chapter 21
Desecration

Show him what real speed looks like," Neahl said to Redmond as they practiced archery in the field. Brion watched in awe as Redmond released ten arrows into the air before the first arrow hit the ground. His technique was so fluid that it seemed like he wasn't even trying. It was almost graceful.

Neahl stepped about ten paces in front of them and began throwing dirt clods into the air. The dirt clods exploded with each shot.

Brion shook his head as Redmond grinned at him after shooting six dirt clods out of the air in quick succession.

"Show off," Brion said.

"Your father was better."

Brion raised his eyebrows in disbelief, while his heart sank. He could never be that good.

"I could step off twenty paces," Redmond said, "toss up a rock the size of my thumbnail, and your father could hit it nine times out of ten."

Brion frowned at the memory of his father and mother. His gaze strayed to the cabin he had called home. It sat on a rise across the field and on the other side of the dirt road with its split-rail fence. That's when he saw it. The door stood open—a black, empty mouth opened wide as if in surprise.

"Have either of you been to my cabin?" he asked without taking his gaze off the gaping black hole.

When they turned to look toward the cabin but remained silent, Brion burst into a run. Had the assassins returned? Would he get his chance to even the score? He vaulted the fences on either side of the road and slid to a stop at the ghastly scene before him. His parents' corpses had been stripped and lay half out of their grave. Their waxy skin had marbled and turned black in places. The smell of putrefaction filled the air. The crumpled remains of the cat lay trampled in the dirt amid his mother's beautiful tablecloth. Brion clenched and unclenched the fist that wasn't

97

holding the bow. He ground his teeth as the hot rage surged into his belly and filled his chest.

Three bounding leaps propelled him through the door of the cabin. It was empty, but it had been ransacked. Everything that could be smashed had been smashed. Floorboards had been pulled up. The straw tick from their beds had been ripped out and strewn around. The trunk with his parents' things had been smashed open. The vandals had left nothing untouched.

Brion came back to the door. Neahl and Redmond stood beside his parents' bodies.

"Who did this?" Brion said.

Redmond and Neahl exchanged glances and shook their heads.

"Someone who was looking for something," Neahl said.

He watched Brion with his head cocked to one side as if he were waiting for Brion to tell him what it was. Brion pinched his lips tight, set his bow against the house, and went to his parents. If he did nothing more with his life than avenge his parents of this disgrace, his life would be well-spent.

The ransacking of his home and the desecration of his parents' grave gave Brion new purpose. He threw himself into his training. Whoever was out there searching for Weyland's secret would never stop until Brion stopped them. He needed every little advantage Neahl and Redmond could give him. They obliged by pushing their creativity to its limits in finding new challenges to throw at him. They made little round targets out of tightly wound wheat stocks, which they either rolled along the ground or threw into the air for him to shoot. Neahl placed targets at various ranges and made him alternate between them, shooting as fast as he could. They made him shoot at targets up in trees. Then they placed Brion up in the trees and made him shoot at moving targets on the ground. They made him scramble back and forth between targets in the woods and the open fields, pausing only to loose an arrow before hurrying on.

One morning Neahl came in as Brion was stringing his bow in preparation for another morning's practice.

"You won't need that this morning," Neahl said.

Brion glanced at him, only slightly surprised. Neahl and Redmond had made a habit of shaking up his schedule so that he didn't become used to any routine. Neahl gave him a mischievous grin and stepped out the door. Brion followed him to the field where he practiced archery. The snow had melted during a warm spell. But it had turned cold again and the ground had frozen solid.

Neahl carried his bow and a quiver full of arrows. Brion eyed him warily. When Neahl smiled like he did now, Brion knew that he was going to experience something painful or embarrassing, usually both.

Neahl stopped and gestured towards the field.

"Run," he said.

Brion raised his eyebrows and looked around. "Umm, where?"

Neahl shrugged.

Brion's gaze ran over the field before he glanced at Neahl again. He narrowed his eyes in suspicion.

"What am I running from?"

Neahl smiled.

"Run fast. One, two . . ." he drew an arrow from his quiver. Brion noted that it had what looked like a leather pad attached to the tip. His eyes widened.

"No," he said in disbelief. "You wouldn't."

"Three."

Neahl nocked the arrow. His smile broadened.

"Hang on a minute."

Brion tried a last minute effort to dissuade Neahl.

Neahl's smile broadened even wider. He was clearly enjoying this.

Brion sprang into motion. He sprinted toward the old stump zig-zagging as he went. He hadn't gone twenty paces when the first arrow slapped into his backside. He yelped and dodged aside. The arrow stung like crazy, but Brion knew that it had not been shot from full draw. At this close range it would have knocked him over and done some damage.

"Neahl, you're crazy!" he screamed.

The second arrow slapped into his back between his shoulder blades like a hammer slamming into his spine. He heard the thrum of the string again and dropped onto his face. The arrow buzzed as it went over his head. He leaped to his feet and sprinted forward again. Another arrow smacked his backside so hard that it gave him a painful dead leg. His muscle cramped into a ball and he stumbled and rolled, knowing the next arrow was already on its way.

He struggled to his feet again just as another arrow slammed into his ribs and knocked the wind out of him. He tumbled onto the frozen earth again struggling for breath. He tried to scramble to his feet, but his leg wouldn't work and his lungs didn't have any air. He heard the thrum of the string and the zip of the arrow. He cringed in preparation for the impact, but it slapped into the earth just beside his head and bounced off into the field.

He curled into a ball with his hands over his head as he waited for the next arrow to hit him. But nothing came. He unrolled himself and looked back to find Neahl bent over with his hands on his knees laughing to bust a gut. At first Brion was confused. Then rage drove him to his feet. He grabbed up one of the arrows and started toward Neahl. He limped awkwardly, but he tried to ignore the pain of the hard knot in his leg. He had made half the distance before Neahl saw him coming and collapsed into another fit of laughter.

Brion grabbed up the biggest dirt clod he could find. He felt the hard, frozen mud with satisfaction. He wanted to hurt Neahl, to get even. Brion chucked the icy clod as hard as he could. It caught Neahl on the shoulder. Neahl tried to respond, but he was laughing so hard he could barely stand. He waved his hands in front of his face. He shook his head and tried to speak. Brion began chucking clods of frozen earth as fast as he could grab them up. Neahl raised his hands over his head and collapsed onto his knees, sucking for breath and shrieking in a high-pitched, unmanly laugh.

Finally, Brion stood over him in impotent rage, the arrow clenched in one fist and a frozen dirt clod in the other. Neahl jerked and gasped. The tears streamed from his eyes, and his squeals of laughter pierced the air. He tried to talk but choked on his words. Brion watched him for a moment before he stomped off to the cottage. As he turned his back, Neahl burst out into another fit of laughter and threw himself face-first onto the frozen earth to pound the ground with his fists.

Redmond found Brion half an hour later in the cottage rubbing lineament into his bruised ribs. Brion noted the poorly controlled smile that twitched at the edges of Redmond's mouth and ignored him. Redmond sat down on a stool beside him, watching Brion massage the still sore leg.

"I wondered when he would get around to it," Redmond said.

Deliverance

Brion harrumphed.

"I know it seems harsh," Redmond said, "but it's a lesson you'll never forget."

Now Brion glared at him.

"I guess I'm having trouble working this one out. Which lesson was I supposed to learn? Not to trust Neahl? How it feels to get shot by an eighty-pound bow at close range? Or is it just to learn to enjoy pain and humiliation?"

Redmond's twitching smile faded.

"You're taking this too hard."

"Am I? When is he going to stop treating me like a snot nosed brat he gets to pick on. When is he going to start showing me some respect? Haven't I done everything he's asked without complaining for months now? I've taken every cut, every bruise, every sleepless night, every insult and I've said nothing. All I want is a little consideration. I may never be as brilliant as my father, but I'm not a complete imbecile who can only learn from a switch and a beating."

Brion glared at Redmond defying him to contradict him.

Redmond pursed his lips and nodded.

"You're right. I'll talk to him," he said. "Now let's go back to the field."

Brion grunted. "Why? You want to join in the fun?"

Redmond gave him a flat stare until Brion slipped on his shirt and followed Redmond out to the filled. The knot in his leg had eased, but it was still painful to walk.

"Here's what you need to know," Redmond began. "Know where the archer is looking, hear the shot, and see the arrow. When you can't see the arrow, you have to know how an archer will think. Never let him anticipate your next move."

"All you had to do was explain," Brion said.

"Maybe, but you won't learn it until you do it. And this skill will save your life. Now run!"

Many bruises later Brion stood with his hands on his hips panting while Redmond grinned at him. Redmond slapped him on the shoulder.

"You're starting to get it. But let's shake things up a bit."

Brion scowled. "Sounds painful."

"Not for you. It's your turn to shoot at me."

A big grin spread across Brion's face. "That's more like it," he said.

Redmond nodded. "You have to see it from both perspectives. See if you can anticipate what I'll do. See if you can think like an archer evading a shot."

Brion nodded reaching for the bow.

"And just to make it worthwhile," Redmond added. "I'll bet my small boot knife that you won't be able to hit me even once."

Brion grinned.

"You're on."

His constant practice with moving targets over the past two months had made him very good at hitting them. He could take a rabbit on the run or a grouse out of the air. How hard could it be to hit a full sized man in an open field?

Redmond waited for Brion to get ready and then ran. Brion came up to full draw, but just as he was about to release Redmond lunged sideways. Brion followed him and released. Before the arrow left the bow Redmond turned aside. The arrow missed him by several feet. Brion already had another arrow nocked. Redmond was putting distance between himself and Brion at a good pace. This, of course made it much more difficult to hit him. Brion let two more arrows fly in rapid succession before he stopped. He couldn't hit him. Why? He watched Redmond carefully trying to find the pattern, trying to see into his mind.

But Redmond didn't seem to be running in any pattern. Then Brion noticed that he seemed to be timing his moves to coincide with the time it took to nock and shoot an arrow. Brion drew and aimed where he thought Redmond might go given his last several zigzags and released. Just as the arrow was about to miss, Redmond turned right into it. The arrow caught him in the shoulder nocking him off balance. He fell, rolled, and came to his feet. This time he came running back towards Brion. Brion got off five arrows before Redmond was too close to shoot without injuring him, but Redmond dodged them all.

Redmond jogged up smiling. He extended his hand and shook Brion's hand vigorously.

"Well done. How did you do it?

Brion grinned. "Practice," he said.

Redmond smirked and nodded waving his hand in a circular motion, waiting for his explanation.

Brion shrugged. "I figured out that you were timing your evasions with my shooting rhythm. Then I just guessed which direction you'd go."

"Exactly. That's what I meant. You had to get inside my head and think the way I was thinking. If you hadn't already had to avoid arrows, you probably couldn't have done it."

Redmond bent down extracting his boot knife and sheath from his boot top. He handed them to Brion.

"But you need to remember that an arrow flies faster than you can run or dodge. At close range or from ambush your chances of avoiding the arrow are slim to none."

Brion nodded as the sweat dripped from his head. "Do you think Neahl would be let me take a few shots at him, just to see how good he is?" Brion asked.

Redmond raised his eyebrows and gave him a dismissive gesture. "You can ask him that one."

Neahl and Redmond quizzed Brion on the Salassani language—made him speak nothing else for days on end. Brion found that it was similar to the common tongue in the south, but placed a different emphasis on the beginning and ending of words and some words were exactly the same but with different meanings.

Neahl and Redmond did everything they could to get him out of his comfort zone. Eventually, they saddled up the captured horse and began teaching him to shoot while riding. When they had first proposed the idea, Brion had laughed.

"How am I supposed to shoot from horseback with a six-foot long-bow in my hands? I don't suppose you noticed that the horse will get in the way."

"It can be done and done well," Redmond had explained. "The trick is knowing how to position yourself to take advantage of your strengths, how to ride with no hands, and how to shoot at a full gallop."

Brion had rolled his eyes.

"That's all there is to it, then? Just ride with no hands and shoot at full gallop." He paused dramatically and continued more loudly. "I'll fall off and break my neck."

Neahl laughed. "You will if you try to do it all at once. Relax, we won't let you get hurt."

Brion raised his eyebrows. "You expect me to believe that after all these weeks of continuous beatings?"

In the end, Brion did learn how to do it. He had to trust the horse and learn to feel the horse's stride so that he could release the arrow at just the right instant. Neahl gave Brion the black mare they had taken from the dead Salassani. She was a surefooted, intelligent beast that responded to knee pressure and whistles. Brion named her Misty because of the silver speckles on her flank.

Misty understood what he needed when he was shooting. She extended her stride to give him time to get off a well-aimed shot. When he tracked Neahl and Redmond or when he was hiding from them, Misty could be exceptionally quiet. And when someone approached, she gave a quiet blowing sound and shuffled her feet. Misty also had the stamina that had made Salassani ponies famous. She could keep up a steady trot all day with a few walking breaks. She continually surprised Brion with what she could do.

Brion also learned how to care for and repair all of his equipment, memorized the map, and practiced hand-to-hand and weapons combat. Even Neahl began to study the new flowing style of fighting Redmond was teaching Brion. The style had a lot of throws, joint locks, and kicks. Brion learned which plants were good for food, medicine, or fire building. They taught him how to determine the weather by examining the clouds, the wind, and the behavior of the animals.

The games of hide and seek also continued. At first, Brion did all the seeking, but eventually, he also hid and found that he could outsmart the two old foxes. An arrow whizzing past their heads told them that he could have killed them. The arrows began to fly with increasing regularity after the first month.

Neahl led Brion deep into the forest where he taught him how to set up ambushes, how to use the landscape and the vegetation to conceal himself, and even how to construct a wide variety of snares and traps. Of course, Brion already knew how to make snares for animals. But Neahl taught him how to make snares that would capture or kill a man. Neahl's knowledge proved to be vast and devious. Brion wondered how he had learned it all; but when he asked, Neahl always said, "Practice."

Chapter 22
The Blue-Eyed Woman

inola stood watching the meat burn in the skillet. She knew they would beat her for it, but she didn't care. It had been a month since they had recaptured her, and she had done everything she could to make them regret that they hadn't let her go. She braced herself for the storm when she heard Addie entering the cabin. Addie was a round woman and not just because she was pregnant. She had pale skin and lips that drooped in a permanent frown. Finola found her cooking bland and her brain muddled.

It had been a long, three months since the raid on Wexford. She had learned to speak Salassani, more or less, in the first two months, but since her failed escape she wouldn't try to speak. Ithel beat her, but the brutality increased her stubborn resolve to resist.

Maybe taking a beating once a week wasn't the best way to handle being a slave, but at least it kept her fighting spirit alive—which is what she needed. Without the hope that she might escape and find her way back to her parents and maybe even to Brion, she would have just given up and died. So she insisted on cooking everything poorly or burning the food when she could get away with it.

Addie screamed from the doorway, rushed into the kitchen and shoved Finola aside. She snatched the skillet from the fire, her face red with rage. Finola stood her ground, sneering at her coldly, belligerently. Before Finola understood what Addie was doing, Addie grabbed up the fire tongs and swung them. Finola ducked, but the tongs caught her right behind her left eye, square on the temple. The blow spun her around with an explosion of pain. She fell into darkness.

Finola awoke to blink at a dark ceiling of thatch overhead. Pain throbbed in her head with the rhythm of her beating heart. She raised a hand to touch a bandage. At least they had bothered to do that much for her. Voices drew nearer. They were speaking Salassani in hushed tones.

Finola understood most of the conversation.

"She's no good, I tell you, Ithel. The sooner you sell her the better."

"But people are talking about her and that redheaded girl. There's even talk that King Tristan may try to buy one of them. If we sell her now, her new owner will just take her to the gathering and sell her for a profit."

"If she stays here, she might kill us in our sleep. She has to go."

"There's always the Hallstat," Ithel said. "But I told you before, something big is afoot. There'll be a lot of wealthy, important people at the gathering."

Feet shuffled against the floor, and they passed out of hearing.

Finola breathed deeply, trying to still the throbbing in her head. She didn't know if she should be satisfied or frightened by what she had heard. Her pattern of resistance was wearing on them. That seemed plain enough. But what had it given her? Nothing but bruises. If she continued, they might sell her to someone in the village who might not have any restraint, or worse, to the Hallstat far across the sea. She remembered Emyr's warning and had no desire to end up in a brothel.

At least Ithel had never tried to *really* hurt her—yet. He had just tried to break her spirit and force her to obey. Her next master could easily be far more brutal. And what if the King did purchase her? She had no idea how the Dunkeldi kingdom even functioned, but she had learned that wealthy men could have more than one wife. Would that be her fate—to exist only to please a king when he tired of his other wives? The thought made her sick.

Fury and despair pressed down upon her in equal measure. Where was Brion? Why hadn't he come for her? If he still lived, he would have come. But maybe he had already tried and been killed. For all she knew, he had been in the rescue party. Finola swallowed the sadness that rose in her throat. Silent tears leaked from her eyes. She didn't want to accept that he was dead. There had to be another reason he had not come.

The next morning, Finola awoke early, and, despite a pounding headache and waves of dizziness, she set to fixing them a fine breakfast. Addie came into the kitchen just as she finished. She stood in the doorway. Her gaze followed Finola with suspicion. Finola smiled and waved toward the table.

"Good morning," Finola said in Salassani. "Breakfast is ready."

She knew her accent was poor, but she hadn't practiced much lately.

Addie stepped into the kitchen with one hand on her wide belly. She eyed the food warily. Ithel stomped in behind her. They exchanged glances. It was comical to see them so baffled by the mere sight of a well-prepared breakfast. Finola had to repress a grin of satisfaction. This transformation after weeks of conflict clearly had left them unsettled.

"I didn't poison it," Finola said, enjoying this little bit of power she had over them.

She picked up a piece of boiled lamb she had just fried in butter and bit into it. It was delicious. The blend of herbs she had used complimented the flavor of the lamb. Ithel glanced at his wife again, sat down, filled his plate, and began to eat. He beamed at his wife and waved at her seat.

"It's good," he said.

Finola ate the leftovers and cleaned up without having to be told. Then, she set about cleaning the house. When Addie came to find her, Finola had already finished and was getting ready to go for water to start on the noonday meal. Addie watched her with a deep scowl.

"Don't think I don't know what you're up to," she said before shuffling out of the kitchen.

Over the next three weeks, as Addie drew closer to the time of her delivery, Finola assumed more responsibility for managing the household. Ithel started bragging about her cooking and made her bake her rich barley-oat rolls for sale in the village. He also gave her more freedom to roam and even to converse with other slaves. Now that she discovered the independence cooperation could give her, she wondered why she had been so bullheaded all these months.

In the market one early, spring morning, Finola saw a strange woman with a long face, protruding chin, and drooping eyes watching her. The woman appeared each time she went to the market. Finola considered approaching her and demanding what she wanted, but she knew a slave was not permitted to speak to a free person unless spoken to. She didn't want to give Ithel any reason to punish her.

After days of enduring the languid gaze and feeling the paranoia at being watched, the woman approached Finola and motioned for her to follow. Finola glanced around, knowing that it might not be a good idea to follow her, but her curiosity overpowered her reason. The woman shuffled sideways, bent over as if she carried a heavy load. She led Finola away from the pungent smells and raucous noise of the market to a quiet side street before she turned.

The woman's eyes were a piercing blue. Her curious appearance left

Finola with the impression that this woman was probably dull-witted.

"You are much desired," the woman said.

"What?" Finola asked. This was the last thing she had expected.

"Men talk of you and of the coming gathering. You need to beware of the man with the ruined face and the dark one. They have heard of your beauty and will try to carry you away."

Finola stood silent for a moment, confused.

"But I don't know a man with a ruined face."

"He knows of you."

"What would he want with me?" Finola asked.

"He has already killed one wife and now he seeks another."

"Killed a wife?" Finola said.

The woman nodded. "But the dark man who sees beyond has great power among the Salassani."

"Beyond what?" Finola interrupted.

Annoyance flashed across the woman's face. "Beyond this world," she said. "He is here even now. If he seeks you, flee. Flee for your life."

"That's easier said than done," Finola said, unable to keep the trembling out of her voice. "I've already tried it." Finola paused. "Why are you telling me this?"

The woman hesitated and chewed on the inside of her cheek.

"Because I am a woman who lost her youth because of bad men. Take care. Protect yourself, if you can. You'll not be safe until you have escaped or until you have wed."

The woman shambled away. Finola watched her shuffling gait until the old woman disappeared around a corner. She didn't know if she should be angry or terrified. Wasn't it enough that they had dragged her from her home and treated her like an animal? Now the brutes were going to fight over her like a piece of meat. The terror quickly turned to anger.

Finola marched back to the market so preoccupied that she didn't see him until she began to retrace her steps toward Ithel's house. He had long, tangled hair and wore a black cloak that trailed behind him. She felt his gaze follow her as she hurried to disappear into the maze of streets.

Chapter 23
The Warning

hat? Are we taking a day off?" Brion said as he joined Neahl and Redmond at the table where they sipped their steaming tea and inspected the map spread before them. "It's about time."

The snow had stopped falling the first week of March. The crocuses and hyacinths began to raise their heads and look out over the soft, muddy soil. Dogwoods began to flower in the hollows. The wind blew in from the south, bringing the birds and the rains with it. But the weather had never stopped Neahl and Redmond. Brion had found himself soaked to the skin and caked in mud following trails, shooting bows, and sparring with fists and feet and knives and swords.

Neahl and Redmond peered at him from over their mugs as he sat and poured a cup from the hot kettle.

"No. No day off," Neahl said. "Just a different schedule." Neahl sipped at his tea. "Today we pack. Tomorrow we leave."

Brion came to his feet, almost spilling the entire kettle on the table. "Tomorrow?"

"Yes, tomorrow."

Brion's blood began to race. Tomorrow. They were finally going to go after the Salassani. They were finally going after Brigid and Finola. Brion sat back down with a dazed expression.

"Am I ready?" he asked. The two brothers exchanged glances.

"Ready or not," Neahl said.

"No. I'm serious."

Brion had trained as hard as he could. He had suffered every indignity Neahl could invent. But he knew that he was still not as good as his father. In fact, he grew more certain every day that he would never live up to his father's reputation.

Redmond waited for Neahl to answer, but when he didn't, Redmond spoke. "If you weren't," he said, "we wouldn't be leaving. But it's time

109

we got started."

A knot landed in Brion's stomach. It didn't seem possible. He had been so busy over the last four months that he hadn't even noticed the time passing. He had thought of nothing else in all that time but getting ready to go rescue Brigid and Finola. But it had always been somewhere off in the future. Now that future had come rushing up. It had finally arrived.

Redmond placed a sheathed dagger on the table in front of Brion. Brion glanced at it and then at Redmond.

"Weyland gave this to me before my first battle," Redmond said. "I want you to have it."

Brion reached out and drew the dagger from the sheath. It had a double-edged blade.

"It's a boot knife," Redmond said. "You never know when you might need one."

"Thanks," Brion said. He sheathed the blade and traced the intricate stitchings on the sheath.

"We gave you enough bruises," Redmond said. "You've earned it."

They spent the day getting everything ready—including extra arrow shafts, fletchings, flax string, points, and wax. They packed their food and clothes, and they each carried an extra bow and an extra quiver of arrows. When they had finished, the sun sagged heavily in the western horizon.

"Well," Redmond said, "why don't we visit the village one last time before we leave?"

Brion hadn't visited the village since before the raid. He was surprised when they arrived how odd it was that he could feel like a stranger amid the folk with whom he had spent his entire life. Even his friends acted as if they didn't know him. None of them had tried to visit him during the long months of training, but he had assumed that Neahl had warned them away. As he sought them out now, they all seemed tense and expectant as if they thought he would jump up and bite them.

Brion avoided the old midwife who seemed to be taking an unusual interest in him today. She seldom came to town, but Brion had often seen her in the woods around his cabin or watching from the road. She had been there on the day he had buried his parents.

Today she seemed to be everywhere, as if she were trying to force him into a conversation. When he spotted his best friend, Seamus, by the old tanner's corral, he ran to meet him.

Deliverance

"Seamus, what's going on?" Brion asked.

Seamus was a tall, lanky kid who had been apprenticed to the tanner. Seamus cast a glance around them and shook his blonde head. "Not here." He gestured toward a nearby shed. The two of them crowded inside. It smelled of old, dead animals.

"Look," Seamus said. "The town gets hit by a raid. Neahl comes in and tells us that your parents are dead and Brigid is kidnapped. But he refuses to help the town. He roughs up a few people and then disappears. A week later, a traveler comes in and spreads the rumor that you shot him while he was riding up the river road."

"What?"

Seamus held up his hand. "I'm only telling you what's been going on here since you haven't bothered to come around yourself."

"Neahl wouldn't let me."

"It doesn't matter. Just listen."

Brion fell silent.

"Then the Sheriff came through and spent an entire morning with the new headman before he rode off to your place. Rumors spread that you and Neahl joined up with a traitor from the southland and that you're going off to start a war with the Salassani."

"They took my sister!" Brion yelled.

Seamus shook his head. "I'm only telling you what they've been saying," he said.

"Who's been saying it?"

"Everyone. Don't you understand? Someone is trying to turn the entire village against you."

Chapter 24
The Test

he words tumbled out as Seamus's face colored to a bright scarlet. They stared at each other. Seamus placed a hand on Brion's shoulder.

"You know it's a suicide mission, don't you?"

Brion met his gaze before he bowed his head. He nodded.

"I know, but I have to try Seamus. She's my sister."

Seamus peered through the crack in the door. "Listen," he said. "I think you're in over your head. Somebody wants you dead. Maybe they took Brigid to get you and Neahl out of here."

Brion considered. "But why? How could a crippled trapper and a couple of kids be a threat to anyone?"

Seamus shrugged.

"What do you think I should do?" Brion asked.

Seamus shook his head. "If I were you, I'd want to go after them, but you just need to keep eyes in the back of your head. That's all."

Brion nodded. "Goodbye then," Brion said.

"I'll keep my eyes open for you while you're away," Seamus said. Seamus shook Brion's hand. "Good luck," he said. "I'll miss you."

Seamus's words chased Brion all the way to the baker's shop. The excitement of the morning had dissipated in the fog of intrigue that encircled them. He hadn't realized how isolated he had become.

He found Finola's father and mother cleaning the ovens. When the latch clicked behind him, they both dropped what they were doing and came around to the front of the counter.

Finola's father, Paiden, was a round man with a patch of white hair that hung down before his eyes. He wiped his hands on his apron before extending a hand to Brion. Brion grasped it. Paiden's hand was warm and strong.

Finola's mother, Shavon, was a tall woman who could have been Finola's sister. She had the same sweet face and soft, blonde hair, but her eyes were a dark gray. She smiled sadly and touched Brion's arm.

"I'm sorry I haven't visited," Brion said.

Paiden shook his head. "We understand what you've been doing."

Brion shifted his weight awkwardly.

"So you're off then?" Paiden asked.

Brion nodded.

"Bring her back for us, Brion. Bring her back."

Brion swallowed the lump that rose in his throat. He nodded. "I will."

Paiden shook his hand again.

"Thank you," Shavon said. "We'll watch for you every day."

Brion nodded and lifted the door latch to leave. Shavon grabbed his hand to stop him. Her hand was dry and cold. She hurried behind the counter and wrapped a fresh loaf of bread.

"We can't do much," she said, "but I . . ."

Brion thanked her and reached for the latch again.

"Brion," Paiden said.

Brion paused.

"They say you're set on starting a war."

Brion pinched his lips into a thin line. "All I want to do is get the girls back," he said.

Paiden blinked and glanced at his wife.

"Watch your back, son. Someone is set to destroy you."

"Do you know who it is?"

Paiden shook his head. "The new headman's involved, that's all I know."

"Be careful," Shavon said.

She gave him a kiss on the cheek.

Brion thanked them, placed the loaf of bread in his satchel, and left the shop. How could he carry the burden of their trust when he didn't even trust himself—when forces he didn't understand swirled around him? Everyone knew that he had become a target, but no one could tell him why or who was aiming at him.

As he stepped out into the street, he found the old midwife waiting for him again. Her ragged clothes sagged about her frame like the skin did around her eyes. She leaned on a walking stick and had a woven basket slung across her back. Her gaze was steady and confident. She pointed at him, and Brion assumed she was asking for money. So he fished a coin from his pocket and held it out to her. She took it, but shook her head.

"You are not your own," she said.

Brion scowled. "What?" he asked.

"Your secrets pursue you," she said.

"What secrets?" Brion glanced around suddenly wary that this might be a trap.

A touch of softness drifted across the old woman's face. "I have watched you," she said.

A shiver ran through Brion. "What secrets?" he demanded.

"There are others," she said.

"Witch," someone called as they passed by. A shopkeeper stepped out with a broom and started waving her away.

"In time," she said to Brion. "All secrets are revealed." Then she spat at the shopkeeper who pushed at her with his broom, and she shuffled off down the road.

Brion tried to understand what she had told him, but after all he had learned, he no longer felt welcome in Wexford. He decided to find Neahl and Redmond.

He found them in the tavern taking one last pull at a mug before their long journey. Brion recognized many of the faces that turned toward him as he entered, but he didn't understand the fear and hesitation he found there. Seamus and Paiden had been right. Someone had been busy turning the town against them.

Neahl and Redmond sat alone with a lot of elbowroom. Some men huddled over their mugs, brooding over their ale. Others played at cards, while still others roared with laughter and shouted over each other. But everyone was intent on ignoring their presence as much as possible. The tavern reeked of human sweat, the sweet aroma of ale, and roasting meat.

Halfway to the counter where Neahl and Redmond sat, a man pushed his elbow back into Brion's path, forcing Brion to bump into it. Beer sloshed from the man's mug. The man set the mug on the table with a bang, shook the beer from his hand, and spun to face Brion.

Brion made an apologetic gesture with his hands, but he couldn't help feeling that the man had done that on purpose.

"Sorry," Brion said.

The man reached out and pushed him hard. Brion slammed into the person behind him, who cursed. But when he saw the big, burly man that loomed over Brion, he apologized and hurried to the corner. Soon the tavern had gone silent. The center of the room cleared. Brion found himself in a circle of onlookers facing a man at least twice his age and much taller. The stranger wore leather breeches and a dirty, linen shirt. His hair was stiff with grime. He had a wild look about him.

"I said I was sorry," Brion repeated.

Fear gripped at Brion's throat. His vision narrowed until all he could see was the angry man with a big nose and narrow-set eyes standing over him.

"You will be," the man sneered.

Brion understood and began to circle away from the man, trying to buy some time. Out of the corner of his eye, he saw Neahl start forward, but Redmond laid a hand on his arm. When Neahl glanced at him, Redmond shook his head.

That tingling excitement that mingled with the fear Brion always had before a real fight made him tremble. He didn't want this fight and certainly not with everyone watching. Still, he had been training every day for months. He wasn't about to forget his lessons now.

The man lunged with a wide, swinging punch aimed at Brion's head. Brion stepped inside the punch, delivering his own. When the man tried to grab Brion in a bear hug, Brion broke the hold, grabbed the man's arm, spun, and dropped to one knee, throwing the man over his head to land on his back with a thud and a rush of air. Brion wrapped the man's arm into one of Redmond's joint locks and began to apply pressure. The man tried to rise or squirm free, but Brion tightened his grip. Soon the man was screaming and writhing in pain.

"I expect you to accept my apology," Brion said.

Brion's fear had been replaced by anger—cold, calm anger.

"I accept," the man yelled. "I accept."

Brion let the joint lock loose. The man cradled his arm to his chest. Brion stood and glanced around the room. Many people he knew watched him expectantly. He didn't know what they wanted him to do, so he just stepped toward Neahl and Redmond. He saw it in their eyes at the same time that he heard the quiet swish of a knife being drawn. He spun.

The man swung the long blade in a deadly arc at Brion's stomach. Brion jumped back, barely avoiding the biting steel. The two began to circle. This man apparently didn't know how to use a knife. He lunged again in the same swinging attack. Brion stepped back just out of reach of the blade, but as the man started to swing it back again Brion rushed in, wrapping his arms around the man's neck, with the knife arm pinned over his shoulder.

He tucked his head low and threw the man to the ground. As he landed on top of him, ribs cracked. Air rushed out of the man's lungs. Brion squeezed with all his strength as his attacker kicked and writhed, doing everything he could to dislodge Brion's hold. Eventually, his writhing slowed to a few erratic twitches. Brion held on until the man went still. The knife fell to the floor with a thud.

Brion came to his feet with the knife in his hands. He wiped the sweat from his eyes and looked down at his attacker. His chest rose and fell, so Brion knew he hadn't killed him. Neahl and Redmond stepped up to Brion. Each grabbed an arm and escorted him from the tavern without a word to anyone.

"He made me smash my loaf of bread," Brion said in annoyance.

Chapter 25
The Threat

The glittering, night sky draped itself across the heavens as Brion rode in silence from Wexford. He didn't know how he should feel. His belly could have been ripped open, but the fight had been easy. He felt bigger somehow. More capable. And yet, he couldn't stop the trembling.

Neahl broke the silence. "Well done," he said.

Brion glanced over at him. "I could have used some help."

"You didn't need any," Redmond replied. "Though I did get a bit worried when he drew the knife." He glanced at Brion. "Excellent choice, by the way. I've never seen anyone choked out with that technique before." He nodded. "I also liked the throw and the joint lock. Nicely done."

At first, Brion couldn't tell if Redmond was making fun of him or not. "I didn't think about it. I just did it," Brion said.

"Good," Redmond said. "That's when you know that you've finally learned something."

"It was also wise not to kill him," Neahl added. "Our High Sheriff Cluny would have had to come all the way down here, and that could have ruined our plans." He chuckled, apparently thinking his comment was funny. Then he changed his tone. "Now you know that you can hold your own against a grown man," Neahl said, "and a big one at that. But you also need to remember that in the heathland the rules change. It's kill or be killed. Understand?"

Brion nodded. He did understand. And the understanding terrified him. He had never killed a man, and he had never felt so surrounded by unknown dangers.

"You know that someone's been turning the town against us?" Brion said.

"I noticed," Neahl said.

The moon dangled over their shoulders in the coal-black sky amid a million tiny dots of silver fire as they crested the rise over which Brion's home lay. Both Neahl and Redmond pulled their mounts to a stop at the same instant.

When Brion craned his head around to peer at Neahl, Neahl shook his head, shrugged the longbow from his shoulder, and slipped an arrow onto the string.

Now Brion sensed it, too—that uneasy knowledge that something wasn't right. Redmond kneed his mount off to the right, while Neahl nudged his horse a few paces to the left, slid from the saddle, and melted into the tall, waving grass beside the road. He clicked his tongue, and the horse whirled and disappeared over the rise.

Brion followed his example and positioned himself on the opposite side of the road. An unearthly silence settled around them to pound in his ears. Redmond signaled them with the raspy call of the short-eared owl, and Neahl motioned for them to advance.

They were near the cabin when Brion saw the shadowy figure crouching behind the old well in the front. It was an ambush. How many more were out there? The dark shadow of the forest came close to the road here, and Brion considered how someone might use this spot to waylay a party on the road. One man by the well, maybe a few in the woods or prostrate in the grass? A shod hoof clicked against a stone. Leather creaked. Someone gave a soft curse.

Two horsemen burst from the cover of trees, bearing down on Neahl. The man behind the well rose up and bent a bow before he screamed and collapsed to the ground, writhing in agony. Apparently Redmond had been ready for him.

Brion faced the horsemen. Neahl had already risen from the grass. Steel flashed in the moonlight. Brion hesitated. The one nearest him bent low over his saddle with a curved saber in his hand. Brion raised the bow and loosed in one, smooth motion. The arrow caught the man in the shoulder, causing him to reel in the saddle with a cry of pain. But he kept his seat, slipped to the opposite side of his horse and kicked it on up the rise. Neahl's blade crashed with that of the last horseman.

"Who sent you?" Neahl said. The man whirled and their blades met again, but he didn't speak.

"Send them a message for me," Neahl said again. He whipped his blade across the man's arm. The man dropped his sword. Neahl cut a long gash on his leg.

"Tell them I'll bleed them before I kill them," he said.

Deliverance

The man spurred his horse at Neahl, who jumped out of the way and smacked the horse's flank with the flat of his blade. He watched the man gallop over the rise.

The third man Redmond had shot by the well had found a horse and angled away from the cabin. Redmond gave chase until he disappeared into the darkness. Then Redmond whirled his mount and galloped to where Neahl and Brion stood watching.

"Looks like someone wants to hurry us along or stop us from going," Neahl said. "Which do you think it is?"

Finola bent low to whisper to Clidna as they strolled toward the market.

"Who was that?" Finola asked.

Finola had rescued the little slave girl from punishment a few days before. She had found her weeping beside a broken jar of water because Clidna knew her master would beat her. Finola had stolen one of Addie's jars to replace it and sent Clidna on her way—better that *she* take a beating than the beautiful, round-faced, doe-eyed, little girl. As they approached the market, they passed the man with the matted hair and the black cloak.

Clidna edged closer to Finola and grabbed her arm in a tight grip. Finola's skin crawled. She could feel his gaze upon her. She refused to recognize it. But the dire warning of the broken woman continued to haunt her.

"He's the Holy Man," Clidna said.

"What does that mean?"

"They say he can see into the future—that he can tell you what your dreams mean. Some say he can heal the sick or even bring the dead back to life. But my people hate him. He's a demon who secretly kills people who challenge him." Clidna squeezed Finola's arm again. "He frightens me," Clidna said.

"But I've never seen him in the village until this last week," Finola said.

"You wouldn't," Clidna said. "He travels between Salassani villages. But he can't come to my people. They'd kill him." She glanced about them and sidled closer to Finola. "He once killed the King's slave because the King insulted him."

Finola gaped at Clidna. "And the King let him get away with it?"

"I told you that he is powerful," Clidna whispered. "When I was small, before I was a slave, our headman died. People said the Holy Man shot him with a demon's arrow because the headman wouldn't sell him his daughter."

"His daughter? Why would any Salassani sell their own children?"

Clidna shrugged. "Some do."

"Does this Holy Man marry?"

Clidna glance up at her, confused. "Why else would he want a woman?"

"Well, I thought he wanted her as a slave."

Clidna shook her head. "No, he wanted to make her his wife. He has two old wives now, and he wants a young one."

The fear tugged at Finola's chest. Could this be the man the broken woman had warned her about?

"What if the woman doesn't want to be his wife?" she asked.

Clidna shrugged again. "She would need a powerful man like my headman to protect her. The Holy Man is a demon." When Finola didn't respond. Clidna spoke again. "He usually gets what he wants," she said.

"Where is he from?"

Clidna shrugged. "He's Taurini, but he's a traveling Holy Man. That's why he wants another woman."

Finola glanced sharply at Clidna. "He wants a wife to travel with him?"

Clidna shrugged again. "Even he gets lonely."

Clidna left Finola to run her errands. But Finola could not stop pondering her words. She took a different route back to Ithel's cabin, hoping to avoid the Holy Man. She hurried around the last corner onto the street where Ithel's house stood and nearly bumped into him. She staggered backward, startled by his appearance. Fear jumped into her throat. She mumbled an apology and spun to hurry up the street. But a strong hand grabbed her wrist.

Chapter 26
Into the Heathland

The morning dawned cool and clear. They set off up the road, leaving Neahl's cabin cold and silent. Brion had his cloak wrapped around him against the chill. The air smelled clean and fresh, the way it only can in the early spring. Brion surveyed his boyhood home as they rode past in silence.

Weeds had reclaimed the hard-packed earth before the door. Grasses peeked over the pasture fence beyond. The blackened stubble of the unplowed fields rolled off to either side of the road. For a moment, Brion imagined that his father and mother stood in the doorway with their arms about each other to wave goodbye and to ensure him that they would be waiting for him when he returned. But the door remained shut. They left the road and climbed the hill to the north of the cabin.

When they reached the crest of the hill, Brion glanced back. The little home he had known all of his life was just visible in the pale light of dawn. No smoke curled up from the chimney. The cow was not in the stall. From this distance, it seemed as if the cabin was just sleeping the way it might have looked a thousand times over the last eighteen years— except for the mound where his parents were buried. Brion reflected on his last visit to his parents' grave early that morning.

He stood over the mound, wishing that he could have said goodbye, wishing that he could have asked them for advice and forgiveness.

"I'll find Brigid and bring her back," he said. "I promise."

As he looked up from the grave, still fighting the tears, he found the old midwife standing beside the shed with her walking stick in her hand.

Brion marched over to her. "Why are you watching me?" he demanded.

She frowned. "Now is not the time," she said. "Find your sister first."

"What secrets were you talking about?"

The old lady studied him. "Even the best of men have their secrets, Brion," she said. "Some secrets are best discovered slowly, one piece at a time."

"What is that supposed to mean?"

"Come to me when you return," she said, and she shuffled away.

Brion wanted to grab her and shake the secrets out of her. But he had let her leave. Redmond and Neahl were waiting for him.

Now, as Brion surveyed his childhood home, a wave of sadness settled over him. How many times had his mother awakened him to the smell of corn fritters frying in bacon fat over the fire? How many hours had he spent working alongside his father, setting traps, skinning animals, scraping the fat from the hides, and stretching them to dry against the walls of the shed? How many nights had they gathered around the fire to sing and to talk—snug and safe during the long, cold, winter months? How many times had Brigid crawled onto his lap when she was small and begged him to tell her a story? So many memories came flooding in all at once. These memories, his father's sword, and his mother's necklace were all that he would carry of his childhood home into the heathland. Would he ever return to build his life in the little cabin his father had promised him? Would Finola share that life with him?

"Whoa." Brion pulled back on Misty's reins. "Take a look at this," he said as Redmond and Neahl stopped beside him.

The scent of heather hung rich and pungent on the moist air. A steady, spring rain had dribbled from the sodden sky for a week as they pushed into the heathland. They had followed the Leetwater River north and kept to the forest as long as they could before venturing out onto the heathland.

Brion dismounted and pointed at the muddy trail. "They're going the same way we are and moving fast," Brion said.

Neahl nodded. "What else?"

"Haven't I graduated from my tracking apprenticeship yet?" Brion asked.

"You never graduate," Neahl said.

Brion studied the trail again. "Looks like a bunch of men on foot, maybe ten or twenty. By the length of their stride, I would say they're in a hurry."

"Look here," Neahl pointed. "You can see how the boot has been whip-stitched around the edges. That's a Carpentini technique."

"You'll want to see this," Redmond called from further up the trail.

Brion strode up to kneel beside him. A Carpentini footprint was super-

Deliverance

imposed on a horse's track.

"Our Carpentini are following someone," Brion said.

He looked up at Neahl for confirmation.

"Probably," Neahl said. "Question is, do we follow them or keep going?"

Brion frowned. "Why would we follow them?"

Neahl shrugged. "To get news. And maybe to knock a few heads."

"I say we keep going," Redmond said. "Our quarrel isn't with either of these groups. We need to find the girls. The fewer people who know we're here the better."

"I agree," Brion said.

Neahl gazed up the trail, looking for all the world like a child who had just been told he couldn't play a fun game or have a delicious treat. But he nodded, and they continued.

They rode until the sun drooped over the western horizon, throwing flames over the mountain peaks as if in joy at being liberated from the low-hanging clouds that had hidden the mountains from view for so many days. They found a small depression where their fire would not attract attention. A swollen stream on the far side of the depression wiggled its way toward Com Lake. Dogwood, witch-hazel, and serviceberry clogged the edges of the stream as if in desperate competition for the water. But they also formed an open canopy where the stream flowed.

The ruins of what had been a substantial farmhouse rested on the hill. The roof timbers had long disappeared, but the rectangle of stones still clung to the landscape. Brion appreciated the location for a farmstead—a ready supply of water, a broad, flat bench above the house. But the place also felt lonely—maybe lost was a better word.

"Would have been a good place for a farm," Brion said.

Neahl reined his horse into the depression. "Most of the foothills were occupied at one time or another," he said.

"Alamani settled this far north at one time," Redmond said. "Until the wars came. Those that survived were driven south."

Brion knew that both Redmond and Neahl were thinking of their old home in Comrie. They had stopped at the ruined village a few days before. Redmond had shown it to Brion, but Neahl had refused to enter.

"What's an Alamani?" Brion asked. He had heard the term before, but never knew what it meant.

"That's what the Salassani call the people of Coll," Redmond said.

"Why?"

"Because that's the tribe we came from. The Alamani drove the other tribes out of the southland when they established the Kingdom of Coll a few hundred years ago. We don't use the name anymore, but the Salassani do."

After caring for their horses and their equipment, they settled down for the night. Though the rain had stopped, the ground was still moist.

Redmond awakened Brion for the second watch and rolled up in his blankets. Brion stretched and tried to rub the sleep from his eyes before he sat in the shadow of a fallen wall of the old farmhouse and tried to become part of it. He held his bow across his knees with an arrow nocked and his fingers on the string.

Brion hated this watch. Fresh from sleep, it was hard to stay awake, especially when it was necessary to remain motionless. One never knew what eyes might be scanning the dark searching for movement. Brion had learned the hard way that movement was your enemy when you didn't want to be seen.

While he sat, Brion found time to ponder the events of the last four months. It still astonished him how much had changed—how much *he* had changed. One day, he had been just another country boy. The next, he was training to be a warrior so he could go on a journey that everyone knew was impossible.

But if Brigid and Finola were still alive, they would be expecting him to come for them. He couldn't imagine what they had suffered at the hands of the Salassani. He couldn't fail them like he had his parents. He knew well enough that his chances were thin. He was counting on Redmond and Neahl to get them to safety. That was all that mattered.

But his mind was troubled with the evidence that someone in Wexford had been conspiring against them. He couldn't understand why—unless it had something to do with his father's secret. Was the Salassani raid linked to the other attacks or not? Could these be the dark things his father had said were in motion? Did the old midwife know what his father had been hiding? Why was he messed up in all of this?

The hair bristled on the back of Brion's neck. He became alert. Something wasn't right. A noise that did not belong on the heathland had pulled him from his reveries. The tiny burrowing owls hooted in the distance, and the wind played in the heather. But this sound was different, and it had not come from their horses. Brion watched to find Misty shifting in her stance. She gave the soft purring sound she used when something was amiss.

Now Brion heard the sound that had disturbed Misty. It came from up the creek. Brion tried to focus all of his senses. He kept his gaze moving and his breathing quiet. He heard it again—the sound of water splashing and the sound of a shod hoof against stone. The sounds were faint at first, but as he listened, they came nearer. He was certain now. Several horses with shod hooves splashed in the creek, making their way towards their camp.

His muscles tightened. There could be only one reason horses would approach their camp in the middle of the night. Someone was trying to cover their trail. But it didn't make any sense if they hoped to sneak up on their camp. Coming up the creek was the worst possible way to do it. They were sure to be heard. That could mean only two things.

Either this was a diversion to deflect their attention away from the real threat, or whoever worked their way down the creek didn't know they were there. Brion glanced at the fire. It had been small. A few red embers remained to cast their pale light against the blackness. Still, the night was dark. From the right position, the embers could easily be seen.

Brion gave the soft hoot of the burrowing owl that served as their nighttime signal. Two long, one short. That told his companions that danger approached. He watched to make sure they had heard the call, but neither of them stirred. He gave the call again, just to be sure.

As the intruders entered the little depression, the noises became louder. Someone hissed and the noise ceased. Brion waited. Because the breeze blew toward the creek, he figured that they had either smelled the fire or seen the coals. Their horses certainly had.

The splashing started again. But this time the splashing moved in two directions. The shadows shifted down by a narrow opening in the underbrush by the creek. The thin sliver of the moon didn't give much light, but the shape of a human head detached itself from the black mass of the bushes. Two more appeared.

Brion's blood raced, and his mouth went dry. This was the real thing. This was what he had trained for. But could he do it? He hadn't done so well on the hill beside his home. He curled his fingers around the string of his bow and tried to swallow.

The bent figures of three or four men squatted by the creek, waiting. The bushes up the creek toward the head of the depression rustled. Brion realized that he faced an attack coming from two directions. One of the men by the creek came to one knee. Brion tensed.

The man raised a short, recurve bow. Brion drew his own bow, counting on the shadow of the wall to conceal his movement. He held the bow nearly horizontal because he couldn't hold it upright from a sitting position. Just as the man began to draw, Brion loosed the string.

Chapter 27
The Holy Man

inola jerked and twisted her arm trying to free herself from the cold, clammy hand that gripped her arm like a vice. She searched for someone, anyone, who might help her. But the street was empty. She stopped struggling and stared at the man who held her, while swallowing the fear that gripped her throat. Bits of straw and leaves and other things Finola didn't want to identify, dangled in his matted hair. The strong odor of human filth assailed her nostrils. His face had a stretched, waxy appearance, and one eye had a milky film near the middle.

He didn't say anything. He just studied her with those dark, menacing eyes that peered out between the stray bunches of hair. But the eyes were enough to tell her what he wanted. They roamed over her body from head to foot. He inspected her for a long, tortuous moment before he dropped her arm. "You will do," he said as he ambled away.

Finola fled to Ithel's house. The terror of the Holy Man's presence chased her like a menacing shadow she could not escape. When she entered the house, she hurried to the wash basin and scrubbed her hands and arms. But the soap and water couldn't remove the clinging sense that she had been touched by something foul and dangerous. A dread like she had never known settled in her chest like a disease. Ithel would be no protection if the priest came for her. He might even be anxious to get rid of her, for the right price.

In late April, Clidna thrust a bunch of tiny, white flowers into Finola's face. "These are for your hair," she said with a pretty little smile.

Finola reached for them.

"Thank you. But I—"

"They're for the celebration," Clidna said. "You have to come."

"Uh—"

"All the slave girls get to dress in white and dance around the May pole. You have to come."

Finola had spent the last few weeks doing everything she could to avoid being noticed. But Clidna's little, shining face melted her heart. She accepted the flowers, fixed her hair, and slipped into the ragged white dress Ithel had tossed to her from the trunk of Addie's old clothes.

She grabbed Clidna's little hand and tried not to think of all the May Day celebrations she had enjoyed as child. Together, they paraded through the streets and danced around the May pole with the other slave girls. For a few, brief moments, Finola almost forgot that she was a mere slave with no rights and no protection.

The music and dancing continued well into the evening, when the Holy Man reappeared. Finola saw him and tried to melt into the crowd that gathered around the bonfire in the village square. As darkness enfolded the village, the Holy Man ascended a small platform and held up a struggling rabbit by the feet. The music stopped. The crowd fell silent.

The Holy Man mumbled something that Finola couldn't hear and plunged what looked like a stone-tipped knife into the rabbit's heart. The rabbit gave a piercing cry of anguish, struggled briefly, quivered, and then hung limp and lifeless from his hand. The Holy Man set the knife on a short table and extracted the rabbit's heart. He searched the crowd until his gaze fell upon Finola. He motioned for her to come. She hesitated, but Ithel shoved her forward. She glanced back at him, hoping that he would not make her, but he gestured toward the stand with an irritated wave.

"Go," he said.

Finola's stomach tightened. Had Ithel and the Holy Man planned this all along? Was Ithel going to give her to the Holy Man right in front of the entire village? Her stomach tightened and twisted like someone had grabbed it in a fist.

The crowd parted for her until she stood at the foot of the stand. The Holy Man reached out a hand dripping with blood and dropped the rabbit's heart into her hand with a smile as if he were granting her a special treat.

The warm heart quivered and spasmed. The bile rose in Finola's throat, and she coughed. She had butchered many rabbits in her life, but never had the heart of a rabbit filled her with such dread and disgust. The blood dripped from between her fingers. Finola blinked and began to turn away when the priest stopped her with a short command.

He raised his hand to his mouth in an unambiguous gesture that she was to eat the heart. Finola swallowed the bile that still lingered in her throat. She craned her head around to see if Ithel might save her. But he didn't come to her aid.

Her entire body went cold and trembled as if it were a freezing, winter day. The silent crowd watched and waited. Feet shuffled. Someone coughed. The smell of burning wood filled the air and mixed with the warm scent of the blood that rose from the rabbit's carcass. The Holy Man gestured again more insistently. His smile had turned to a scowl. Finola stared down at her hand.

She couldn't eat it raw. Her stomach would not allow it. The bile burned her throat. She raised her hand, then lowered it again. The Holy Man shouted something that Finola couldn't understand. He stepped toward her with a raised hand as if he meant to strike her, when a short, broadly-built man stepped beside her, grabbed the heart from her hand, and swallowed it whole. The flutes and drums struck up another lilting tune, and the crowd erupted into singing and dancing again. Finola raised her gaze to the man who had rescued her. He wore bright red and blue paint that glistened in the light of the fire. The thanks she had been prepared to give him froze on her lips. Her throat constricted.

His face looked as if the skin had melted like fat in a skillet. She struggled to know what to do. The strange woman's warning of so many weeks ago echoed in her mind. The man with the ruined face who had already killed one wife was seeking another.

He smiled, but the twisted skin made it more of a grimace. Finola spun away and wiped the blood from her hand onto the white dress. She hurried to where Ithel pushed his way toward her. His face was livid.

"Why have you shamed me?" he yelled.

"What?" Finola stared at him in confusion.

"The Holy Man selected you for the honor, and you wouldn't take it."

Finola didn't try to hide her confusion. For a moment, she thought that he might strike her, but he only glared, red-faced and fuming.

Her confusion turned to anger.

"Honor? What kind of honor is that?"

"It is the way," Ithel said. "Now my family will never be selected again. You have shamed us."

Ithel glanced up at the Holy Man who stood watching their exchange. "Maybe I *should* sell you," he mumbled as he turned away.

He left her standing in the square surrounded by the jostling crowd. Finola whirled to face the Holy Man and the man with the ruined face, who both stood watching her. And she remembered. The man with the facial burns was the same man that had wanted to buy Brigid. The man Emyr had shamed.

Terror propelled her through the crowd. She tore the white flowers from her hair and flung them to the dirt. For the first time, she looked forward to leaving for the Great Keldi—anything to get her out of this village and away from these vile men.

Chapter 28
Suitors

The next day, Ithel bade his wife and child goodbye and led Finola, with a group of villagers who were also attending the gathering, out onto the high heathland. It spread out before them, rolling over the horizon until it collided with forested slopes of the purple mountains still capped in snow.

To be back on the open heathland filled Finola with a sense of liberation and hope she hadn't had in months. But she knew it was foolish to allow her feelings to get away from her. The long months of waiting would soon be over. She would be sold to the highest bidder, and if she didn't find a way to escape soon, she would never escape. Her imagination led to wild daydreams of finding Brigid and fighting their way free. But she knew these dreams were hopeless.

As they climbed higher into the foothills of the Aldina Mountains, the man with the ruined face joined their party. Ithel didn't seem surprised by his appearance. She learned that his name was Gilroy, and his intentions were clear to Finola. He talked freely and kindly to everyone, and he even contrived to ride beside Finola on occasion. He spoke to her in quiet tones about frivolous things.

But Finola never answered him—never looked at him directly. If she could find a way to punish all these fools and go her own way, she would do it. She would do it even if it meant dying alone in the heather. What she needed was a plan. She needed help. She checked the small knife she had tucked under her saddle. If it came to it, she would use it.

Brigid watched the line of slaves file past with growing revulsion. Emyr had set out for the Great Keldi with her in early May. Now he gestured for her to step off the path to let the slaves pass. They shuffled up the trail like a long, exhausted snake. Their chains clinked. Men, women, and children passed her with heads hanging low. Several men on horseback followed along beside them, lashing out now and then with a whip if one stumbled.

When she glanced back at Emyr, she found that he had been watching her rather than the slaves. He had a strange expression on his face that she couldn't interpret.

That evening, while they camped by a small stream, Emyr approached her.

"Can I have a word?" he asked.

Brigid kept scrubbing the dishes. "Now?"

"Yes."

Brigid set the dishes down, stood, and followed him to a clump of heather several paces from the camp. The other travelers were all seated around their fires or were occupied in various camp duties. No one paid them any attention.

"I saw how you looked at those slaves today," Emyr said.

Brigid dropped her gaze to her hands.

Emyr continued to speak. "I just wanted you to know that I've decided not to sell you at the gathering."

Brigid's head snapped up.

"I won't let you be chained like an animal," Emyr said. A strange intensity came into his eyes. "I just wanted you to know."

Something gripped Brigid's stomach. She couldn't tell if it was relief or anxiety. "Why are we going then?" she asked.

Emyr shrugged. "It is the way."

Brigid scowled. If he told her that one more time, she might just slap him, master or not.

Chapter 29
Battle in the Dark

It was an easy shot. The man knelt fifteen paces away from Brion. He jerked in surprise as Brion's string slapped. The arrow buried itself into his chest with a loud thud. The other men sat startled for an instant before they let out their war cries and rushed into the camp. Neahl and Redmond rose as one.

Two more attackers fell. Brion dropped the last and spun to meet the group that came rushing from the other side. Brion shot the lead man, but before he could get off another clear shot, Neahl and Redmond were in his way.

The attackers loosed a volley of arrows and sprinted into the camp. Neahl dropped and rolled as an arrow passed through the air where he had been standing. He came to one knee and dropped another attacker. Redmond leapt to one side, dodging two arrows and felled two more men in rapid succession. He shot so fast that Brion had barely seen him nock the second arrow.

At that instant, Brion became aware of his mistake. He had allowed himself to become engrossed in the battle. A scrape on the wall behind him told him that he was not alone. He sprang to his feet with his bow half-drawn when a body launched itself from the stone wall and slammed into his chest. He fell backward. His head slammed into the rocky earth. The glint of a knife flashed toward his throat. Brion threw up his crossed hands to catch the arm as the knife drove towards his heart. He was going to die—here in the shadow of an old farmhouse, just like his father. Then he saw the opening.

Brion swung his right leg up and hooked it behind the man's head. Using all of his strength, he forced the head to the ground while clinging to the man's arm. The man was strong but Brion's legs were stronger. He pulled on the arm with all his might, extending his legs. Brion knew from experience that this created tremendous pressure in the elbow and the shoulder.

133

The shoulder tore from its socket with a jerk. The man groaned and released the knife. It clattered to the ground as the arm went limp. But Brion didn't let go. Neahl had used that trick on him more than once—to go limp as if defeated only to seize the advantage once the attacker had loosed his grip.

Brion had also learned never to give up a good position until he had a better one. He wasn't going to get one better than this. So he kept the pressure on even after the man began to plead for him to let loose. He craned his head around to see how the others had fared. He found Neahl bending over two of the bodies while Redmond stood beside him, dividing his attention between Brion and the surrounding darkness.

"I think you can let him go," Redmond said.

Brion released the pressure and rolled quickly to his feet. His head throbbed, but he was otherwise uninjured. The man tried to sit up. He gasped and stopped. He clutched at the arm Brion had dislocated.

Brion watched him, trying to decide how he should feel. The old hatred he had felt when he had kicked the dead Salassani back by his cabin still lurked deep in his chest. But somehow, seeing this man crumpled in pain and knowing that he had just killed at least three men, didn't give Brion the satisfaction he had expected. Where was the sense of triumph? Where was the sweet joy of revenge?

"Search him," Redmond told Brion.

Brion bent and searched the man's body. When he finished, Brion helped him to a sitting position against the rock wall. The man's smudged war paint looked something like a serpent's mouth. His hair and eyes were dark. He didn't show any fear, but Brion caught his gaze straying to their weapons.

Neahl came to stand beside them. He loomed large in the dark night. He slipped his knife back into its sheath.

"Ten dead and this one," he said. "They must have thought we were the Carpentini that have been tracking them."

"What do we do with him?" Brion asked.

Redmond shook his head. "Looks like our choices are to kill him or leave him here where he may well die anyway."

Neahl considered. "I don't like killing an unarmed man, even a Salassani."

"Then let's tend his injuries, Redmond said, "and leave him with some food from his own supplies. We can scatter the horses into the heather.

By the time he catches one and gets back north, it'll be too late."

Neahl glanced at Brion. "What do you say? Kill him or leave him?" he asked.

Brion glanced at the man who had just tried to knife him. His right arm dangled by his side. He watched them, aware that Brion would be deciding his fate. Brion shook his head. The man probably had a wife and children.

"I guess we leave him," he said.

Brion went to retrieve the horses the men had left in the creek while Neahl and Redmond searched the dead. When Brion returned, he found Neahl and Redmond arguing.

"It's barbaric." Redmond's tone was harsh.

The blush of morning was beginning to brush the rolling hills of the heathland. By this pale light, Brion could see that Redmond's face was flushed.

"But," Neahl said, "it serves a useful purpose, and we're supposed to ensure that no blame can be cast on King Geric for our activities."

Neahl's face was tight in anger.

As Brion approached, Redmond whirled away and knelt to tend to the injured man's shoulder.

Brion glanced around at the corpses. The bile rose in his throat. The stench of excrement and urine was already rising from them.

He had never killed a man before, and, even though this had been the result of an unprovoked attack in the dark, he still felt a strange, disembodied remorse. He hated them, and he pitied them. He knew full well that he could join them before this journey ended. He probably would.

Only then did he note the dark stains on the sides of their heads. One ear had been cut from each man. He remembered seeing Neahl slip his knife into its sheath.

Neahl handed Brion his spent arrows.

"Never underestimate the power of fear," Neahl said. He glanced at the mutilated bodies and strode away.

Redmond called Brion to help him reset the Salassani's shoulder back into the socket.

"Did you see what he did?" Redmond said as they worked.

Brion nodded.

"He's crazy," Redmond said. "He did this when we tracked down the Salassani that raided our village when we were young men. It's barbaric."

Brion had never seen Redmond so angry. Redmond seized Brion's arm.

"I don't want you to do this," he said. "If he wants to, then let him, but don't let him convince you to start down this path. Where does it lead, Brion? Think where it leads."

Brion nodded.

Redmond watched him for a moment to make sure he understood. When they finished setting the shoulder, Redmond sat back on his haunches.

"Well, no point in trying to get any rest now," he said.

Half an hour later, they were gathered around their prisoner.

"We're going to let you live," Redmond told him in Salassani, "on the condition that you remain here for one week. Then you can try to find a horse and go on your way. Tell no one that you saw us here. The Carpentini caught you and killed the rest of your band. Understand?"

The man nodded.

"Good. If you follow us or reveal any information about us, we'll kill you."

The man nodded again. Then the man gestured towards the bodies of his comrades.

"Won't you bury them?"

Redmond shook his head. "We don't have time."

"Why did you cut off their ears?"

Redmond glanced at him, mounted, and rode away.

Neahl and Brion waited to let him scout the way before they followed with the string of eleven Salassani ponies trailing out behind them.

Once they had scattered the ponies, they reined their mounts to the north, keeping to the foothills of the Aveen Mountains. They settled into the routine of rising early, traveling all day, stopping late, caring for their gear, and practicing archery, hand-to-hand combat, or sword play. Then they ate a quick meal and bedded down for the night. Brion tried to give Misty a good rub down every evening. They made good time with little incident until the terrible cry of an enraged beast brought them up short.

Chapter 30
Into the Mouth of the Beast

he roar rolled over the hills of the heathland followed by the squeal of a terrified horse. Neahl and Redmond exchanged glances before kicking their mounts into a gallop. Brion followed. He couldn't imagine what kind of animal could make such a terrifying roar. When they crested the hill, they found wild pandemonium in the valley below. Packhorses fought their hobbles, neighing in terror as they jumped and kicked against the restraints.

A man wearing a long, dark cloak stood between the horses and a massive creature, which reared up on its hind legs and bellowed an ear-splitting roar that raised the hairs on the back of Brion's neck. Brion had never seen one, but Redmond had described it to him. It was a great northern bear. Paws the size of a plate with claws as long as daggers swatted at the man. A mangled horse lay kicking weakly beside him as its blood flowed into the dirt from a gash in its throat.

The man held his sword at the ready. The bear swatted at him again. The man darted in and slashed at the bear's belly before leaping to safety. The bear roared again, dropped on all fours, and charged. By this time, Brion, Neahl, and Redmond had nocked arrows and were galloping down the hillside to the stranger's defense.

The stranger evaded the charging bear, but the bear wrenched the sword from his hand and sent him sprawling in the dust. He came up on one knee with a long knife at the ready just as the bear bore down upon him. He disappeared under the monster.

Three arrows appeared in the bear's side. When the bear raised its head, it held the stranger's head full in its mouth. Brion couldn't see how the man would survive. But the hand that held the knife kept stabbing blindly. Brion released two more arrows into the bear's side before it let go of the man's head and turned toward them.

Brion and Redmond galloped to either flank of the bear while Neahl faced it head-on, sending an arrow straight through its eye. Brion and

Redmond aimed for the heart. The bear charged Neahl, but his horse danced sideways to avoid the attack. The bear stumbled, wheeled, and charged again. Neahl buried an arrow in its throat as his horse danced aside again. This time the bear's front legs gave way, and it plowed head-first into the trampled heather. It tried to raise its bulk from the dirt, but failed. It struggled and quivered before it lay still.

Redmond leapt from his horse and knelt beside the injured man. The man blinked up at Redmond through the blood that dribbled from a dozen puncture wounds.

"You know," the man said in the common tongue. "I thought my mother-in-law had bad breath. But that bear was the worst."

Brion, Neahl, and Redmond stared at the man in surprise before Neahl began to laugh.

"You're not Salassani." Redmond said.

It was a statement, not a question. They sat around the fire while strips of bear flesh they had skewered on the ends of green sticks sizzled over the open flames.

The man smiled.

"Mixed blood," he said.

Brion could see it in his face despite the injuries and the cloth bandages Redmond had applied. He had a long nose like some did in the south-land, but the dark eyes and hair of the Salassani. The uninjured parts of his face were marked by the small pox. His finger played with the pointed handlebars of a thick mustache.

Neahl gestured toward the horses and the bundles.

"You trade?"

"On my way to Aldina Lake."

"A bit off the beaten track, aren't you?" Neahl said.

The stranger gave a slight nod and kept smiling. How he could smile after staring down a bear's throat was beyond Brion.

"That's often the best way to avoid trouble," he said. "But I've got an appointment with a band of Bracari at the northern spur of the Aveen. Then I'll turn northeast again." He paused. "Name's Airic."

Neahl introduced each of them. Brion saw recognition in the man's expression, which surprised him and made him suspicious.

"My thanks for your timely rescue," Airic said. "I owe you my life."

Deliverance

His hand drifted to the back of his head where Redmond had stitched together a particularly nasty gash. "How may I repay you?"

"That depends," Neahl said as he handed Brion the arrows they had extracted from the bear's carcass. Brion began cleaning them of the dried gore.

Airic studied them and held up his hands. "I don't take sides in anything," he said. "I mind my own business. 'Keep your beard close to your chest.' That's what I always say. Sticking it out where it doesn't belong is a good way to get it pulled."

Brion smiled at the imagery.

"All I care about is my trade," Airic continued. "As I said, I'm on my way to Aldina Lake for the Great Keldi." He stopped and watched them with raised eyebrows.

Brion glanced at his companions, but kept cleaning the arrows.

Neahl spoke. "We also mind our own business. And that business takes us north."

Airic nodded. "I'm not gonna try to guess what that business might be, because it's none of my business." He grinned, making his mustache quiver. "But I did hear tell of a couple of beautiful young ladies and a boy that were taken in a raid near Mailag last winter. I heard tell that they would be taken to the Great Keldi where they are expected to bring a fair price."

Brion tried not to show any emotion, but the quick flick of Airic's gaze to his face showed that he had given away his interest.

"Why are you telling us this?" Redmond asked.

"Just making small talk, friend. As I said, I don't take sides. But, if these girls are as pretty as I heard tell, I might buy one for myself."

Again his gaze flicked to Brion's face. Brion picked up another arrow, wondering what this man intended, struggling to keep his emotions in check.

"A man gets lonely traveling the heathland," Airic said.

Brion's face grew hot despite all of his effort. The smile that twitched at the side of Airic's mouth showed that he enjoyed Brion's discomfort.

"Did you hear which band they were with?" Neahl asked.

"Justin led the main band," Airic said. "I don't know where the kids are, but there's talk that men are lining up to buy the girls. Word is the boy is half-Salassani already." Airic eyed them again expectantly.

Brion pulled out the little file he used to sharpen the broadheads on their arrows and set to filing them.

Neahl nodded. "Since you have no interest in anyone else's affairs," he said, "I wonder if you have heard tell of any movement at Dunkeldi to, maybe, pay a visit to Laro Forest?"

"Ah, now that you mention it," Airic said with a smile. "I do recall someone saying that King Tristan had planned to vacation in Brechin this summer or maybe, if things went well, the beach country of Whit-horn in the south." Airic rotated the roasting meat. "He is said to prefer to travel with a large party of vacationers who can sometimes get row-dy." He emphasized the last word with raised eyebrows.

Brion knew that Whit-horn was the southernmost territory of Coll. The Dunkeldi king could only vacation there if he had conquered the entire kingdom. Apparently, this Airic enjoyed speaking in riddles. And Neahl seemed more than happy to play along. But how could a simple trader know of such things? Brion's suspicions seemed confirmed. There was more to this man than he let on.

"Does King Tristan have a preferred method and route of travel when he vacations?" Neahl asked.

Airic pursed his lips. "I think he prefers horseback, though some of his entourage prefer boats. But I haven't heard if there are any definite plans that way."

Neahl nodded. "Are any other royal details being discussed publicly?"

Airic shook his head. "Not that I know of."

Neahl massaged his chin. "How long before you return to Brechin?"

Airic shrugged. "If the gathering goes well, I hope to be back home by mid-summer."

"Will you be traveling alone?"

Airic place a pot on the fire. "That depends on what is for sale at the Great Keldi and how much it costs."

Brion noted the wicked grin, but still found himself wondering if Airic was teasing or if he was serious. He couldn't decide if he liked this man or not, but he knew better than to trust him—not after the way he had so astutely discerned their real purpose in the heathland.

Neahl sat back. "Well, we may see you at the Great Keldi," he said. "Just out of curiosity, how does a mixed blood happen to be trading with the Salassani?"

Airic made a dismissive gesture. "Well, my mother was from Brechin," he said. "She was captured and sold to the Taurini where she eventually married the village headman as his second wife. He treated my mother well, but I was the child of a second wife who didn't own any property." He dumped some leaves into the pot. "My mother always wanted me to return to her family in Brechin. So when I came of age, I left. I've been wandering ever since." He shrugged. "You know how it is. When you're a mixed breed you come from both and belong to none."

"So you took up trade between the two?" Redmond asked. He picked up an arrow from Brion's pile, pulled out his own file and ran it over the broadhead.

"It seemed like a good idea. When I get tired of one society, I can always escape to the other."

"Are you married?" Brion asked before he had considered it.

Airic flashed him a broad grin.

"No need to worry about your little beauties," he said. "I have a lovely Alamani wife back in Brechin."

Brion's face burned. But he hadn't been worried about the girls. Or had he?

"I think this meat is charred enough," Airic said as he tugged a piece of smoking meat from the spit. Melted fat splashed into the fire causing it sizzle and pop. "Shall we take our revenge upon the beast?"

Airic joined their group and they rode with him for a couple of days before they parted. Airic had made a point of speaking directly to Brion.

"I'll keep my eyes and ears open for them, lad," Airic had said. "If there's anything I can do to help them, I'll do it."

Brion didn't know what to say. They hadn't said anymore about the girls since that first meeting, and he had half-suspected Airic of ulterior motives. But he nodded and mumbled a thanks.

As they rode along in silence, Brion considered what Airic had told them. He and Neahl may have been playing verbal games, but their meaning was clear enough. The Dunkeldi king meant to invade Coll that summer. They were the only people to know, and they were heading north, deeper into Salassani territory. Then, he considered Seamus's words. Maybe they weren't the only ones to know. Maybe they had been manipulated into the heathland to add the final spark to ignite the flame. A raid from Coll, no matter what its purpose, could be seen as an act of war. They were being led into a trap. Maybe Seamus was right. Maybe they were meant to die in the heathland after starting a war.

The Aldina peaks loomed out of the far horizon—purple, snow-capped mountains that floated in the distance as the terrain rose and fell. The green, rolling hills dotted with the ruins of hamlets, round towers, and farmhouses gave way to an open and empty landscape where the heather became sparse and was replaced by bushes with long, gray leaves that had a rich aroma Brion had never smelled before. Redmond called it "sage."

The terrain became more broken and the hills and valleys deeper. The antelope disappeared to be replaced by large deer with wide ears that flicked about. Short junipers with shaggy bark also began to dot the landscape. The valleys were wooded with patches of aspen and birch.

The whole terrain made Brion feel lonely. But it also enchanted him. The smells were different, more pungent, the colors less vibrant, and the wind sharper. At first, the open heathland had left him feeling exposed. Now, he sensed an eerie attraction to it, as if the wild, untamed land knew him and accepted him.

Fresh Salassani trails crisscrossed their path and only constant attention and careful maneuvering allowed them to travel without encountering any more Salassani. Once, they saw a band of riders moving fast to the east. Occasionally, Redmond or Neahl would backtrack on their trail to ensure that they weren't being followed. Despite all their efforts, as they entered the narrow, steep-sided valley that led to the pass, they discovered a small band of Salassani on their trail.

Redmond came in late from searching the back trail with the news.

"I counted seven. They're warriors, but I couldn't tell which tribe."

Neahl cursed. "Now it'll be impossible to conceal that we have taken the pass." He paused. "Well Brion, this is what you've trained for. Where would you set the ambush?"

Brion glanced at Redmond, who nodded. They all understood that they had no choice. They couldn't afford to attempt a rescue with a band of Salassani hunting them. And they couldn't get out of the valley without being seen.

"I don't think it's an accident that they're following us," Brion said. Neahl pursed his lips. "I mean," Brion continued, "I think someone sent them after us."

"Explain," Redmond said.

Brion told them what Seamus had said, feeling rather stupid for not telling them sooner. Somehow the fight at the tavern and the rigors of the trail had driven it from his mind.

"I think we've been lured up here for something else. Maybe they just want to kill us, or maybe they want us to start a war for them," Brion said.

Redmond and Neahl considered.

"But why kill your parents?" Redmond asked.

Brion opened his mouth to tell them about his father's secret and his admission of treason. But he closed it. He would not break the last promise he had made to his father. That promised had been sealed with his parents' blood.

Brion shook his head.

"If someone wants to start a war," Neahl said, "there's not much we can do about it. But I won't let the Salassani have Weyland's child. War or no war."

Brion nodded. Sometimes he wondered if Neahl forgot that he wasn't his father—that he was barely eighteen and totally inexperienced. Worse still, Brion had been ashamed of his father's crippled arm. He didn't deserve to be confused with his father. But he was all Brigid had left, as his father had told him with his dying breath. And Brion would save her, no matter the cost. He had to.

Brion shifted in his saddle and surveyed the country around them. He pointed up the canyon where it narrowed. The walls became steeper and rockier.

"Let's see how long that narrow section lasts. It might be a good spot."

They kicked their horses toward the gap. It ran about forty paces. Its walls formed the shape of a V with large boulders and rock outcroppings on either side. From the right position, a couple of archers could pin down anyone who came through.

"Let's keep one person here at the exit," Brion said. "He can hide without being seen from below and can keep anyone from getting out this way."

He scanned the area and continued. At about the middle, he found an outcropping on either side that could provide cover.

"The other two should be here on opposite sides. We'll need to lead the horses on a bit in case they have a scout out front. If necessary, he can be dealt with after he passes so as not to alert the others to the ambush." He stopped. "Did I miss anything?"

"Let's give it a try," Neahl said.

Brion concealed himself on the valley wall opposite Neahl, while Redmond covered the exit. From this position, Brion had a clear view of most of the valley floor.

They sat in silence for more than an hour before the first sounds of horses' hooves striking stone echoed up the gap. Brion had been watching a hawk soaring high above, when the sound reached him. He glanced at the tiny feather on the upper limb of his bow to check the wind direction. The wind blew up through the valley, which meant that their pursuers' horses wouldn't catch their scent and give them away. Brion had forgotten to consider this and made a mental note not to forget it again.

Brion resisted the temptation to rise up and peek over the rock. To do so would have silhouetted his head against the skyline. He had made that mistake too often in the last four months to repeat it here.

The sound of a single horse came louder, moving slowly. He had guessed right. They had sent a scout to check for any trickery. A few moments of silence were followed by the sound of rocks sliding as someone scrambled up the side of the valley. Brion cursed himself. His blood began to race. He had miscalculated.

Quiet footfalls approached and passed above him. Brion tried to become a part of the rock. He had chosen his position carefully. No one coming up the trail could see him, but anyone coming down or backtracking would have a plain view of his position. The scout trod softly along the ridge, his head constantly moving from side to side. When he came to the end, he studied the floor of the valley. Redmond's foot poked out from where he was hiding about twenty paces away, and Brion wondered why the scout hadn't seen it. Brion tightened his fingers on the string of his bow, waiting for the scout to turn and see him. Sweat dripped into his eyes. But he did not stir.

The scout stepped up to stand on the rock where Redmond lay concealed. He surveyed the valley and turned to retrace his steps. Brion held still, not even daring to breathe.

The scout stopped. He bent to study the ground. Then his head snapped up, his eyes moving. Brion read the alarm in his face. The scout whipped an arrow out of his quiver and placed it on the string in one, fluid motion. He knew they were there.

The man's gaze roamed the landscape, his body tense and alert. Brion considered rising up to shoot, because he knew he could get the shot off before the man could respond. But Neahl and Redmond had beat into him the importance of patience. Movement gave a person away. If a person sat still, they could be difficult to see, even in the open.

The man's sweeping gaze paused and focused on Brion.

"My I sit?" Gilroy asked. He spoke with a lisp, because his lips had been so badly melted that they never fully closed.

Finola didn't answer. They had spent the last week climbing up the broad trail that led into the heart of the Aldina Mountains. Pine trees towered over their heads and rustled in the cold wind that blew down from the mountain peaks. They had stopped to camp in a clearing beside a gurgling creek. Finola had just finished washing the dishes from the evening meal and was wiping them dry.

Gilroy sat beside her. He had seized every opportunity to ride beside her on their assent, attempting small talk now and then. He joined them every evening around Ithel's fire.

"I've wanted to speak to you," he said. He glanced at her before studying the little waterfall that splashed over the stones. "I want you to know why I look the way I do." He shifted. "When I was still a boy, raiders set my home on fire. I went in to save my baby sister, but she was already dead. I brought out her little melted body anyway. The flames did this to me." He pointed to his face. "I'm not a bad man," he said.

Finola glanced at him and set the pot she had dried in the pile of dishes.

"Killing your wife doesn't make you a bad man?" She knew she shouldn't have said it, and she braced herself for the blow of his fist. But Gilroy stared at her, tight-lipped for a moment before standing and walking away.

Finola watched him take a place by the fire. She picked up a bowl and ran the rag over it. What did he want from her? First, he nearly got himself killed trying to buy Brigid, and now he weaseled his way into Ithel's friendship and tried to talk to her like they were old friends. She had not forgotten the old woman's warning. She would sleep with her knife in her hand from now on.

Chapter 31
Ambush and Revelation

Brion knew the scout had seen him because the man's eyes widened and his muscles tensed. Brion drew and loosed. The man leapt aside. Brion's arrow narrowly missed him. Before Brion could reseat another arrow on the string or the scout could draw his own bow, an arrow appeared in the scout's chest with a thud. He grunted and crumpled forward. He slid part way down the slope before coming to rest against a gnarled cedar tree that clung to the rocks. Brion heard the slap of boots on stone from the other side of the valley. He peered over the rock to see Neahl sprinting toward the scout's horse. He leapt onto its back from the rocks above and kicked it into a gallop through the narrow gap. Redmond hurried to the fallen scout, waving for Brion to help him. Together, they dragged his body over the rise and slid it into a crevice in the rocks. Then, they worked to eliminate any sign that they had been on the ridge. Neahl's birdcall echoed through the canyon. They hurried to where they had left the horses.

"It's no good waiting now," Neahl said. "They'll know something's wrong when their scout doesn't return, especially when they see the gap. We either ride on and seek another opportunity or we ride back and seek battle."

"We better ride back to meet them," Redmond said. "Once they reach the gap and discover that their scout didn't return to report it, they'll be on the alert."

Neahl looked at Brion. Brion nodded.

"Then we have to move now," Neahl said.

Neahl slapped the scout's horse into a gallop up the canyon, sprang into his own saddle, and galloped back the way they had come. Redmond and Brion followed. They had ridden about a mile, when Neahl called them to a halt in a hollow with short junipers on either side and a large sandstone outcropping. They hid the horses around the bend in case they needed to make a quick exit.

Deliverance

Neahl positioned Brion and Redmond each on opposite sides, well-hidden from view, and concealed himself on the top of the outcrop. They didn't wait long before the riders came into view. As they entered the little depression, Neahl cried out in a loud, deep voice.

"Halt."

The astonished men drew rein on their horses. Several of them placed arrows on the strings of their bows.

"Who's there?" one of them called.

Neahl replied in Salassani. "I am the demon who guards the pass."

Brion wondered what Neahl had up his sleeve. The men exchanged glances. He had a good view of the half dozen men gathered in the hollow. They seemed more confused than frightened by Neahl's odd declaration.

Something flew down from the rock outcrop and landed in the dirt beside the horses. The men leaned forward. Brion couldn't see what it was, but he understood what they called it.

"Ear," they said. "It's an ear."

They exchanged startled glances.

"I'll give ya one chance," Neahl said.

They hesitated.

"What of our companion who rode the trail ahead of us?"

Neahl tossed another ear at their feet.

"You may share his fate, if you wish."

One of the men yanked his horse around and rode out of the depression. Two more followed him.

"We would see your face," the apparent leader called, still trying to hold his ground.

An arrow shrieked past his head.

"My face will be the last thing you see before you die."

The other two men said something to the leader who reluctantly followed them back down the trail.

Neahl was smiling half an hour later as they prepared to ride out. He had fixed the two ears to the tree by shoving them onto a broken branch, while Redmond had checked to make sure the men didn't circle back on them.

"Just a little reminder to make them think twice before they venture up this trail again," Neahl told Brion. "Remember what I told you; never underestimate the power of fear."

"But why would they be afraid of a couple of ears? I mean," Brion swallowed, "it's a bit revolting, but why would it make them afraid?"

"Two reasons," Neahl said. He held up one finger. "First, because the Salassani only mutilate their victims when they wish to ensure that their souls can't go on to their underworld. It's considered a terrible thing to inflict this infamy on anyone."

He gave Brion a mischievous grin.

"And two," He held up another finger. "They already believe this pass to be inhabited by demons. One of the demons they tell their children about feeds on human ears. That's what gave me the idea. So I just manipulated their willingness to believe that some supernatural power is at work and played on their fears of being trapped soulless and bodiless in this world. It's a potent combination."

"It's barbarism," Redmond muttered as he came back to the little depression.

Neahl smirked at him. "Yes, it is. But, by using it, we just ensured that these men will not venture to follow us again any time soon, and we did it without having to kill them all needlessly." He paused. "I know you think that I am still driven by my lust for revenge, but I think I just proved you wrong."

Neahl kicked his horse into a trot.

Redmond exchanged a glance with Brion that said, "I'm not convinced," before he rode on.

As they rode, the realization of what had just happened began to weigh on Brion. He had been tasked with selecting the spot for an ambush, and it had failed. If Neahl hadn't been there for him, he might well be lying dead amid the rocks right now. Why hadn't he considered that a Salassani scout would check a place like that? Neahl's ambush had been much more effective and much better executed. Some of the confidence Brion had acquired from his first three fights began to wane. It was easy to make a deadly mistake—too easy.

"I didn't kill my wife," Gilroy said.

He rode beside Finola as they dropped down over the pass. The wind nipped at her nose and cheeks. Patches of snow crunched under her horse's hooves. From the high table where they rode, Finola could see over the forest of pines below to the blue lake just visible in the valley bottom far in the distance. The ring of snowcapped peaks stabbed toward the sky all around the deep, mountain valley. Gray clouds billowed about the peaks.

"I don't really care," Finola replied.

Gilroy ignored her.

"I found her sleeping with another and I . . . I beat her a bit. She ran away and froze to death."

Finola wondered how he had convinced a Salassani woman to marry him in the first place. Not only was it difficult to look at him, but despite his recent attempts at gentility, she knew he was still a brute.

But why was he telling her this? All he had to do was convince Ithel to sell her to him. She wouldn't have any say in the matter one way or the other. And yet, he had been trying to make her like him ever since they left for the Great Keldi. And what was Ithel doing? He didn't discourage Gilroy, but he gave him little encouragement. Ithel had other plans. But what were they? The Holy Man? The King?

"I've always wanted a family," Gilroy continued.

Finola wanted to say, "Congratulations, go bother someone else." But she said nothing.

"My wife never conceived."

Finola steeled herself for yet another awkward conversation and then decided against it.

"It's going to snow," she said.

"What?" Gilroy glanced up at the sky.

Finola kicked her horse into a trot.

The ascent through the high mountain pass strained Brion's endurance. The broken trail wiggled its way amid towering pines and treacherous landslides. It meandered past crystal-clear pools and lichen-covered waterfalls, squeezed between soaring peaks, and traced the edge of cliffs that dropped away a thousand feet to bare stone.

High up in the canyon where the wind always blew cold and wet from the high peaks, they took shelter from a sudden and violent snowstorm in a lean-to Neahl cast up amid the howling wind.

Brion was gratified as they sat around the fire in the lean-to during the storm to see Redmond and Neahl stretching stiff joints. He wasn't the only one finding the mountain trail punishing. He awoke once during the long night to the sound of quiet voices.

"Have you ever heard what happened to Lara?" Redmond asked.

Neahl shifted. "Last I heard she was living in Dunfermine."

"Did she ever marry?"

"I don't know," Neahl said. "But I do know she was very hurt when you left. I think she waited for you to come back."

They were silent for a while.

"I'm sure it would come as no comfort to her now," Redmond said, "but I never forgot her. I often imagined I would come back and find her waiting for me." He sighed. "But I don't blame her for moving on. She deserved someone better."

Neahl rolled onto his back. "After all she went through at Comrie," Neahl said, "and all the time she waited for you while we were in the heathland, she deserved at least a goodbye."

"I know," Redmond said. "I had promised to marry her, you know."

"I figured as much."

"I even gave her mother's silver star pendant before we went back to the war."

"I wondered where that went," Neahl said. "After Cassandra died, I couldn't look it. It should have been hers."

"I know," Redmond said.

They fell silent. Brion stared into the darkness. Redmond had mentioned Lara once before when he had first returned. Brion considered questioning them about Lara and Cassandra, but decided against it. It would be prying, and, if Redmond or Neahl had wanted him to know, they would have told him.

The long, cold days of trudging were followed by long, cold nights. One day bled into another until they finally crawled over the top of the pass and began the descent. The weather had warmed, turning the trail unto a slushy torrent of melting snow. But once they reached the other side, the snow disappeared.

Still, the descent wasn't any easier than the ascent had been. The path was steeper, and they had to pick their way across several rockslides that buried the trail. Four more days brought them down into a pine forest on

Deliverance

a large bench. From a rock outcrop where they paused to rest, they could see the blue waters of the great Aldina Lake far below them.

"The tribes gather on the south side of the lake by a large bay," Neahl said. "There's a great, black stone where they hold the Great Keldi. I've never seen it, but I've heard that anciently they used to sacrifice a young girl there. Today, I believe they use a lamb or a goat." Neahl pointed to the east. "Anyway, that's our road. From here on, we have to be cautious. The Aldina inhabit these mountain valleys."

Brion's nerves were on edge for the next three days as they worked their way down the mountains. They were so close. What if something went wrong now? What if they couldn't find the girls? What if the girls weren't even there? What if one of them was killed or injured in trying to make the rescue? What if Airic had lied about the girls being sold at the Great Keldi? So many things could go wrong, and he knew that he was the weakest link in all of their plans.

Two more days brought them to a high bench with a large meadow. They worked their way back to a rocky hillside where they discovered a small, dry cave. The rocks stood out from the hillside to form a natural corral that hid the cave from view.

"Good place for a base camp," Neahl said. "We can hide here while we work out what to do."

Neahl unrolled a couple of bundles he had carried tied to the back of his saddle. Brion recognized the Salassani clothes. Neahl also had three short bows and three quivers of arrows rolled up in them. The feather fletchings on the arrows were smashed from being packed, but, with steam from a small fire, they were easily set right.

"Where did you get these?" Brion asked.

"Borrowed them from our Salassani friends we met back on the heath-land," Neahl said. "They didn't need them anymore."

"So we're all going into the camp then?" Redmond asked.

Neahl nodded. "Can't be avoided," he said. "We'll melt into the crowd. We can all understand them—more or less," he glanced at Brion with one raised eyebrow.

Brion returned his gaze, not sure at all that he would understand the Salassani.

Neahl continued. "We each search a section of the encampment during the day and meet back here at night. With any luck, they'll be here already or will arrive soon, and we can get on with this."

Once they had fitted the clothes and practiced shooting the short, re-curved bows, they slipped out to scout the gathering. When they crawled to the edge of the bench above the lake to peer out over the valley, Brion's heart leapt into his mouth.

Chapter 32
The Great Keldi

Tents blanketed the plain. People milled about, thick as locusts. A large stage had been erected in the center of the tents where a great, black stone rose up at least twenty feet into the sky. Several large pavilions stood off to one side in a long row. Beyond the tents, horses milled about in an open field. To the side sat a field set up for contests or games.

Brion had never seen so many people in his life. He watched them, dumbfounded by their numbers. How could they possibly hope to succeed? What if the entire encampment came after them? It wouldn't matter how much he had trained or how good they were. The impossibility of the task they had set for themselves overwhelmed him. He had been so foolish and arrogant to think he could do anything against so many.

The blue lake spread out in all directions. The northern Aldina Mountains rose up to white peaks in the distance. The lake extended beyond Brion's range of vision, and he wondered if this was what the sea looked like. It was hard to conceive of so much water and so many people all in one place.

They crawled back from the bench and made their way back to the cave. Brion was shaking his head.

"I had no idea so many people even lived, let alone that there could be so many Salassani."

Both Redmond and Neahl laughed.

"Didn't you ever take this kid to the city?" Redmond asked as he sat down to oil his weapons.

"There didn't seem to be any need."

"Well, look at him now," Redmond said. "He's crippled by the sight of a few Salassani."

Brion bristled. "I'm not crippled, and that's not a few Salassani. There are as many Salassani as there are herring when they run up the river. I don't think I could even count them."

153

"There's probably only about five or six thousand down there now," Neahl said. He handed Brion the oil and raised his eyebrows. Brion drew his knife and began wiping it down. Neahl continued. "But there will be a good eight or nine in a couple of days."

"Thousand?" Brion paused. "I've never seen a thousand anything except maybe wheat seeds or ants. How many Salassani live up here?" Brion fumbled with his knife.

"Pay attention to that blade," Neahl said.

Brion sheathed the knife.

"Maybe thirty to forty thousand if you throw in the Carpentini," Neahl said with a casual flip of his hand.

Brion gaped. "And we're supposed to walk right in and stroll back out with three girls and then just ride over the mountains?"

Redmond grabbed the oil from Brion.

Brion sat back and passed a hand over the back of his neck. "I feel like I'm getting ready to poke a stick into an anthill—only this time they don't just bite."

Redmond chuckled. "That's a good comparison. But you're missing the point. The fact that they are here in large numbers is to our advantage."

Brion opened his mouth, but Redmond stopped him with a raised hand.

"With so many unfamiliar Salassani wandering around," Redmond said, "no one will be surprised to see three men they don't know. Neahl and I can ask questions. You just watch and listen. Finding them should be easy enough. Getting them out will be more difficult."

Brion snorted. "Ya think?"

Neahl sheathed his sword. "We'll come to that when we have more information," he said. "For now, let's just learn what we can."

The next morning, Redmond painted Neahl's face like a bear head with bright blue and red paint. Neahl painted Redmond's face with a wolf's head. They were both remarkably good at the painting.

"Your turn," Redmond said to Brion.

"But I haven't earned any paint," Brion said. After all, his ambush had been a failure.

Redmond and Neahl exchanged glances. "You've had three successful fights already," Redmond said. "I think we'll give you an elaborate eagle's head."

154

Deliverance

Neahl raised a questioning eyebrow, but Redmond ignored him. When Redmond had finished, Brion asked them how they had learned to paint so well. They both smiled.

"Practice," they said together.

Brion shook his head. "If I hear that word from either of you again, I might just shoot you."

Brion stared at the mob of people milling about and jostling each other in the wide meadow between the stage and the rows of merchant stalls. His pulse throbbed in his ears and sweat glistened on his upper lip. How could there be so many people? At that moment, he would have rather faced an army of angry Salassani than step into that throng alone. But he had to do it for Brigid and Finola. So he gathered up what courage he could find and sauntered into the sea of tents and people.

Once he entered the maze of stalls, what he found sent his mind racing in astonishment. He had never seen such a vast array of goods. Some he recognized from his village, but others were wondrous. He found exotic pottery with bright blue and pink glazes, multi-colored glass cups and bowls, textiles woven in intricate designs. Artists not only sold their goods but also had little shops where they made their wares. Blacksmiths, silversmiths, saddlers, engravers, fletchers, armorers, and many others worked in their shops, gossiping as they plied their trades.

Brion tried to listen to the conversations at the tables. To his dismay, he found so many dialects and accents that he couldn't understand much at all. He roamed about in constant fear that someone would ask him a question. He tried to look as surly as he could so that no one would want to talk to him.

By midday, Brion worked up the courage to buy some grain for the horses to give them a treat. He selected a seller that wasn't doing much business and waited until no one was around. He approached the feed stall and pointed to a sack of barley. The old man mumbled something.

"Sorry?" Brion said in his best Salassani, trying to keep the panic down. He hadn't understood a word the man said. The man peered at him before he repeated himself.

This time Brion caught the amount. "Six bits." Brion counted out the money and handed it to the old man as the strong smell of horse manure wafted over him. He glanced over his shoulder to find a young man about his own age standing behind him.

Brion hefted the bag onto his shoulder and stepped aside. The young man was tall and stocky with coarse, filthy clothing. His auburn hair hung loose around his shoulders. He studied Brion with honey-colored eyes. Then he inclined his head. Brion returned the gesture.

The young man handed the grain seller a bag that clinked. The seller pointed to several large sacks stacked by the wall of the tent and grunted something. As the stranger extended his hand to pick one up, Brion noted the tiny brand on the back of his hand. It spread out in the shape a bird with outstretched wings. Brion stared, despite himself. He had seen that mark scribbled onto the parchment he had taken from his father's trunk.

The young man paused, searched Brion's face, and gestured toward the tents with a nod. Brion understood that he wanted him to follow. Brion hesitated and trailed behind him despite the nervous wriggling in his stomach and the thought of Neahl berating him for letting himself be lured away from the crowd.

Something about the stranger intrigued him. He was dressed like a slave, but he didn't carry himself like a slave. And he had that mark on his hand. It couldn't be a mere coincidence.

Brion followed him through the tents back to the horse corral. The man pushed his way into the corral, well out into the huge mass of horses.

"I know who you are," the young man said without any ceremony. "And I know what you're doing." He spoke in the common tongue.

Brion glanced around unsure what to say.

When he opened his mouth the young man shook his head.

"Don't bother denying it. We don't have time. They know you're here. You have to act before the King gets here. Whether you know it or not, you are part of a bigger plot to—"

He stopped speaking and jerked his head around. Voices lifted above the shuffling and snorting of horses. "You can't be seen here." He dropped a small piece of metal into Brion's hand in the same shape as the brand on the back of his own hand. "If you get back south, take this to the Duke of Saylen. He'll know what it means." Then he disappeared amid the horses.

Brion ducked out of sight and worked his way back to the tents where he slipped back into the crowd. When darkness fell, he disappeared into the thicket of pines that surrounded the clearing and hurried back to the cave.

He found both Neahl and Redmond waiting for him. They each had a pile of arrows beside them as if they had been straightening arrows all day.

"Well?" Neahl questioned.

Brion dropped the little bag of grain he had purchased and surveyed them. "Did you know a man can take a bag of sand," Brion said, "heat it up until it glows red, and then blow it into a cup or a bowl?"

They both laughed.

"This kid has led a sheltered life," Redmond said. He wiped an oily rag down an arrow shaft and lifted another from the pile.

"I meant did you find anything?" Neahl said.

"I didn't understand them very well," Brion said.

Neahl handed Brion some arrows.

"Unlike you," Neahl said, "we spent more time listening and searching and less time gawking at Salassani wares."

"I wasn't gawking."

"Relax," Neahl said. He peered down a shaft and rolled it against his finger. "I found out that the girls are in different groups. Finola and Brigid aren't here yet, but some people are anxious to see the famous beauties."

Neahl put pressure with the heel of his hand on the shaft and peered at it again. "I couldn't find any news of Maggie, which worries me. If they don't bring her to the market, it may be impossible to find her."

"The King is supposed to come for the high ceremony at the great rock," Redmond said as he dropped another shaft into the pile. "It's whispered that he wanted to convince some of the hesitant headmen to join him in a raid on the south. The rumor is that he wants to take back the lands they lost to Coll on the borders of the Laro Forest."

Neahl sighed and applied pressure to another arrow.

"If he's the king, can't he just command them?" Brion asked.

Redmond peered at him from over a shaft. "He's only the King of the Dunkeldi."

"But I thought—"

"The other tribes are autonomous," Neahl interrupted. "They often follow his lead. But he has to convince them to follow him. Otherwise, he could never create an army large enough to invade Coll."

"Well," Redmond said, "let's hope we can get this job done and get back before we get caught between two armies. I have a feeling this summer is going to be an unpleasant one for all of us."

"They know we're here," Brion said.

Redmond and Neahl both stopped what they were doing.

Brion told them how he had met the slave with the brand and showed them the little figure of the eagle.

Redmond and Neahl exchanged glances.

"This is deep water," Neahl said.

Brion swiveled his gaze between them. "What?"

"Apparently someone has been feeding the Salassani information about us all along," Neahl said, "and this slave has just given you an old royal symbol that hasn't been used for almost twenty years. Not since the coup."

"An eagle?"

"Yes," Neahl said. "That's a dangerous symbol in Coll. Don't let anyone know you have it."

"What about the Duke?" Brion asked.

Neahl shrugged. "Not a problem worth worrying about at the moment," he said.

"What could it mean?" Brion asked.

"My only concern," Neahl said, "is to get the girls safely away. I won't get tangled up in anything else."

"Well," Redmond said, "looks like we have two days to find the girls before King Tristan arrives."

Brion said no more but retreated to his bedroll to struggle with his conscience. Neahl and Redmond didn't know about the papers and the ring that he kept carefully concealed in his saddlebags. He hadn't looked at them since he had taken them from his father's trunk—not since that first night. It wasn't as if he had had time. But now the curiosity to know what they contained roared up inside him.

If they contained a royal seal of the deposed monarchy, could the papers be the treasonous secret his father had tried to tell him about before he died? Had the assassins and vandals been searching for the papers? What could they contain that would justify the murder of his entire family? But Brion would have to read them to find out, and he hadn't known the language they were written in. For a moment, he considered showing them to Neahl and Redmond to see if they could read them, but he had promised not to reveal the secret to anyone. It was the last promise he had made to his father, and he would keep it.

Finola edged closer to the tent flap. Ithel was conversing with someone in quiet tones.

"You agreed to sell her to me at the Keldi," a man said. Finola recognized the low whine of the Holy Man's voice.

"I said I would consider it," Ithel said. "And you already have several wives."

"I don't want her for a wife."

"What then?"

The sounds of the sleeping camp filled the space left by Ithel's question.

"She is a bargaining chip," the Holy Man said. "That is all. The King will not forget the death of that child."

"You want to give her to the King to replace the girl you killed?"

"I didn't kill her." The Holy Man's voice rose in anger. "If the King wants his servants to live, he should beat them less. There was nothing I could do."

"If the King wants her," Ithel said. "I'll sell her to him myself."

A long pause followed. Finola leaned close, grabbing the cloth of the tent and twisting it in her hands. She knew that Ithel had hoped to sell her for a substantial profit at the Great Keldi.

"I will pay you well," the Holy Man said.

"Take another," Ithel said.

"She must be special. The King has to be satisfied."

"Emyr will sell."

"I have asked," the Holy Man replied.

"You didn't offer him enough," Ithel said.

Feet shuffled. "You will pay for this," the Holy Man said and the sound of his footsteps faded amid the tents. Finola rushed back to her sleeping mat as Ithel stepped in. She pulled the blanket tight as if its folds could keep her safe. Her worst nightmare was coming true, and there was nothing she could do to stop it.

Chapter 33
Discoveries and Danger

rion hadn't been in the market area for more than an hour when a commotion rippled through the camp. The word "slaves" filtered through the crowd. His heart began to race.

He hurried toward the center of the commotion. A long line of ragged men, women, and children staggered into the camp. They each had a rope around their necks that linked them all in a single file. Their hands were bound and the men had manacles around their ankles that clinked as they walked. The children stared around with wide, frightened eyes, while the men and women kept their heads bowed, their gaze on the ground. Brion searched each face with growing apprehension for any sign of Finola, Brigid, or Maggie. But they weren't there.

A wail rose up off to Brion's right. A woman rushed out of the crowd to snatch a girl up into her arms. Brion couldn't hear what she said, but he thought he heard the word "child." He watched in amazement.

These slavers were so brazen they would even bring a Salassani child they had captured in a raid to the fair where they must have known the child's parents would be waiting. The woman tugged at the child in an attempt to drag her from the line. The slaver shoved her away and pulled the child from her grasp. An argument ensued. It was clear that the woman demanded they release her child and that they demanded payment in return.

A tall, sandy-haired Salassani with elaborate wolf's head war paint came out of the crowd to stand beside the woman. For a moment, Brion imagined he was the father, but it soon became obvious that the woman didn't know him. He talked with the slavers and handed them a small bag of coins. They opened it and counted it before unlocking the girl from the chain. She rushed into her mother's arms. The tall, young man watched them for a moment before striding away. The crowd wavered and dispersed.

As Brion watched the woman and her child, he pondered on the savagery of a people who enslaved their own. Why wouldn't they just stop the practice like the Kings of Coll had done generations ago? Who did it benefit?

Brion looked away, absorbed by his abhorrence over this barbaric practice, when something flashed copper at the edge of his vision. He spun back to search the crowd. He was sure he had seen a copper head. He shoved his way through the throng toward the flash of color, but it had disappeared. Hours of wandering amid a maze of tents convinced him that it had been his mind playing tricks.

As he made his way back to the booths, the hair stood up on his neck and arms. He craned his neck around to find a man dressed in black standing in the shadow of one of the tents, watching him. A sword protruded from under his cloak. It wasn't the slave he'd met earlier. But somebody was watching him. Brion worked his way back into the crowd while circling back around to where the man had been standing. But the man had disappeared.

Twilight came early to the mountains as the sun dipped behind the snowcapped peaks. Nightfall found Brion picking his way through the woods to their little cave. He arrived first and sat alone, brooding over the day's events. First, the flash of red hair in the crowd and then the silent man who watched him. He was so nerved up by the time Neahl and Redmond came in together that at the sound of their approach he sprang to his feet and yanked his sword from its scabbard.

Neahl and Redmond stopped.

"Expecting someone else?" Neahl asked.

Redmond appraised him. "Taking it easy in camp, while we do all the work?" he said.

Brion shrugged, feeling stupid.

"Just surprised," he said.

Neahl smirked at him.

"Well *we*, at least, have been doing our job," Redmond said.

They sat around the cave, chewing on dried meat and fruit. They tried to avoid building fires when they didn't need them now that so many people were about.

"Any news?" Brion asked.

Neahl nodded and swallowed. "They're both in the camp."

Brion jumped to his feet, dropping his jerky in the dirt. "I knew it! I thought I saw a redhead in the crowd."

Neahl tore a loaf of bread in half. "I caught a glimpse of her in the market with a Salassani warrior. Finola's here, but her master isn't letting her out on her own. Apparently, she likes to escape." Neahl wiggled his eyebrows at Brion and ripped off a piece of jerky.

Brion grinned. That was Finola. She was the most stubborn person he knew when she had set her mind to something. "Let's go get them."

"Whoa, lover boy," Neahl said.

Brion flushed.

"We will, but we don't know where they're staying, and we have to work out the details. Did anyone hear any news of Maggie?"

They both shook their heads.

Neahl frowned. "I was afraid of this. I don't think we're going to find her."

"Let's not give up yet," Redmond said. He drank from his waterskin. "One more day and we should know where the girls are. If Maggie is going to be sold, she should be here tomorrow."

"And the King comes the day after tomorrow," Neahl said.

"Someone was watching me," Brion said.

"Yep," Neahl said. "Man in a black cloak wasn't it?"

Brion nodded.

"He's been watching us since we arrived," Neahl said. "That's one more reason we need to get on with this."

Emyr played with the hilt of his sword while Brigid avoided looking at him. The light of the morning sun fell on the east wall of the tent behind Emyr, giving the tent fabric a rich glow. Emyr cleared his throat.

"You know I'm not going to sell you," he said.

Brigid nodded and set her sewing down.

"I . . ." He paused and swallowed. "I want you to stay with me."

"Do I make a good slave?" The words came out before she considered them. Pain slipped across Emyr's face. He shook his head.

"I don't want a slave. I never did. I only took you so you wouldn't be killed."

"So, why not sell me, then?"

"Because I want you to stay with me, but not as a slave."

"I don't need a brother." Brigid passed a hand over her eyes.

"No, you insist on misunderstanding."

162

Deliverance

Emyr stood up and turned his back on her. Brigid picked up the roll of thread and began fiddling with it. She did understand him, and his awkward proposal startled and angered her. She picked up the sewing again and began twisting the thread around her finger. How could he expect her to accept the man who had destroyed her family—no matter how sorry he said he was? She opened her mouth to reply, but he faced her again.

"I know this is hard for you," he said. "I just want you to think about it. It doesn't matter what you say. I won't sell you." He lifted the tent flaps and strode out.

Brigid threw the roll of thread after him. It smacked the tent and fell to the ground with a soft thud. She was a slave and no matter how much he tried to pretend otherwise, she was in his power. He could do whatever he wanted with her. What if she refused? Would he free her? If he did, what would that mean? She had to live somewhere, with someone. She could always try and escape. But where could she go in these mountains? She had no idea how to survive or even which way to go. All she knew was that home was to the south.

Still, Emyr had come for her when she had been kidnapped. He had never treated her unkindly. He had a way of looking at her that made her heart beat faster. And what if Brion never came? Would it be so bad? Emyr would protect her. He would be kind to her. It was a far better option than what was available to all those women and girls curled up in the nasty stalls of the slave tent. What choice did she have? If Brion was really dead, she had no one to return to anyway.

Brion and Redmond stood before the stage, pretending to watch the midday tumbling act when Redmond elbowed Brion's shoulder and nodded to one side of the stage. Brion's heart leapt into his mouth. A surge of desperate relief flooded him. He stepped forward, but Redmond restrained him with an iron grip on his arm. Tears stung Brion's eyes.

He couldn't believe it. Brigid stood to one side of the stage, watching the same performance. She seemed older and maybe even taller. But she didn't have that starved and defeated look the other slaves had.

It was all Brion could do to restrain the desire to rush to her. He glanced up at Redmond, blinking the tears from his eyes. Redmond shook his head. Brion squirmed in an agony of anticipation. All those

163

months of waiting, hoping, and struggling, and here she was a few feet away from him, and he couldn't even speak to her.

When Brigid left the stage area, Redmond began easing through the jostling bodies. It wasn't hard to find Brigid amid the crowd of dark-haired people. Heads turned to follow her progress. Brion noted with considerable annoyance the interest of more than one young man. They followed her past the line of vendors and into the thicket of tents on the outskirts of the gathering. They hurried to keep up, but she soon disappeared. A few discreet questions from Redmond led them to the tent.

"Let me make sure she's there, please." Brion begged.

Redmond shook his head. "She doesn't know me. It's better that you don't give her any reason to act differently. It would be noticed."

"Please."

"No."

Brion dropped his gaze. He knew that Redmond was right, but it was difficult to let him go on without him. He bent to fiddle with his boot while Redmond approached the tent entrance. Redmond stood outside and clapped his hands in the Salassani way. Presently, an old woman parted the flap.

Redmond asked for directions. The woman spoke sharply to him and closed the flap. Redmond rejoined Brion, and they began to work their way back to the vendor's area.

"Well?" Brion whispered.

"She's there."

"What are we going to do?"

"Wait," Redmond said.

Brion cast one last agonized glance at the tent flap that separated him from his sister and followed Redmond. Amid the tables, Brion noted the tall Salassani who had paid to have the child released from slavery. He touched Redmond's arm and pointed him out.

"That's the one I told you about," he whispered.

Redmond said nothing. His gaze followed the young man with more than casual interest. Brion thought he noted some sign of confused recognition in his gaze.

That evening, they found Neahl checking his equipment. Brion could tell by the way he avoided looking at them that Neahl had news. Neahl waited for them to settle down and begin eating before he spoke.

"Find anything?" he asked.

"We saw her," Brion blurted. He had been bursting to tell him. "Brigid, I mean, we found her."

Neahl nodded. "I thought as much."

"Looks like she's the slave of an old woman," Redmond said, "though I saw a warrior's gear in the tent. I'm guessing the man who captured her still holds her. I don't know if he intends to sell her or not, but she looked like a permanent slave to me."

"Hmm," Neahl said. "The slave market doesn't open until the day after tomorrow. The gathering officially begins with a big feast. Tonight, plenty of alcohol will be flowing."

"Did you find any word of Finola?" Brion asked.

Neahl grinned as he wiped down his saddle. "I thought you would never ask. I spoke with her today."

"You what?" Brion leapt over and hugged Neahl.

Neahl pushed Brion away. "Restrain yourself," he said.

Brion's face suddenly burned, and he backed away feeling foolish.

"She was baking in a little shop in one of the camps to the west of the larger encampment. I bought a muffin. It was good."

"What did she say?"

"She said 'thank you' in perfect Salassani."

Brion collapsed back to the ground. "You mean she didn't recognize you?"

"Oh, she knew me," Neahl said. "But she has brains enough to keep silent and not let on. She lost her composure for only a second before she recovered."

He shook his head as he tossed Brion the oily rag and pointed toward his saddlebags. "That's some girl," he said.

Brion's insides began twitching and writhing. He grabbed the saddlebags and began rubbing in the oil. The girls were so close. He rubbed harder. Neahl smiled at him.

"What about Maggie?" Redmond asked.

Brion stopped rubbing and glanced around at them feeling guilty. He had forgotten about Maggie. He imagined Mullen's face when they told him they hadn't been able to recover his child.

"I don't think she's here," Neahl said. He set the saddle aside and picked up his own saddlebags. "In the last two days, I've examined every outlying camp, and I've checked the slave quarters. I've asked every slave dealer for a young Alamani girl and none of them have one." He shook his head. "I just don't think she's here."

"What are we going to tell Mullen?" Brion asked.

Neahl shrugged. "We'll tell him we tried. What else can we do?"

"I think we should act sooner rather than later," Redmond said.

"I agree. We can't wait for tomorrow. The King may be here by then," Neahl said.

"What's our plan then?" Brion asked.

"We go in tonight," Neahl said, "and we ride back the way we came. That road offers the quickest route to the plains, and it provides a lot of opportunities to ambush anyone who follows. The Aldina might know it, but the other Salassani aren't accustomed to using it."

Neahl smiled at Brion. "We slip in and grab them with as little noise as possible," he said, "and we slip out with no one the wiser."

"Sounds too simple," Brion said.

"It always does," Redmond said.

They spent the rest of the evening ironing out the details and packing their gear. Redmond disappeared, but came back a few hours later carrying half a dozen goose eggs. Brion watched Redmond poke a hole in each end and blow out the contents.

"What are you doing?" Brion asked. He noted that Neahl also watched with interest. Redmond raised his eyebrows dramatically.

"I'm cooking up a surprise for our friends down below."

"With an egg?" Brion asked.

"Yep." Redmond heated a mixture that smelled of sulfur and tar over some red coals, being careful not to spill any. While it was cooling, he plugged one end of the egg with a small, wooden plug. Then he carefully poured the mixture into the eggs and sealed both ends with wax. He set the finished eggs aside in a nest of grass. He then extracted four copper cones from his saddle bag, placed an egg in each one, and returned them all to the saddlebag.

Brion watched all of this with a growing sense that Redmond had lost his senses. "What are those—uh—things supposed to do?" Brion asked.

"You'll see. When it happens, you'll know."

Deliverance

Finola lay awake long into the night. She had seen Neahl. He had recognized her. If Neahl was there, Brion might be, too. She had nearly cried out when her gaze finally penetrated all the red and blue paint. But she had swallowed the scream, smiled instead, and handed him a muffin. He had nodded and winked. The hope that had drowned in her despair arose anew—hotter and more vibrant than before. They had come. They had finally come.

She knew he was planning a rescue. It could be tonight—or tomorrow night. How would they get out of the camp? Did Neahl know where Brigid was? Maybe they had already rescued her. Finola rolled and faced the tent flap.

Gilroy had become a regular feature at their evening fire. And the Holy Man had found her and watched her. He had tried again to convince Ithel to sell her to him. It was only a matter of time before one of them made a move. Neahl needed to come soon or it might be too late.

Finola slipped her hand under the wad of clothes she used as a pillow and closed her fingers around the knife. She always kept it close by just in case. She didn't know how to fight with one, but she had slaughtered many chickens and rabbits. It wouldn't be any different to slide a blade across the throat of one of those villains. She wasn't going anywhere with anyone without a fight, and she would rather die than be dragged away to be the plaything of some Salassani pig—even if he was a king.

Chapter 34
The Great Escape

The celebration began as the sun slipped behind the snow-capped peaks. The alcohol flowed freely, and the music and laughter rang through the clear, mountain air. Brion watched the dancers on the stage and the wild shadows they cast in the light of the blazing torches. He waited where he could see Brigid's tent, drew lines in the dirt with the toe of his boot, and fingered the hilt of his sword.

A metallic crash broke into the merrymaking, followed by a pause as if every Salassani in the valley held their breath. Then pandemonium erupted. Women screamed. Another crash created more confusion. Horses neighed. Their hooves beat the earth. The entire encampment awoke in a chaos of frightened people yelling and scurrying about. Brion heard the word "fire" over and over again. Somehow Redmond had made magic with those goose eggs. Now was the time. Brion wiped the nervous sweat from his hands and strode toward the tent.

His heart pounded in his ears. He had to force himself to breathe steadily and to walk slowly. Brion quietly poked the knife into the fabric of the tent, making a long slit. Voices came from within. A light flickered. Brion withdrew the knife. A man said something in Salassani he couldn't understand. He heard the clanging of metal. The flap flew back, and Brion caught a glimpse of the tall warrior hurrying toward the market with a naked sword in his hand.

Brion bent to peer into the hole and found himself staring at a knife. He blinked. Brigid watched him, but said nothing. Over her head, Brion could see the old woman standing at the flap.

"Brigid," he mouthed. "It's me, Brion."

He motioned for her to come.

Shock and then recognition flashed across Brigid's face. She jerked her head around to peer at the woman who stood with her back to her, peeking through the flap at the front of the tent. Brigid swung her head back to stare at Brion, wide-eyed. She hesitated, checked that the old woman still had her back to her, grabbed the cloak she had been sitting on, and stepped through the slit. Just as her back foot passed through, a cry came from inside the tent.

"Run!" Brion shouted.

They dashed through a cloud of smoke. Flames spread into the market area. People scampered about in total confusion. Someone called for water.

Brion chanced a glance back and found the old woman chasing after them. He cursed to himself. But he and Brigid were fleeter of foot. They zigzagged in and out of the crowd, leaving the woman behind them. She called for help, but her cries drowned in the sea of voices and chaos.

Brion dived behind an overturned table so they could catch their breath and get oriented. The tall warrior stood by the burning stage, craning to see over the crowd. He suspected something.

Brigid squeezed Brion's hand and pointed to the warrior. Brion nodded. He pulled Brigid along as they ducked behind the tables and tents. Brion glanced back to see the tall warrior pushing his way through the crowd—his gaze fixed on them. Fear gripped Brion's chest. He needed to reach the short bow concealed in the brush on the edge of the encampment. He didn't have time to get caught up in a fight. One arrow and he could get Brigid away.

He stopped behind the last tent to see if the warrior had gained on them. To his astonishment, the tall, young slave who had smelled of horse dung rushed through the crowd toward the warrior. At first, Brion thought the man was going to join the warrior in the chase, but he plowed right over the warrior as if he were in a panicked flight. The slave strode a few more steps after the warrior tumbled to the ground and then stopped, looked right at Brion, and waved a hand at him to run. Brion stared for just a second in open astonishment before he grabbed Brigid's hand and dragged her toward the trees.

When they reached the edge of the encampment, Brion checked to make sure no one followed. He retrieved the bow and led Brigid up the creek to where Redmond would be waiting for them. They would have to ride further up the lake to meet Neahl and Finola.

Finola awoke to the sound of screaming and the flash of a candle in the tent. Ithel had already buckled on his sword and was pushing the flap aside. He scanned the area outside the tent and dashed off towards the commotion. A thrill rushed over Finola. Now was her chance. If Neahl didn't come, she was going to make a break for it. Finola slipped on her cloak, stuffed a loaf of bread into her pocket and grasped the knife in her hand. Booted feet pounded past the tent. The chaos spread. She waited. Nothing happened.

Finola lifted the flap and peered out into the night. Shadows cast from massive flames danced and leapt on the walls of the tents around her. People hurried about. Screams and yells came from the market area. This wasn't the sound of celebration.

Then, she saw him. Neahl emerged out of the shadows and waved at her to come. The exhilaration stopped the breath in her throat. She rushed to meet Neahl. But the thrill of joy at this promising bid for freedom died as quickly as it had begun.

Neahl whirled to lead the way, but two warriors stepped into her path. An involuntary cry of fright escaped her lips. They caught her.

"Looking for some excitement, my pretty?"

The voice crawled up her spine. The two men jerked her around to face the Holy Man whom she now saw had been standing in the shadows of one of the tents.

"You really must wait for the King. You will make a pretty concubine."

Finola spat in his face and kicked out at him with her boots. If she could just get her hand on her knife. The Holy Man wiped the spit from his face and sneered at her.

"Take her to my tent," he commanded. "But don't injure her. The King will want her unblemished."

One of the men holding Finola jerked, gasped, and crumpled to the ground. Neahl's blade scraped as he yanked it from the man's ribs. The Holy Man's other warrior dropped Finola's arm and yanked his sword from its sheath. The Holy Man reached for her. Finola snatched her knife from her belt and raised it with a snarl to stab him to the heart. But he caught her arm.

Out of the corner of her eye, she saw Neahl deflect the warrior's blade. But she couldn't watch the fight. The Holy Man began to drag her away. She clawed at his eyes as she struggled to wrench her wrist from his grasp. Someone cried out behind her. A body fell to the earth.

An instant of quiet was followed by a huge fist that crashed into the

Deliverance

Holy Man's jaw. His knees buckled. Finola yanked her hand free. Neahl grabbed her wrist, and they sprinted into the darkness. As they sped away, the Holy Man began shouting in a garbled voice as if his jaw were broken.

Once they had entered the trees, Neahl stooped and picked up a short, recurve bow. He appraised Finola. She nodded, telling him that she was okay. He led her off under the canopy of pines. They hadn't gone far when Neahl crouched and pulled Finola down beside him. He placed a finger on his lips. Then he crept forward. Two men stood beside a saddled horse. One held its reins.

"This isn't a Salassani horse or saddle," one of the men was saying.

"Could be the traitors we heard about," the other man said. "Maybe they're here."

Brion found Redmond waiting with the horses.

"Everything go all right?" Redmond asked.

Brion nodded and pulled Brigid into a giant hug. Tears streamed down her face.

"I didn't know if you were dead or alive," she said. "I thought I would never see you again."

Brion held her, fighting back his own tears. He tried to swallow the lump in his throat. "I'm sorry it took so long." He cleared his throat. "But you're safe now."

"Not yet," Redmond said. "We need to get moving if you want that statement to come true."

Brion helped Brigid onto the horse and swung up behind her. They rode off into the night, leaving the sounds of commotion behind them.

Neahl nocked an arrow. Finola watched him wrap his thumb around the string, draw, and release. As soon as the arrow had left the string, he whipped another from his quiver and shot. The first arrow slammed into the man holding the reins. He grunted and fell sideways. Just as his companion realized what had happened, the second arrow buried itself into his back. He cried out in shock and pain. The horse shied away.

Neahl motioned for Finola to come. They sprinted to the horse. Neahl lifted her into the saddle. He bent, made two swift cuts with his knife

171

and sprang up behind her. Someone called out. Pounding feet crashed through the woods. Neahl kicked the horse into a gallop.

An arrow zipped past Finola's head. Neahl pushed her down close to the horse's neck and urged the horse to greater speed. Just as they broke free of the trees, Finola heard a slap. Neahl jerked. He cursed once and rode on in silence.

Two horses were waiting for them. Neahl didn't stop. He waved them on. But Finola recognized Brion and Brigid. Her throat tightened, and she blinked at the stinging of tears in her eyes. After all these months of waiting and hoping and fearing, here they were riding to safety.

Finola didn't recognize the other man who rode up beside them.

"You've been hit!" The tall man called over the sound of the galloping hooves.

"I noticed," Neahl growled.

"Stop and let me tend it."

"There's no time! They're following us. We've got to get them away from here."

"Neahl—" the man began.

"There's no time! There's a Holy Man back there raising the alarm and four dead Salassani to show them our trail."

Neahl let go of the reins with one hand and reached behind him. Something snapped and he tossed it away.

Just then shouts echoed through the woods. Neahl cursed again. Men on foot and on horseback materialized from the shadows in front of them, sprinting to cut them off.

To Finola, it seemed as if these men had been waiting for them. Arrows whistled past their heads as they thundered past. Neahl handed Finola the reins and swiveled in the saddle. His bowstring slapped. It slapped two more times before Brigid gave a cry of warning. Finola saw them, too. Six or seven horsemen bore down upon them from the front. They were trapped between two parties of angry Salassani.

Chapter 35
Betrayal in the Night

Brion spun his head around to see the new threat.

"To your left," Neahl shouted.

Brigid reined Misty to their left. They hurtled through the trees. Branches snatched and clawed at their bare skin and clothing. The riders in front of them veered to cut them off. Brion managed to get an arrow off despite the fact that, with Brigid sitting in front of him, he couldn't come to full draw.

"Take this," Brion yelled. He shoved his bow into Brigid's hand. His mouth went dry. Terror wrenched his stomach. Then, they were among the jostling horses and cursing men.

Brion yanked his sword free. A Salassani rider bore down upon them. Brion deflected the blow from the man's sword and flicked his sword into the man's throat. The Salassani gave a strangled cry and swayed in his saddle.

Brion kicked Misty on. The horse lunged and screamed and bit at whatever came within reach of her teeth. The cries and clash of battle filled the air. Neahl's battle cry rose above the chaos as he cut a path through the horsemen. Brion couldn't see or hear Redmond, but he didn't have time to look. It was all he could do to maintain his seat behind Brigid while fending off his attackers.

Brion lunged and parried. Misty spun this way and that. A glancing blow with the flat of a sword nearly knocked Brion from the horse. A hand grabbed Brigid and tried to drag her away.

"The redhead," someone yelled.

Brion spun to face the attacker. He blinked at the pain in his head as Brigid drove her knife into the man's arm. The man cried and let go. Misty plunged on. But a large man on a great, black stallion, whose clothes glinted gold in the darkness, barred the way.

"Stop," he commanded. He possessed the air of authority and spoke as if he expected to be obeyed. But Brion was crazed with terror for his friends and for himself. He would do anything to save them—anything to escape.

Misty plowed into the black stallion. Their swords clashed. Brion tried to break away but the man pressed him. Misty circled to face him, and then turned so that Brion could engage. The man was fast and careful. Brion had never faced such a skilled swordsman. Neahl and Redmond had trained him hard, but nothing could have prepared him for this man's speed and agility with the sword.

"Down," Brion yelled to Brigid as he pushed her down onto the horse's neck. He needed to get her out to the way, so he could maneuver more effectively.

Fear and doubt filled Brion's mind. This man was good. Maybe better than he was. The rider's blade nicked Brion's leg. Brion grimaced at the pain, but kept searching for a mistake or weakness he could exploit.

After another brief exchange, the rider dropped his sword point just enough to allow Brion to snap his own wrist up. His blade bit into the rider's shoulder. The rider bellowed. The sword slipped from his hand. Brion kicked Misty, and she lunged away toward the trees. Brion could hear the yells over the pounding of Misty's hooves.

"The King. To the King," they cried.

This confused Brion. Why would the King have been waiting for them? But he didn't have time to ponder it. He sheathed his sword and retrieved his bow from Brigid. Brion craned his neck around to see a single rider break from the melee. He tried to find Finola, Neahl, and Redmond, but the crowd of thrashing horses, cursing men, and clashing steel pressed in so close that he couldn't distinguish anyone amid the impenetrable shadows. He couldn't leave them.

Brion waited until Misty had galloped into the deeper shadows of a small ravine before he pulled her to a stop and backed her behind a thick patch of briars and vines.

"Are you all right?" he asked Brigid.

"Scared," she replied.

"Me too."

The pounding of hooves reached them before the shadow of the loan rider skipped between the trees. Brion raised the bow. He inhaled slowly to still his panting long enough to get off a clean shot. He aimed low preferring to hit the horse rather than miss all together. He held his breath and let the string slip from his fingers. The string slapped. The arrow leapt from the bow to disappear into the darkness. An instant of silence was followed by a thwack, the scream of an injured horse crashing and thrashing, and then silence.

Brion nocked another arrow as a shape lifted from the ground near the thrashing horse.

"Emyr," Brigid whispered.

Brion raised the bow. The shadow disappeared. More pounding hooves echoed through the wood. Brion hissed, and Misty surged into a gallop.

Three more riders pounded into the ravine riding up close behind him. Brion cursed. He had been stupid to stop—so overconfident or so scared that he wasn't thinking straight. Now he had let them catch up with him. But what of Finola and Neahl and Redmond? How could he leave his friends behind? Still, what choice did he have? He was outnumbered. If he went back, Neahl would curse him for a fool. But Finola? He couldn't leave her. Not now.

Brion gave the reins to Brigid again.

"Let Misty pick her own course," he said as he swung around to face their pursuers.

Now rage replaced the terror of battle. Rage at his inability to control what was happening to them and a rage at the Salassani for what they had done.

A slight figure clinging to the neck of the horse led the pursuit. The rider was inexperienced—maybe just a young warrior trying to earn his war paint. Brion raised the bow. The rider passed through a ray of moonlight that slipped through the canopy of pines.

Brion lowered the bow in surprise. It was a woman. It was Finola. His heart leapt and then fell. Why wasn't Neahl riding behind her?

Terror gripped Brion's stomach. Not Neahl. Not now. He canted the bow and aimed at the rider pressing close behind Finola. He would kill them all if he had to. They would not take Finola and Brigid again while he lived.

"Brion, no!" Finola cried.

Brion hesitated.

"Ride, you fool!" Neahl's hoarse voice rose above the pounding hooves. Relief flooded into Brion's chest making it hard to breathe for just an instant. He swallowed the knot that rose in his throat.

Now he could see that the third rider was Redmond. So he dropped the arrow back into his quiver, swung back around, retrieved the reins from Brigid, and gave Misty all the rein she wanted. She galloped for almost a mile before she slowed. Her hooves ate up the ground in a steady trot that never faltered. Mile after mile she worked her way through the darkness. The others followed.

After what seemed like hours, Redmond called them to a halt at a small stream. The night was dark under the canopy of pines. Brion slipped from his saddle and helped Brigid down.

"Is everyone okay?" he asked.

"I'm good," Redmond said. "Finola? Neahl?"

Neahl grunted. "We can't stop long," he said.

"I'm fine," Finola said.

The sound of her voice brought tears to Brion's eyes. He stepped over to where she stood watching him. He just stared at her, drinking in the face he had so longed to see. Even in the shadows, dressed in the trousers and tunic of a Salassani slave with her hair windblown, she was beautiful. A knot rose in his throat. A million things ran through his mind, but none of them managed to make their way to the tip of his tongue.

He reached out to grab her hand. She let him lift it before she pulled him into a tight embrace. Brion simply held her. It was enough.

"You're almost certain to get an infection now," Redmond said as he finished stitching up Neahl's wound. The bloody broadhead lay on a rock next to them. They had ridden through the night until they stopped to rest the horses in a bright, little glade surrounded by towering pines. A small dolmen had been erected by the ancients in the center of the glade. Three, wide, flat stones had been jammed into the earth and a fourth lay balanced on top. It provided them some shelter from the rising sun.

Neahl grunted. "The Salassani sure gave us enough time to treat our wounds, didn't they?"

Redmond smirked at him. "Maybe not, but when you're dying from an infection you can tell me if that comforts you."

"Anyway," Neahl said, ignoring Redmond's comment, "stealing the girls away was the easy part. Now we have to cross hundreds of miles of heathland with the entire Salassani nation hunting us."

Finola sat down next to Brion. "I'm glad you all finally came," she said. Then she scowled. "But what took you so long?"

There was accusation in her voice. Brion regarded her with amazement. Here they had just risked their lives to rescue them, and all she could say was, "What took you so long?"

"It wasn't exactly easy to find you," Brion said.

Finola slugged him. "We've been beaten and abused for months." She punctuated each word with a blow from her fists. "Forced to serve and wait on people who treated us no better than their dogs. I want to know what took you so long!"

Redmond smiled as he packed his medical bag. "I'm Redmond by the way," he said. "Brion speaks fondly of you."

"That won't work," Finola replied.

"Well," Brion tried again. "It's a long story."

Finola sat back and folded her arms. "I'm not going anywhere."

Redmond tied the bag to his saddle. "I am," he said. "And before you launch into your tale, make sure that you have everything packed up and ready to go in a hurry. I'm going to scout behind us. We can't afford any more surprises." He glanced at Finola. "I suggest that you get some rest, because when I get back, we're riding." He slipped his longbow from its protective sleeve, braced it, and pulled the quiver of arrows over his head. With a nod to Neahl, he mounted and rode back the way they had come.

Brion, Finola, and Brigid brushed and watered the horses before replacing their saddles and repacking their gear.

As Brion unsaddled the new horse, he gazed over its back at Neahl. "I'd like to hear how you ended up on a different horse," he said.

Neahl winked at Finola. "Finola pushed me off," he said. "She said I was so big I just got in the way."

"I should have," Finola said.

Brion waited.

Neahl shrugged. "It seemed like the best way to get Finola out of there. Besides, its rider no longer needed it."

"So you just jumped onto another horse?"

"Yep."

Brion shook his head. Neahl was impossible. Brion pulled his longbow out of its oiled canvas cover. He tossed the recurve aside, retrieved Neahl's longbow, and strung it for him.

As they went to sit down, Brigid picked up the recurve and tested it. She grimaced as she pulled the string to the corner of her mouth. Brion watched her.

"Wow! I can't believe you can draw that."

She let it down and shook her right hand. "It still hurts," she said.

Brion gave her a questioning glance.

"I'll tell you later."

Now Brion appraised her more carefully. "Hey," he said. "You're as tall as me."

Brigid's gaze flicked up to his head before a broad grin spread across her face. "Not your little sister anymore, am I?"

"Okay," Finola interrupted. "If you two are finished, I want to hear your reasons for leaving us in the hands of the Salassani for five miserable months."

Neahl gave a chuckle. "Before you get too heated, you need to consider what would have happened if Brion had gone after you alone or if he had gone before he was ready." He paused, giving her a moment to consider. She just raised her eyebrows in stubborn defiance. "He would have died," Neahl said. "He would have been killed if we hadn't prepared him. That's why we waited."

She rolled her eyes. "Okay, but what took so long?"

"I had a lot to learn," Brion said.

Finola gave him an irritated glance. "I'm sure you did."

"You're not the only one who's been beaten and attacked!" The words burst out of Brion's mouth as his frustration with Finola rose.

Finola simply stared at him in apparent shock and confusion before she cast him a withering scowl. Brion knew that he had just triggered a storm, and he rushed to head it off. "You try being trained by Redmond and Neahl," Brion said. "Their methods aren't exactly gentle."

All three of them turned to Neahl who grinned broadly. "We had to make it realistic," he said.

Brion hurried to tell her how Neahl and Redmond had trained him for four months and how they had been attacked three times while still in Wexford. He tried to avoid the more embarrassing moments of his training, but Neahl was more than happy to fill them in. Then Brion recounted their journey northward across the heathland.

When Brion told of his first real battle, Neahl cut in. "He did well," he said.

Brion paused. From any other person, he wouldn't have given the comment a second thought. But Neahl did not give idle praise. In fact, he had never praised Brion at all. Brion's cheeks flushed. Finola and Brigid exchanged confused glances. Brion hurried to finish his tale.

When he was done, Finola nodded. "Okay," she said, "but don't ever let me hear you compare being trained to fight to being a slave. There is no way you can understand what it's like." She paused and punched him hard as if for good measure. "And next time, you had better not take so long."

"There better not be a next time," Neahl said.

Brion gave Finola a helpless gesture as she launched into an account of her captivity. She didn't hide anything. She told them about the beatings and even pointed to the purple scar by her eye. Rage exploded inside Brion when she told how Ithel had mistreated her and how the Holy Man and Gilroy had competed for her. If he ever got the chance, he would punish all three of them.

When Brigid told about her second capture and Emyr's rescue, Brion bent to study her hand. It had healed nicely, though a jagged scar spread on either side. She seemed reluctant to talk about Emyr, but Neahl wanted to know everything about him. She told him how Emyr had saved her and that he had always treated her kindly. But even Brion could see that she was not telling them everything.

"You recognized him," Brion said. "Back in the ravine. You said his name."

Brigid reddened. "It *was* him," she said. "He's persistent."

Brion scowled, but Brigid plowed ahead. "I have to tell you something," she said. "Emyr told me that he had been paid to kill our entire family."

"What?" Neahl said.

"He said that papa had powerful enemies."

Neahl shifted in his seat with a grimace. "Your father had powerful friends. That's how he got his land. But I don't know of any powerful men in Coll that would want him dead."

"That's what he said," Brigid said with a shrug.

Brion raised an eyebrow at Neahl. "First the raid," Brion said, "then the assassin, the attack before we left, the High Sheriff, the Salassani who followed us into the canyon, the slave. I don't think those men we had to fight our way through last night just happened to be there."

Neahl frowned and nodded. "Agreed."

Brion rose to his feet. "Wait a minute," he said. "The assassin and the attackers at our cabin, they weren't trying to kill us. They were trying to scare us."

Neahl scowled. Brion persisted. "That assassin had plenty of time to shoot me if he had wanted to. And that ambush was a joke. They weren't serious."

Neahl considered.

"And we thought we were just coming to rescue the girls," Brion continued. "We've been played, Neahl. They never meant for us to get this far."

Neahl inhaled. "I think you're right," he said. "So let's prove them wrong. We'll get these girls home and then deal with whoever has betrayed us."

Thinking of his home reminded Brion of the promise he had made beside his parents' grave. He reached inside his shirt and drew out a delicate, silver chain. "I almost forgot," he said. He extended the necklace toward Brigid. "I brought this for you. I've been wearing it since . . . ." He swallowed. "I brought it for you."

Brigid reached out a trembling hand to take the necklace. Tears brimmed in her eyes. "They're both dead then," she whispered. She held the necklace tenderly.

Brion hesitated, afraid to tell her. He had had months to come to grips with the loss. But Brigid had spent that time hoping and longing that somehow they had survived. He nodded.

Brigid's tears spilled down her chin. Her face twisted in despair. "What are we going to do?" Her lips trembled.

Brion hugged her. "Go home," he said.

"Can we make it?" Finola asked.

Brion looked over Brigid's shoulder at Neahl, who blinked and nodded. Brion wasn't so sure. If Neahl took an infection, there was no way they were going to get him out of these mountains with the Salassani on their trail.

He released Brigid and lifted Finola's hand. "We have to," he said.

Chapter 36
Pursuit

The hairs on the back of Brion's neck rose. He became alert, listening for the normal sounds of the mountains. He had taken the watch to allow Neahl and the girls to get a bit of rest. Everything had gone quiet. A breeze blew in from the east, carrying with it the scent of rain. The sun had risen high into the sky where clouds as fluffy as lamb's wool hung suspended in the pale blue. Brion glanced at the horses. Misty had her head up. Her nostrils flared and her ears flicked. Her speckled flank quivered as she shuffled her feet. She had smelled something. Something was out there, and it was upwind of them. Misty gave the quiet purring sound she used to give an alarm.

Brion whistled the birdcall that Neahl had made him practice a million times. Neahl's eyes popped open. His gaze swiveled to Brion and to the horses. His hand crept slowly to the handle of his bow.

They waited until the pounding of horse hooves broke the silence. Redmond thundered into the clearing. His long, lanky form bent over the horse's neck, his cloak streaking out behind him. Neahl struggled to his feet, grimacing in pain. Brion leapt up and raced towards them. The girls sat up. Redmond gestured for them to mount.

"Aldina," he said panting. "Coming this way."

"Are they following us?" Brion asked.

"No, but they'll be here in a moment. I nearly stumbled onto them. They're very close. Hurry!"

Brigid mounted the extra horse Neahl had stolen in their nighttime battle, while Brion lifted Finola up behind him. He tried to ignore the thrill of having her arms wrapped around him. He wished he had time to savor it.

Neahl could still lift himself up into the stirrup because the arrow had injured him in his right hip. But he couldn't swing the stiff, right leg over the horse's rump. Redmond rode up to him and lifted it for him. Neahl's face drained of color, but he made no sound.

Just as Neahl found his seat, Misty neighed in warning. Brion spun in his saddle to see a huge brown bear lumber into the clearing one hundred paces away. It stopped, as surprised to find them in the clearing as they were to see it break from the trees. The image of Airic with his head in the bear's mouth leapt into Brion's mind.

Redmond's and Neahl's horses shied, but Misty gave another warning snort. Brion kicked her into a gallop. He had to get Finola out of there. The bear coughed and rushed after them. It was incredibly swift for such a large beast.

Brion couldn't believe that anything so large could cover ground with such speed. But it had angled to cut them off, and it was closing the distance. Still, they reached the edge of the clearing first. The horses slowed to pick their way over a narrow, rocky outcrop. Brion glanced back. The bear had almost reached them.

Four arrows flew at the bear. Brion had rushed his shot, so his arrow caught the bear in the foreleg. Two arrows slammed into its chest. The fourth, shorter, arrow pierced its eye. The bear roared, but checked its onward rush and rose up on its hind legs, wagging its head back and forth as it tried to dislodge the arrow protruding from its eye socket. Red froth flew from its mouth. Two more arrows buried themselves in its chest. It dropped to all fours, swatted the air with one massive paw and wheeled away from them.

At that moment, a cry rose up from the far side of the clearing. Brion spun around in the saddle to see half a dozen Aldina warriors emerge from the trees. They gave chase with loud, battle cries. Neahl cursed. Redmond hissed to his horse, which leapt into the lead. They had no time to consider what would become of the bear.

Brion kicked Misty up over the rocky outcrop just behind Redmond and into the widely-spaced spruce and pine trees that loomed over them. The thick canopy blocked out much of the sunlight. The air became cool under the pines, smelling of mold and decay. The pine-needle blanket muted the pounding of their horse's hooves as they loped like shadows through a forest shrouded in half light.

Fortunately, their horses had had several hours' rest. They rode them hard for a good mile while maneuvering to avoid the dense tangles of briars that filled the small hollows. They neither heard nor saw anything more of their pursuers until two of them appeared in the woods in front of them.

Deliverance

Brion cursed. The Aldina, who knew these mountains better than they did, must have guessed that they intended to take the pass and had sent these two to cut them off. The riders came at them head-on with bows raised. An arrow sped over Brion's head. He heard the hiss of the fletchings pass his ear.

Neahl raised his bow and canted it sideways but didn't check his horse. Redmond and Brion both followed his example. Another arrow flew wide of Neahl. The riders came on. Neahl released, followed by Redmond. Neahl's arrow grazed the front horse's neck and buried itself into the rider's leg. But the rider kept coming. Redmond's arrow dove over the second horse's head, plunging into the second rider's belly. He toppled from the saddle with a cry.

Brion aimed at the remaining rider who had now torn Neahl's arrow from his leg. He raised his bow. Redmond had taught Brion to aim at the horse's head. That way if the arrow flew high, it would strike the rider. If it flew low, it would strike the horse. Brion aimed for the spot between the horse's ears, waited for the pause in stride and released. The arrow flew true. It grazed the horse's ear and struck the rider in the chest. But just before the arrow struck, the rider loosed his own arrow. He toppled from his horse, clutching at the shaft.

The Aldina's arrow arced up streaking straight toward Brigid.

"Brigid!" Brion shouted a warning.

Brion watched in horror as it reached the top of its arc and begin to plummet toward her as if in slow motion. Brigid yanked on the reins, but her exhausted horse responded too slowly. The arrow grazed Brigid's leg and slammed into the horse's flank. The horse reared and bolted in a wild, careening flight.

Brigid cried out and clung to the horse's neck, like a rag doll caught up in a gale. The others followed.

After a terrifying ride through the wood, Brigid managed to get the horse under control. It stood blowing and quivering, its sides dark with sweat and stained with blood.

Redmond leapt from his saddle and helped Brigid down before he tied the horse to a tree and patted its muzzle, speaking softly in its ear. He gave it some water to calm it down before he attempted to examine the wound.

"Are you all right?" Brion asked.

Brigid nodded with wide eyes and windblown hair as Redmond examined the horse's wound.

"The arrow fell out on its own," he said. "Looks like it entered at an extreme angle. The wound isn't deep."

"Did the arrow hit you?" Brion asked Brigid.

She fingered a hole in her pant leg. "Just grazed my pants."

Redmond grunted and moved to tend to the horse. He sprinkled a red ocher powder on it, gave the horse more water and remounted.

Another three hours of steady walking brought them to the narrow valley that led up to the pass they sought. The rock-strewn path narrowed, forcing the horses to walk single file, picking their way over the numerous rocks and roots. The path remained narrow for a good mile before it opened up again onto a high bench. They came out onto the plateau and kicked their horses into a trot. But the horses were winded and soon began to stumble. Redmond's horse began to favor its right hind leg.

When they had crossed the bench and climbed up a steep embankment, Redmond called them to a halt. They dismounted. Neahl slid from the saddle and collapsed to the ground. His gray, ashen face glistened with sweat, and his hands trembled. Redmond made him drink the tea he had prepared earlier that morning, while Brion and the girls watered the horses and let them graze.

Brion caught Brigid smiling at him as he helped Finola down and then made sure she drank and ate before he did. He ignored Brigid. She had teased him about Finola for years. Brion checked Redmond's horse and pried a rock from the crevice of the hoof. He hoped this would keep him from going completely lame. When they came back to where Redmond and Neahl sat, they found them arguing.

"You've taken an infection'" Redmond said. "I'll have to drain it and clean it again."

"There's no time." Neahl scowled.

"It won't take but a moment. Sit down and shut up."

Redmond retrieved his bag and worked quickly while Neahl tried to get something to eat and drink. Redmond lanced the wound and drained the yellow pus. Then he washed it with brandy and applied the red powder. He finished, gulped down some water, grabbed a piece of dried meat, and helped Neahl into the saddle.

Soon they were riding again. The broken ground, the steep incline, and the exhausted horses slowed their pace. The forest of pine closed around them again.

They entered another narrow canyon. Great boulders rose up on either side of them. They rode on at a steady pace, stopping only to water the horses from shallow, swift-flowing streams. The ground became wet and slippery. The horses often stumbled. Brion had felt Finola's grip on his waist slacken. She was tired.

"They can't take much more of this," Brion said to Redmond.

"I know," Redmond said.

Brion read the concern on his face. "The Salassani will be coming, won't they?" Brion asked.

Redmond nodded. "They'll ride through the night if they have to—especially now that we've killed or wounded more than half a dozen of them and disrupted their most sacred gathering."

"They were looking for us," Brion said.

Redmond glanced at him.

"Those warriors we met last night expected us. They were between us and the pass—waiting. They knew we would be coming."

Redmond considered. "I think you're right—which means we have to expect more surprises." Then he let out a long breath. "Let's find a place to rest."

Brion understood that he meant a good, defensible place to rest. They came upon a large boulder that commanded a view of the trail behind them for a good one hundred paces.

They unsaddled the horses, and Brion and the girls brushed and watered them and then let them graze while Redmond tended to Neahl.

After he finished, Redmond came to Brion and pretended to help him with the horse. He whispered in his ear. "He needs rest. That wound is infected. Who knows what kind of filth they put on that arrow. The point punctured the bone. I don't think it broke it, but there's a good chance that it's cracked." He shifted nervously. "This riding must be causing him excruciating pain. I don't know how he's lasted this long. We can't stop, but if we go on, it could kill him."

Redmond's voice was filled with anxiety. Brion glanced over at Neahl. He sat against a rock, sipping at the cold tea Redmond had given him. He did not look good.

"Is he going to be all right?" Finola asked as she came up to them.

Redmond didn't answer.

They rested for a few hours before resaddling the horses and riding on.

Night found them near the end of a long, steep valley. They paused again for a couple of hours while Redmond treated Neahl. Finola and Brigid fixed a warm supper over a small fire.

Brion had protested at the fire, fearing it would attract the Salassani. But Neahl had insisted. "A warm meal in the belly is the best antidote to despair," he had said.

Brion relented, but soon discovered that a warm meal was no antidote to exhaustion. As the heat of the stew expanded into his belly, Brion let his head rest against the tree. One minute he was chewing, the next he was asleep.

He awoke with a start to the sound of voices and choked on the stew. When he recovered, he could finally make out what they said.

"I can't walk, and I can barely ride," Neahl said. "I'm slowing you down. You know it, and so do they. There are only four more behind us. I can stop them here and come after you once my hip has healed."

Brion sat up.

Redmond was shaking his head. "You know there's more than four coming after us. If we keep a steady pace, we can outlast them."

"You're not being realistic." Neahl replied. "We knew something like this might happen."

Brion stood up. Finola clasped his hand. He glanced at her. Her eyes brimmed with tears. Brigid sat with her head down, clutching the recurve bow. Her tangled red hair hid her face.

"Get me up to the top of that outcrop," Neahl said. "From there, I can hold off an army."

Redmond shook his head. But Neahl placed a hand on his arm. "I'm glad you came back when you did," Neahl said. "I couldn't have done this without you. Brion will need you now. Get them safely away from here." He paused. "I've nothing to go back to now anyway."

Brion swallowed hard, blinking rapidly. He understood that Neahl had chosen to die to give them the time to get away. He waited for Redmond to continue arguing, but Redmond dropped his head and turned to the horses.

In another half an hour, they rode on. Redmond and Brion had to physically haul Neahl into the saddle. His face burned red, and he continued to sweat.

An hour later, they reached the outcrop. When they found it, Neahl positioned himself so that he could see the trail for fifty paces in either direction, while a gnarled old tree shielded his body from view. They left him with two quivers of arrows and food and water for several days. He insisted that they take his horse so that the Salassani didn't get their hands on it and use it to follow them.

They lingered on the outcrop, fighting the need for speed and the desire to stay with their friend.

Finola approached Neahl first. "Thank you," she said. "I can never tell you how it felt to see you standing at my booth. I'll never forget you." She hugged him and then went to Brion. He wrapped his arms around her.

Brigid hugged Neahl, sobbing into this shoulder. She could find no words.

Brion let go of Finola and shifted awkwardly from foot to foot before he too hugged Neahl. "I don't know what to say," he said.

Neahl held him at arm's length. "You're your father's son," he said. "He would have been proud of you. Now get your sister and Finola safely out of these accursed mountains."

While the others remounted, Redmond approached Neahl. "I can't leave you like this," he said.

"You have no choice. Get them safely away, brother. That's all I ask."

Redmond bowed his head. Neahl grasped his arm until Redmond raised his gaze. Neahl stared into his eyes. Redmond nodded, mounted, and rode away.

A few hours before dawn, Redmond called Brion and the girls to a stop. They were halfway up the pass. The dark shadows of the mountains rose up on either side of them. The wind had picked up, bringing the scent of snow.

Redmond approached Brion.

"I can't do it, Brion. Not again. I can't leave him to die."

Brion swallowed. He had been waiting for this. He had seen the expression on Redmond's face. But to hear him say it now, high up in the pass with the descent and all of the lonely heathland still in front of them was almost more than he could bear. He felt as if a fist had grabbed his innards and had twisted them into a knot.

He had relied on Redmond and Neahl from the beginning, and now he would be on his own. He couldn't do it. But he had no choice. He couldn't ask Redmond to leave his brother behind again.

"I know," Brion said.

"You take the girls," Redmond said. "You know the way from here. Once you're out of the pass, head straight for Com Lake. If we can, we'll meet you there at the village. If you find yourself in real danger, there's a large rock that juts out into the lake just beyond the village."

Brion nodded.

"If you crawl down by the water, there's an entrance to a cave where you can shelter. It will hold four or five people. I'll look for you there."

Brion nodded again. Redmond grasped his hand hard. He struggled as if he wanted to say something, but no words came to his lips.

"We'll watch for you," Brion said as Redmond released his hand.

Redmond's determined expression told Brion that Redmond didn't expect to ever see them again. Redmond nodded, leapt onto the horse, and kicked it into a canter. Brion watched him clatter over the rise. When he turned, he found Brigid and Finola standing hand in hand watching him. Brion blinked back the tears and swallowed the lump in his throat.

"We should keep moving," he said, his voice thick with emotion. "We still have some hours before dawn."

Neahl listened to the sound of their departure until it disappeared into the night. He settled in to wait. It was strange how knowing he was going to die gave him an incredible feeling of peace. In some ways, dying would be a welcome release—a release from all the years of bitter guilt, shame, and hatred. He had never told anyone what had happened up on the high heathland when his beautiful, young wife, Cassandra, lay dying in his arms. The secret would die with him.

Neahl tried to stay awake, but he dozed fitfully. The sun had climbed well into the sky when he saw them—first one and then two. They skulked along the edge of the clearing below. Two dozen more appeared. He saw their horses just beyond the trees where they had left them. Apparently, the Salassani expected an ambush and had dismounted to inspect the pass.

Neahl recognized the tall Salassani warrior who had been Brigid's master. The careful way he moved and watched told Neahl he knew how to follow a trail and that he didn't take chances. The young man glanced up to the crag where Neahl lay hidden. Neahl read his mind. He was thinking that an attacker would select that spot to post an archer.

The young man paused and said something to the others. He was going to come on alone and check the pass. Neahl raised the bow. It was time to die. But he wouldn't die alone.

Neahl's arrow flew true. The man furthest back crumpled without a sound. Neahl had learned this trick from a Salassani years ago who had used it to hunt sage grouse high up on the Daven Fens. If you shot the one at the back, the rest would just keep coming. But if you shot the one in the front, it would spook the entire flock. Men weren't much different from grouse.

Three dropped before one of them cried out in pain. The others spun around to find their companions sprawled amid the grass still wet with the morning dew. After a few moments of confusion in which Neahl shot one more Salassani, they sprang into action. Some rushed the pass while others scrambled back to their horses. No one knew yet where the arrows came from. Neahl loosed again and another man fell. This time, he had been clearly visible on the outcrop.

Several men shouted and more of them rushed the pass. Neahl shot again, but the men were now alerted to his presence. Two of them jumped out of the way of his arrows. Then they were beyond his sight in the pass. He faced the approach. The tall warrior appeared, but when Neahl loosed an arrow, he dodged behind a tree. Soon other men began to appear in the trees and boulders around the outcrop. Neahl still had a commanding position and was protected by the tree and the boulder, but he had to expose himself to shoot. A couple of wild arrows flew his way. Horse hooves clattered on the trail below. Then the men rushed.

Neahl shot one more before they were too close. He dropped his bow and yanked his sword from its scabbard. His right leg would not support him so he leaned against the tree. An arrow pierced his thigh. He couldn't acknowledge it. Two men fell to his sword.

Horse hooves pounded down the trail. A terrible battle cry rang out. The men paused. Some spun to face the new threat. In rapid succession, two more fell with arrows through their bodies to writhe on the ground. Then the horse was among them. Steel flashed in the early morning light. The men scattered.

Emyr watched the charge and understood. The two warriors were giving the girls time to escape. They must have sent them on with the young warrior he had seen running away with Brigid. He gathered five men, including Ithel, and sped up the trail. He would let the others deal with these two, if they could. Brigid was his first concern. She was his only concern. But he suppressed a twinge of doubt as he jogged off up the trail. He was certain that he should know who these men were. He had wondered about them ever since Brigid had described the big man to him. She hadn't mentioned the tall thin one, but in his mind the two went together. Why?

Neahl watched Redmond leap from the horse and rush to reach his side. But a small group of Salassani formed to oppose him. Two of them stood their ground after the first few strokes, but the others fled. Neahl sank to his knees. Relief and panic swept over him at the same time. Redmond had come back for him. After all these years, he had come back for him. They would die together as they should.

A snarling Salassani launched himself toward Neahl. Neahl saw him coming through a haze of pain. He heard Redmond shout. He struggled to raise the sword. It had become so heavy. He watched the arc of the incoming sword slicing through the air as if in a dream. With a last great effort, he brought his own sword up to crash with his enemy's sword, but not with enough force to stop the blow. The Salassani's blade bit into his shoulder. Neahl blinked and swayed, but he swung his own blade in an awkward backhand stroke that disemboweled the man. The man screamed and clutched at the wound as if he hoped to keep his guts in. He fell sideways to roll off the edge of the precipice. Neahl swayed and fell into darkness.

Chapter 37
On Their Own

Brion staggered over the last rise and began the descent toward the heathland beyond. The gray light of evening had already settled into the mountain valleys and canyons that stretched out in front of him. The horses had given out hours ago, and they had had to lead them on foot up the narrow, rugged trail, stopping often to let them rest and graze. Brion needed the horses. He had to be careful not to overtax them. Even Salassani ponies could tire, despite their famous stamina. They had been running for three straight days with little sleep. The sky had turned a steely gray and drizzled rain upon them as if it were spitting on their despair.

He glanced back. Finola and Brigid stumbled after him with downcast eyes, their hair matted to their heads. He called them to a stop by a stream where someone had erected a small stone trough to collect the water. They let their horses drink and graze while they settled down to a quiet dinner of dried fruit and meat with some bread that Redmond had purchased at the gathering.

"My backside has never been so sore," Finola said.

"Mine either," Brigid said. "I think I prefer walking, at least for now."

Brion smiled despite the weariness. "You'll harden to the trail soon enough," he said.

"Uh, huh," Finola grunted over her mouth full of bread.

"What's your plan from here, Brion?" Brigid asked.

Brion glanced up at the dark clouds rolling in over the snowcapped peaks. Did he have a plan?

"That storm is going to hit us tonight or tomorrow morning," he said, "so we had better be as far down the canyon as we can get. I know a good spot to wait out a storm, but we have a long way to go to get there, and the trail is rough. I don't like the idea of trying it at night, but I don't think we have a choice."

"Do you think Redmond and Neahl have a chance?" Finola asked.

Brion swallowed his jerky. He shrugged. "If only four or five men come after us, then I'm not worried about them. But if any more come, I don't know. Neahl was weak, and Redmond is only one man."

"He'll come," Brigid said quietly. She slipped a slice of dried apple into her mouth.

Finola glanced at her. "Who?"

"Emyr," she said. "He's the best tracker in the village, and he's stubborn and dangerous. I've seen it. He'll keep coming."

"What are you saying?" Brion asked.

Brigid swallowed. "I'm saying," she said, "that he's as good as Neahl or Redmond or you at tracking and fighting. He'll see my rescue as an insult he has to avenge. I think he'll avoid Neahl and Redmond once he knows I'm not there. If he can go around them, he will. He doesn't take unnecessary risks. And he's cunning. I just think we need to be careful."

Brion considered her for a long moment, pondering what she had said. He knew that Redmond would either die defending Neahl or he would stay with him until Neahl died. Even if some Salassani got past him, he would read the weather and hope that Brion could get far enough ahead to escape their pursuit.

"Okay," Brion said. "You two get some sleep. I'm going to leave a surprise for anyone who follows us."

"What about Neahl and Redmond?" Finola asked.

Brion nodded. "I'll warn them."

The girls both gave him questioning looks, but he ignored them and went to Misty's side. He stroked her affectionately before moving back up the trail.

An hour later, he had managed to rig a snare that would send a man-sized boulder rumbling across the trail. He surveyed his handiwork with satisfaction. Neahl had taught him well. The thought of Neahl brought a crease to his brow. He couldn't escape the nagging fear that his protector and friend was back there somewhere, dying, sacrificing himself so that Brion and the girls might live.

He fashioned a wooden cross and placed it in a crevice so that Redmond would see it if he came up the trail. Redmond had told him once that in the southlands people used a cross as a symbol of death. Redmond at least would understand what it meant.

When Brion returned to the girls, he found Finola asleep, but Brigid had waited up for him. He sat beside her.

Deliverance

"Are we going to make it?" she asked.

Brion draped an arm around her shoulders and pulled her close. He remembered when she had once asked if they would be safe during a terrible thunderstorm when she was just little. She had that same expression of concern and trust now.

"I don't know," he said. "But I'm going to do my best to make sure that we have a chance."

Brigid nodded. "You need to get some sleep."

Brion shook his head. "You first."

Now Brigid shook her head. "I'm not as important as you. If you get so exhausted that you start making mistakes, we could all die. You sleep. I'll watch."

She held up the Salassani bow.

Brion gave her an approving nod. "Good shot by the way. Right in the eye."

"It was luck," she said. "I was aiming for his chest."

Brion laughed. "I missed too," he said.

Dusk the next evening found them wading through several inches of snow and chilled to the bone. Brion pushed them until they found Neahl's lean-to. The wind filled the canyon with low, mournful sounds that gave it the feel of a haunted graveyard. Brion left the girls to set up camp in the lean-to while he set another snare on the trail behind them.

By the time he came in, several more inches had fallen.

"Hungry?" Finola said from the far side of the fire.

Brion grinned. "Haven't had anything warm in, what, four days?"

"Well, it's just dried meat and vegetables," Finola said. "But it'll warm you from the inside out."

Finola volunteered for the first watch, and Brion gratefully rolled up in his cloak beside the fire. He awoke to the low moans of the storm to find Finola poking the fire back to life. Brion watched her for a moment before rising up on one elbow.

"How are you?" he asked.

Finola checked a tart reply. But she considered and bowed her head. "It was hard," she murmured. She threw some sticks on the fire.

Brion sat up. "I know," he said. "I'm sorry. We did the best we could."

"I know you did."

193

Brion sat next to her and held her hand in his. It was dry and warm from the heat of the fire.

She raised her head. Her eyes misted. "I'd given up hope, you know. I thought you had abandoned me—or worse."

"I'm sorry," Brion said again. "I tried to come after you once I learned that you had been taken, but Neahl made me wait. In the end, he was right. The Salassani would have killed me."

Finola nodded. "I know. But it was still hard." Then she told him about little Johnny. "I tried to save him," she said. "I'll never forget how he looked at me when they told us he would be going with the other men. It tore me apart." She blinked. "Then there was Clidna. She was a beautiful, innocent child. I'm afraid for her. That brute of a master might seriously injure her someday. When he does, nothing will be done to him, and Clidna will have to bear all of the blame."

"I wish it hadn't been so hard for you," Brion said. He placed what he hoped was a comforting arm around her shoulder. "I wish I could take it back; make it all go away."

Finola shook her head. "The beatings I could stand," she said. "But watching those little children suffer was the worst."

Brion pulled her to him. "We're going to make it home, Finola. I promise."

"I hope so, Brion," she said. "But even if we do, all those little children will remain slaves." Finola raised a hand to brush at a twig in Brion's hair. The gentleness in her expression made him want to pull her close again. She kissed him on the cheek and then pulled away from him and picked up her knife. "Once we get out of this weather, I want one of you to start teaching me how to use this thing. I'm *not* going to be captured a second time."

Brion raised an eyebrow. "I'm not sure I want to. You might decide to use it on me sometime."

"If you don't behave, I might," she replied with a wicked smile.

Brion watched as Finola settled into the quiet, rhythmic breathing of sleep. How he had longed to be with her. He resisted the urge to reach out and brush aside the hair that had fallen before her eyes. Brion could hardly believe that they were together, and yet, they were so far from home. Her safety rested heavily upon his shoulders. If she came to harm because of him, he would never forgive himself.

He sighed and pulled the oiled pouch that held his father's papers from his saddlebag. The curiosity to examine the papers had gnawed at him for days, ever since the slave had slipped him that little golden eagle. Someone had betrayed them. That slave seemed like the most likely culprit. But, if he had, why would he interfere when Emyr was chasing them? Maybe the papers would tell him something.

Brion set aside the notes his father had written to his mother and examined the seal more carefully. The blue wax had cracked, but the coat of arms of the Duke of Saylen was perfectly clear—a stag in a tear-drop shield. Brion unfolded the papers and bent to the light of the fire. To his surprise, he could read the writing. It was Salassani. Why hadn't he thought of that before? Brion studied the words, trying to make them out. But this was an official document with words and phrases Brion didn't know. Still, he understood enough.

What was his father involved in? A short letter used Weyland's name and said he would keep the secret. Brion came to the page with the drawing of the eagle. It was scratched in the margins of a sales slip for a baby boy aged six months. The paper was dated eighteen years before.

Brion's head reeled. His father's secret wasn't a ring and papers. It was a person. A royal baby from a deposed king sold into slavery, and his father was acting as a courier? For what? Now he understood his father's fear. If anyone in the Kingdom of Coll knew he had these papers, he would have been a marked man. And apparently someone did know.

The riddle of his parents' murder started to make sense. But if his father had been guilty of treason, so had the Duke of Saylen. And why send the Salassani to kill them? Why lure him and Neahl and Redmond into the heathland? Could it be possible that Brion had managed to get himself tangled in more than one plot? And who in all of this was betraying them? The Sheriff? The Duke? Who else could it be? As desperately as he wanted to return home, home now seemed like it might just be more dangerous than the heathland.

Two more days' descent, first through knee-deep snow and then over loose rock, brought them to a tiny lake. As they descended in elevation, the temperature rose. A few delicate, white, purple, and blue flowers began to appear beside the trail. Birds and squirrels chattered around them.

Spring had finally reached even these high glens, though it would have to wait to reach the high passes.

"Time for a lesson," Finola demanded each time they paused for a rest.

So Brion taught her the different ways to hold a knife and the most vulnerable spots on the body to attack.

"A knife isn't the best weapon in a fight," Brion explained, "because its range is short, and your options are limited. But it's a good last defense, and it's good for quick, sneak attacks. A knife can do far more damage than most people think. So remember this." He held up the knife and demonstrated his words. "A knife is most effective as a slashing weapon. Stabbing may seem more dramatic, but a slash across the belly or armpit is going to do far more damage and cause far more bleeding than a simple stab wound."

Finola nodded.

"The trick is to close the distance for your attack," Brion continued, "and escape before your opponent can respond."

Brion taught her one or two defenses against common attacks, and they practiced these at each rest stop. Brigid taught her how to slash and how to dash in and out quickly. The lessons meant that none of them rested much during their breaks. But it did help to ease the tension and to keep their minds off the friends they had left behind and the enemies who may be following.

By the time they reached the crystal lake nestled between two cliffs in a long valley, the moon had risen high overhead, casting weird shadows amid the trees. They led their horses down the sliding shale into the valley. The moonlight glistened on the water in a quiet magic that made them all stop to watch it for a moment.

Finola leaned over to whisper into Brion's ear. "It's beautiful. I wish we could stay here for a while."

Brion squeezed her hand. How many times had he imagined being alone with Finola in just such a setting?

They settled in for a few hours of sleep, curled up in their cloaks and blankets for warmth. Brion took the last watch. He wanted to explore the trail behind them for any sign of pursuit. He had become so accustomed with Neahl and Redmond to have scouts out checking their trail that he felt as if he were blundering through the pass blind. He had to know.

Brion set off with his bow and quiver of arrows and his father's short sword strapped to his back beside the quiver. He couldn't afford to have it at his side getting tangled in the bushes. The sword was short enough that he could still unsheathe it. The girls knew to be ready to ride at first light. He would be back by then.

Brion shadowed their trail, doing the best he could to leave little sign and to make no noise. The moon had gone, but the diffuse light of morning filtered into the mountain pass. He had traveled less than an hour when a quiet sound caused him to duck behind a rotting stump and freeze. He crouched in a dense stand of mixed pines and birch on a long plateau where he had explored away from the trail in case their pursuers had avoided the main path.

The sound had been ever so soft, but it didn't belong. He searched the wood. The sound came again off to his left. A flash of red appeared through the trees not twenty paces away and then the swish of a horse's tail.

Someone was moving through the woods on horseback. Brion realized how foolish he had been. He should have kept running. This Salassani either knew or suspected that he was there. Why else would he take such care when he was in pursuit?

As Brion scanned the trees, the form of the man on horseback materialized from the chaos of the undergrowth. He passed behind a tree and stopped. Brion seized the opportunity to kneel behind a large rotten stump, hoping to conceal his shape. The man kicked his horse to the next tree.

Brion slipped his fingers onto the string. The Salassani passed behind the fork of a large birch. Brion drew. The Salassani stopped with his head and shoulders exposed in the fork of the two great branches.

Brion pulled his back muscles taut, kept the arrow in his peripheral vision, focused on the man's ear, and released. A mere fraction of a second passed between the quiet thrum of the string and the impact of the arrow. But it had given the man time to turn towards the noise. The arrow caught him in the eye. He slipped from the saddle without a sound. His horse shied and bolted, dragging the injured man for a short distance before his boot slipped free of the stirrup.

Brion nocked another arrow, but remained crouched behind the stump. He had expected more men to rush forward. But after the Salassani's death struggle ceased, silence descended over the wood. Nothing stirred.

Brion tried to control the tremors that always overtook him after a real fight. He didn't have time for it. He crept to kneel beside the dead man.

The bile rose in his throat. His arrow had passed clean through the back of the skull. The fletchings showed where the eye should have been. Brion tried to swallow. He wanted to just leave the man as he was, but he knew he couldn't afford to lose the arrow. He didn't know how many he would need before this was over.

So he fought down the sickness that kept rising in his throat, rolled the man's head to the side, and pulled the arrow the rest of the way through. He cleaned it as best he could with the man's cloak before dropping it back into his quiver. He rose and scanned the area one last time, trying to decide if he should go after the horse. But he didn't have time. The girls were in trouble. He rushed back the way he had come.

Brion raced through the trees, cutting directly over land without bothering about the trail. He needed speed now. Why had he been so stupid? Why had he left the girls? He had wasted valuable time. He came back to the trail at the narrow cleft that led down to the lake. He glanced down and stopped in shock. Distinct hoofprints had appeared on the trail Brion had checked not more than two hours before. Brion jerked his head up, scanning the trail as far as he could see in front of him. He scrambled down the cleft and over the loose shale.

Brion reached the flatlands surrounding the lake and was sprinting through the trees when a cry echoed off the canyon walls. Finola. It had been a cry of warning. He lengthened his stride, racing with all his speed. The brown grass whipped at his legs. Branches tore at his face.

As he came through the trees, he saw Brigid standing by the lake with the bow drawn. A Salassani man sprinted toward Finola and the horses. Brigid released. The arrow caught the man in the thigh. He stumbled and fell, but rolled to his feet. Finola stood with her knife drawn.

Brion nocked an arrow and paused to shoot. His arrow grazed the man's head. As he whipped another from his quiver, he saw the ripple in the grass not twenty feet from Brigid. He spun and released an arrow at the spot without taking time to aim. Someone cried out. Brigid saw where Brion's arrow had gone and aimed her own bow in the same direction. Her arrow flew. A man rose up with a cry from the grass to rush her. Brion dropped him with an arrow in his side. Brion whirled back to Finola. The man had reached her. Brion sprinted toward her, desperate to reach her in time. He couldn't risk a shot with the man so close to her.

Something shifted in the grass to his right. He tried to check himself and turn to face it, but he was too late. The man slammed into him. They fell in a tangle of arms and legs. Brion released his grip on the bow. His hand sought his knife, and he drew it out as he drove his elbow into the man's chest. The man grunted and slacked his grip. Brion brought his fist up into the attacker's chin and kicked himself away. He rolled to his feet, sweeping the sword from its sheath in the same instant. The man rose and drew his own sword.

Brion faced the young man who had been Brigid's master. Anger rose up in him like he hadn't felt since the raid had left him orphaned. Here was the man responsible for it all. Brion crouched and began to circle. Today was a good day for revenge.

Chapter 38
The Battle of Crystal Lake

inola stood her ground as Ithel hobbled toward her. The broken arrow protruded from his thigh. Blood dribbled into his eyes. She was finished running. If she could, she was going to even the score right here and right now.

Ithel's face twisted in an awful grimace. "You little witch," he said. He cocked back his fist to punch her the way he used to, but this time he meant to hurt her. Finola could see it in his eyes.

She ducked and slashed at him with the knife. His fist glanced off the top of her head as he twisted to avoid the slashing blade. She lost her balance and stumbled sideways. He lunged to grab her. She regained her balance and held up the knife. Ithel read her intent at the last moment but couldn't avoid it. The knife slashed a long wound along his hip. He roared, grabbed her by the throat with one hand and shook her. His other hand clamped on the hand that held the knife. "I'll kill you," he said through gritted teeth. "You've been more trouble than you're worth."

He squeezed. Finola struggled. Her eyes felt like they might pop from their sockets. Her lungs stretched to the point of bursting. The world began to grow gray. He was squeezing the life out of her. He was going to kill her like he had promised all those weeks ago when she had first runaway. And she couldn't stop him.

Ithel grunted. His grip loosened. His eyes opened wide. Air rushed into Finola's lungs. She twisted her hand free from his grip and slashed upwards at his armpit the way Brion had taught her. She slashed down across the side of his throat before she scrambled away.

Blood sprayed her face as she ducked to avoid the swinging fist. Ithel staggered after her, one arm dangling uselessly. Finola saw the arrow buried in his side. She looked around to find Brigid nocking another arrow. Behind Brigid, Brion was locked in combat with Emyr.

Ithel staggered to his knees. He reached a bloody hand toward Finola and whispered something before he fell headlong into the grass. Finola's

200

knees trembled. She started toward Brigid, but Brigid had whirled away and rushed toward Brion and Emyr, shouting Brion's name as she sprinted through the tall grass.

Emyr faced the young man he had followed for days. Now that he saw him, he realized that he must be Brigid's brother. This was why he hadn't simply killed the young man from his hiding place, as he could easily have done. The young man had been distracted. He could have cut him in two with one stroke of his sword. But something had stopped him. Now he realized that it was because he had believed that the young man was Brigid's brother all along. Brigid was rushing toward them, screaming the name of Brion. Emyr knew he could not kill Brigid's brother. If he did, he would lose her forever. But he did need to survive.

Brion's eyes filled with hate and anger. Emyr understood it. He would have felt the same. Brion feinted with the sword. Emyr parried it and jabbed with his own. Then Brion came in. His attack was swift and well-executed. Emyr found his skill sorely tested just to keep the blade from his own chest.

He stepped sideways and brought up his foot in a powerful classic Salassani kick that Emyr had found to be effective. Brion backstepped and brought his elbow down on Emyr's ankle. Emyr backed out, trying not to limp at the terrible pain.

Brion was good. He had been well-trained, and Emyr had underestimated him. Brion came in again, this time with two quick feints. Emyr sidestepped the incoming knife just in time. He counterattacked but landed only one kick. It glanced off Brion's thigh—not enough to slow him down.

They separated, each panting from the exertion. Emyr needed Brion to make one mistake—just one. They exchanged several more blows, the metal ringing in the quiet, morning air. They circled and exchanged blows again. Brion never let Emyr inside his defenses, and he was skilled at penetrating Emyr's. Still, Emyr managed to keep him at bay.

Emyr feinted to the right and attacked in an upward slicing blow that had disemboweled more than one opponent. But, to his dismay, Brion was already there with a strong sword stroke deflecting Emyr's blade into the dirt. Brion kicked his foot up in Salassani fashion, catching Emyr in the groin. Emyr grunted as the young man sliced a wound across the back of Emyr's sword hand. Emyr momentarily lost feeling in the hand. The sword slipped to the ground.

Brion stepped in, bringing in a powerful elbow strike to Emyr's nose. His nose broke with a loud crack and a burst of pain. Emyr stumbled backwards, tears blurring his vision, blood spurting everywhere.

Brion sprang forward with a cry of victory. He raised the sword.

"No! Brion, no!"

The cry broke through the cloud of battle. It was filled with desperation and terror.

Brion paused. Emyr ripped the knife from his neck sheath and rolled to the side coming to one knee. Brion watched him, his sword prepared for the killing stroke.

Emyr spit the blood from his mouth and wiped at his eyes.

Brigid ran up to Brion.

"It's him," Brion growled, never taking his gaze off of Emyr. "He killed our parents."

"No, he didn't, Brion. The others did."

"But he was there. He kidnapped you and made a slave out of you."

"I know." She laid a hand on his sword arm. "But he also saved my life. I don't want you to kill him."

"Brigid," Brion began. "You don't understand."

"I understand more than you think. And I know him better than you do. Let him go, Brion." Tears trickled down Brigid's cheeks.

An agonized expression twisted Brion's face. He shook his head. "I can't, Brigid. I can't. He deserves to die."

Finola stepped up to Brion and touched his arm. "It's okay, Brion. Brigid's right. Let him go."

Brion hesitated. "He'll come after us."

"No, he won't," Brigid said. She leveled her gaze on Emyr.

Emyr saw his opportunity and accepted it. He straightened and raised his hands in a submissive gesture. He saw the tears spring to Brion's eyes.

"You can't ask me to do this," Brion said.

"I will go," Emyr said. Emyr kept his eyes on Brion as he picked up his sword. Then he turned his back deliberately and strode away. Unless he misread this young man, he would not kill a man from behind. Still, he forced himself to continue walking without looking back, half-expecting the pain of an arrow in his back. But nothing happened.

Deliverance

Brion watched Emyr go, resisting the desire to separate his head from his shoulders with one slash of his blade. He stood with his sword in one hand and the knife in the other, grinding his teeth, trapped in indecision as his enemy simply strolled away.

The revenge he had sought for so long had been stolen from him by his own sister. And by letting this man escape, he had guaranteed that they had to keep running. Or worse, he had ensured that they would not escape at all. He had been so foolish.

Blood trickled down his arms from the superficial wounds he had received.

Brigid hugged him tight, tears streaming down her face. "It's over," she said.

Brion pushed her away. "No it isn't." He glanced at Finola, whose brow wrinkled in concern. His gaze ran over the droplets of blood on her face and clothes. He stepped toward her, suddenly terrified that she had been injured. "Are you all right?"

Finola nodded.

"Are you sure?" Brion reached up to wipe the blood from her face.

Finola grabbed his hand and squeezed it. "Thank you," she said.

Brion was confused. "For what?"

"For being more than a vengeful killer."

Brion stared at her. Is that what he had become? Was he becoming like Neahl, driven to kill to avenge his parents? He didn't know what to feel. But he couldn't escape the nagging doubt that he had made a terrible mistake in letting Emyr go. "Then let's go," he said.

Now Finola looked confused. "Why?" she asked.

"Because we don't know how many more will come." He waved a hand to where Emyr had disappeared into the trees. "He'll be back with more."

They had paused in their descent beside a brilliant waterfall that spilled down the rocks from the lake above. Thousands of white rivulets trickled down amid the colorful lichens creating quiet music. The scene jarred Brion's nerves because it was too pretty, too pure. They had just fought a desperate battle, and he hadn't done what he set out to do. He had failed again. But this time he had failed because Brigid and Finola had stopped him. Why would they do that? After all their talk of how awful it had been to be slaves, how could they just let the man responsible for it all walk away?

"I've never seen anything more beautiful," Finola whispered as if she were afraid of spoiling the scene. When Brion didn't reply, she glanced over at him. "Are you all right?" she asked.

He nodded and kicked Misty into a walk. They rode on for hours, dismounting when they needed to rest the horses, but never stopping their descent through the mountain canyons.

Nightfall found them camped beside the stream fed by the crystal lake. The wind blew down the canyon so Brion risked a fire. He had killed two rabbits with his bow earlier that evening, and they settled in for the first roasted meat they had had in days.

Brion tried to ignore the fact that Finola kept watching him and exchanging knowing glances with Brigid.

After they had eaten, Finola finally spoke. "Talk to us."

Brion ran the wax down his bowstring and paused. He didn't look at them. "Neahl and Redmond are probably dead," he said.

"Why do you say that?" Brigid asked.

"Because that many Salassani couldn't get past them if they were alive." His anger and despair rose as he talked. "Without them to guard our backs, more will come, and they will have this Emyr fellow to guide them." He waved his hand in a gesture of disgust.

"He won't do that," Brigid said.

"What?" Brion paused in his waxing.

"I know him. He won't lead any more Salassani after us."

"You spent days telling us how determined he was, and now you expect me to believe that he'll just give up? We just let the man responsible for this entire stupid mess walk away, and now he has been humiliated. You don't think he's going to seek revenge?"

Brigid shook her head. "Listen to me, Brion," she said. "I understand how much you and Redmond and Neahl sacrificed to rescue us. But I lived in Emyr's house for almost five months. I watched how he behaved. He told me himself that he wasn't Salassani, but a slave who had been adopted. I'm sure that now that he knows you're my brother, he won't come after us."

"You can't know that." Brion threw the wax into his bag.

"Listen," Brigid continued. "He apologized to me more than once for leading that raid. When he saw that Papa was a cripple, he tried to stop it. The best he could do was save my life. When one of the men challenged him about it, he killed him instead of me."

Brion gaped at her. "He apologized? Ah, well, that makes everything better, of course."

"No it doesn't!" Brigid yelled coming to her feet. "Stop being such a useless toadstool. You can't say that he killed our parents because he didn't. I was there. I saw what happened."

Brion studied her for a long moment, clenching his jaw in anger and confusion. He picked up a rag and began oiling his bow. "Why are you so keen to defend him?"

Brigid dropped her gaze and sat down. "Because I know him. I know what kind of man he is. He's not like the others. He's not like Ithel."

Brion studied her. Her answer didn't satisfy him. There was more that she wasn't telling them. He wanted to check their back trail to be sure Emyr wasn't trailing them, but after the ambush by the lake, he didn't dare leave the girls alone again.

Two days later, while they prepared to stop for the night beside the crumbling ruins of what looked like a hunting shack, Emyr appeared silhouetted in front of a large patch of white aspen trees a hundred paces away. Brion raised his bow to shoot. Emyr disappeared. Brion began to race back up the trail when Brigid called him back.

"Wait, Brion."

Brion stopped.

"If he meant mischief, he could have worked it by now."

"I can't *believe* you," Brion said. "What do you want me to do?"

"Let him alone."

"Why?"

Brigid shook her head. Tears brimmed in her eyes. "I don't know. I just don't think he's a threat anymore."

Brion watched her, trying to understand what was going on in her bright, red head and returned to his place by the fire.

Each morning after that, Emyr either showed himself or left them an offering of rabbits or grouse that they would find just outside their camp in the morning.

"He's playing with us," Brion said.

"He's keeping us fed," Finola said.

As they reached the end of the pass and entered the long, narrow canyon that led to it, the pines and aspens began to thin. The junipers and cedars replaced them. A few patches of small, scrubby heather began to appear. Some were already flowering in delicate white.

A thunderstorm that rocked the earth that night with the crash of thunder and split the sky in brilliant, blue flame changed the entire landscape. The torrent of rain soaked them through and roared through the gullies. Overnight the heathland blossomed. As far as they could see the next morning, patches of blue, white, red, and purple heather had sprouted up. Flowers of every kind dotted the landscape.

"I thought I would never see anything as beautiful as that waterfall, but this . . ." Finola paused.

"I never knew anything like this existed in the world," Brigid said.

The wild heathland called to Brion. He wished for just a moment that he could shrug off the terrible burden of responsibility that rested on his shoulders and wander the hills and valleys with Finola by his side. Just to see what was there, what new surprises the wild, untamed land held. But he couldn't. Not yet.

Two nights later, Brigid sat the last watch with her back to an old, gnarled cedar. She breathed in the rich aroma of the tree and stretched as she watched the faint glow just beginning to peek through the darkness to the east. She held the Salassani bow in her lap with an arrow nocked on the string. But her mind wandered over the last several months. So much had changed. What would she and Brion do when they finally returned home? Could they manage the trap lines by themselves? If not, what would they do? Sell the land? And go where?

She felt the presence before she heard the sound. Her muscles stiffened. She gripped the bow, preparing to give the alarm. An arm encircled her from behind pining her to the tree. The rough bark pushed into her back. A hand found her mouth before she could scream a warning. She struggled until a quiet voice breathed into her ear.

"Shh. It's me, Emyr."

Brigid relaxed. The hand came free, and the arm released her.

Emyr sat beside her with his arms around his knees. He gazed out towards the coming dawn.

"What are you doing?" she whispered.

"I was just lonely," he said.

"You better not let Brion catch you here. He doesn't trust you."

"There's no reason why he should."

"Why are you following us?"

Now Emyr looked over at her. "I thought you'd know."

A tingle rippled through Brigid's belly. She did know, but she had been working hard not to think of it. For days, she had been struggling with the guilt of knowing that she could never form a relationship with the man that had ruined her family while she secretly hoped he would come for her like he had before.

Emyr read her silence and looked away. Brigid felt confused. She knew he had misjudged the turmoil that rolled around in her thoughts and in her heart, but she didn't know how to explain the contradictory rush of emotions his appearance had created.

"Thanks," she managed.

"For what?"

"For bringing us food and for not killing my brother."

"You know as well as I do that he could have killed me."

"But you could have killed him when you surprised us. Why didn't you?"

Emyr shrugged. "It felt wrong."

"What are you going to do?" Brigid tried not to look at Emyr. She didn't want to see his expression.

"Don't know. That depends on you."

Her cheeks grew warm. She hoped he couldn't see it.

"Well, I had better shove off before Brion wakes up," Emyr said.

He stood. Brigid reached up and grabbed his hand. "Come again," she whispered.

A smile slipped across Emyr's face. He nodded and melted back into the shadows.

Chapter 39
Unlikely Rescue

rion kept running, day after day, convinced that the entire Salassani nation now hunted them. Their Salassani ponies proved that their reputation for endurance was well deserved. Some days they were able to put thirty miles behind them. While others, the pace was much slower as they maneuvered to avoid the main trails and Salassani patrols.

By the signs left in the dirt, it appeared that every Salassani in the heathland was on the move. New trails crisscrossed the heathland. Flocks of ravens following war parties, and clouds of dust appeared with frightening regularity on the horizon. The entire heathland crawled with Salassani. He hoped that all of this activity had not been caused by their little rescue.

That thought gave him pause. He kneed Misty over to where Brigid rode at a steady walk.

"Brigid?"

"Hmm?"

"Why wasn't Papa in the village?"

"What?"

"On the morning of the attack. He told me he was going to the village."

Brigid frowned in confusion. "He never went to the village. After you left, he told me to stay inside and help Momma, and he got his sword. He was outside when they came."

Brion puzzled over this surprising news. His father had lied to him and sent him away from the cabin on a job that would have taken him all morning. "What did Momma say?"

Brigid pondered. "She kept looking at the door, and she said, if anything happened, I was to go out the back window and hide."

"They knew," Brion said. "That soldier that was speaking to Papa must have told him something."

"But if they knew, why didn't we all just leave for the day?" Brigid asked.

Brion shook his head. "I don't know. And why wouldn't Papa warn Neahl?"

"What are you suggesting?" Brigid asked.

Brion frowned. "I don't know. But something isn't right with this whole thing. Momma and Papa knew something. Maybe they just didn't know what day the attack would come."

Brion shook his head. If his father were involved in treason over this royal baby, why wouldn't he try to get his family out of harm's way? Why would he wait at the cabin, unless...

"He didn't think they would attack us," Brion said.

Brigid stared at him. "But he had his sword."

"Papa wasn't a fool," Brion said. "If he thought you and Momma were in danger, he wouldn't have left you there. I know he wouldn't."

"Then why did he get his sword?"

Brion continued as if she hadn't said anything. "He thought they were coming to get something, not to kill us."

"What? What would they be coming to get?"

Brion studied Brigid. He almost told her what Weyland had said to him the night before the attack. He almost told her about the ring and the papers. His father had been wearing the ring. Had he thought they were coming for the ring?

"A secret," he said. "Papa was hiding a secret."

That night after Brion had delivered the watch to Brigid, he awoke to the sound of whispered voices. His eyes popped open. Brigid's shadow perched between the tree and the rock. But another shadow folded itself into a mound beside her. Brion's fingers closed around his bow. The voices drifted to him on the still morning air.

"It's a beautiful night." It was a man's voice.

"What do you want me to do, Emyr? I mean, my brother risked his life to save me, and my father's best friends probably died doing it. Both my parents are dead, and it all happened because you led a raid on our family." Brigid's voice choked. "What do you want from me?"

Brion listened to the long silence.

"Your forgiveness."

A boot scratched against stone and the shadow unfolded itself. "I love you, Brigid. I'm sorry for what I did." The shadow slinked away, but stopped. "You need to warn Brion to be careful. The heathland is crawling with Salassani. I've never seen anything like it. King Tristan is massing an army from all the tribes." He paused. "And I think someone might be following your trail. I'll stop them if I can." Then his shadow melted into the gray of the coming dawn.

Brion ignored Brigid at breakfast. Her betrayal of his trust could not be forgiven—not when she so callously risked their lives. It was a good thing he hadn't revealed the secret he had been carrying with him all these months. But he said nothing to her because he couldn't decide how best to handle it.

His anger was soon forgotten, however, when later that day he spied a group of horsemen. He lay concealed on the top of a rise, amid the remains of an old watchtower from which he examined the ground he planned to travel. The horsemen were riding hard and riding straight toward them.

Brion scrambled down from the rise and leapt onto Misty's back. He gestured for the girls to follow him as he galloped down the valley to a stand of mixed birch and cedar that hugged the slope.

He hurried the girls into the trees. They dismounted while Brion rushed back on foot to do what he could to erase their trail. He had barely returned to the thicket when the first galloping horse pounded into the valley. They held their breath as a dozen riders thundered past them.

Brion led them southwest away from the riders and toward the Aveen Mountains that loomed large on the horizon. As they crossed one of the many streams that cut through the heathland, Misty gave her quiet purring sound and bobbed her head. Brion stopped mid-stream. He spun in the saddle to searched the trail behind him.

"Hurry," he called, waving frantically at the girls to cross. He kicked Misty through the water and wheeled her about on the bank. "Hurry," he waved again before searching for a place to conceal the horses.

Finola and Brigid were halfway across the stream when an arrow buried itself into the side of Finola's horse. The horse reared and screamed. Finola tumbled into the stream. The horse splashed to the bank and bolted into the junipers. Brigid reined her horse around to come back for Finola just as the rest of the horsemen came over the rise.

Deliverance

"Run!" Brion yelled. "Run!"

Finola staggered to her feet dripping wet, grasping at Brigid's stirrup.

A Salassani lowered his bow at Brion. Brion kneed Misty aside and shot the man from his saddle before he could release. The man's arrow flew wild. He rolled to the ground. Brion divided his attention between the girls and the oncoming riders.

Brigid kicked her horse out of the stream. An arrow buzzed over her head. She bent low, crouching as she tried to reach the cover of the trees. Brion's next arrow dropped the first rider. His third dropped the horse out from under another. His fourth dropped another rider as he splashed into the creek.

Brion kicked Misty between the girls and the approaching riders, desperate to shield them. Brigid turned in the saddle and loosed an arrow at the next rider to splash into the creek. She caught him in the side. Finola scrambled to the top of the bank and dashed toward the trees. Brion tumbled another man from the saddle before he was forced to draw his sword.

As Finola reached the line of the trees, an arrow plunged into her shoulder. She let out a cry and stumbled into the bushes.

"No!" Brion screamed. His worst nightmare was coming true. Not Finola. This couldn't happen to Finola.

Brigid jumped from the horse's back just as an arrow buried itself into her saddle. Another arrow buzzed past her as she dove out of sight.

Brion struggled to keep the panic down. He needed to concentrate. He needed to focus. But Finola had been shot. He caught glimpses of Brigid helping Finola into the trees and then of Brigid standing with the bow dangling useless in her hands, watching the battle.

What was the matter with her?

"Get out of here," he screamed. Two Salassani broke away from Brion to go after her.

"Run! Hide!"

He struggled in growing desperation to cut his way to them, but, every time he thought he had an opening, a Salassani closed it. He couldn't win, not against so many. He would die a warrior's death here on the lonely heathland. He had failed, just as he had done before. Maybe he had been doomed to fail all along.

Out of the corner of his eye he saw an arrow appear in the back of one of the riders that had galloped to attack the girls. Before the other reached the bank, he also fell into the muddied waters of the creek. Brion didn't have time to consider who had shot the arrows or even to watch what happened. He faced a storm of steel that threatened to cut him to ribbons.

A blade slipped past his guard and sliced a gash above his eye. He whirled to parry another blow. He misjudged and the blade slid across his forearm, opening a long gash. He twisted his wrist and flipped his sword across the man's belly before lunging to avoid another blow. Three remaining riders crowded around him, but Misty, his wonderful Salassani pony, kicked and bit and whirled so effectively that the riders couldn't close in on him. Still, they were wearing him down.

He couldn't last forever. He blinked at the blood that slid into his eyes. The sword grew slippery in his grasp. His throat burned and his chest heaved. The murderous blows tested all the strength and skill he could muster.

Three Salassani circled him, seeking an entrance. A wave of dizziness swept over Brion. He reeled for a moment. He was losing too much blood.

He knew that he couldn't keep them off for much longer. He didn't know where the girls were, but he hoped they had kept running and made good their escape. Now would be a good time for Redmond and Neahl to catch up with them, if they were still alive. Brion parried a blow to his head, but his return stroke proved sluggish and awkward. His sword had become heavy in his hand.

A battle cry rang out over the clash of steel. A lone Salassani warrior broke from the concealment of the trees with a sword raised. Brion's last reserve of hope melted away. It was over.

Two of the Salassani reined their mounts around to face the newcomer. But he swept into them, nimble as a cat. In a few seconds, both of them were down. One of the Salassani that Brion had unhorsed scrambled to attack the newcomer, who parried his blow, gave him a sharp elbow into his face, and then stabbed him with his sword. The last remaining Salassani wheeled his horse around and kicked it into a gallop back over the stream and up the valley. The newcomer sheathed his sword, jerked a short, recurve over his head, nocked an arrow, and shot the Salassani from the saddle before he had made it forty paces.

He turned to Brion, lowered the bow, and watched him. Brion wavered in the saddle. He thought he recognized the man, but his vision swam.

Deliverance

He blinked, trying to bring it into focus.

Redmond? he thought. He swayed. Misty danced under him to keep him in the saddle. Brion slumped forward onto Misty's neck. The blackness reached for him.

Chapter 40
Friends and Foes

rion awoke to a raging pain in his head and a body that felt like it had been trampled by a horse. Voices spoke quietly beside him.

"When did you learn to use a bow?" It was a man's voice.

"My father taught me," Brigid said.

"Remarkable man, your father. Didn't he ride with the two warriors we passed back in the pass?"

"You passed them?" Brigid's voice rose in excitement.

"Yes, I left the others to deal with them. My only interest was in you."

"Are they alive, then?" Finola said.

"Don't know. I don't think they could survive the attack of a couple dozen Salassani. One of them was badly injured. I doubt he survived."

"Which one?"

"The big one."

Brion opened his eyes. He lay in a hollow with a pile of boulders off to one side and scraggly junipers on the other. The sky above was clear and blue.

Emyr squatted beside a small fire. Brion noticed that he had washed all of the Salassani paint from his face. Finola had her back to Emyr, her shoulder bare and creamy white in the afternoon sun. Blood stained the shirt that she pulled down to expose the arrow wound.

A wave of jealousy rushed over Brion, followed by outrage that this murdering Salassani would dare to sit so openly among them and to touch Finola. He reached for his bow, but pain lanced up his arm. So he dropped his left hand to his knife instead. He bent to rise.

"You're lucky," Emyr said to Finola. "The arrow passed through the muscle and didn't break the bone. I think you'll be fine. But it's going to hurt for a quite a few weeks, and you'll need to be careful with it."

Brigid saw Brion rise and bent to lay a hand on his shoulder. "Not yet," she said. "Just lay back."

Brion's gaze shifted to Emyr. He brushed Brigid's hand away.

Brigid glanced at Emyr and back at Brion. "He just saved your life," she said. There was an impatient edge to her voice.

Brion scowled trying to remember what had happened. "He's a Salassani," he said.

Emyr sat back while Finola lifted the blood-stained shirt back up over her shoulder.

"He carried you from the battlefield," Brigid continued, "and he tended your wounds. Stop being a baby."

Brion glared.

"We would all be dead right now if it wasn't for him," Brigid continued. "Those Salassani weren't trying to capture us."

Brion struggled with the hazy memories of the battle. Was she telling the truth?

Emyr packed his things into a leather pouch before stuffing them into his pack. "They weren't all Salassani," he said without looking at them.

This gave Brion pause. He tried to remember what the men had looked like, if he had heard them speak.

"What do you mean?" Brigid asked.

"One was Alamani and four others were Hallstat mercenaries."

"Our own people are hunting us?" Finola asked.

Emyr shrugged and cinched the strap on his bag.

Brion struggled to understand. How had they known where to find them? Why were they all dressed like Salassani warriors? He scowled. Was Emyr lying to confuse them?

Brigid brushed the hair out of her eyes and gave Brion a playful smile, perhaps hoping to deflect Brion's attention away from Emyr.

"You sure managed to get yourself all cut up," Brigid said. "Didn't Neahl teach you that was a bad idea?"

Brion smirked at her. But he raised his right arm and flexed his fingers. The dull ache ran all the way up his forearm. He remembered the sword cut and experienced a moment of panic as the image of his father's withered hand flashed into his mind. Would he be crippled already?

"How bad is my arm?" he said.

If Brigid saw the terror in his eyes, she chose to ignore it. Instead, she said, "Emyr?"

Emyr glanced over at Brion. "It wasn't bad. You'll heal. The sword stroke ran the length of your forearm—not across it. No tendons were severed."

The words released the tension in a rush. Brion flexed his fingers again to see if he could make a fist. He felt a pull all along his forearm, but he could still use his hand. He began to breathe easier. Then he remembered Finola again and felt stupid and childish for having panicked over a mere cut when Finola had taken an arrow full in the shoulder.

"Is Finola okay? Tell me what happened. I couldn't see," he said.

"I'm okay," Finola said.

Brion grimaced as he raised himself up and struggled to her side. He searched her face. "I'm sorry," he said.

Finola leaned forward and gave him a peck on the cheek. "I thought I'd lost you," she whispered in his ear. "Never do that again."

Brion was about to explain that he hadn't exactly invited the men to attack them, when Brigid cleared her throat dramatically. "Excuse me," she said, "but I'd rather you kept the lovey dovey stuff for private occasions."

Finola and Brion shared a smile as Brigid launched into an account of how Emyr had shot one of the Salassani who came after them and how she had shot the last one before Emyr could finish him.

"After you passed out, Emyr helped us stop your bleeding and moved us into a different valley to get us away from there. Then he treated your wounds. He had to stitch your head closed. You're gonna have a nice, long scar there."

Brion raised his hand to prod gently at the puckered stitches on his forehead. Finola laid her hand on Brion's good arm. That look of tenderness she sometimes had crept back into her eyes.

"You'll be dashing with a scar over your eyebrow," she said.

"Are you sure you're okay?" Brion asked.

She winked at him. "It's just a scratch."

"Uh-huh," Brion said. Finola never liked having the attention on her.

"How many got away?" he asked. He didn't want to speak to Emyr directly. He wanted to ignore him because Emyr's presence complicated everything. But he had no choice.

"None," Emyr said.

"Were they all dead?"

Emyr shook his head. "Two were still alive."

"Did you question them?"

Emyr nodded.

"Well?"

Emyr smiled. "Only one of them could talk. He said that King Tristan has called all the warriors of the heathland to his banner and that he has ordered every Salassani who crosses the heathland to kill any Alamani they find—especially any men traveling with Alamani women."

Brion nodded. "That explains why they attacked us before they even knew who we were."

"Maybe," Emyr said. "It appears that Tristan thinks you were sent to assassinate him."

"What?"

"Well, you did stick a sword in his arm."

"Me?"

"Didn't you notice the older fellow in the rich clothes riding a black horse?" Emyr raised his eyebrows at Brion's surprise. "That was the King."

Brion blinked.

Brigid laughed. "That's a sure way to start a war."

Brion glared at her and shook his head. "That's just what the Sheriff told us not to do."

Emyr kicked dirt over the little fire and stomped it out. Brion knew he had only risked a fire so he could treat their wounds. Fires during the day had a bad habit of attracting unwanted attention.

Emyr bent and picked up his bow and quiver of arrows. "I'll be back," he said.

"I won't be able to draw my bow for a while," Brion said. "It's too heavy."

Emyr turned to him.

"Could you get me a Salassani bow to use?" Brion asked.

Emyr nodded to a pile of gear by the horses. "Finola already asked for one. There are a couple by the saddles."

Brion glanced at Finola.

"I'm sick to death of being the target," Finola said.

Brion smiled. "We'll practice together, then."

Brion waited until Emyr had climbed the hill. "So, how long has Emyr been visiting you while you were on watch?" he said to Brigid.

Finola glanced at Brigid, whose face began to redden.

"He just saved all of our lives," Brigid said.

"That's what you said, but it doesn't change the fact that you have been letting him stroll right into our camp without telling either of us."

"Brion," Finola began.

Brion held up his hand. "No, Finola. Brigid has been going behind our backs and potentially endangering all of us."

"What?" Brigid demanded.

"The heathland is overrun by Salassani, and we have one who has been following us for two weeks. It didn't cross your mind that he might communicate with them?"

"No!" Brigid said. "He wouldn't. He didn't. In fact, he warned me to tell you that someone could be following us."

"And of course, you didn't say anything because you were afraid that I would figure out what you were up to. I'm not stupid, Brigid."

Brigid opened her mouth but didn't reply.

Brion sighed and studied his injured arm. "I don't understand how a girl can fall in love with the man who's responsible for the death of her parents and her own enslavement."

"I never said—" Brigid began to protest, but Brion kept talking.

"It won't work. Think about it. Are you willing to become a Salassani? He can never be Alamani. People won't let him."

Brigid opened her mouth to respond, but Finola stepped in to arbitrate. "Look," she said. "You two aren't going to get anywhere by arguing about it. Why not just ask him what his plans are and see what he says? Besides, it's going to be a few weeks before either of us are healed. We could use a little help until then."

Brion frowned. "Okay, but no more secrets, Brigid. We have to trust each other. We don't have anyone else."

Brion felt a pang of guilt for not sharing the secret he had kept from everyone, but it wasn't his secret to give. He also didn't tell her about the problems that they were likely to face when they returned to the village. There would be time for that later.

Emyr scanned the rolling hills around them from the ridgeline just above the rocky hollow where he had left the others. They were well concealed. He had selected the spot so they would not be seen while he tended their wounds. They needed time to work through what they were going to do with him.

He had made his decision back by the lake when he had decided to follow them, to offer them what protection he could. He had hoped that, in time, Brion's hatred towards him might soften. Now he was glad that he had followed them if for no other reason than they would probably all be dead if he hadn't.

Still, he marveled at what he had seen Brion do. He had never seen it equaled, though he had heard stories of accomplished warriors with seemingly magical reflexes and an ability to read their opponents' thoughts.

Brion had picked off the members of the band that had posed the most immediate threat, thus slowing them down and interrupting the flow of their attack. He had also displayed incredible swordsmanship. No warrior he knew could have stood so long against so many opponents, but this young man, who couldn't be much older than he was, had done so while slowly dwindling their numbers. Had he remained uninjured, he certainly would have prevailed. It was an incredible feat.

Emyr shifted to gaze around. A trace of smoke or dust lifted into the clear sky. He waited until a horseman rode over a rise a good half-mile away trailing a line of horses. A child or a young woman sat astride one of the packhorses. The pack train disappeared into a valley for a long while. When they next came into view, Emyr knew it was the trader from Coll who came to the fens peddling his wares. Emyr made a decision. He rose from his hiding place and jogged to intercept them.

As Emyr approached, Airic's right hand slipped down to loosen the sword at his side and he glanced back at the girl who seemed tense and frightened. Emyr stopped a good twenty paces away and raised his hand in the Salassani greeting. He could now see that the second rider was a little girl, maybe four or five years old. Airic returned the greeting. Emyr approached and Airic opened his mouth in a wide grin, causing the handlebar mustache to jump and quiver.

"Ah, Emyr." he said. He raised his gaze to search for Emyr's companions. "Are you this far south alone?"

Emyr shook his head. "I'm not alone. But I need information."

Airic stopped smiling and glanced back at the girl.

"Do you have any news from the gathering?" Emyr asked.

Airic studied him before he dipped his chin in acknowledgment. "I have, though I confess that I'm surprised you haven't."

"I've been on the trail for a while."

"Well, I heard there had been some trouble and that the Salassani were swarming the mountains searching for three men from Coll." Airic pat-

, ted his horse's neck. "It didn't sound too hospitable for a fellow like me, so I decided to hightail it out of there."

Emyr scowled. "Haven't they caught them already?" By now, word of the battle on the ridge should have reached the gathering and spread all over the heathland.

Airic appraised Emyr.

"Last I heard, a party went after them into the South Pass," he said.

"How many days since you left the gathering?" Emyr asked.

Airic laughed. "I wasn't at the gathering, friend, or I wouldn't be here. They were, um, how do you say it? Eliminating everyone who looked like an Alamani."

Emyr frowned in surprise. "They were killing Alamani?"

Airic nodded.

"Even slaves?"

Airic nodded again.

"Why?"

Airic shrugged. "These three Alamani tried to assassinate the King."

Emyr understood. That's what the dying man back by the creek had told him.

"Word is that the assassins had at least one traitor who helped them set fire to the King's tent."

"That's nothing but old woman's talk," Emyr said. "I was in the camp when they attacked. The King wasn't even there."

Airic shrugged again. "That's what I heard."

Then he gave Emyr a sideways glance. "If you were there, how did you get to be here?"

Emyr waved a hand at him. "Follow me, and I'll show you."

Brion started as Emyr appeared at the edge of the hollow with a rider and a line of horses trailing behind him.

"I knew it," Brion cried.

He reached for his bow, but thought better of it as the cut on his arm stretched and pulled. He yanked his knife free with his good hand and scrambled to his feet. A wave of dizziness washed over him, and he staggered.

Finola cried out and raced toward Emyr. Brion stumbled after her in alarm. But his entire body fought against him. His legs didn't want to bear his weight. His head throbbed.

"Maggie!" Finola gasped. "Maggie!"

Finola dragged Maggie off the packs into a great hug, then winced and fell to her knees. She favored her injured shoulder. Tears coursed down her cheeks. "Are you okay?" she asked through her tears. "I thought I'd never see you again."

The girl nodded and hugged her neck. Finola lifted her with one arm and carried her back to the camp.

At the sight of Maggie's little form clutched to Finola's neck, Brion felt a lump rise in his throat. He stopped. He had always admired Finola's ability to love little children. And now he would not have to go back to Mullen empty-handed. They had found his little child at last.

"I see I was right," Airic said as he dismounted.

Brion sheathed his knife. He could see the puffy, red marks on Airic's face, souvenirs from his fight with the bear.

Emyr gestured toward them. "This is how I came to be here."

Airic furrowed his brow. "Are you the traitor, then?"

Emyr shook his head. "It's more complicated than that."

Airic extended a hand to Brion. "Good to see you, lad," he said.

Brion shook his hand. "Tangle with any bears lately?"

Airic grinned and sat beside the little pile of coals left over from the fire. "Nah," he said with a dismissive wave of his hand. "I've had that fun already. But I think your story is one I want to hear."

Finola cradled Maggie in her lap, while Emyr sat beside Brigid. After introductions, they managed to explain to Airic what had happened. He nodded, unable to conceal his astonishment. When they finished, he sat shaking his head.

"I don't think anyone would believe me if I told them your story," Airic said.

"How did you find Maggie?" Finola asked.

"Ah, well. I wasn't exactly looking for her. But when I saw her all small and frightened sitting with the other slave girls in the Bracari camp, I wondered if she might not be the one Neahl had asked me about. She seemed so, well, new."

He reached over and patted Maggie's leg.

"So I asked when she had been taken, and they told me only a few months ago. I couldn't leave her there. No sensitive child like her should be forced to endure that kind of life. So I bought her and told them I was taking her to my wife. When I heard of the trouble at the gathering, I assumed it was Neahl. So I hurried south in search of him." He paused and surveyed the group. "I thought he would be with you."

"We left them in the pass," Brion said. He pulled at the bandage on his arm. He couldn't say what he knew to be true.

Airic's eyes opened wide as if he understood. He picked up a rock and rolled it between his fingers. "That's too bad." Then he glanced at Brigid. "We're going to have to do something about that hair."

"What?" Brigid eyed him with suspicion.

"That red hair can be seen for miles. You'll draw every Salassani to you like bees to honey." He glanced at Finola. "The Salassani are looking for two Alamani women. It would be a good idea if they disappeared."

Brigid and Finola glanced at each other.

"He has a point," Brion said.

"You're not cutting my hair," Brigid said with her hands on her hips the way Rosland used to stand when she was annoyed with Brion.

Airic smiled. "I have just the thing," he said. He retrieved a couple Salassani jerkins made of leather and two leather helmets from his packs.

Finola balked. "They stink," she said.

"And we'll look ridiculous," Brigid added.

"Ah, but they may just keep you alive." Airic smiled. "No one will know you're women unless they get up close and see the roses in your tender cheeks."

Brigid smirked and Finola cast him an exaggerated frown. "Don't even try that stuff on us," Finola said.

Airic laughed and sat back down while Brigid and Finola braided each other's hair to fit under the helmets and donned their new outfits.

When they were finished, Airic tossed a twig on the coals. "What now?" he asked.

"Tomorrow we make for Comrie," Brion said.

"Comrie?" Airic questioned.

"It's an old, abandoned village on Com Lake."

"Right," Airic said. "I've heard of it. Didn't the Salassani destroy it back before the heath wars?"

Brion nodded.

"Redmond and Neahl lived there at the time."

At the mention of the name Redmond, Emyr's head shot up, and he listened with interest.

222

"Ah, now everything falls into place," Airic said. "I knew I had heard of those two before. Didn't they have a partner? Weren't there three of them?"

Brion nodded. "The third was my father, Weyland."

Airic grinned and glanced at Emyr, who looked away. "Didn't know you'd stir up a hornet's nest with your little raid, did you, Emyr?"

Emyr shook his head, but didn't say anything. Brion glanced at him and then studied him. Something in Emyr's expression caught his attention.

"What?" he said to Emyr.

Emyr frowned. "I've heard of this Comrie, when I was young," he said.

"Well the Salassani still talk about the three rogues who hunted Salassani and ate their ears." Airic said. "I don't think there's a Salassani child who hasn't been told those stories to frighten them into good behavior. Is there, Emyr?"

Emyr shook his head in agreement.

Brigid smiled. "If they only knew Neahl, they wouldn't be so afraid of him."

Brion snorted at her ignorance. "You've never seen him fight for keeps. He isn't always the doting fellow who likes to bounce little girls on his knee. He's the last person I would ever want hunting me, and that's after I've spent four months trying to learn everything he would teach me. He's the most dangerous man I know."

"Which brings up the question," Finola said. "How long will we watch for them at Comrie? How can we know if they're even still alive?"

Brion studied the ground. Finola had voiced what he had been too afraid to think.

Airic looked over at Emyr. "What do you think?"

Emyr hesitated, choosing his words carefully. "Look," he said. "I first want to say that I'm sorry for all of this." He made a sweeping gesture with his hands. "I only followed the Salassani way as I had been taught to do since I was a child. I would take it all back if I could."

An uncomfortable silence settled over them.

Emyr continued. "You have no reason to trust me. If I were in your boots, I wouldn't be able to do it. I would have killed you the first chance I got. But I want you to understand that, for me, there's nothing left in the heathland to return to—even my grandmother is dead."

"What?" Brigid said. "Dealla? When did she die? How?"

Emyr blinked at her without expression. "She was trampled in the crowd as she tried to follow you."

A hand flew to Brigid's mouth. Tears spilled down her cheeks. Finola sat next to her and draped an arm around her shoulder.

"I'm so sorry," Finola whispered.

Emyr nodded. "I know. But now, I have no reason to go back. I no longer wish to follow the Salassani way."

"What will you do?" Airic asked.

Emyr shrugged and fiddled with the knife in his hands. He flipped it back and forth with surprising dexterity. Brion kept waiting for him to cut himself.

"I've thought that I might go into the south countries across the seas. I may find a use for my skills there," Emyr said. He bowed his head. "You should also know," he continued, "that all of the men who raided your home are dead, except for me. I killed one of them, one never came back from riding after a big man we saw on the road beyond your cabin, and Brion killed the other two."

Brion gave him a questioning glance. Emyr explained. "Your rock snare carried one of them down the mountainside. And the man you shot through the eye back on the mountain above the lake was the one that killed your father and mother."

They sat in silence for a long while.

Brion mulled over everything Emyr had said. Knowing that he had killed the man who had murdered his parents closed something inside him. The rage disappeared. He sighed and made up his mind about Emyr. But he would not forgive the man who sent Emyr on that raid. Someday he would find out who he was.

"I don't know about Redmond and Neahl." Emyr said. "I don't think their chances were good."

Chapter 41
Mistaken Identity

As they pushed deeper into the foothills of the Aveen Mountains toward Comrie, they entered a land widowed of its inhabitants. Old fields could still be seen where stone walls had been erected. Tiny hamlets lay in ruins and the burned-out hulks of isolated farmhouses dotted the landscape. Stark, white bones lay tangled amid the branches of the heather, reaching from the earth as if the bones of the dead simply wished to be remembered. The landscape put Brion in a thoughtful, brooding mood.

He edged Misty next to Airic. "Can I ask you a question?" he said.

Airic had given a packhorse to Finola, and they rode at a steady pace, with Emyr scouting the trail ahead of them.

"Do you know anything about a royal symbol in the shape of an eagle?"

Airic snapped his head around to gape at Brion in open astonishment. "Why, have you seen one?"

Airic's reaction startled Brion, and he hesitated.

"Uh, I heard someone talking about it, and I wondered what happened."

Airic edged closer to Brion. "Don't ever let anyone hear you talking about this in Coll," he said.

Brion watched him, without trying to hide his confusion.

Airic glanced around. "That eagle is the symbol of the last royal family," he said in a low voice, "the House of Hassani. They were deposed in a bloody coup almost twenty years ago."

"I've heard about it," Brion said.

"As well you should," Airic said. "The entire royal family was murdered. Only two escaped. The Duke of Saylen and some say a child, a prince."

Brion tried not to sway in the saddle at the shock. "You're joking," he said.

Airic gave him a sad smile. "No one knows what deal the Duke cut, but he alone retained his title and his life when King Geric seized the throne." Airic watched Brion. His gaze shifted to the back of Brion's right hand where it held the reins and back to Brion's face. "If they thought that someone knew the whereabouts of the lost child, they would stop at nothing to silence him."

Brion gazed out over the open heathland. A coup, the Duke, a royal baby, treason? What could his father have known about all of this? What had he been doing?

"But how could anyone prove that he was the prince?" Brion asked.

Airic's gaze wandered to Brion's hand again. "It is believed that he was branded on the right hand with an eagle."

Brion gaped. He had seen the lost prince, even spoken with him while standing amid the jostling horses at the Great Keldi. The slave was the lost prince. And the prince had saved him. He had said that he knew who Brion was.

"Brion?" Airic said.

Brion looked at him again.

"You must never speak of this to anyone. The King's son..." Airic stopped himself. His fingers played with his mustache. His brow furrowed. "You would risk the lives of everyone who knew you. Do you understand me?"

Brion nodded. "I think I do," he said.

Brion pondered what Airic had said. If the ring was the royal seal, then that must have been what is father was hiding. If the young man he had seen with the mark on his hand was the lost prince, the current royal family would have good reason to seek the ring and the papers. But if his father had been waiting to give the ring to whomever he thought was going to call, they must have belonged to some other faction—someone who wanted to keep the secret safe. The powerful enemies Emyr had mentioned must have been the current royal family. There could be no other explanation. It would also explain why Alamani disguised as Salassani had been hunting for them in the heathland.

Six days after the battle at the creek, Emyr returned with news that a large Bracari war party had crossed their path several miles ahead of them and that he had seen several other parties all moving in the same direction.

"I can't believe this," Brion said throwing up his hands. "We hardly saw anyone on our way north, now the whole heathland is alive with Salassani."

"And they're all hunting us," Finola added.

Airic rode up to them.

"The King needs to be warned," he said.

Brion gave him a questioning glance. "I thought you said you didn't take sides? What did you say about your beard?"

"Keep it close," Airic replied. "And I intend to. But if Geric isn't warned, the Salassani will sweep in, and you'll see nothing but slaughter. Tristan is set on revenge." He paused. "He means to finish Coll once and for all."

Something about the way Airic looked at him when he said this troubled Brion. There was something out of character about it—something not right. He remembered his conversation with Redmond on the other side of the pass. Was Airic the one who had betrayed them? He had known all about them, and he had gone north where he certainly had the opportunity to warn the Salassani.

Brion considered challenging Airic on the matter right then, but decided against it. He was in no shape for a fight at the moment, and Airic might still prove useful. But he would deal more carefully with him from now on.

"What do you have in mind?" Brion asked instead.

Airic shrugged. "Get off the heathland for one thing and then send a message to the King."

"Easier said than done on both accounts," Brion replied.

Now both Brion and Emyr ranged to the sides and the front of the others, keeping a careful watch on the trails that crisscrossed the heathland. Evening found them deep into the foothills of the Aveen. They camped in a secluded, wooded valley well away from the main trails and the abandoned buildings.

Finola tended Brion's wounds each morning and night. Then Brion waited while Brigid treated Finola. Brion wasn't about to let Emyr do it again. And it didn't seem right for Brion to be touching her bare shoulder, even though he found the sight of it rather interesting. He insisted that Brigid checked the wound carefully to make sure that the pink flesh around it had not begun to fester. After Neahl's infection, he lived in constant dread that Finola would take one, as well.

"You look good in a helmet," Brion said as Finola gently washed and bandaged his arm.

She grinned. "Soon I'll be a better warrior than all of you combined."

Brion laughed. "Well, you already look like a Salassani warrior maiden," he said. "And you're getting good at the bow."

"I wish my shoulder would heal more quickly so I could practice more."

Maggie came to sit in Finola's lap watching Brion with big, brown eyes. Her initial shyness was starting to wear off, and she had started following Brion around asking questions.

That evening Maggie studied Brion as he sat by the fire checking his arrows for straightness.

"What are you doing?" she asked.

"Straightening my arrows."

"Why?"

"So they'll shoot straight."

"You mean they can shoot crooked?"

Brion laughed. "Not exactly. They just won't fly where I want them to if they aren't straight."

Maggie pondered for a moment.

"If I bend the Salassani arrows, they can't shoot me?"

Brion stopped laughing. Emyr glanced around at them before studying the ground.

Finola swept Maggie up into a hug. "No one is going to shoot you, little one," she said. Finola frowned at Brion from over Maggie's head. He knew that Finola was thinking of their conversation about how the children always suffered the most.

This shattering of Maggie's innocence when she should have enjoyed playing with the other village children, unconcerned about the petty affairs of the adults in her world, sobered Brion. She understood what had been done to her, even though she couldn't understand why. She had probably seen people die already, and she believed that the Salassani captured people just to kill them.

A solemn silence descended upon them after Maggie's questions. That, combined with the exhaustion and worry, cast a shadow over the rest of the evening. They ate a subdued dinner, lost in their own gloomy thoughts until Airic volunteered to sit the first watch. Of them all, he was most rested.

Deliverance

The long weeks of running and living under the constant fear of discovery punctuated by short, violent battles were beginning to take their toll on Brion. He gratefully accepted Airic's offer, placed the strung Salassani bow with an arrow on the string within reach, rolled up in his blankets, and fell into the welcoming oblivion of sleep.

Brion jerked his eyes open. Something was wrong. His hand found the soft, leather-covered handle of the bow. He lay on his side listening and searching the area in front of him without moving his head. He knew that Airic had been sitting behind him. Brigid lay close to him. Finola and Maggie lay beside her. Emyr was on the other side of the fire where orange coals still glowed. Everything seemed to be as it should. Then he saw it. A shadow appeared beside Emyr. It grew larger and larger.

Brion tightened his grip on the bow. Why hadn't Airic given the alarm? The thought stopped him. It could be that Airic couldn't give the alarm—that something had happened to him. Or maybe he had betrayed them. Brion prepared to jump to his feet and rush to the large tree not five feet away, from where he could cover the girls from any attacker.

The flash of steel by Emyr's sleeping form propelled Brion to his feet at the same moment that Emyr came up to grapple with his attacker. Brion sprinted for the cover of a juniper as he released an arrow at the shadow that lunged toward Emyr.

As he scrambled behind the juniper, he glanced back to where Airic had been hidden. To his surprise, Airic was standing. Someone stood behind him. Brion cursed. His arm had not yet heeled. He wasn't ready for a fight. He nocked another arrow preparing to rush to the next tree before they could attack him where he was hidden.

Emyr threw his attacker to the ground, but the man grabbed Emyr and pulled him into a bear hug. Brion couldn't shoot at either attacker without the possibility of hitting his friends.

"Brion," a voice called.

Brion paused in confusion. He recognized the voice. It couldn't be.

"Stop trying to kill us," the voice called again.

It was Neahl. A rush of joy brought the tears to Brion's eyes. Brion stepped out from behind the tree, the bow poised to shoot just in case.

Redmond pushed Airic toward them with a knife to his throat. Neahl dragged Emyr to his feet, but kept his sword under Emyr's chin.

"Make one move, and I'll open you up to your navel," he growled.

Emyr watched him but showed no sign of fear.

In that moment, Brion understood. "Wait," he said. Then he began to laugh. "Wait, you don't understand." He tried to speak but the joy at seeing Redmond and Neahl alive combined with the realization that they had misread everything seemed incredibly funny. He laughed like an idiot. All three girls came to their feet—their eyes opened wide in the darkness, their heads turning this way and that, trying to make sense of the strange scene.

"What's going on?" Brigid asked.

Neahl grimaced. "We're waiting for happy boy here to tell us," he said.

"Neahl?" Brigid said and stepped toward him. "Neahl, it's you." She rushed toward him.

"Hang on a minute," Neahl said, holding out an arm to stop her. He glared at Brion.

Brion finally managed to regain control. He shook his head at Neahl. "I could have shot you."

"You did," Neahl said.

"What?" Brion stepped toward him in concern.

"You grazed me. Now stop laughing like a lunatic and explain to me why this Salassani is still alive."

"Neahl," Brigid began.

He stopped her with a raised hand.

Brion shook his head again. "Look," he said. "You two have it all mixed up. Emyr saved our lives."

Redmond lowered his knife. Airic inhaled dramatically. But Neahl didn't relax.

"I suppose you're referring to the battle site we passed?"

Brion nodded. "If it hadn't been for him, they would have killed us."

Neahl smirked. "He led them there and waited in the bushes while they attacked you."

"No," Brigid said.

Brion opened his mouth to say something, but he could only stare wide-eyed and disbelieving at Emyr. All of his doubts came flooding back with a vengeance.

Emyr faced Neahl. Brion watched his expression, but, in the darkness, he couldn't tell if he looked guilty or surprised.

"May I speak?" Emyr asked. No one answered him, so he continued.

"I didn't do it. I thought they had passed on. I don't know why they came back."

Neahl sneered. "I read your trail," he said.

Emyr appraised him. "Then you read it wrong," he said.

Neahl leaned in close, his face twisting in rage. Emyr didn't flinch.

"Neahl," Redmond called.

Neahl paused and glanced at him.

"Neahl, Brion." Redmond gestured for them to gather to him.

Neahl hesitated and nudged Brigid. "Keep an eye on him," he said.

When Neahl strode away from them, Brigid stepped up to Emyr and clasped his hand. Finola smiled. Brion considered saying something, but decided against it. Brigid had made her decision.

When they had gathered, Redmond spoke.

"Okay, Brion. Tell us what happened. Why have you allowed him to join you? He obviously thinks that you have."

Brion shrugged. "Brigid trusts him."

"What?" Neahl glanced back at Brigid and scowled. "What's gotten into her head?"

"Do you trust him?" Redmond asked.

"I didn't at first. But after the battle by the lake, he followed us, left us food, and scouted the trail for us. After the last attack, he kept us all alive. He apologized for what happened and said that he no longer wanted to be a Salassani." Brion paused considering. "I guess I do trust him. I think he's proven himself."

Neahl snorted in disgust. "Brion, this is the man that kidnapped your sister and killed your parents."

Brion shook his head. "He didn't kill my parents. Brigid was there. She saw what happened. Emyr saved her life even though he had been ordered to kill us all. The rest are dead, except Emyr. I killed the last two." Brion glanced back at the others who stood watching them. "I haven't admitted this to anyone," he said, "but when they ambushed us by the lake, he could have just as easily cut me in two. But he didn't. He could have killed me after the last battle, too. I was unconscious. He could have slit my throat and taken the girls. But he didn't. And he's not a Salassani. Brigid told me that he was Alamani and captured as boy. I think he means to leave the heathland." Brion paused. "For all these reasons, I trust him."

They stood in silence for a moment.

"Well, that's good enough for me," Redmond said.

Neahl glared at him. "Not so fast."

"What do you want him to do?" Redmond asked not trying to hide his impatience.

Neahl considered. "All right. But I'm not taking my eyes off of him. If he takes one misstep, I'll stick an arrow into him."

Brion grinned. "It's good to see you," he said and embraced them both.

"Sorry for the rude awakening," Redmond said as they returned to the group. "We had to be sure."

They all stood around in uncomfortable silence until Brion spoke. "You know, it would have been easier just to wait until morning and ask."

Redmond laughed. "But it wouldn't have been nearly as much fun."

"Is that what you call it?" Airic asked. "I'm going to have nightmares of that knife pressed against my throat for the rest of my life."

Redmond approached Emyr. "Sorry for the rough handling. But you understand that we couldn't have known."

Emyr nodded, dropped Brigid's hand, and surveyed Neahl. "He won't forgive so easily," he said.

Redmond pursed his lips. "Make sure you earn his forgiveness," he said. "Your band killed his best friend and nearly killed him. That kind of thing is not easily forgiven, nor should it be."

Emyr bowed his head and nodded.

The excitement drove the sleep from them. Maggie sat in Finola's lap with wide eyes, too shy once again to speak.

"What happened to you?" Brion asked Neahl and Redmond. But Neahl raised his crippled hand.

"No," he said. "I've earned the right to hear your story first."

Brion recounted the last few weeks with input from Brigid and Finola. Then Neahl and Redmond told them of the harrowing battle on the ledge and how Neahl had nearly died of his injuries. Redmond had allowed Neahl a week to recover and had then thrown him in the saddle and jogged along beside him in their desperate attempt to catch up with them.

"Neahl was practically frothing at the mouth," Redmond said, "when we came across that battle by the lake and Emyr's tracks following you. We've run day and night for two weeks just to catch you."

Redmond gestured to Emyr. "Okay Emyr, it's your turn."

Emyr shifted in his seat. "What do you want to know?"

"Well," Redmond considered. "Why not start with how you came to live with the Salassani."

"Don't remember much," Emyr began. "I was traveling with my mother when I was four or five. I think we were moving to a new village." He reached out and poked a stick into the fire. "The Salassani came upon us. My mother tried to keep me from them, but they pulled me away and knocked her into the river. I saw her struggling in the water as they dragged me away. I lived with the Taurini until Mortegai adopted me and raised me to be a warrior."

"Mortegai," Redmond said. He glanced at Neahl, who frowned.

"Yes," Emyr said.

"I met a Mortegai once," Redmond said.

Emyr nodded and fixed his gaze on Redmond. "My mother's name was Lara."

Redmond stared at him in silence for a long, quiet moment. Confusion, followed by understanding, slipped across his features. Redmond lowered his head into his hands. Finola and Brigid exchanged confused glances. Brion switched his gaze between Redmond and Neahl. He remembered the conversation he had heard while they thought he was asleep in the lean-to. Neahl's face remained impassive, but his eyes narrowed.

Redmond raised his head. "I thought there was something familiar about you from the first time I saw you. You move like Lara's father." Then he paused. His eyes opened wide as the implication of what Emyr had said finally registered. "I . . ." he began.

"I'll want some proof," Neahl interrupted.

Emyr reached into his shirt and withdrew a small, silver chain with a round pendant of woven silver. A delicate star had been woven on the inside. "I tore this from my mother's neck as she fell into the river."

Redmond watched the pendant swing back and forth before he stood and strode into the shadow of the trees.

"Well," Finola said. "I have no idea what that was all about. Anyone want to fill me in?"

Brigid nodded her agreement.

Brion waited for Neahl to explain, but he didn't say anything. He just stared into the fire. After a few moments of awkward silence, Brion spoke. "I don't know much about it, but I understand that Lara and Redmond were close before he left."

Finola made a large O with her lips.

Brigid looked to Emyr. Her eyes brimmed with tears. She sat next to him and squeezed his hand. "You're Redmond's son?" she whispered.

"Wait, what?" Brion said.

Brigid lowered her eyelids and gave him her, "how can you be so thick" expression.

Emyr nodded to Brigid. "I think so," he said.

"How long have you known?" Brigid asked.

"A few days."

"Whoa," Brion said. "You're gonna have to explain because I got lost right after the 'My mother's name was Lara' bit."

Emyr smiled. "My mother told me my father was a great warrior named Redmond." He replaced the silver chain around his neck. "I just put the pieces together after I heard you mention his name."

Brion whistled. "What a nice welcome-to-the-family," he said. "Your own father's been hunting you for months, and your own uncle just about slit your throat."

Chapter 42
And So We Run

Exhausted from a nearly sleepless night, the band rode on, pushing south as fast as they could without killing the horses. On a short break later that morning, Brion crouched beside Redmond as he filled their waterskins at the stream.

"Even after all these years it's hard to hear," Redmond said.

"What?"

"That Lara is dead and that the young man I have been trying to kill is my own son."

Neahl came to stand beside them.

"I should have been there for her," Redmond continued. "If I had known. My own son." He glanced up at Neahl. "My own son, Neahl."

"She's not dead," Neahl said.

"What?"

"I told you that I heard that she was living in Dunfermine. But I didn't tell you that I had heard it just last year. I think she's still alive."

Redmond stared at him. "I'm such a fool." Then he snapped his head around to peer at Neahl. "Did you know?"

Neahl shook his head. "I saw her only once after you left. She must have had the child by then. But she didn't say anything." Then, he rubbed his chin and grinned. "I guess this solves our problem of what to do with this particular Salassani," he said.

"It does?" Redmond asked.

Neahl grinned and slapped Redmond on the back. "If he proves he's worth trusting," he said. "We teach him to be a man instead of a Salassani."

Redmond went to where Emyr sat running a coarse stone over his sword and sat beside him. "You must think that I am a villain to have left your mother alone and pregnant," Redmond began. "But I swear to you I didn't know. Truly, I didn't. No matter what happens after today, I want you to understand why I left the island and why I stayed away for so long."

Emyr nodded, but kept sliding the stone over the sword.

Redmond explained how he had left to protect Lara from the Salassani assassins he knew were hunting Neahl and how his horse had bolted during a battle. When he had returned to find that Weyland and Neahl were boasting that they would kill him, he had left the island in his foolish pride. "So, I am sorry for what you've suffered," Redmond said. "I should have been there for you."

He was about to continue when Emyr raised his hand and shook his head. "Don't apologize. I have had a good life. I have known love and belonging. I raided like all Salassani, but I have never killed unless I had to. I have always tried to be the warrior my mother said that my father had been."

Redmond blinked rapidly and swallowed. He laid a hand on Emyr's shoulder.

"Together we'll find her," Redmond said.

Maggie crawled out of Finola's lap and approached Emyr.

"Is he your papa?" she asked.

Emyr glanced at Redmond, who smiled and nodded. "I am."

The following day, everything changed. Brion and Emyr returned from scouting the trail ahead, leading Airic's horse with his body draped over the saddle.

Maggie wiggled from Finola's grasp and dropped to the ground beside their horse. She hurried up to Brion and Emyr as they lifted Airic from his horse and laid him gently amid the heather.

"Why is he sleeping?" Maggie asked.

Brion swallowed the knot in his throat and exchanged uncomfortable glances with the others. Finola dismounted and knelt beside Maggie. "He's gone Maggie," she said.

Maggie gazed at her, struggling to make out what Finola meant.

"I mean he's dead," Finola tried again.

Maggie stepped to Airic's side and knelt beside him. She laid a small hand on his cheek.

"Airic," she said. She knit her brows in confusion. "Why is he cold?"

Finola sniffled as she lifted Maggie into her arms. Brion could only watch in grim sadness as the child struggled to understand.

Deliverance

"He's dead Maggie. He isn't going to wake up," Finola said.

Maggie started to shake her head. "No," she whispered. She squirmed from Finola's grasp again and grabbed Airic's face between her two small hands. "Airic! Wake up!" she yelled. When he didn't respond, she pounded her fists on his chest. "Wake up!"

Finola scooped her up and pulled her close. Maggie buried her head into Finola's shoulder and wept.

"What happened?" Finola asked. She choked on a sob. Tears trickled down her cheeks.

Brion had been standing beside Emyr as if in a trance. They stirred for the first time since Maggie had approached Airic. Redmond and Neahl stepped up to them.

"We were circling back," Brion said, "when we found his horse wandering through the heather. Airic had been scouting our right flank so we followed the horse's trail and found Airic in the clutches of a Salassani while another lay dead at their feet. We shot the man, but Airic was already wounded."

Emyr pointed to his side. "The shaft pierced his side beneath the right arm and broke off inside him. No man could have survived such a wound."

"There wasn't anything we could do," Brion said, casting Maggie a pleading glance. He wanted them to understand that they had tried to save him.

"Were there any more?" Neahl asked.

Brion shook his head and glanced at Emyr who also shook his head. "We found no sign of anyone else," Brion said. "These two must have been scouts, but I can't understand why they would kill Airic."

"Every Salassani knows of the wandering trader," Emyr said. "No one bothers him. It's an unspoken rule. But the King did order that all Alamani be captured or killed." He shrugged. "Looks like they tried to capture him, and he fought them."

"Before he died," Brion said, "he warned us to watch for the man with a burned face and the Holy Man. Then, he said something about his saddlebags and papers we had to take to the King. He also said that now that the Taurini have come, we only have a few days."

Redmond stepped up to Airic's horse and rifled through the saddlebags. He pulled out an oiled leather bag with a wax seal on it.

Neahl grabbed the packet from Redmond, broke the seal, knelt, and unfolded the papers on the ground. They all gathered around. Neahl scanned them before he looked up at Redmond. His expression registered his astonishment.

"By the King's beard, Redmond," he said. "King Tristan has made an alliance with the Hallstat. He plans a four-pronged, simultaneous attack that is to begin when the Taurini, Bracari, and Carpentini attack Dunfermine." He handed the papers to Redmond. "This is all out war, Redmond, and King Geric has no idea that it's coming."

"Then, Airic has been one of Geric's agents all along," Redmond said. "No wonder he was so welcoming. He probably knew all about us."

"What do we do?" Brion asked. He considered telling them what he had read in his father's papers, but decided against it. Now was not the time.

"The Taurini will find their dead scouts eventually," Emyr said. "I think we should be on our way."

"What about the two men he warned about?" Brigid asked.

"Exactly," Finola said.

Brion suppressed the surge of jealous anger and shrugged. "What can we do," he asked, "but run?"

Brion glanced down at Neahl, who had remained kneeling. He found Neahl staring at him, his jaw slack and his eyes wide in an expression of complete shock. He held a small piece of paper in his hands.

"What?" Brion said.

Neahl blinked, looked down at the paper as if for confirmation and folded it, stuffed it in his pocket, and stood. "We'll have to ride night and day to get this news to the King," he said without looking at Brion. He gestured at the three girls. "And to get them out of the way before two armies clash." He gave Finola a wry smile. "Or their two disappointed lovers find us."

This comment earned him a spiteful scowl from Finola and a slap on the arm from Brigid.

"We ride as soon as we've buried Airic," Neahl said.

The moon rode high in the sky before they stopped to steal a few hours' rest. They passed the ruins of Comrie as the sun peeked over the heathland, but they didn't linger. The sun beat down on their shoulders before they dropped out of the southern end of the valley. They had left

Deliverance

Airic's baggage behind and commandeered his horses for the desperate flight toward Coll. They used them as spares to give their own horses a much needed rest as they pressed on mile after weary mile.

Redmond scouted the trail ahead while the rest remained bunched together, trying to be as inconspicuous as possible. Maggie rode in front of Finola, where she dozed and drooped from exhaustion. The dust of the heathland coated Brion's throat and clung to his sweat-streaked face.

He considered calling another halt to give the horses and the girls a rest when Redmond came galloping up to them. He gestured to the east where a cloud of dust lingered over the heath-covered hills. "It's a party of Salassani," he said. They've seen us."

"Ride for the river," Neahl said. "We'll split up there and lose them."

Brion took Maggie from Finola. "Stay close to me," he said as they kicked their horses into a gallop.

The sun had dipped toward the west when they reached the banks of the Leetwater. They wove their way in and out of the thicket of trees and shrubs that lined the bank before Neahl called them to a halt at a wide and shallow ford.

"Redmond and I are going to circle back to slow them down," he said. "Brion, you know the way from here."

Brion nodded.

Neahl continued. "You and Emyr work your way down the river doing what you can to lay false trails. We'll meet you at the fork. Brion knows which one I mean."

Brion nodded again. The image of the map he had spent so many months memorizing came into his mind.

"Good. We should meet you there by morning. If not," Neahl paused, "ride for Mailag."

With that, Redmond and Neahl kicked their horses back up the trail and disappeared into the trees.

After the open heathland, the woods pressed in on Brion. The rich smell of earth and decay filled his nostrils. The cool air chilled his clothes and made him shiver. In the woods, his horizons shrank to a few feet or paces and with it his sense of security. On the open heathland, he could see an enemy approaching sometimes for miles. Here, he wouldn't see them until they were right on top of him.

But the oak and maple trees that might conceal an enemy could also be used to conceal his little band. So, Brion and Emyr rode a twisted trail through the forest, leaving false trails and switchbacks and splitting up—sometimes riding in the river and streambeds. They ate hasty meals while riding and stole short breaks to let the horses rest, drink some water, and crop the grass. Without the horses, they would never make it.

The twilight of evening filled the forest with gloom. Animals called to one another. Trees groaned as if in conversation. Every sound sent a jolt through Brion. Every shadow seemed to conceal an enemy.

No one spoke as the coolness of the forest enfolded them. No one had the energy. The girls sagged over their saddle horns. Maggie had cried for Finola, and Brion had lifted her back into Finola's arms.

"How are you all holding up?" Brion asked.

None of them spoke, they simply looked at him and blinked in weariness.

Brion kicked Misty up to where Emyr led them through the trees.

"I don't know how much more of this they can take, Emyr," he said.

Emyr shrugged. "My adopted father taught me to accept what you can't control and to face what you can't avoid."

"Sounds like good advice."

Emyr smiled. "Then he said, 'If the odds are against you, live to fight another day.'"

Brion grinned. "So in other words, when you have to face someone you know you can't beat, it's best to scamper away like a deer and get the heck out of there."

Emyr slapped him on the back smiling. "And so we run."

Brion began to laugh, but the sound froze in his throat. He raised his hand to call them to a halt. He touched a finger to his lips and then hooked his fingers on the string of his bow. Brigid and Emyr followed his example.

The splash of water and the clip of a hoof on stone drifted through the trees. Brion scanned the area, desperate to find someplace to hide. But they couldn't move without making so much noise a deaf man would be able to find them. Brion peered up the trail to where it passed through an opening not thirty paces in front of them. The gray of evening was rapidly descending into the dark of night.

A horse snorted. Brion tensed, praying that none of their horses answered. But he need not have worried. They were too tired to even shift their feet. The figures of two horsemen appeared through the trees. He could just make out their shapes as they approached the open path.

Chapter 43
Into the Dark

he two shadows loomed bulky and misshapen in the fading light. Brion waited, every muscle tense, ready for action. He should have shot first before they were seen, but uncertainty stayed his hand. It could be Redmond and Neahl searching for them. Or it could be the two men Airic had warned them about.

Maggie awoke in Finola's arms with a grunt. The horsemen stopped. Finola clamped a hand over Maggie's mouth, but it was too late. The riders had heard the noise.

Brion still hesitated, hoping the men would simply ride on. After a long, tense moment, in which the riders waited in silence, one of them reined his horse toward them. A breeze stirred the leaves around them and washed over Brion's face. He was sweating.

In that instant, Emyr raised his bow and loosed. The thrum of the string was followed by the quiet zip of the arrow. One rider crumpled in the saddle with a grunt. The other shouted something in Salassani and kicked his horse toward them.

The words galvanized Brion into action. It wasn't Redmond and Neahl. He and Brigid loosed their arrows. Brigid's arrow hissed past Brion's ear. Two quiet thumps sounded. The man screamed. The horse reared and crashed away. The sounds of its desperate flight disappeared into the distance until the brooding wood swallowed it.

Emyr leapt from his horse and caught the reins of the first rider's mount. The man slumped over the horse's neck. Emyr reached up and dragged the man from the saddle. The man fell heavily to the forest floor. Emyr kicked him onto his back and leveled his sword at his throat.

"Who are you?" Emyr demanded in Salassani.

The man groaned. The broken shaft of Emyr's arrow protruded from his chest. He mumbled something Brion couldn't hear.

"Where are you going, and why are you in these woods?"

Again, the man mumbled something. Emyr shook him with his boot. But the man didn't respond. Emyr stepped down the trail to the other man, but hurriedly came back. "They're both dead."

"What did he say?" Brion asked.

Emyr shrugged. "He said his name was Tyrnon. It's a Taurini name. That's all."

"How did you know it wasn't Redmond and Neahl?" Brion asked.

Emyr tapped his nose. "The Taurini cook with a spice that smells like onions and rotten eggs. Can't you smell it?"

Brion shook his head. All he could smell was horse sweat.

The horses stumbled across the stream at the fork of the Leetwater a few hours before dawn. Brion settled them into a cove a couple of dozen paces from the river after he made certain they could escape out either direction should danger approach.

He took the first watch while the horses cropped the grass and drank their fill. The girls curled up together and instantly fell asleep. Brion laid his cloak over them before he went to sit with his back to an old oak. Emyr joined him with his bow across his lap.

"I lied to you," Emyr said.

Brion raised his eyebrows. "What?"

"That Taurini said that they were hunting escaped slaves. Apparently, King Tristan has put a bounty on your heads."

"So why didn't you say so?"

"Because I didn't want to frighten the girls," Emyr said. "They've endured enough."

Brion pondered for a moment. "Well, that's all the more reason to keep running. I don't know about you, but I'm rather partial to my head."

Redmond and Neahl arrived as Emyr had come to relieve Brion from the watch. They let their own horses rest while they grabbed a few hours of sleep. By mid-morning, they roused the others and shared a meager breakfast.

Neahl grinned in satisfaction when Brion told him about the bounty. "Good," Neahl said. "It's nice to be feared again."

Brion shook his head. "You really are crazy. You know that? Every Salassani in the heathlands is after our blood and all you can say is that you like being feared?"

Neahl nodded. "I told you," he said. "Fear is your best weapon. By making them fear us, we will have to kill less of them, and they will be more cautious how they approach us. Their fear increases our chances of surviving."

"What about my fear?" Finola said.

Neahl smiled at her. "You let your fear drive you, but not control you. Panic is your worst enemy."

He then recounted their ambush of the Salassani war party that had followed them. "We only slowed them down and broke them up," Neahl said. "But more will be coming. They don't want us to take word to Dunfermine or Mailag that an army is amassing in the heathland."

He surveyed them as he wiped his fingers on his trousers. "This is where we'll have to split up," he said. "We've made good time, but we're still a good day's ride on fresh horses from Mailag and three or four days from Dunfermine. Dunfermine has to be warned. For all we know, an army may already be between us and the city."

Neahl gestured toward Redmond and Emyr. "Can you two find a way through?"

Redmond nodded.

"Good," Neahl said. "I'll take Brion and the girls to Mailag. Brion can get them to Wexford from there. He can collect Finola's parents and wait for us at my farm."

He glanced at Brion.

"I doubt you can stay at your cabin now," he said. "But I have to warn the King. Just stay put at my farm until I come for you. I'll get a fresh horse and ride to Brechin. From there, I can catch a boat to Chullish. If all goes well, I should be there in three to four days."

"And what if all doesn't go well?" Redmond asked. "They know where we're headed. Don't sacrifice caution for speed."

Neahl nodded. "Brigid, Finola, any questions?"

The girls exchanged glances. Neahl gestured to the bows both girls held.

"Keep your bows ready," he said. "The next couple of days are going to be exhausting. But, you have to keep your wits about you."

"You mean we aren't exhausted yet?" Finola said with a wry smile.

Brion grinned. "She still has her wits," he said.

Neahl gazed around at them. "Let's go."

Redmond came to Brion and hugged him tight. "Take care of them all," he said to Brion. "Don't let Neahl do anything crazy."

Neahl harrumphed.

Redmond hugged Brigid and Finola in turn. "Good luck," he said. "Don't let Neahl bully you too much."

Emyr came behind Redmond, saying his goodbyes. "I haven't thanked you," he said to Brion," for sparing my life. I won't forget it."

Brion shook his head. "You saved all of our lives, so we're at least even."

Emyr stepped to Brigid. Tears brimmed in her eyes, but she did not let them fall.

"Goodbye," Emyr said. "When this is over, I'll come for you."

Brigid nodded and pulled him into a fierce hug. "I'll be waiting," she whispered.

Redmond hugged Maggie who cried quietly. "It'll be all right, little one," Redmond said. "In a couple of days, you'll be with your parents. Keep your chin up. You have to help Finola be brave."

Maggie glanced up at Finola, who nodded.

Redmond extended his hand to Neahl. "Well, brother. We part again. I can't always be here to take care of you."

Neahl embraced him. "But you came back when I needed you most."

They all stood around awkwardly for a moment before Redmond and Emyr mounted and rode off into the trees. Their horses splashed across the stream toward Dunfermine.

"It's time we were moving, too," Neahl said. He limped to his horse and mounted.

They crossed to the south side of the Leetwater and passed through the patch of woods onto the open heathland beyond. As they climbed the opposite bank, Finola pointed to a dust cloud that rose up on the far horizon. A large band of horsemen crested the rise, galloping toward the ford. Crows soared and whirled over them like a dark raincloud.

Chapter 44
Unwelcome Suitors

eahl cursed.

"Great," Brion said. "You see what your bounty has brought us?"

Neahl shook his head. "How much more punishment do they want?" Neahl said. "Well, let's go." He kicked his horse into a gallop.

"We can't outrun them," Brion called after him. Their horses were exhausted. Even Misty was beginning to miss her step.

"Then we'll find a place to stop them." Neahl called back.

They pushed the horses hard until they reached a high outcrop. It was the last spur of the Aveen Mountains before the lands dropped down into the broad, rolling hills where the heathland began the transition into the Oban Plain further south. Along the banks of the river, a tangle of undergrowth and the occasional patch of oaks or birch marked its passing.

Between the river and the high outcrop, boulders spread out in irregular piles as if a giant hand had torn them away from the outcrop and tossed them about. Neahl led them through the maze of boulders and reined his horse to a stop. Its legs trembled and its sides heaved. Froth flecked its chest.

"I'm sick and tired of this," Neahl said. He glanced at his horse. "She can't take any more." He surveyed the area. "Brigid, keep following the river. Keep the horses at a trot or a fast walk so you don't kill them, but don't stop for anything. Use that bow if you need to. If we haven't caught up with you by the time you reach Mailag, go straight to the Sheriff. Tell him that Neahl sent you with news. Tell him what has happened." He handed her the packet of documents they had found in Airic's saddlebag. "Put this in your saddlebags and guard it with your life."

"Neahl—" she began.

He cut her off. "We went into the heathland to bring you out alive. We never expected that all of us would make it. Don't waste all of our effort.

Get to Mailag. You've only got half a day's ride ahead of you. I swear that no Salassani will get past us."

Brion's heart pounded in his chest. He knew the party behind them outnumbered them ten to one. He didn't have much hope of coming out alive or of being able to stop all of them.

Finola watched him with wide eyes. "Why are men so bullheaded?" she said. "Do you think you're gonna impress us by getting yourselves killed?" When neither of them answered her, she threw her hands up. "You don't need to sacrifice yourselves," Finola said. "Remember what Emyr said. Sometimes it's better just to run."

"I have no intention of sacrificing myself," Neahl replied. "But I'm sick to death of running from the Salassani, and this is the best place to ambush them. Out on the plains, we don't stand a chance. They will catch us for sure and in the open. Now get out of here."

Brion saw that Neahl had managed to get Finola's fire up.

"Brion," Finola said. "You're better alive than dead. Remember that."

Brion swallowed and nodded.

Finola frowned and then glared at Neahl. "You, I'm not so sure about," she said.

But Brion read the worry in her gaze. He reached over to touch her hand.

"Be careful," he said.

Brigid wheeled her horse around. Finola yanked the Salassani bow she had strapped to her saddle and adjusted the quiver she had slung onto her back. She cast one last worried glance at Brion and followed Brigid. They disappeared into the stones and boulders. A sick knot gathered in the center of Brion's chest as he watched them go. Would any of them make it alive?

Neahl dismounted, concealed his horse, and brought out his extra quiver of arrows. Brion followed his lead.

"Keep Misty behind the outcrop where you can reach her," said Neahl. "Wait to shoot until you are certain of hitting them and then take out as many as you can as fast as you can. If you have to shoot the horses, then do it. We want to even the odds before it comes to hand-to-hand fighting. We're stopping them here."

Neahl stopped by a giant boulder and placed a hand on Brion's shoulder. "I know I've been hard on you, Brion, and I know that sometimes you've resented it. But this is what I was training you for. You have to be better than they are even when you're exhausted. You understand?"

Brion nodded. "I know," he said. "Without your training I would have been dead several times already."

Neahl smiled. "I only polished what you already had, Brion," Neahl said. "I don't praise you nearly enough. But you are almost as good as your father at the bow already and a far sight better than he was as a tracker and a swordsman. I'm proud of what you've accomplished in so short a time. Today we fight as equals."

Brion swallowed the knot in his throat. Neahl would never know how much that statement meant to him. He was willing to die just to have heard those words.

Brion bowed his head and turned to assume his position. Neahl restrained him. "There's one thing I need to tell you. Just in case." He paused. "I've never told anyone this, not even Redmond. But I want you to understand why I . . .why I am the way I am." Neahl glanced down and kicked at a rock. "Her name was Cassandra." Pain swept across his face. "I shot her."

Brion opened his mouth but couldn't find any words. Shock coursed through him. Cassandra was Neahl's wife.

Neahl swallowed and blinked. "It was my arrow in her side."

Tears filled his eyes. Brion had never seen Neahl cry, unless he was laughing. Brion's stomach felt like lead.

"The Salassani was riding away with her," Neahl said. "I couldn't lose her. So I shot. But I missed. When the Salassani saw her slump forward and saw the arrow, he just kicked her off the horse like a sack of potatoes and rode away. I killed her, Brion." He moaned. "She died in my arms."

"Whoa," Finola said. She reined her horse to a stop. "Did you hear that?"

They listened. The sound of pounding hooves drifted to them on the afternoon breeze. They hadn't gone far from where they had left Brion and Neahl, but they couldn't take the chance that Neahl had changed his mind.

"Run!" Finola said. She kicked her horse toward the trees along the riverbank with Brigid close on her heels. Someone shouted behind them. The branches whipped at their faces as they ducked into the shadows. The horses slowed and pushed their way through the undergrowth.

When they came to a small clearing, Finola stopped and examined the area. A game trail cut into the trees toward the river. She motioned for Brigid to conceal herself in the trees while she backed her horse into the brush on the other side of the clearing where she could have a clear shot. She angled the horse so that she could shoot from her left side and still kick it into the cover of the trees when it was time to escape. She had just learned to use a bow, and she knew that she wasn't very good. But what choice did she have?

The crashing of the pursuers grew louder. Finola swallowed the knot that kept rising in her throat, and she motioned for Maggie to remain silent. She nocked an arrow and waited. Brigid did the same. If it were Brion and Neahl, they would know soon enough. If it wasn't, they were prepared to fight.

"I will not be enslaved again," she said to herself. She shifted her foot so she could feel the knife in her boot push against her ankle. She had gone through too much to let them take her. If Brion and Neahl hadn't been so bullheaded, they would have been here with them now. Then the idea occurred to her. What if they were already dead?

The first horseman broke through the underbrush. Finola's arrow found his chest with a hollow thump, and he rolled off the side of his horse. The horse continued into the clearing and stood there as if it didn't know what to do. The second rider appeared and Finola recognized him. It was impossible to mistake the shriveled flesh that puckered the skin around his eyes and mouth.

Brigid's bow sang. The arrow bit into his shoulder. He screamed in rage as he burst from the underbrush. Finola shot again, but in her haste the shot flew low and wide. It buried itself into his horse's flank.

She didn't wait to see what happened. She kicked her horse into the trees again, ducking low to avoid the branches. Brigid had already done the same and was ahead of her on the game trail. Maggie whimpered, but she clung to the saddle as they crashed into the deeper shadows of the wood. A branch tore the leather helmet from Finola's head. But she ignored it. They broke from the underbrush and galloped with all the speed they could muster.

Finola fought the weariness creeping into her limbs. She could feel the horse tiring underneath her. They couldn't keep running. *What would Brion do?* she thought.

Brigid must have been thinking the same thing because she starting jabbing her finger toward a rocky outcrop that overlooked a stream and little meadow. They raced toward it, splashed through the stream, and dismounted at the base of the outcrop. They led the horses up and over to a sheltered area where they could not be seen from the stream and crept up to the crest. Finola concealed Maggie in the shadow of a boulder and scrambled to perch behind an old, gnarled juniper, wrinkling her nose at the sharp scent. Brigid found a vantage point beside a boulder, and they waited.

The scene that opened up before them would have warmed Finola's chest with its quiet beauty at any other time. The stream gurgled along toward the river, oblivious to the plight of the young women who hid trembling with weariness and fear among the crags. Junipers and cedars scattered about the outcrop, their shaggy bark hanging in long strips. The occasional birch stood out like the uninvited guest. Finola gazed out over the meadow, hoping she had made the right choice. She had no confidence in her ability to hit a moving target from this height, but she was going to try if she had to.

The low crashing of pursuit grew louder. She exchanged a worried glance with Brigid and tried to become part of the juniper. The rough bark pressed into her cheek. This could be the place where she would die.

The riders broke from the underbrush and sped past the outcrop without even looking up at it. There were only three. But Finola tensed with terror as she recognized the Holy Man riding hard behind the others. The ruined woman in the market had been right. He was dangerous. But what madness could possibly make two men so desperate that they would risk their lives just to capture two girls? It didn't make any sense.

She watched with growing relief as they passed through the clearing and disappeared into the cedars. She waited, hardly daring to breathe. Could it be possible? Quiet returned to the outcrop. The sound of the bubbling stream reached them. A breeze lifted the leaves of the birch trees. Finola stood and motioned to Brigid when the arrow slammed into the juniper beside her head.

Finola dropped to the rock. The bow bounced out of her grasp and clattered away from her. Someone yelled in anger down below. She heard the slap of Brigid's bow and a cry. Finola peeked over the rock to find Gilroy and the Holy Man scrambling up the crag towards them. Finola scooted to the other side of the rock and motioned frantically to Brigid. Brigid jumped up and bounded from boulder to boulder until she disappeared from Finola's view.

Where were the men? Finola listened. Rocks clattered. Finola bent and pulled the boot knife from its sheath. She hugged the stone, listening, waiting. A boot scraped. Metal clanged. Maggie screamed.

The terror in Maggie's voice catapulted Finola from her hiding place. As she scrambled toward the cleft where she had left the girl, a hand shot out and grabbed her wrist. Another clutched at her hair, jerking her head back. The reek of the Holy Man filled her nostrils. Finola writhed in his grasp.

"Not so fast, pretty one," he whispered in her ear. "You are too precious to lose."

Brion stared in stunned silence. He understood the desperation that had caused Neahl to risk the shot. He had experienced it when he had sprinted toward Ithel and Finola high up in the mountain glen. But what do you say to a confession like that? This did explain why Neahl was so taciturn and grumpy. Why he was so driven to hate the Salassani. He was trying to wipe away the guilt of his own mistake. For the first time, Brion sensed that he finally understood Neahl in a way he never understood his own father. And, in fact, Neahl had become like a father to him.

"Well," Neahl said, "now you know." He searched Brion's face as if he wanted to know if Brion would condemn him for his weakness.

Brion nodded. "I'm sorry," was all he could say.

Neahl wiped at the last of the tears. They settled into an uncomfortable silence. Brion searched for something to change the subject. But Neahl slapped him on the back. "Well," he said, "let's give these Salassani pigs what they deserve."

Neahl positioned himself on a high rock to the left of the trail that wound its way through the valley of stones. The river surged along amid the tangled undergrowth to Neahl's back. Brion climbed up on top of the outcrop. From there, he had a better view than Neahl did. The rocky bluff upon which he crouched stretched out for a mile along the river.

The river snaked out into the distance where it disappeared behind a rise. The heather was in full bloom, though it now grew in small patches as the heathland met the vast southern prairie that stretched out before him to the south. The outcrop would funnel the Salassani beneath Brion and between him and Neahl. Neahl had chosen the spot well.

Deliverance

Brion waited less than twenty minutes before the Salassani galloped into view. They wouldn't have made it to Mailag even if they had kept running. Neahl had been right to stop. At least this way they weren't caught on the open plain.

Brion tried to swallow, but his mouth was dry. His hands trembled. He was facing his death, and he knew it. It was hard to believe that this would be his last day on earth. He thought of Finola and Brigid riding to safety. This thought steeled his nerves. He would stop the Salassani here. He hadn't started this fight, but he was going to finish it. And Brigid, Finola, and little Maggie would be safe. That was why he had come into the heathland. It had always been a suicide mission. He might as well die fighting.

As the Salassani filtered into the rocky funnel, Brion was surprised to find that only twelve men pursued them. He wondered where the others had gone and figured they must have split to follow Redmond and Emyr. He smiled despite his agitated nerves. They had no idea what kind of warriors they were trailing. Brion communicated to Neahl that they were in view and how many there were. Neahl signaled to wait.

So Brion waited. The riders slowed and wound their way among the boulders following their trail. The lead rider came within easy bowshot. Brion wondered why they would be so foolhardy as to follow them into this area without sending out a scout first. But he guessed that they figured they had the advantage of numbers and that Brion and Neahl were running scared. If that was true, those notions were about to be rudely shattered. Neahl gave the signal. Brion raised his bow, drew, and released.

Brigid heard Maggie scream and cursed herself for not staying by the girl. She heard the sounds of a scuffle, but could see nothing. She knelt behind a juniper to catch her breath and decide what to do. She had planned to come around to Finola's side so she could see what Finola had meant with her wild hand gestures. She had seen the man with the bow and had shot him. Maggie's scream told her that the others had climbed the crag. But she didn't know if Maggie had been found or if Maggie had seen Finola be captured or killed. Terror tightened Brigid's throat. She wished Emyr were here. He would know what to do.

Brigid crept along from boulder to boulder and tree to tree, following the sounds of the struggle. Then she saw him. The ruined face man crouched by a fallen tree with his hand clamped tight over Maggie's mouth. One shoulder was soaked with blood. He craned his head around to peer under the branches.

Maggie's wide eyes fixed on Brigid. Tears streaked the dirt on her face. Brigid froze. She didn't dare shoot for fear that she would hit Maggie. She couldn't move for fear that he would see her. The sweat dripped into her eyes. She began to tremble. What could she do?

A terrible strangled cry ripped through the trees, followed by crashing and cursing. The ruined face man spun around and crouched, peeking over the tree toward the cliff face. His back was toward Brigid. She raised the bow and drew the string to her ear. She couldn't aim for his body. The arrow might pierce through him and injure Maggie. So she aimed low at the damp backside.

Just as the arrow flew, Finola scrambled into view. Her jerkin and shirt were torn, almost revealing her bosom. The ruined face man stood, and Brigid's arrow caught him in the back of his thigh. He bellowed and dropped Maggie, who fell to her hands and knees and scrambled away. The man yanked on the shaft and whirled to face Brigid. He drew a knife from his sheath, cocked back his arm, and threw.

Brion watched his arrow arc through the sky and sent three more after it in rapid succession. He saw at once that he had misjudged the distance on the first shot. The arrow fell low, but it still struck the rider in the groin. The others flew true. Neahl had done the same, though they both targeted the same man for the initial shot. Two of Brion's arrows found their targets. All three of Neahl's found his. Four men tumbled from their horses. The Salassani scattered.

Brion found one more target, but missed his next two shots. The men were weaving in and out of the boulders, heading toward them, and Brion had only a small window of time to release. Neahl also struggled to find his targets, but two horses stumbled and went down. Three men were still astride as they burst past the outcrop and disappeared from Brion's view for a moment amid the boulders. He watched for the men who had been dismounted, but they were skulking low, scampering from one rock to the next.

Misty gave a warning snort and Brion jerked his head around. Two men worked their way onto the outcrop above him. He couldn't understand how they had managed to do it without him seeing them. But the three riders that bore down on Neahl were the more immediate threat. Neahl shot one from the saddle before he was forced to draw his sword. Brion shot the second horseman in the back before he spun to face the two men hurrying toward him. Neahl would have to fend for himself.

Brion spun just in time to see one of the men rise up on his knee and shoot. Brion jumped to the side. The arrow whipped past him. Brion drew and loosed before his feet hit the ground. The man crumpled. But the second Salassani had already launched himself at Brion. Brion twisted to the side, deflecting the sword stroke with the Salassani bow. The string snapped as the blade cut through it and bit into the limb. Brion twisted the bow trying to wrench the blade away from his attacker. A knife appeared in the man's other hand.

Brion kicked the man's chest, spun on his toes and slammed his other foot against the side of the man's head. This gave Brion time to draw his own sword. The man recovered, and Brion barely had time to deflect the blade. As the blades clashed, the scar on his forearm pulled painfully. But he ignored it.

Brion whipped out his knife and assumed a fighting stance—sword in one hand, knife in the other. The man circled. As Brion followed him around, he could see that Neahl had dispatched the rider, but was fighting against two Salassani on foot. Neahl favored his leg. Desperation to go to Neahl's aid burned in Brion's chest. He had already failed to save his father and mother. He couldn't fail Neahl, as well. Or at least they should die together.

Finola watched in terror as the silver blade twirled end over end. The sight was strangely beautiful. Brigid stood her ground. She drew her bow, aimed, and loosed. The knife and the arrow passed each other in mid-flight. Both flew true. The arrow sank into Gilroy's chest with a terrible scraping thump. Brigid twisted in a vain attempt to avoid the glinting blade. It slammed into her side and bounced off to clatter amid the stones. Brigid buckled from the force of the blow and sank to her knees with a groan.

Brion feinted with the knife and swept the sword at the man's legs. The Salassani recognized the feint and jumped over the blade. He stepped in for an attack of his own, but Brion slashed him across the belly with a backhand strike of the sword. The man's eyes opened wide. He staggered backward and sank to his knees. Brion whirled. Neahl had his back to the rock while two men hammered at his defenses. Brion had never seen Neahl fight like this. His motions were so slow that he seemed drunk or half asleep.

Only then did he understand what it had cost Neahl to ride so soon and so far after such severe injuries. He hadn't had time to heal before he had been forced back on the trail and into battle. The injuries and the exhaustion were starting to take their toll.

Brion scrambled down the steep hillside sliding with the loose stones that gave way underneath him. His arms and legs received a beating, but he barely noticed. He had covered half the distance to Neahl when another rider came out of nowhere onto the trail in front of him.

Brion dodged the sword stroke, drove his knife blade into the horse's belly and swept the man from the saddle with a powerful stroke of his sword as the horse bawled and reared, tearing the knife from Brion's grip. Neahl had fallen to one knee. Brion yelled and rushed the two Salassani. One of them spun to face him.

Brion struggled against the exhaustion. He had also been injured and had been running for weeks with precious little rest. His forearm burned. His head wound throbbed. The Salassani smirked, whipping his blade through the air.

"Time to die, boy," he said in the common tongue.

Finola and Maggie scrambled over the broken stone and fallen branches to Brigid's side.

"I'm all right," Brigid said.

"How can you be all right?" Finola demanded.

"The handle," Brigid said. "The handle hit me, not the blade." Her gaze searched Finola's face. "Where's the Holy Man?"

Finola clutched at the torn shirt, and her expression hardened. She said nothing, but bent to lift Maggie into her arms.

Finola paused and looked down at Gilroy. He had fallen with his head resting against the trunk of the uprooted tree. His eyes were opened wide, and he sucked in little gulps of air that whistled threw his ruined lips. He blinked.

"I loved you," he said. His lips quivered. "I wouldn't have let him take you."

Brigid stared at Finola, but Finola's features didn't soften. She hugged Maggie closer and turned to work her way back down the crag. Brigid glanced once more at Gilroy, feeling pity for this ruined man. If things had been different, maybe he wouldn't have died like this.

"I'm sorry," she said.

Gilroy blinked at her. Then his gaze followed Finola.

When they reached the bottom, Brigid found the beautiful stream fouled with the body of the Holy Man. His blood spread out to stain the crystal water. His filthy robes twisted and turned in the current. His head bent at an awkward angle. Brigid glanced up at the cliff towering above them and then at Finola. Finola ignored the body. Her grim expression cut off any questions Brigid might have had. Finola lifted Maggie into her saddle and climbed up behind her. Brigid followed, wincing at the pain in her ribs.

Brion stepped back to counter the powerful kick. But this man expected the counter and avoided the swinging blade that would have cut his leg in two.

His smirk faded. "You want to play foul," he said.

Brion didn't answer. Sweat stung his eyes. Adrenaline pounded in his ears. The whole world concentrated on this man and his swinging blade.

"You'll never make it," the man breathed. "I know who you are."

Before Brion could process what that was supposed to mean, the man feinted high and came in low. Brion blocked the blow but wasn't fast enough to retaliate. Despite this man's skill, Brion noted that he had a habit of flicking his eyes to where he intended to attack if only for a brief second.

The man's eyes flicked, and Brion leapt in the opposite direction, swinging the blade in a wide arc. The man stumbled in surprise and gave an agonized cry as Brion's blade caught him in the back with a sickening crunch. The blade was wrenched from Brion's hands as the man sprawled amid the rocks. Brion spun to find Neahl on his feet again, but fighting desperately, still unable to finish his last attacker.

Brion drew the boot knife that Redmond had given him and rushed toward Neahl. He let out a cry at the same moment an arrow appeared, as if by magic, in the Salassani's back. The man stiffened. Brion and Neahl both lunged at the same moment. Neahl's blade pierced his belly while Brion's ripped across his throat. The Salassani fell without a sound.

Horse hooves clattered against the broken rock and a lone Salassani disappeared back up the trail, bent low over the horse's neck.

Brion whirled at the sound of another approaching horse, terrified that the rest of the Salassani had circled around to trap them. But he found Brigid sitting astride her horse with an arrow on the string. She had lost her helmet. Her hair was a tangled mess and her clothes were torn and dirty. Finola sat beside her with Maggie in front of her. Finola was in no better condition. Her jerkin had been cut revealing her creamy-white shoulder.

While Brion stared at Finola, Neahl sank to his knees.

Brigid dropped from her saddle and rushed to Neahl's side. But Finola kept her seat.

"Are you injured?" Finola asked. Brion couldn't read the expression on her face.

Brion glanced at the new blood that oozed from the cuts on his arm and shook his head. "What happened?" Brion asked. "Why did you come back?"

Finola frowned. "We were nearly killed," she said.

Brion gaped. He remembered that there hadn't been as many Salassani as he had expected. His astonishment turned to fear. "Are you all right?" He started toward her. But the anger that flashed across her face made him stop.

"My two disappointed lovers found us," Finola said.

Brion glanced behind Finola's horse, half-expecting the two men to materialize from the prairie grasses.

"They won't be chasing us anymore," Finola's voice was low and her eyes hard.

Brion stared at her as the horror of what could have happened tightened his throat. Finola dismounted, and he glanced at the long cut in her jerkin. "Did they . . ." he couldn't complete the sentence.

Finola glanced at him. Brion saw the shame and the fear mingle on Finola's face. She bowed her head.

"One tried," she said. "But I killed him."

Brion embraced her. "I'm sorry," he said.

"I know," Finola said. "It's not your fault." She let him hold her for a moment before she pushed him away. "Neahl is injured," she said. She pulled a pouch from her saddlebags, leaving Maggie where she sat.

Brion reached up and touched Maggie's leg. "Are you helping Finola stay strong?" he asked.

Maggie nodded and pinched her lips tight.

Finola joined Brigid, and they helped Neahl lie on the ground.

"Are you badly hurt?" Brigid asked.

Neahl shook his head. "I've had worse. I just haven't recovered my strength yet."

Brigid fingered the long cut on Neahl's arm while Finola poured some water over the cut above his eye. Neahl blinked at the water dripping into his eyes and smiled at Brion.

"Thanks," he said. "If you hadn't thinned the ranks, I wouldn't have made it."

Brion nodded. "I almost let you take them on by yourself just for fun, but I thought I might give you a hand."

A strangled gurgling noise caused Brion to look back to the man he had struck down on his way to Neahl's side. Brion stepped over to him, thinking it would be merciful to finish him quickly. But Brion hesitated.

The man was laughing. He was laughing even as he choked on his own blood.

"Alamani cur," he said to Brion. "You tell him I cursed him with my last breath."

"Who?"

"Your father."

"My father is dead."

The man gurgled again and choked. His spasmed coughing was pitiful to see. He had nearly been cut in two. Brion found it difficult to look at the horrible wound, knowing that he had done it.

"Who are you?" Brion said.

The man tried to breathe before his body relaxed, and he stared at Brion with dark, unseeing eyes.

Brion found Neahl watching him expectantly, as if he had understood what the man had said. Brion opened his mouth to ask Neahl what the man had meant, when Maggie screamed and pointed up the hill.

Brion spun to find a rider on the ridge behind him. He cursed in confusion. The Salassani who rode away couldn't have circled around already. And why would he?

Brigid scrambled for her bow. Brion reached for one dropped by a Salassani. He couldn't believe it. The whole heathland swarmed with Salassani. He struggled against the despair and frustration. At this rate, they were never going to make it. They were so close, only half a day's ride, and they kept finding Salassani at every turn.

But the man didn't ride down the hill. He raised his hand in the lowland greeting. Brion hesitated. He couldn't see the man's face clearly, but he didn't appear to be a Salassani. The man waited.

"Well?" Brion said.

Finola had already bandaged Neahl's head and was working on the arm.

"Let him come down," Neahl said. "But keep him at a distance. If he so much as flinches, fill him with arrows."

Brion raised his hand in greeting. As the man's horse worked its way down the rocky slope, Brion became more and more convinced that he was not a Salassani. He rode the larger horses bred in the Kingdom of Coll, and on his tunic he wore the crossed swords of the House of Coll.

"Stop there," Brion called. He knew full well that men from Coll, as well as the Salassani, were hunting him.

The man stopped.

"Who are you and what do you want?"

"My name is Jerome. I'm a scout sent by the Sheriff of Mailag to search for Neahl, Redmond, and Brion of Wexford."

Brion glanced at Neahl.

"You've found them," Neahl said.

"I thought as much. Only Neahl would be fool enough to lay in ambush for a dozen Salassani with a boy and three girls."

Neahl struggled to sit up.

"You old villain," Neahl said and laughed. "I thought for sure you would've died in a tavern brawl by now."

"May I approach?" Jerome asked.

"Only if you promise to keep your hands out of my pockets," Neahl replied.

Jerome came forward smiling and dismounted. He shook his head and knelt beside Neahl.

"You've always had a knack for trouble. You're the only man I know who spends his life looking for it," Jerome said.

Neahl raised his right hand to him. They clasped hands.

"It's been a long time," Neahl said.

"Looks like we may live long enough to see another heath war," Jerome said.

"Does the Sheriff know?" Neahl asked.

"He suspects. He hoped you would have more information for him."

"I do. The war is here."

Jerome considered. "Well, then I guess we had best be moving on. While these nice, young ladies patch you up, I'm just going to see if we can find someone with enough breath to talk."

Brion watched while Jerome examined the battle site, bending to search the bodies of the dead men. Once he saw the flash of steel and the twitching of a dying man. Jerome came to a Salassani with an arrow in his groin and another arrow in his shoulder sitting with his back to a boulder. He squatted beside him.

The man made a swipe at Jerome with a knife. But Jerome was quick. He parried the blow, knocking the knife from the man's hand. He questioned him for a moment and left him. As Jerome turned, the man reached for the knife. A cry of warning rose in Brion's throat, but the man snatched the knife and drove it into his own heart.

Brion wrinkled his brow. His whole being filled with disgust. He was sick of death and of killing. He was sick of how cheap human life had become. But what else could he have done?

Jerome knelt beside Neahl again.

"Well, that one accused you and another tall, lanky Alamani of killing the son of a Taurini chieftain." Jerome gestured to the man Brion had killed. "This might be the chieftain." He glanced at Brion. "Anyway, that's why they came after you so hard and because some Salassani priest said one of the girls was his property?"

Brion glanced at Brigid and Finola. Finola glared at Jerome.

"I'm no man's property," she said.

Jerome shrugged. "Just telling you what he said." When Finola didn't reply, Jerome continued. "They also had orders to stop any Alamani they found lurking in the heather," Jerome continued. "He said something about a bounty, too." He smiled. "You've been busy."

Neahl grinned. "Just like old times."

"Well, I guess they didn't like you much," Jerome said. "But what did he mean about fire falling from the sky."

Neahl shifted and stretched out his legs. "Just a trick Redmond cooked up," he said.

Jerome nodded. "I heard he was back. Where's he been?"

Neahl shrugged. "In the southlands all this time."

Jerome considered. "He may be a useful man to have on hand." He scanned the battlefield. "Well, what shall we do with all these Salassani?"

Neahl shrugged. "Leave them."

Jerome gave him a sidelong glance. "Do we leave their ears?"

Neahl grinned. "Redmond says I'm a savage, so I guess I'll let these keep their ears." Then Neahl glowered up at Brigid and Finola. "I thought I told you two to get out of here."

Brigid and Finola bristled.

"We did," Finola snapped. "But you let four of them get past you."

Jerome opened his eyes wide in surprise. This was apparently news to him.

"No one got past us," Neahl said.

"You're not the only one who had to fight for your life." Finola glared at Neahl.

"And lucky for you we came back when we did, isn't it?" Brigid said with an air of prideful disdain. "I believe we saved your life."

Neahl shrugged. "Brion and I had him," he said.

Chapter 45
Homecoming

Five days later Brion, Finola, Maggie, and Brigid crested the hill that overlooked Wexford. They had spent a day in Mailag with Neahl before setting off at a leisurely pace toward home. They all stopped as if by command when they reached the crest overlooking the village. The scatter of buildings filled the wide hollow along several streets.

Brion was keenly aware that no parent would be welcoming them home. Their home would be silent, empty, and lonely. He wasn't sure how he should feel at this moment—the moment for which he had trained, and worked, and suffered, and struggled for so long. Now that it was here, he experienced a great emptiness and uncertainty. He glanced at Brigid. She reached a hand up to finger the necklace he had given her. The spear she had picked up from the Salassani battle site rested across her thighs. A tear glistened on her cheek. Brion reached out his hand to her.

"Welcome home," he said.

They rode down the hill and into Wexford. Dogs barked. Someone called out.

"They're here! They're here!"

People hurried from their houses. Mullen was the first to reach them. Tears streamed down his face. He pulled Maggie from the saddle and hugged her fiercely.

"My girl," he whispered. "My little child."

"Papa," she said with a shy, little giggle.

A woman rushed up to Mullen and tore the child from his arms. "My baby," she said in between sobs. "My baby."

Mullen reached a hand up to grasp at Brion's leg. "Thank you, son. Thank you." Tears slipped down his cheeks. Brion nodded, and they all dismounted as the villagers gathered around.

Brion searched for Paiden and Shavon, Finola's parents, but they weren't there. He pulled himself from the crowed and hurried with Fino-

261

la toward the baker's shop to find the windows broken and blackened beams stabbing up through the gutted roof.

Finola grabbed a young lady who had followed them. "What happened? Where are my parents?"

The girl glanced around. Fear filled her eyes. "Things have changed," she said.

Finola shook her. "Tell me."

"I can't."

A large man appeared behind the girl, and Finola let her go.

Brion recognized him as the man that had attacked him in the tavern all those weeks ago. Now, more than ever, he was convinced the man had been sent to pick a fight with him. Seamus's warning came back to him, and he felt foolish for even thinking that he could return to the village.

"You're not wanted here," the man said.

"Where are my parents?" Finola demanded.

"They moved on, and so should you."

"We'll move on when we're good and ready," Brion said, the anger and frustration rising hot in his belly.

He hadn't fought his way through the entire Salassani nation to be cowed by the new village thug. The new headman barked an order from where he stood framed in the doorway of the tavern. The thug glared at Brion and strode away. The rest of the townspeople left them alone in the street in front of the burned-out bakery.

"Welcome home," Brion said again, letting the sarcasm fill the space between his words. They all knew that they had no home anymore. And Brion knew why. His father's papers held the secret, and he was going to have to find the Duke of Saylen if he wanted answers.

Seamus approached with a broad grin on his face. He wiped his hands on a leather apron. His blonde hair was longer now. He embraced Brion, and Brion wrinkled his nose at the strong scent of the tannery.

"I can't believe you made it," Seamus said as he pulled away.

"We almost didn't," Brion said. "How are you?"

Seamus bobbed his head indecisively. "Surviving. Looks like you beat the odds though."

Seamus glanced at Finola who stood staring at the burned out bakery.

"They went to Dunfermine," he said. "The headman ran them out of town a few days ago."

"Why?" Finola said.

Deliverance

Seamus shrugged. "Because they kept insisting that Brion and Neahl had done nothing wrong. They were stirring up support for you in the village. So they were driven out."

Brion glanced around to where Mullen was carrying Maggie back to his shop.

"What about Mullen?" he asked.

"He's never said a word against you as far as I know," Seamus said. "But he knows how to keep his head down."

Brion reached out to Finola. "I'm sorry," he said. "We'll go find them."

"Brion?" Brigid said. The note of warning in her voice made him spin around. He expected to see the big thug returning with more support.

But the old midwife stood not three feet away, watching him with dark eyes sprinkled with filmy, white clouds. Her brow ridges were heavy, and her face sagged. She bent under the weight of her years, appearing much older than the last time Brion had seen her so many weeks ago.

The woman raised her walking stick and pointed it at Brion's chest. He imagined that she was going to scold him for causing so much trouble in the village. But she didn't.

"Brion of Wexford." Her voice was soft and invited confidence. "It is time for the secrets to be revealed. I know who you are."

Brion raised his eyebrows. This was the second time someone had said this to him recently.

"Four boys were born into tribulation," she continued, "yet only three remain."

"I'm sorry." Brion said. "I don't understand you."

"Your father will come for you."

"My father is dead." Brion's chest began to warm in frustration.

The old woman poked her stick at Brigid.

"Her father lies dead where you buried him. A pile of stones covers a child in the woods."

"What?" Brigid said.

Brion exchanged glances with the girls.

The old woman continued, "I saw him born, and I saw him die." She shifted her stick to point at Brion again. "I delivered you, and I gave you to Weyland."

"What are you saying?" Finola asked.

"Your true father comes for the ring, the papers, and the son he gave into Weyland's keeping."

263

The breath caught in Brion's throat. He tried to swallow. Brigid grabbed his hand. He stared at her. Her green eyes were wide in confusion and disbelief. *His* father?

Brion's world flipped on its head. His stomach tightened. Everything he had always believed about himself seemed perched on the edge of a knife.

Weyland had been involved in a plot to save the royal baby from the coup. Was that the baby she was talking about? Brion remembered the little pile of stones he had stumbled across in the woods the day the assassin had attacked them. Was that where Weyland had buried his real son? The papers made it clear that Weyland didn't have the royal baby. It had been sold into slavery.

Brion's pulse began to race.

"My father," he said, "is the Duke of Saylen?"

"No," Brigid said. Tears leaked from her eyes. She squeezed his hand.

"Whoa," Seamus said. His blue eyes opened wide.

"Why should we believe you?" Finola demanded.

The woman smiled. "A young man is fortunate to have two beautiful protectors," she said. She reached out a twisted hand toward Brion and dropped a delicate woman's ring onto his palm. The ring was golden with a tiny image of the stag in a teardrop shield—the coat of arms of the Duke of Saylen. "It was your mother's," the old woman whispered. "I took it from her lifeless finger."

Brion stared at her, something in her voice had changed. Her demeanor had softened the way it had when she had spoken almost on this very spot the last time he was in Wexford. Brion knew that she wasn't telling him everything. She turned to leave.

"Wait," Finola said. "Who are the four babies?"

"I have named two," the midwife said. She pointed at Brigid. "She has found the third." Her stick pointed back to Brion. "He must recover the fourth." She smiled and shuffled away.

Brion stared after her.

"Does she mean Emyr?" Brigid asked.

Brion faced her. A chill swept through him. He nodded. "And the lost prince," he said.

The setting sun stretched the cabin's shadow over the sunken depression where Weyland and Rosland lay buried. Brigid knelt with her head bent beside the grave. Her shoulders trembled. Brion stood with Finola's hand clasped in his. Her hand was cool and smooth and reassuring. The revelation of the old midwife had pierced him to the core. How could he reconcile himself to it?

"Do you believe her?" Finola asked, squeezing his hand.

Brion bowed his head. He didn't want to believe. He had loved Rosland and Weyland. "I have something to show you," he said. "Brigid?"

Brigid stirred and looked around at him. She ran a hand over her cheek, leaving a dirty smear. Brion waved her toward the cabin.

The cabin had been searched again in their absence. When they entered, Brigid stopped in the door. "It wasn't enough that they killed our parents, they had to ransack our home, too?"

No furniture or floorboard had been left untouched. It took some time to clear a spot on the floor for them to sit. When they were all seated before a newly kindled fire, Brion brought out the bundle of documents and the golden signet ring. He passed the ring around as he explained how Weyland had given him the ring just before he died and how he had found the papers tucked away under the floorboards in Weyland's and Rosland's bedroom. Then he read them the Salassani documents. When he finished, he set them on the floor between them.

"I don't believe it," Brigid said. "I won't. You're my brother."

Brion smiled as he experienced a sudden rush of affection for Brigid. "And you'll always be my sister," he said.

Brigid frowned. "Papa would have said something," she said, sounding much less confident.

"He tried to tell me the night before the raid," Brion said. "You interrupted him just as he was going to explain. I didn't understand until today, but he said that it would be hard for me to understand what he had done and that I shouldn't judge him too harshly."

"But—" Brigid began.

"No wait," Brion interrupted. "Just before he died, he said something else. He said, 'They didn't get it.' All this time, I thought he was talking about the ring. But he was talking about me. They had come to take me. That's why he sent me away from the cabin and fought them himself. He expected someone to come for the ring and the papers. But they were sent to destroy our father's secret—me."

Brion tried to swallow the lump that rose in his throat. "He died to protect me, and he and Momma died because they had taken me in and given me a home."

Finola wrapped an arm around his shoulders. Brigid sniffled.

Brion continued. "Then he said, 'You're all they have left.' And he made me promise not to desert them. I thought he was talking about you and Momma, but maybe he also meant this lost prince."

"Sounds like he wanted you to find the prince," Finola said.

"I found him."

"What?" Brigid and Finola both gaped.

"I saw him at the Great Keldi," Brion said. "He had an eagle brand on his hand, and he gave me this." Brion handed them the little golden eagle.

"So what are we going to do?" Brigid asked.

"Well," Brion said. "We need to find Finola's parents first, then we can—"

"Brion," Finola interrupted. "I want to find my parents more than anyone. But Dunfermine is surrounded. If they're stuck in the city, there's no way we're going to get in to search for them now."

"Neahl said to wait for him here," Brigid added.

Brion sighed. "All right, then. We'll wait for Neahl. But in the meantime, I intend to find out as much as I can about these four boys 'born into tribulation.'"

"What do you mean?" Brigid asked.

"The grave," Brion said. "I'm going to dig up that grave."

ABOUT J.W. ELLIOT

J.W. Elliot is a professional historian, martial artist, canoer, bow builder, knife maker, woodturner, and rock climber. He has a Ph.D. in Latin American and World History. He has lived in Idaho, Oklahoma, Brazil, Arizona, Portugal, and Massachusetts. He writes non-fiction works of history about the Inquisition, Columbus, and pirates. J.W. Elliot loves to travel and challenge himself in the outdoors.

Connect with J.W. Elliot online at:
www.JWElliot.com/contact-us

Books by J.W. Elliot
Available on Amazon and Audible

Archer of the Heathland
Prequel: *Intrigue*
Book I: *Deliverance*
Book II: *Betrayal*
Book III: *Vengeance*
Book IV: *Chronicles*
Book V: *Windemere*
Book VI: *Renegade*
Book VII: *Rook*

Worlds of Light
Book I: *The Cleansing*
Book II: *The Rending*
Book III: *The Unmaking*

The Ark Project
Prequel: *The Harvest*
Book I: *The Clone Paradox*
Book II: *The Covenant Protocol*

Heirs of Anarwyn
Book I: *Torn*
Book II: *Undead*
Book III: *Shattered*
Book IV: *Feral*
Book V: *Dyad*

The Miserable Life of Bernie LeBaron
Somewhere in the Mist
Walls of Glass

If you have enjoyed this book, please consider leaving an honest review on Amazon and sharing on your social media sites.

Please sign up for my newsletter where you can get a free short story and more free content at: www.JWElliot.com

Thanks for your support!

J.W. Elliot

Writing Awards

Winner of the New England Book Festival for Science Fiction 2021 for *The Clone Paradox (The Ark Project*, Book I*)*.

Award Winning Finalist in the Fiction: Young Adult category of the 2021 Best Book Awards sponsored by American Book Fest for *Archer of the Heathland: Windemere.*

Award-Winning Finalist in the Young Adult category of the 2021 American Fiction Awards for *Walls of Glass.*

Award-Winning Finalist in the Science Fiction: General category of the 2021 American Fiction Awards for *The Clone Paradox (The Ark Project*, Book 1).

Chet Kevitt Award for contributions to Weymouth history for the publication of *The World of Credit in Colonial Massachusetts: James Richards and his Daybook, 1692-1711.* Awarded by the Weymouth Historical Commission, 2018.

Writers of the Future Contest
    Honorable Mention for *Recalibration*, 2018.
    Honorable Mention for *Ebony and Ice*, 2019